# SATAN'S DAUGHTER

## AND OTHER TALES FROM THE PULPS

# SATAN'S DAUGHTER

## AND OTHER TALES FROM THE PULPS

## E. HOFFMANN PRICE

*Introduction by*

## DARRELL SCHWEITZER

**WILDSIDE PRESS**

# SATAN'S DAUGHTER AND OTHER TALES FROM THE PULPS

*Part of the Pulp Classics Series,*
*selected and edited for Wildside Press*
*by John Gregory Betancourt*

"Satan's Daughter" originally appeared in the January, 1936 issue of *Spicy Mystery Stories*. "Pit of Madness" originally appeared in the April, 1936 issue of *Spicy Mystery Stories*. "The Walking Dead" originally appeared in the November, 1935 issue of *Spicy Mystery Stories*. "Every Man a King" originally appeared in the November, 1943 issue of *Speed Adventure Stories*. "Revolt of the Damned" originally appeared in the June, 1938 issue of *Double-Action Gang*. "Crystal" originally appeared in the August, 1936 issue of *Spicy Detective Stories*. "Night in Manila" originally appeared in the October, 1935 issue of *Spicy-Adventure Stories*. "Murder Salvage" originally appeared in the April, 1941 issue of *Spicy Detective Stories*. "Triangle with Variations" originally appeared in the August, 1935 issue of *Spicy Detective Stories*. "Scourge of the Silver Dragon" originally appeared in the December, 1935 issue of *Gold Seal Detective*. "Drink or Draw" originally appeared in the December, 1943 issue of *Speed Western Stories*. "She Herded Him Around" originally appeared in the February, 1941 issue of *Spicy Western*. "You Can't Fight a Woman" originally appeared in the November, 1943 issue of *Speed Adventure*.

Published by:
Wildside Press, LLC.
www.wildsidepress.com

# CONTENTS

# INTRODUCTION

E. (FOR EDGAR) Hoffmann Price (1898-1988) was truly one of the grand old men of the pulps, who sold his first story to *Droll Stories* in 1924 but rapidly made a name for himself in *Weird Tales* for such tales as "The Stranger from Kurdistan" and the swashbuckling Pierre D'Artois series. A man with far more worldly and cross-cultural experience than the usual pulp writer, he was able to create authentically exotic backgrounds better than most. He had been a soldier in the U.S. Cavalry in the Philippines and was a veteran of World War I. He graduated from West Point in 1923 with, among other things — particularly useful for a writer of action stories — practical knowledge of horsemanship, the use of sword and pistol, and military tactics.

But he was not destined for a military career. He became a professional astrologer, a Theosophist, a practicing Buddhist, and, in an era in which this was particularly unusual, a close associate of Asian communities in California to the extent that he had a Chinese name, Tao Fa, and used to sign letters with his printed "chop" of Chinese characters — for him, not an affectation.

He was a world-traveler, a connoisseur of fine wines and rare carpets, and not adverse to doing real research when the occasion warranted. In order to write detective stories, he made friends with police inspectors, coroners, and sheriffs. Even when writing for the lowliest and trashiest of pulps, he did his best. He wrote in the introduction to *Far Lands, Other Days*:

> When the "spicies" appeared, my agent figured that my taste for lewd nude women might earn us a few bucks from immoral, if not immortal prose. Though the *Spicy* mags were trivial tripe and trash, I took each story seriously. Despite the limitations of the formula, all the built-in juvenility and silliness, I researched and wrote as honestly as I could. *Spicy-Adventure Stories* was a proving ground. The $50 sales paid for groceries. Each was a step toward becoming a regular writer, appearing in real magazines.

*    *    *

THE MAGAZINES *Spicy Mystery Stories, Spicy Detective Stories, Spicy-Adventure,* and *Spicy Western,* all put out by the perhaps ironically named Culture Publications in the 1930s, were known idiomatically as "the hots" in those days. You took them home in a plain brown wrapper. You *really* didn't want your mother, children, or respectable wife to find you reading them. The ladies in such stories lost their clothes with surprising frequency. Covers and story situations involved lots of bondage, torture, and violence, much of it a tease. Close analysis of the texts will reveal what parts of the female anatomy had to be described in each story with prescribed euphemisms and what parts could not be described at all. The illustrations, even in a medium noted for luridness, are astonishingly explicit, pushing the boundaries of what could be sent through the mails or displayed in public to the absolute limit at the time — and indeed these magazines were often sold under the counter.

E. Hoffmann Price became a regular contributor to the *Spicy* magazines. Most collectors today accumulate these very rare and expensive magazines to look at the pictures, or as museum curiosities, but if they actually read any of the stories, most likely they are the ones by Price or Hugh B. Cave, who wrote under the ironic pseudonym of "Justin Case." Price published a few stories as "Hamlin Daly," but otherwise put his own name on his *Spicy* work. He regarded them as honest apprentice work, nothing to be ashamed of.

He later did achieve his ambition of breaking into "real" magazines. He completely mastered the pulp medium and published in *Argosy, Adventure, Golden Fleece,* and others which required good writing and authentic detail. One month he was able to look at a newsstand and see his name on thirty different magazines. He continued to write for the pulps until they collapsed in the early 1950s, then went on to other pursuits for a time (astrology, Oriental studies) before returning to writing in the late 1970s with two novels of Chinese magic, *The Devil Wives of Li-Fong* and *The Jade Enchantress,* plus a western, four science-fiction novels, and a variety of shorter works. He also wrote vivid memoirs of his days as a pulp writer, which proved very popular. He was, after all, the only colleague who ever met Robert E. Howard and the only one who ever collaborated with H.P. Lovecraft not as an apprentice, but as an equal. These were collected in an excellent Arkham House volume, *The Book of the Dead,* in 2002. Price remained a dedicated writer to the end of his very long life, literally dying on the job, in front of his keyboard.

Here are pulp stories at their pulpiest from a master of the form. Enjoy!

— Darrell Schweitzer
June 7, 2004

# SATAN'S DAUGHTER

*It was Lilith the wife of Adam . . .*
*Not a drop of her blood was human,*
*But she was made like a sweet soft woman."*

— Dante Gabriel Rossetti

WHEN Morton Reed, unaided except for a leather-faced, white-bearded Arab servant, began to dig in an unpromising spot half a dozen miles from Koyunjik, his fellow archaeologists devoted their spare moments to helpful mockery; but they remained to marvel when Reed uncovered a buried city where every tradition claimed there should be nothing of the kind.

And inevitably the big American universities chiseled in on the discovery; which perhaps was no great imposition, as Reed's only resources were his lean, bronzed hands and enthusiasm that gleamed from his deepset, dark eyes to relieve the grimness of his gaunt, angular face. One man can't excavate an entire city.

STANDING on the crest of a mound near the now crowded excavations, Reed watched a hundred sweating natives dragging a monstrous winged and human-headed bull from the oblivion of forty centuries. He smiled ironically, nestled in the crook of his arm a small parcel wrapped in a grimy turban cloth, spat contemptuously, and turned his back on the diggers.

"Let them have that rubbish," he muttered, striding toward his shabby tent at the further crest of the mound. "I've got mine."

A necromancer is one whose magic art makes the dead speak. An archaeologist is one whose spade uncovers forgotten centuries. Sometimes the distinction between the two becomes dismayingly thin.

Once in his tent, Reed examined his prize. It was a green basalt image of a woman standing on the back of a lion. She wore a tall tiara, and her delicately aquiline Semitic features were sweetened by the shadow of a smile that lurked at the corners of her sensuous mouth. That vague, disquieting smile made Reed feel as though he had exhumed some living thing.

Her body was a suave succession of curves, and about her waist was a

11

broad girdle from which trailed carved pendants reaching well past her hips.

On the foot of the pedestal was a cuneiform inscription; but a wrathful muttering from the rear distracted Reed's pondering on the text.

"I betake me to Allah for refuge against Satan," growled old Habeeb, Reed's Arab servant. He fingered the blue amulet that he had worn suspended about his neck ever since they had begun excavating.

Reed recognized the symptoms of superstitious terror.

"What's the trouble now?" he brusquely demanded.

"Throw the accursed thing away, *sahib*," muttered the Arab. "That is the image of Bint el Hareth."

That meant, literally, Daughter of Satan — El Hareth was the name by which the angels called their renegade brother.

"Cousin of a jackass," retorted Reed in Arabic, "that is only the lady they used to call Anaitis, a couple of thousand years before Mohammad made the world safe for the one true God."

But old Habeeb muttered and cursed as he collected dry camel dung for the evening's fire.

Master and servant ate in silence.

Habeeb was thinking of Bint el Hareth, the queen of demons, who rode by moonlight attended by myriads of seductive, night-prowling *lilin*, whose whisperings lure solitary travelers into the trackless desert to their doom. Reed was equally perturbed, but for another reason: he would have to guard his treasure day and night, lest the otherwise faithful and devoted Arab destroy it.

AS SOON as he had swallowed the last savory morsel of *pilau*, Reed stretched his weary length on the thick-napped Mosul rug spread on the dirt floor of his tent. He watched Habeeb descending the slope toward the campfires of the archaeologists' native workmen. From afar came the mutter of a drum, and the monotonous reiteration of the old song about what happens to the wandering dervish when he met the sultan's forty daughters . . .

But that, reflected Reed as he again regarded his green basalt treasure, would be nothing to a meeting with the model who centuries ago had posed for this image of Bint el Hareth —

Then he cursed that chanting in the distance. They had changed to a new song. One that Reed had never before heard in all his wanderings. A sensuous, seductive rhythm, for all the crudity of the hoarse voices that blended to produce it. Reed caught himself nodding to that disturbing cadence. It reminded him of silk and white flesh and all that an archaeologist abandons —

It seemed finally as though something age-old and evil and alluring had begun to whisper to him in the undertones of that barbarous melody.

Then, suddenly, he realized that he was listening to music that could come from no group of Arab laborers. He sensed that he was no longer alone.

The full moon was rising over the low-lying knolls beyond the Tigris. Something was advancing through the moon glamor toward the entrance of his tent. A woman wearing a tall, glistening tiara. Her shapely body was a succession of fluent, rippling curves that smiled through a gown that left him wondering whether its fragile fabric could endure even a breath of evening breeze.

A native girl. Her flesh was a warm, rosy amber, and he caught the glint of moonlight in her incredibly large, dark eyes. They were dark and somber, and the fascinating sweetness of her face was subdued by the wistful, almost melancholy mouth.

Reed's eyes strayed down the gracious lines of her throat, and the firm, full blossoming breasts and inward sweep of her waist. He caught his breath, and for an instant cold thrills overwhelmed the warmth that had surged through his veins.

Beneath the gossamer that rippled with the sway of her hips was a broad silver girdle agleam with uncounted sapphires that glittered frostily in the moonlight. He heard the soft tinkle of the jeweled pendants that reached half way to her knees. For an instant it seemed that the basalt image had come to life!

Then Reed assured himself that she must have been prowling in the excavations by moonlight and had discovered a tiara and a jeweled girdle worn uncounted centuries ago by some perfumed favorite of a Babylonian king. She had found the treasure, and was displaying it to the best advantage in order to strike a bargain.

If she removed that silver girdle . . .

And then fresh wonder again subdued the desire that her shapely smiling curves had aroused. Her lovely face was a duplicate of the green basalt features of Bint el Hareth!

Utterly impossible — but there she was, standing in the doorway, silhouetted against the moon.

"I knew I could finally find you," she was saying in Arabic, "if I waited until the moon rose."

THE night had become a witch-glamor that chilled and at the same time inflamed Reed's blood; then he told himself that it was after all not so strange that a village girl should strikingly resemble the green basalt statuette in face and figure. She was substantial, and the moonlight did not sift through her body, but only through the tenuous gauze that enveloped her.

"I have been waiting for you, *Malika*," Reed replied. "For a long time."

Digging for long buried ruins is lonely work, and even scholars have their human moments. This girl was one for whom any man might have waited. She was glamor that walked by night.

Her slender fingers loosened the tent's lashings, and as the flap slid down into place, she deftly knotted the cord again.

Reed struck light to the gasoline lantern hanging on the tent pole. As he turned back toward his rug, the girl was at his side. He felt the warmth of her body, and the soft promising pressure of her gracious curves. The scent of her dark hair dizzied him, and the glow in her eyes told him that she had not come to trade in stolen antiques.

"Gorgeous," muttered Reed, seating himself on the rug and, catching her hand, he pulled her down beside him.

She shook her head, and her smile was a sweetness in the desert as she murmured, "No . . . I am Bint el Hareth."

The Daughter of Satan — a perturbing play on words. But her presence was warm and dizzying, and by the glow of the gasoline lantern none of her loveliness was hidden except by the broad jeweled silver girdle and its tinkling pendants. Even her feet were bare — tiny feet, nails tinted with henna.

Her arms moved like amber serpents as she set aside her tall silver tiara. Her hair cascaded in shimmering ripples down about her shoulders hiding her breasts, and reaching toward her silver girdle . . .

THE far-off mutter of Arab drums was now drowned by the pounding of Reed's heart. He caught her in his arms, and as he found her lips, his fingers slipped between the scented strands of her streaming hair, and caressed the veiled amber curves of her yielding body.

Lovely as her shapely form had been to the eye, it was incredibly more wondrous to the touch . . . satin smooth, firm, yet yielding . . . a succession of soft mysteries that sent fire rushing through his veins.

Her arms twined about him as her lips surrendered to his caress, at first tentative and quivering, then maddeningly possessive.

A strange, endless kiss — such is what the Arab story-tellers in the bazaars of Cairo described. More than contact. It was a mutual enlacement and union of lip and tongue.

Her ecstatic shudder, and the sighing exhalation of breath as she finally drew away, goaded Reed to flaming frenzy. But somehow, without ever wholly breaking from his embrace, her lithe body evaded complete surrender. She was eager and glowing, yet evasive . . .

"Not now," she whispered as his hands vainly clawed the heavy silver girdle about her waist. "Later. This is only a meeting and a promise. Don't try. That girdle is locked on. You can't remove it. Not *tonight*. . . ."

Reed had heard of jealous husbands and of fathers who applied such devices to keep feminine frailty from going too far in unguarded moments.

She sensed his next thought even before he could speak it.

"Neither a file nor a locksmith could help us," she whispered. Then, shaking her lovely head and smiling sadly, she added, "A jealous king was once in love with me. He was old and grizzled and knew that I would out-live him —"

"Who?" Reed wrathfully cut in.

"Naram Sin of Agade," she whispered, pillowing her head on his shoulder.

Naram Sin had been dead for more centuries than Reed had years!

Then she continued, "If you want me, we will meet in Kurdistan. I am here on stolen time. But later — when the signs of heaven permit — it will be otherwise. Study the inscription on the base of that statuette. Learn the ritual to chant when the planets rise to their appointed places. Then I will materialize from moon glamor and star dust. But think well, Morton Reed . . . before you summon me in Kurdistan, first look at what remains of my long forgotten lovers . . . see what Naram Sin, King of Agade, paid for my kisses . . ."

Her voice subsided to a sighing murmur. She was kissing Reed's throat. The maddening touch of her lips suddenly became an excruciating pain. He gasped and thrust her aside.

Blood trickled down his chest. Her thirsty lips were redder now.

Bint el Hareth was more than a play on words. She was a night-wandering female demon!

His color receded, but before he could break from her embrace, she caught his hand.

"That is the law. And if you are ever to meet me in my house in Kurdistan — if you are ever to unlock the silver girdle —"

Her finger tips indicated the soft curve just below her collar bone.

Reed knew what she meant, but he hesitated.

"It won't hurt," she whispered. "And the smallest drop will be enough . . ."

The evening was already a madness. Reed bent down and brushed aside the heavy blue-black veil of hair. His teeth sank into the flesh he had so fiercely kissed. He felt the moisture of blood; but as it touched his tongue, there was a savage roaring in his ears, and his entire body seemed enveloped in a shroud of consuming flame. His knees sagged, and intolerable dizziness sent him plunging headlong through a paradoxical blend of incredible brightness and impenetrable gloom. He was falling . . . falling . . . dropping everlastingly through space . . .

When his descent finally ended, he was still conscious, yet immeasurably dazed . . .

HIS fingers were digging into the nap of a Persian rug. Bit by bit the blacknesses faded. He was in his tent, under the white glare of a gasoline lamp.

He was alone. His lips tingled, and there was a stinging at the base of his throat. Then he remembered and tentatively touched the bite.

His hand came back unstained; but clinging to his finger was a long, wavy strand of blue-black hair.

And that seemed to prove that she had been more than moon-glamor and desert wizardry.

He seized the lantern and bounded to the door of the tent. And when old Habeeb returned from the camp of the Arab laborers, Reed was still circling the tent, seeking footprints that would indicate the direction she had taken.

The search was vain. The old Arab muttered under his breath as he watched. He seemed to realize that his master was seeking something that would not have left any trace.

For a long time Habeeb eyed the green basalt statue of a woman standing on a lion. He sniffed the lingering fragrance in the tent.

"Bint el Hareth was walking by moonlight! I betake me to Allah for refuge against —"

"Shut up!" snapped Reed. "Or you'll be taking refuge from my boot! Tell me about this Bint el Hareth."

"She is a peril that walks by night," Habeeb explained. "She sends fools — begging your honor's pardon — out into the desert to find the key to her silver girdle. And they do not come back."

"Nevertheless, I'm going to find her."

"Don't worry, *sahib*," was the old Arab's ominous answer. "She will find *you*. But it is possible that you may yet escape."

"Dammit! I don't want to escape. I want to find her."

"Patience, *sahib*." The old man smiled thinly and stroked his white beard. "They always do. What I meant was there is a way to avoid destruction. Only, no Arab has ever been able to use that method."

"And what's that?"

"It's really very simple." An ironic light burned in Habeeb's narrowed eyes. "She is insanely jealous. Therefore avoid all other women, and she will not destroy you with her deadly kisses." He sighed, shook his head, and repeated, "But that, of course, is utterly impossible for any Arab . . ."

Reed nodded. Simple enough, after all. Keep your mind on archaeology. A tough contract sometimes, but it could be done.

"And now, *sahib*," resumed the old Arab, after an interminable silence, "I am going my way. You are the forgotten of Allah."

Before Reed could detain him, Habeeb was stalking out into the darkness.

And for the remainder of the night, Reed studied the cuneiform text on the pedestal of the statuette. As Bint el Hareth had said, it described a fortress in northern Kurdistan. And the ritual to be chanted when the certain stars rose to the slits that cleft the dome of the turret was simple to an archaeologist . . .

REED finally set out for Kurdistan. His few belongings were packed on a donkey. Into that perilous, bandit-infested region no white man dared venture openly, so he went as a wandering native.

The news of his mission seemed somehow to precede him. But that helped rather than hindered. The superstitious natives regarded him as a madman and thus an object of reverence. One whose wits were in paradise must be a saint . . .

Weeks later, he reached his destination: a gray ruin perched on a foreboding crag that commanded the valley in which nestled a Kurdish village.

What he found in the ruins was dismaying confirmation of what that strange girl who called herself Bint el Hareth had said. In a circular vault in the foundation were arched crypts. In each lay the body of a man. There were bearded, hawk-nosed captains, nomads in sheepskin jackets, dignitaries in silks now crumbled to dust. Their bodies were skin stretched over bone. They were as hollow as insects baked dry in the sun. Reed had heard of mummies made by nature; but on the forehead of each was the red imprint of a woman's lips. This was a promise — and a warning.

The last kiss of Bint el Hareth?

But as his first wave of horror subsided, he resolved to stay. In this desolate waste there were only the women of the savage mountaineers — certainly no temptation!

Then he searched the age-old ruin. Only a single turret was intact. In its uppermost stage he found the vaulted dome pierced by slits. Its circular wall was buttressed by monstrous winged bulls with human heads, bearded and mitred. Placid, sinister guardians of the cabalistic circle were outlined in mosaic on the floor beneath the crown of the dome.

The madness of his quest no longer troubled Reed. He had dug too many buried marvels from the earth to doubt that Bint el Hareth would make good her promise. And that single strand of black hair told him that she had been more than illusion.

He had long since traded his donkey for provisions. Now he had but a pair of empty saddle bags. And as the sun dipped toward the western hills, Reed descended into the valley to buy food.

He strode down among the mud huts of the village. The chattering of the crowd subsided. His story had gone before him. And awed, furtive whispers of the natives told him that since the ruins were haunted by demons, he must indeed be a saint to survive such peril.

He shouldered his haversack, now stocked with grain, cheese, and mutton. But before he could turn to ascend the slope, he saw that the Kurds were not as fanatic as he had expected. His supposed madness was an unneeded protection. At the further extremity of the village a white man sat cross-legged at the door of a mud hut. In front of him was an array of bottles and bandages.

Filing toward him was a line of natives, men, women, and children. A missionary doctor, dispensing iodine, pills and religion. At his side, handing him instruments and antiseptics, was a girl with copper-colored hair, and skin like Jersey cream.

REED, despite his better judgment, joined the throng of ailing natives. The red-haired girl's young, heart-stirring loveliness reminded him of the years since he had seen a white woman. She must be the ruddy faced, grey-bearded doctor's daughter. He crowded closer, trying to catch her voice above the guttural Kurdish chatter and babbling.

The simple severity of her unadorned, faded blouse and sturdy tweed skirt could not mask the gracious loveliness of her figure. Her mouth was sweet and generous, and her slender arms were made to close about a lover's neck.

And despite his recollections of Bint el Hareth, Reed's hungry glance strayed toward the shadowed hollow between her pert breasts as she stooped to unwind a bandage from a grimy ankle. Then, straightening up to get a roll of fresh lint, she caught Reed's trenchant gaze.

She returned his steadfast regard. The ghost of a smile for an instant brightened lips shaped to murmur endearments between kisses exchanged by moonlight; then she remembered that that bronzed, bearded man with the haversack on his shoulder was another tribesman. She hastily turned toward the tray of instruments, but not before Reed noted the flush that crept from her cheeks down the whiteness of her throat.

Warm and human and sweetly curved — Reed's teeth gritted, and he resolutely turned. Bint el Hareth was a night-wandering witchery guarded by a silver girdle; and this red-haired girl was only a woman. Yet he was trembling from head to foot, and his brain was a reeling confusion as he pictured those warm roundnesses that could be cupped in his hands. That is, if he went back and revealed himself as a scholar and a white man.

As Reed reached the fringe of the village he caught a glint of steel in the shadows of a ravine that opened into the valley. There was a yell, abruptly checked. A file of horsemen came charging from cover. A bandit raid!

It was none of Reed's business. He had paid for his supplies. He could reach the ruins during the confusion of the attack; but he knew what would happen to the red-haired girl. Flinging aside his haversack, he ran down the street shouting a warning. The traders bounded from their booths. Muzzle-loading rifles, repeaters, and curved swords blossomed from every mud hut; but before the defense could be organized, the raiders had closed in. A second detachment followed, and a third.

The warning had only postponed the end. A man dropped at Reed's side. He snatched the Kurd's rifle and poured lead into the wave of advancing horsemen. The gun jammed. Clubbing it, Reed beat his way through the milling throng. The red-haired girl was somewhere at its further edge.

A bearded tribesman, charging on horse through a huddle of screeching women, wheeled as he saw Reed. His dripping blade rose. Reed parried the scimitar cut, felt the glancing steel rake his shoulder, but he carried through, smashing home with his clubbed gun. The enemy ducked, but the rifle butt, driving through, crashed across the horse's head. The beast reared, unseating its rider. And before the raider could regain his feet, Reed closed in. Kicking, jabbing and grappling, they wallowed in the red street. Horse and foot charged over them, but Reed kept his hold of that corded throat; and as the enemy's dagger hacked and slashed him, he smashed the raider's head against a boulder.

Reed regained his feet. He had won a sword.

The village was now a howling butchery. Crackling flames were gutting the woodwork of the traders' booths. The shouts of the raiders and the shrieks of the surviving villagers drowned the voice that Reed still hoped to hear.

He plunged headlong into the tangle, hacking right and left with his curved blade. He saw the red-haired girl huddled in a narrow passageway between two houses. Her garments had been torn to shreds, and her flesh was raked and bruised. She was scrambling to her feet, still clutching the short dagger that had cut down a bandit. But before she could kick clear of her dead captor, another raider saw her and closed in.

Reed ploughed into the nightmare of murder. His reckless wrath and the confusion gave him his chance. He was hacked and battered and bleeding, but he made it — and in time to catch the bandit before he could whirl. The raider pitched forward in a gory huddle, shorn from shoulder to hip. Reed jerked the girl to her feet.

"Head for the ruin on the cliff," he shouted. He paused to pick up an abandoned rifle and a bandolier of cartridges.

Once their path was blocked by a pair of looters; but before they could recognize Reed as an enemy, they dropped in a vengeful mill of steel.

The archaeologist and his companion were now in the clear; but before they were beyond the red glow of the burning market stalls, half a dozen bandits saw the girl's red hair and almost bare body and took up the pursuit.

Reed knelt, snapped the rifle into line. Three shots — wild, hasty shots, but two of them pitched to the ground like bags of grain. The survivors broke for cover.

Reed followed the red-head.

Not a word as they clambered up the precipitous ascent. They needed their breath for escape. Finally, as Reed half dragged his exhausted companion into the deepening blackness of the ruin, he said, "The moon will soon rise. And I can pick them off as they come up the slope."

He struck light and dipped some water from a green-scummed, rain-fed cistern. But before he could wash the smoke and grime and blood from his slashed body, the red-haired girl interposed.

"Let me help you — thanks, I'm all right — only a few scratches. But who are you? I couldn't believe it when I heard you speak English."

He ignored the question.

"Sorry about your father," he commiserated as she bandaged his superficial wounds. "But when this riot quiets down, I'll get you a native escort to Kirkuk. Or somewhere."

Her dark eyes widened. Then she said, "That was my uncle. I'm an orphan, and when he came to Kurdistan, I accompanied him. So — well, I've really no place to go."

She rearranged the tattered remnants of her dress, but there was no concealing the tempting roundness of her breasts and the fine gracious curves that swelled upward to meet the scraps of a skirt that now only reached half way to her knees. She was lovelier than Reed had realized, down in the village, and the glow of the fire coaxed alluring lights from her eyes as she sat crouched there, knees drawn up and clasped with her long, slender hands.

Despite the terror of the earlier evening, she was smiling as though the languorous warmth of the fire had blotted out all but the present moment.

She wasted no word on gratitude. None was needed. But the silence and her white presence were an eloquent torture.

Reed leaped to his feet and stalked into the further darknesses. He had to get rid of that tantalizing loveliness. The stars were marching to their ordained positions. Bint el Hareth would soon appear; but that time was too far off for him to endure that red-haired stranger's presence.

Even as he pondered, nature conspired to defeat him. The penetrating chill of the mountains pierced his heavy woolen cloak. The girl was clad only in a few ragged threads.

He stalked back into the courtyard, slipped out of his cape, and flung it about her shoulders. She caught his hand, and murmured, "You'll be terribly chilly. You needn't keep such a close watch. If the bandits knew we were here, they'd have been up here before now."

The touch of her fingers was seductive as a kiss. Reed seated himself on the rug beside her. He tried to ignore the warmth of her body as she drew closer and flung part of the heavy cape about his shoulders.

"There's plenty for both of us."

Her face was now a white vagueness in the gloom. Her bare legs had become seductive witcheries that tapered invitingly from slender ankles to the scanty refuge of fragments of a skirt.

The firm pressure of her breasts against his side was maddening. She was infinitely more real than any night-walking demon. Reed's resolution melted as her warm breath fanned his cheek and her red curls brushed against his throat. The gloom had become a whirlpool of long imprisoned desire.

He caught her in his arms. Instead of drawing away, she pulled together the edges of the voluminous cape to imprison the warmth of their bodies. But it was her contented sigh that was ruinous.

Peril and the night had brought them together, but it was not until Reed's hand touched a firm, bare breast that they realized how far apart they were. She shivered, and not from the evening chill. Her half-hearted protest was a languorous murmur, and her arms closed about him as his free hand slid down the inward carve of her waist, and crept caressingly down the tattered wisp that still clung to her hips.

"Our chances of getting back to civilization are zero," she murmured. "I ought to make you stop . . . I would, too . . . but we shouldn't waste the hour we've gained . . . I'd hate to die before I ever lived . . ."

The bandits could return. He owed them a blood debt for those he had cut down during the raid. He would die — without ever finding Bint el Hareth.

Her voice was now an inarticulate murmur, and her breath was coming in short, quick gasps. Their lips met, and Reed knew that the red-haired girl had drunk as deeply of loneliness as he had during all his wandering . . .

AND when, a long time thereafter, Reed noticed that the rising moon was invading their corner of the court, the witchery in her dark eyes convinced him of the exceeding folly of persisting in his pursuit of a phantom of the night. They would leave in the morning; turn their backs on that sinister ruin and let Bint el Hareth walk alone by moonlight . . .

The red-haired girl seemed to sense his unspoken thoughts.

"We've both been awfully lonely," she whispered. "Oh, how I hated that village — but that's all over, and maybe you'll forget — whatever it was that made you look at me that way when you left the fire."

But before Reed found words, he heard a faint stirring somewhere beyond the gate. Instinct warned him. He snatched the loaded rifle and crept to the gateway.

The raiders had returned. They were creeping up the slope, dark blots in the moonlight. Something had conquered their overwhelming fear of that devil-haunted ruin.

Reed's rifle snapped into line. A crackling blast. The savage whine of the bullet that ricocheted from a rock down the slope. Moonlight was deceptive. He had wasted a precious cartridge.

"Run for the tower," he shouted as he slammed the bolt home. "I'll hold 'em!"

There was no answering fire. No sound. Only those dark, creeping blotches that relentlessly advanced, slipping from cover to cover, tempting him to waste his ammunition until they could close in.

He fired in desperation, but the derisive whine of wild bullets mocked him. His rifle was now empty. The bandolier of cartridges was by the fire. As he turned to retreat, a dozen gaunt Kurds popped up from concealment to charge up the slope.

Reed bounded toward the baggage lying near the embers; but before he could seize the bandolier, he heard the red-haired girl's voice. She was vainly struggling with the massive door that led to the turret.

"I can't open it!"

Three long leaps brought him to her side. The massive iron grille-work screeched as Reed savagely wrenched it open. But the raiders were now in the court. A savage, triumphant yell; but, strangely enough, not a shot was fired.

It was a close race, but Reed won by a hair. He thrust the girl across the threshold, then jerked the gate shut and slammed the massive bars into place. The Kurds could not break in without siege engines.

They were safe, but unarmed and without food.

"You fools!" Reed ventured a bluff. "This ruin is haunted. The demons will tear you to pieces."

"The peace upon you," the leader respectfully countered. "But we know that you are a saint. Your holy presence will protect us. We do not intend to harm you. We only want the red-haired girl. Our chief ordered us to get her. We will wait until hunger and thirst drive you forth with the girl."

The Kurd salaamed and turned his back.

As Reed followed his companion up the lordly staircase, he fully realized the irony of fate.

He had mocked Bint el Hareth in her own home, almost within arm's reach of her. And the girl whose loveliness had made him waver was with him. But he could carry on by surrendering the red-haired girl. Even though Bint el Hareth blasted him for his weakness.

Surrender her now. In the end, they would be starved out anyway.

"I'll go back," his companion said. "That'll give you your chance. They'll get me anyway."

But hearing it from her lips seemed to alter things.

"Stay here!" he snapped. "I'm going to the top story to think it out. There must be some way."

But Reed knew that there was no escape. The turret overlooked a precipitous drop of hundreds of feet. The bandits guarded every exit.

AS HE entered the upper chamber of the turret, the emptiness and desolation seemed vibrant with life. He glanced through the slits in the vaulted ceiling. *The stars were rising to their appointed positions.*

Reed frowned perplexedly. Some calculation had been in error. The stars that governed the return of Bint el Hareth would soon be at the marks sculptured by some forgotten astrologer.

Bitterness now corroded Reed's heart. Bint el Hareth would appear, and her jealousy would destroy him.

He raised his arms, lifted his eyes to the slits in the ceiling, and cursed the stars as they relentlessly marched toward their culmination; but they did not hear.

Reed was not afraid; but the iron was biting deeply into his soul. He seated himself on a block of granite and for a long time stared at the vague, mitred and bearded gods whose faces loomed monstrously in the shimmering gloom. They were remorseless as fate, but less malignant.

Reed's skin began to twitch. The gloom was becoming a live and vibrant creature. He wondered who would carry his body down to the nethermost vault to place him with those others who had been blasted by Bint el Hareth's wrath. How could a man's body become like the shell of a sundried insect?

Let her appear. Let it be over with. She might smile before she blasted him. He rose, and taking his position at the circle, he began reciting the ritual.

Scarcely a dozen syllables had thundered from his dry lips when he felt eyes probing the darkness behind him. He whirled.

The red-haired girl was at the threshold. Her body was a vague white glamor, and her face was a heart-shaped blot.

"Get out!" barked Reed. "I'm trying to think! Don't disturb me."

Instead of retreating, she advanced. Reed's hand flashed out to detain her. She eluded him and stepped toward the circle at the center.

That was the ultimate sacrilege!

But before his wrath could find voice, the red-haired girl spoke.

"Your fate is still in your hands, Morton Reed. Your choice is still yours."

How could she have called him by name?

But that was swallowed by a greater wonder: she went on to speak of his search for Bint el Hareth!

"But how — how can you know —" he finally gasped.

"Because —" She paused. He could just distinguish the whiteness of her hands against the waist band of what remained of her skirt. It slipped down in a heap about her ankles. "Because I am Bint el Hareth."

Her words burned into his brain as his eyes saw what gleamed at her waist: a broad silver girdle, flashing with uncounted sapphires. This was some monstrous trickery! Down there in the court, by the dying embers of their fire —

"How —"

"Raise your eyes, Morton Reed," she softly murmured, "I have other features as well . . ."

HER voice had in some inexpressible way changed. It was low and vibrant and heart-stirring and strangely modulated. Despite the alluring vagueness of her body, he was certain that its contours had unaccountably altered. Some strange change was going on before his very eyes. And as Reed looked her in the face, he could no longer be sure that her hair was red, or that it was not the deceptive play of brightening starlight that seemed to make her cheekbones ever so slightly more prominent and give her features a faintly aquiline cast.

"I am indeed Bint el Hareth," she continued. "It was written on the books of fate that that red-haired girl be killed in the raid. What difference if I borrowed her body, or shaped one for myself of moon glamor and star dust? I have already reshaped her to the form you desired."

"Then — down there — in the court —"

Bint el Hareth smiled.

"That was still her body, and some of her lingering personality."

"Then you're not jealous?"

She shook her head. "Old Habeeb gave you a garbled tradition. Not my wrath, but my more than human kisses left my lovers as you saw them. They accepted their doom and were glad.

"The choice is yours, Morton Reed. Those bandits down there cannot touch what little is now left of that red-haired girl's flesh.

"Deny and disown me, open the gateway, and go in peace. Your life will be long — but you will never forget the silver girdle that you could not remove."

She paused and ran slender fingers through her hair and withdrew a small key.

"And this," she continued, handing it to Reed, "is the key of doom. If you still have the courage and the will."

The night had become a maze of wonders. Reed saw that Bint el Hareth had blossomed in the light of stars risen to their culmination. Then for a moment he pictured those desiccated bodies ranged in the crypts below.

"It would be worse to wander with only the memories of a girdle without a key," he finally said.

Key in hand he stepped into the circle; and the splendor of her eyes foreshadowed the consuming fire of her uncounted strange kisses . . .

AND all the while, the leader of the Kurdish bandits watched his men heaping wood in front of the iron grille.

"That should be enough," he at last decided. It had taken a long time to find enough fuel in that barren waste. It took almost as long again before the massive bars reached a red heat. Then sword-strokes bit into the glowing metal, and the bandits poured through the breach.

Sunlight was filtering through the slitted dome of the upper chamber when they reached its threshold.

*"Wallah,"* muttered the bandits, "where is that red-haired *feringhi* wench? Not even a cat could have leaped through those small slits."

Then they saw Reed lying in an alcove between a pair of winged bulls. They recoiled, then paused to wonder what dream could leave such ecstasy on any man's face.

"The saint is sleeping," whispered the leader. "But see the print of her lips on his forehead. Doubtless — though Allah is the knower — he utterly destroyed her for trying to seduce him."

*"Ay wallah,"* echoed another in an awed whisper, "let us leave, before this pious man likewise destroys us for disturbing his sleep."

# PIT OF MADNESS

BAYONNE seemed incredibly ancient and lovely to Denis Crane as he headed from the wine shop to the Biarritz Highway and across the sombre parkway toward the Gate of Spain. The cathedral spires were silver lance-heads reaching into the moonglow, and the city was a pearl gray enchantment afloat on a sea of writhing river mists: yet that blood soaked soil whispered to Denis Crane as he walked.

This was unholy ground, honeycombed with crypts in which Roman legionnaires had worshiped Mithra, and watched frenzied devotees slash and mutilate and emasculate themselves in honor of bloodthirsty Cybele. This corner of France was the home of witch and wizard and warlock.

A shiver rippled down Crane's lean, broad-shouldered body as he glanced to his left and saw the ominous cluster of ancient trees that over-shadowed the low gray cupola of the spring where Satan and Saint Leon once had met —

Another medieval legend. Well, and here is the causeway, and just ahead, rue d'Espagne, with the yellow glow from the windows of Basque wine shops breaking its narrow gloom.

But the scream that came from his left told him how far from warm humanity he was, however near the lights might be. It was the sobbing, desperate outcry of some woman whose last gasp could not quite voice her terror.

Crane's suntan became a sickly yellow in that spectral, mist-filtered moonlight. He wheeled, stared into the swirling grayness of the dry moat that girdled the thirty-foot city wall. His face lengthened, tightened into grim angles, and his eyes narrowed as he listened. Silence — sinister . . . poisonous. . . . Then that dreadful wail again. It was closer now, and though it was inarticulate he knew that the woman was crying for help and despaired of getting it.

An everlasting instant, and she burst from the mist and into the foreground at the foot of the causeway that blocked the moat. Her abrupt appearance shocked Crane, though he knew that it was but the illusion of fog and moonlight.

Her hair was a streaming blackness, and her body a pearl-white glow. Her feet and legs were as bare as her torso. All she wore was a flimsy shawl caught at the shoulder, draping slantwise to veil one breast, and flaring out, to shroud the opposite hip. Crane distinguished no feature but her mouth. It was distorted in a cry she could not utter.

He plunged down the steep slope of the causeway and into the moat. Her legs gave way, pitching her headlong to the sand. She lay there, arms sprawled out. As he reached her side, she shuddered and slumped flat, no longer making instinctive efforts to protect herself.

Crane rolled her over into the crook of his arm. He saw then what mist and motion had masked: her throat was savagely torn, her breast and stomach clawed and lacerated. Her face was a gory crisscross of bruises and slashes. The filmy fragility of the shoulder-to-hip shawl had not hampered her assailant enough for him to tear it from her body.

Neither pulse nor breath was perceptible. Though her sweetly curved body was blood-splashed, her wounds could not have killed her; but terror and despair could have.

Her face must have been as lovely as her body; but horror blinded him to the sleekness of her hips and the shapeliness of her legs and firm young breasts. His eyes narrowed as he recovered sufficiently from the shock to interpret certain significant signs.

Her hands had the incredible softness of one utterly a stranger to the lightest work; but what she still clenched in her fingers was a startling revelation.

It was similar in shape to a military campaign badge; purple, with a rosette of the same color. A decoration awarded to an elect few.

But most revealing of all was the silken shawl. It placed her beyond any question. There was only one house in Bayonne where the girls paraded in such costume; and that place was on the street that ran along the city wall.

Then he noted that she was breathing; and a slash on her inside arm was bleeding. It might not be dangerous, but it was near an artery. He drew a clean handkerchief from his breast pocket, and devised a tourniquet.

The town was asleep, and he'd have to carry her to the house on the wall; but first give that tourniquet a twist. He fumbled for a pencil —

But Crane's first aid was not completed.

The sand of the moat bottom gave no betraying crunch; the mist thinned moonlight cast no warning shadow; and Crane's intuition was an instant too late. He dropped the battered girl, but before he caught more than a fleeting glimpse of the dark figure which loomed monstrously above him in the grayness, a flying tackle carried him crashing to the ground.

The impact knocked him breathless. Iron hands clutched his throat; but Crane's fist hammered home. Splintered teeth lacerated his knuckles, and blood gushed, drenching his face. His opponent, snarling scarcely articulate curses, jerked back. Crane's boot lashed out.

But the moonlight was blocked by another figure with monstrous, outspread wings. Bat wings, it seemed. It dropped, boring headlong, toppling Crane backward. A spicy, pungent odor, an odd blend of incense and cosmetics stung his nostrils. Then, still grappling with the thing which had swooped out of the upper mist, he crashed against the gray masonry of the bastioned wall. Crane's hard head had not a chance against a fortress built to defy a battering ram, but his shoulders absorbed enough of the terrific impact to save his skull Some lingering vestige of wits told him that once out of action, he no longer interested the enemy.

Minutes elapsed before he could fight off the numbness and inertia that clogged his will. But he finally rolled over and clambered to his knees.

He was alone in that gray, ghoulish moonglow. The girl was gone. He saw the prints of his own feet and those of the mysterious assailants that had swooped down on him. Blood flecked the sand, and one untrampled spot still held the imprint of that savagely slashed girl's breasts. It had not been illusion; but for a moment Crane's blood became ice.

The laundry marks and monogram on the handkerchief he had bound to the girl's arm would damn him beyond redemption when her body was found. And aside from that, he could not hope to obliterate the traces of the struggle in the moat.

The French police, inhumanly efficient, would inevitably connect him with the outrage. When he returned to his quarters, the *concierge* would note the time of his arrival. The proprietor of the wine shop on the Biarritz Road would remember when he had left, and the direction he had taken. And every foreigner is conspicuous in sleepy Bayonne.

Damn those experts with their omniscient microscopes! Their chemical tests which would detect the faintest trace of blood on his clothing.

And someone, watching from some darkened window of a house on the wall, might observe him as he left the moat, might already have heard and noted the encounter.

Only one move for Crane: find that girl, dead or alive. Hit first before the merciless *Sûreté Générate* connected him with the work of night-roving ghouls. And find the man whose decoration she had clutched.

As he hastened down the moat, he followed the girl's small, shapely footprints along the sand. Wrath burned him as his first fear left. Though that gaudy shawl branded her, she was still a woman, and the victim of something monstrous and deadly; something too eager for her torn flesh to bother with Crane beyond hammering him out of action.

Or had the two spectral assailants already arranged to frame him?

Half way to the sombre Lachepaillet Gate he noted the spot where her bare feet first marked the moat-bottom sand. He entered the walled city and hastened to his room at the Panier-Fleuri. The concièrge regarded him with bleary eyes that suddenly sharpened. But she said nothing.

Once in his room, he cleaned up, then stretched long legs toward rue Lachepaillet. He should report to the police; but who would believe such a story, told by an insane American, trying to implicate one who wore that coveted purple decoration the size of an A.E.F. campaign badge?

Crane jabbed a pushbutton. A trim, sharp-eyed girl in black admitted him and led the way to a spacious hall whose walls and ceiling were a solid expanse of mirror.

A bell tinkled, and a half a dozen girls lounging on upholstered benches lined up on parade as several others emerged from a rear apartment to join them.

They wore satin slippers and knee length silk hosiery. Their professional smiles, and the flimsy chiffon shawls draped from right breast to left hip completed their costume. Not a bad array; though some had overplump legs, and breasts that would have been the better for a brassiere. A few were lovely in face and body, but there was something infinitely repulsive about that grotesque multiplication of bare flesh in those mirrored panels whose angles probed the concealment of chiffon shawls and made the glaring room a patchwork of feminine curves.

Crane caught a freshly mirrored whiteness and turned toward the door. The shock for an instant numbed him. A full moment elapsed before he realized that he was not looking at the girl who had vanished from the moat.

She had the same gracious inward dip at the waist, the same heartwarming flare of the hips, and one lovely breast peeped alluringly through the heavy strands of hair that trailed down over her left shoulder. Her blue eyes were almost black. Their troubled darkness matched the sombre droop of her lips.

Tears had smudged the mascara of her lashes and a trace of redness lingered. Crane perceived the tensity of her body and saw her fingers twisting the trailing fringe of her shawl.

Why had she been reserved from the lineup? Why that startling resemblance to that savagely mutilated girl in the moat? Why that black fear in her eyes?

The girl's fingers sank insistently into his wrist, and he felt the firm pressure of her hip and shoulder against him as she paused in the doorway.

More than her resemblance to the girl in the moat told Crane that this was the one who could give him the most help — or damn him soonest. He followed his hunch.

*"Allons!"* he whispered. "Let's go."

He tossed the three hundred pound keeper of the house a purple Banque de France note, and followed the girl in the scarlet shawl up a flight of stairs and into a sombrely furnished room.

Her name was Madeline, but all the coquetry of the game was missing, though she contrived a friendly smile as her fingers plucked the shoulder knot of her shawl.

Crane checked her.

"What's wrong?" he demanded.

"Diane — my sister," she answered. "I'm terribly worried. She hasn't come back. That awful Arab — or Turk —"

Crane frowned. That was an odd touch. Who ever heard of an Algerian wearing that decoration?

As she spoke, she abstractedly kicked off her slippers and leaned back among the cushions. She regarded Crane curiously, seeing that his face was gray and grim.

"What's the matter . . . don't you like me?"

"That will keep!" His voice was harsh and low. "Tell me about that Arab. What was wrong with him?"

"Some of the things he did, the first night he was here. Before he took Diane — wherever he's taken her. It was in the room next door, No, he didn't hurt her at all — I mean the other girl, not Diane. But he frightened her terribly. I saw him leave. His pupils were like black saucers. *Mon Dieu!* Such eyes. Like Satan eating opium."

She was wrong. Opium contracted the pupils, but her very intensity gave Crane the picture.

"Are you sure he didn't wear the Order of Saint Léon?"

"Mumm . . . no, of course not! But he dropped something in her room, and she showed it to me, and left it here." Madeline slid to her feet and stepped to the dresser. She returned with a small silver watch charm. It was a tiny peacock with ruby eyes; an exquisitely tooled bit of metal.

"A soldier who'd served in Syria once told me," explained Madeline, "that that is a symbol of the devil-worshipers. That's what's been worrying me. If I'd known in time, I'd never have let her go. But why should you care?"

"I'm a damn' fool who can't mind his business," Crane smiled grimly. "I've got to find your sister." She sceptically eyed him.

"Then you don't want me? But you paid —"

Crane shrugged. "If you knew, you'd understand."

"Oh . . ." Very slowly, like a dying echo. She caught him by the shoulders, stared him full in the face; and bit by bit she read that the sombre riddle in his gray eyes concerned her missing sister.

"I didn't realize you knew Diane . . ." Her arm slipped about his neck and she drew closer as she continued, "I'll go with you. I'll help."

She had guts. Crane's smile lost his bleakness. For a long moment their glances blended. She sighed, and her breasts crept through their screen of dark curls. Her smile was a revelation, and suddenly Crane's blood quickened from the soft caress of her arm and the warmth of her body.

*"Tenez!"* protested Crane. "Stop it, you damn' little fool. I've got some business to attend to —"

"You wouldn't buy me," she whispered. "Somehow, that's rather wonderful . . . but you like me just a little, don't you? Wouldn't that make it different?"

Somehow, it did; and Crane's sensible effort to break away failed. She was lonely and worried. He couldn't repulse her friendliness.

"Cut it out!" he growled, though his protest was weakening. He laughed harshly, thinking of the one about the mail-carrier who hiked on Sundays; but Madeline seemed no longer one of those who lined up in that mirrored hell glare. She had become a bright flame in the foulness that crept through the mists of that fiend-haunted gray city.

Those were not bought lips that clung thirstily to Crane's mouth, and the shudder that rippled down her throbbing body was instinctive . . . and as her arms closed about him, Crane defied the peril that was gathering outside. He could not repulse the first glow of friendliness in that drab lupanar . . .

Madeline's eyes were tear-sparkling when she slipped from Crane's arms and said, "I know now that she is dead."

"The devil you do!"he snapped, feeling decidedly stupid about the interlude that might in the end cost him all but his head – literally, as they use the guillotine in France.

"Yes. Or you'd not have lingered, with that wrath in your eyes. So I know you can't find her alive."

No use explaining his true motives. He took a key from his pocket.

"Go to the Panier-Fleuri. Stay under cover. What you told me about an Arab has entirely upset my assumption. I thought you could tell me about someone wearing the Order of Saint Léon. But no matter – I've got a fresh hunch. Now run along."

They waited for the cessation of laughter and footsteps in the hall. A latch click. Silence, except metallic voices from the reception room on the ground floor.

Crane watched Madeline slip toward the further stairway. A moment later, looking from the window that overlooked the narrow black alley that skirted the rear of the house, he saw the white blur of her face, and caught the gesture of her hand.

She was on her way. He slammed the door and strode down the main stairway. He forced a laugh at the doorkeeper's vulgar farewell; but as he crossed the threshold, he began to see that his investigation, despite the delay, had gained him an ally if the police should catch up with him.

But that silver peacock was an ominous hint. Devil worship . . . some damnable Asiatic cult. He'd heard it existed in the mountains of Kurdistan.

Yet for all that thickening menace, the riddle in some respects was less baffling in the light of reflection.

Diane had been headed off by the monsters that had swooped down on Crane from the lip of the moat. They must have held to a straight line across the parkway. That gave him a start toward tracing the point from which she had made her futile break.

The mist was thinning, yet enough remained to envelop Crane in a spectral veil that protected and at the same time hampered him. He was unarmed; but he paused long enough to remove his socks, stuff one inside the other, and then slip in a rock the size of his fist. Very pleasant, if he got the edge on the two who had laid him out.

For half an hour he circled, trying to pick a course that the two monsters would have used to head off the mangled fugitive.

"Her instinct would drive her to the closest route to safety," he reasoned. "To her sister. Then if the Gate of Spain was the closest, her direction must have been more to my left. Otherwise she'd have gone through the Lachepaillet Gate."

Half an hour search vindicated the hunch. A shred of scarlet chiffon. A splash of blood.

He looped left. He found footprints heading toward the Gate of Spain — her pursuers, eager to cut off a flight that would betray their rendezvous.

Ahead of him a masonry lunette loomed low in the mist. One of the outer defenses erected by Vauban — or perhaps something much more ancient, and conceived by no honest engineer.

Crane now crept through the mists until a whiff of stale tobacco warned him of a watcher's presence.

He rose and boldly stalked toward the lunette. A jet of light flared in his face, blinding him. He was challenged in French.

"I've got to see the *émir* at once!" Crane bluffed, using a plausible Arabic title that would flatter anyone of lower rank.

The sentry protested. The *émir* was not to be disturbed. The ceremony had started. Crane shrugged and offered him the silver peacock.

"Hurry, idiot!" growled Crane. "Tell him I'm here!"

The flash shifted toward the silver token. The drawn pistol was holstered and an empty hand reached for the symbol. And then Crane's bludgeon cracked down. The guardian collapsed. Crane caught him and the flashlight.

The fellow was wearing a gown, and a hood from which hung a mask to conceal his face. Crane donned the disguise. This was no time for qualms.

The memory of that mangled girl nerved his arm. He raised the pistol, smashed down with the barrel. Then he picked his way down a narrow casemate inclining sharply into the earth.

Furtive flashes of his light guided Crane. He descended a stairway of archaic masonry, crumbled treads whose rubbish litter had been swept against the walls. A splash of fresh blood guided him.

Finally there was an indirect glow ahead. Drums were thumping, and voices muttered in eerie rhythm. Some satanic ritual was in progress.

Reasonably, Crane should now notify the police; but that brained sentry left him with no retreat. More than ever, his story had to be good.

He halted at the jamb of an arch opening into a vaulted chamber illuminated by flickering wax tapers. Its circular walls were pierced with other arches that led to further and darker crypts.

Upward of a score of scarlet-robed and hooded figures were informally gathered in groups. They sat on low wooden tripods the size of coffee tables. Their muttered conversation was low-voiced and unintelligible, but Crane sensed the tension that gripped them, felt their awe and soul-stabbing anticipation.

There was one, tall and commanding, who strode from group to group. Red-masked faces jerked abruptly upward at his approach.

But most revealing of all was the blank arch opposite Crane. Stretched out on a massive block of stone lay a woman, bound hand and foot: Diane, recaptured for the ritual from which she had escaped. Her body was to serve as an altar, perhaps to feel the thrust of a sacrificial knife. Black candles burned about her, diffusing acrid fumes which half obscured her; but Crane saw that she breathed. The tourniquet with his initials, however, had been removed.

Since Diane was alive; he need not find that damning handkerchief, provided that he could extricate her. But though he was armed with the sentry's pistol, the odds were far too great for open attack.

Then he saw that the figure on the two foot, brazen crucifix behind that altar of bare, lacerated flesh was inverted. That final detail sent frost racing through his blood. Those hooded figures had gathered for the Black Mass, the evil ritual of modern satanism, utterly different from the oriental devil-worship. Crane wondered how that silver peacock fitted into the tangle.

From one of the passages at the left came bestial snarls and half human mutterings: some monster held in reserve for the ultimate horror of that mad gathering.

The lordly figure in black clapped his hands. The devotees shifted into crescent formation. Crane joined them as they moved toward the altar.

The Black Monster was donning a priest's stole and cope. Six red-robed acolytes filed from a passageway. Three carried thuribles from which poured blue-black, pungent fumes; the others had trays of hammered copper, all heaped with diamond shaped lozenges. They passed among the gathering, swinging their thuribles and offering wafers to the devotees.

Crane tasted one of the confections; but instead of swallowing, he palmed it. It reeked with hasheesh and datura, blended with other oriental drugs he could not identify; but the two he recognized warned him. Both were brain-searing aphrodisiacs. Those wafers of illusion would make the partaker a crazed beast gnawed by outrageous fancies and delusions. That would give Crane his chance to act.

And all the while that bestial mumbling and groaning and the vibration of pounded iron echoed from the further crypt.

Crane watched the high priest of Satan make a foul mockery of the genuflections of the Mass, saw him spit upon the reversed crucifix, heard him chanting in a high, malignant voice.

Crane could scarcely understand the ritual, but some phrases of ultimate blasphemy were all too clearly burned into his reeling brain.

"Satan, Lord of the World, defend us against an unjust god who created only to damn . . . defend us against hypocrisy that mocks with the lure of redemption . . . hear the voice of the damned, O Lucifer, Son of the Morning! Satan, to you we make our prayer, Just and Logical God . . ."

Finally, the priest faced about and mocked the caricatured crucifix.

"And You, O Thief of Homage and Deceiver of Mankind, I compel you to become incarnate in this bread . . . by the mockery you have ordained, I who am ordained command you and you will obey . . . yea, while we draw blood anew from your wounds . . . and press fresh thorns of vengeance on your brow . . . this I can and this I will do . . . Accursed Nazarene . . . Traitor Son of a Traitor God . . ."

A low rumbling mutter drowned his amen; then with an inverse gesture of his left hand, the priest blessed the gathering and in mocking accents completed the blasphemy: *"Hoc est enim corpus meum!"*

He spat upon the consecrated bread, stolen from some consecrated altar; he scattered the fragments among the frothing, slavering devotees. They closed in, maddened with blasphemy and Asiatic drugs. They groveled, clawing and growling as they fought for the fragments.

Crane joined them. It was too early for a break. He had to outwit the un-drugged acolytes.

First voices, then the tearing of the scarlet robes told him that women were among those who writhed and panted and grappled on the floor. Hoods and masks yielded to clawing fingers. Soon they forgot blasphemy. The Asiatic drugs were biting deep.

In a moment the vault had become an animation of the bestial carvings of a Tantric temple, Women in jewels and costly gowns, and men in formal evening dress were clawing each other with a fury that stripped clothing to shreds.

A golden-haired fiend with crazed eyes and hungry red mouth emerged unpaired from the tangle and twined eager arms about Crane. A few scraps that glittered with green sequins trailed from her hips and what remained of a brassiere clung to breasts that throbbed from her fierce, drugged passion. Her legs were white serpents and her quivering body was a multitude of consuming flames, and her loose hair blinded and choked Crane as he swallowed his horror of that uncontrollable madness.

Yet he had to play his part. That black-robed demon's eyes glittered fiercely from behind his mask as he circled the arena, watching their ever fouler fancies cropping out . . .

That golden-haired woman's madness was cleaner than what was on every side. And despite his qualms, Crane's blood surged in irrepressible response to her savage frenzy . . .

Yet even as he yielded to that vortex of passion, a remote corner of his brain remained untainted. He plied her with answering kisses, felt the shudder of her hot flesh, but that one sane morsel was wondering. And at times he saw what was about him.

He recognized a black-bearded man whose face had appeared in every major newspaper of the world . . . another, who had led a victorious army . . . and one who from the sidelines told premiers what to say . . .

The Master gestured, and an acolyte dashed to the passageway at the left.

Crane's fist smashed home, driving away a black-haired woman who sought to displace his companion. Her body was raked and bitten and slashed, but she was seeking more savage company . . . Crane saw how Diane had been mangled. Her terror hinted that she had not been drugged . . .

Then Crane saw what had been released when those unseen iron bars clanged open. A tall, gray-haired man whose deeply lined face had once been handsome and commanding. He wore what remained of full evening dress. The ribbon that had crossed his shirtfront trailed like a streamer as he approached; and on it Crane saw the ribbons of civil and military decorations.

He recognized the man. He knew now from whose formal garb that purple rosette had been torn. His mouth frothed, and his eyes burned insanely. He snarled bestially and plunged into the surging orgy.

This was a man whose whispers shook Europe. Now he rolled vilely in that tangle of writhing flesh.

But why — Great God, *why?*

The Master laughed and gestured. The sullen ruddy glow of the tapers was drowned in a blue white, dazzling radiance, pitilessly revealing what shadows had shrouded.

Then Crane saw and understood.

A motion picture camera was covering the hideous show. That damnable film would place those drugged dignitaries forever in the power of that master of blasphemy. He had tricked them from Biarritz with hints of sensational ritual, drugged them, and the record of their unspeakable wallowings would doom them. Satanism had a logical purpose: political blackmail.

Time to move. The Master was distracted by his own show. Crane kicked clear of his companion, reached for his pistol.

It was gone! Lost in that writhing vortex.

He bounded to the altar, snatched that mockery of a crucifix, and whirled toward the Master. A pistol crackled. Crane felt the stab of hot lead, hurled himself aside as bullets spattered the masonry. The acolytes closed in. The brazen crucifix crunched home. But the survivors overwhelmed him, hammering and kicking and grinding him into the flagstones.

The Master joined them. Crane, battered and stunned, heaved up out of the gory tangle, clawed the mask aside. He slashed at that swarthy, aquiline face. He missed, ducked a knife thrust, and closed in. This was the *émir*, the Asiatic enemy whose grip on the drugged dignitaries would buy state and army secrets, upset an African colonial empire.

Crane bored in, but the enemy was fresh and he was dizzy and battered. They crashed to the floor, Crane underneath, vainly trying to drive home one good blow. He jerked clear of a second knife thrust; but the next raked his ribs. The vault became a roaring redness until he perceived nothing but those implacable eyes and that savage, brazen leer.

But that last stroke did not fall. The surging tangle of madmen, sated of all but blood lust, swept Crane and his enemies against the wall. As the acolytes strove to club them into reason, Crane made the most of his respite.

He snatched an abandoned thurible by the chains, swung it like a flail, flattening the Master's skull. He swung again, but the chains whipped athwart a devotee who intervened, and the weapon was jerked from Crane's grasp. He turned toward the altar, ploughing through the writhing tangle. He tripped and was dragged back into the whirlpool of madness, a yard short of his goal.

A pistol roared as he struggled to his feet.

Madeline had followed him.

Crane jerked the weapon from her fingers and blasted the acolytes back as she struggled with her sister's bonds.

Another shot. The cameraman toppled from his perch behind the altar. The pistol was empty. Crane seized the machine and smashed it across the head of a surviving enemy. The film reservoir spewed out its reel of yellow celluloid, fogged beyond redemption in an instant.

The knots yielded. Crane seized the half conscious girl and with Madeline at his heels, skirted the groveling tangle of drugged devil-worshipers. There were no acolytes left to pursue. And presently they reached the mist and moonlight . . .

"As you learned," explained Diane, hours later, in Crane's rooms, "I was just frightened helpless by your dashing down to meet me. The *émir* didn't intend for me to be clawed to ribbons. But *Monsieur le Général Mar* —"

"Forget his name!" interrupted Crane, "Later, I'll tell you why."

"*Eh bien,*" resumed Diane, "through error he prematurely took some of those drugs sooner than the *émir* intended. Before the ritual started. And you saw —"

"Plenty." Crane shuddered. Then he glanced at Madeline. "You little fool, you had to follow me!"

"But yes. I suspected that through no fault of your own you had been involved and were following some insane American impulse to do what you thought the right thing. So I followed, to help if I could. I feared she was dead, so I hesitated to call the police."

"Damn lucky you didn't!"

And then Diane interposed, "Monsieur Denis, how can I ever express my gratitude —"

"Madeline," interrupted Crane, "has already taken care of that. And having had my fill of sunny France, I think I'll leave for Spain in the morning."

# THE WALKING DEAD

WHEN WALT CONNELL heard the diffident tapping at the back door, he assumed an expression of judicial sternness. Plato Jones, who spaded Connell's garden, must be returning with a fantastic story to account for a week's absence and the six dollars which Connell had given him to buy some orange wine. But it was Plato's wife who tapped at the door, a plump, comely negress with a small parcel under her arm.

"Evenin', Mistah Walt," she began. "Mah man Plato ain't come back yet."

Tears were streaming down her face. Connell was saddled with a problem. Being adopted by a negro entails responsibilities: the colored man brings tribute of game, fish, and vegetables; the white patron reciprocates with old clothes and by bailing the negro out of jail at reasonable intervals.

"That no good man of yours probably drank my orange wine and now is afraid to come back," Connell accused.

"No suh, no suh!" Amelia protested. "Plato don't drink nuthin'!"

"Well, maybe I can help," Connell temporized.

"Yass, suh, Mistah Walt!" Amelia beamed through her tears. "Ah knew you'd take care of yo'ah cullud folks."

She thrust into his hands a paper-wrapped parcel.

"Ah don' baked yo'all a chocolate cake for yo' lunch when you go to get dat no good niggah! And ah fixed up some salted cashew nuts, too."

African guile had caught him totally off guard. He had accepted the present. Nothing to do but resign himself to a sixty-mile drive down the Mississippi Delta where the *Cajuns* convert undersized oranges into fragrant, blasting wine; a no-man's land, where a century or more ago, Lafitte's pirates found refuge.

THE NEXT morning Connell thrust Amelia's gift of chocolate cake and cashew nuts into the parcel compartment and headed down the west bank. He spent the forenoon searching small town jails as he worked his way down the Delta, but no news of Plato. His last chance was Venice, at the end of the highway.

Venice was half a dozen shacks plus a general store not much larger than a piano box. The girl behind the counter was uncommonly attractive. One of those substantial *Cajun* women, with luxurious curves, and plump, firm breasts as inviting as her amiable smile. Connell, however, managed to shift his glance to her dark eyes and began his oft repeated query concerning Plato and his red flivver.

Marie shook her head. Her eyes suddenly became somber as she said, "You're too late."

"What do you mean?" Connell, catching her by the wrist, felt her tremble.

"I didn't have any orange wine," she began, lowering her voice almost to a whisper. "So he went back."

Something was distinctly salty.

"You'd better tell me," he said in a quiet voice that impelled her attention.

Marie was wavering, but she was afraid. Finally she compromised, "We can talk better in back here."

Connell followed her to the rear of the tiny store. The crude, primitive room contained an oil stove, a small wooden table. In the further corner was a bed.

"You won't never see your nigger again," began Marie, drawing up a chair for Connell. "Not with walking dead men like they got at Ducoin's plantation."

*"Walking dead men!"* he echoed, leaping to his feet. "Who's Ducoin? What —"

But Connell's query was cut short. The Cajun girl's hand closed about his arm, drawing him to her side.

"I'll tell you later," she whispered. Her dark, smouldering eyes were still haunted, but her lips suggested reasons for delay.

Under other circumstances, Connell would have welcomed the hint, but something about her furtive glance and unnatural eagerness combined with her sinister remarks to repel him. But Connell made little progress. As he drew away, her arm slipped about his neck and her ripe, voluptuous curves pressed him closely as she pleaded, "Don't go . . . I'm terribly scared . . ."

She was. But Connell wasn't. And that warm, plump body was as inflaming as orange wine. He drew her to him, stroked her black hair, caressed firm flesh that trembled at his touch, and tried to entice her further remarks about walking dead men.

However, it did not work as he intended. His presence did reassure her, but the contact made his pulse pound like like a rivetting hammer, and the sudden rise and fall of her breasts showed that it was becoming mutual. . . .

Marie's dark eyes were no longer haunted by anything but a desire to get closer. Presently she forgot to brush away an exploring hand, and yielded her eager lips.

And then Connell learned that the Delta offers more than orange wine. . . .

IT WAS close to sunset before he remembered Plato and renewed his queries.

"Honest, I couldn't help it," Marie protested. "I didn't have any wine left and just as the nigger was going to leave, in comes Ducoin with a load. And he tells the nigger to come along, he'd fix him up. And I didn't dare warn him."

"Wait till I get at Ducoin!"

"Don't!" implored Marie. "He'll know I told you. And you can't do nothing. Plato's a walking corpse by now — and I'll be one, if Ducoin finds out —"

She tried to detain Connell, but he broke clear before her full-blown fascinations could conspire with her sinister hints. She had merely delayed the quest; and Connell headed up the river, toward that mysterious plantation.

Ducoin's house loomed up above the surrounding orange groves, nearly a quarter of a mile from the highway. Its remnants of white paint made it resemble a gaunt, ancient tomb. As Connell pulled up, he saw a Model T parked in a clump of shrubbery. Plato's decrepit red Lizzie!

And then Connell received a shock. A file of negroes emerged from the orange groves. Their black faces were vacant. They shambled toward the left wing of the house with the grotesque gait of animated dummies.

The sodden, lifeless *clump, clump, clump* of their feet sounded like clods of earth dropping on a coffin. Their arms dangled limp as rags.

Connell shuddered. No wonder that the ignorant *Cajuns* considered them walking dead men.

*Clump, clump, clump.* The most poverty stricken and oppressed negro laborers jest and chatter at the end of a day's work; but these black men stalked in silence broken only by the shuffling crunch of their flat feet.

Following the file came a white man who wore boots and riding breeches. His heartless, handsome face was tanned and deeply lined. Intelligent but relentless. His dark eyes were as cryptic as his smile as he confronted Connell.

"Looking for someone?"

"Yes. A nigger named Plato," answered Connell. "Are you Pierre Ducoin?"

"That's the name," admitted the taskmaster. "But there's no strange nigger on the plantation."

The more Connell saw of Ducoin the less he liked him. There was something uncanny about the man.

As Connell hesitated, something compelled him to glance towards the veranda that ran the full length of the house, some ten feet above the ground level. Framed by a French window was a girl whose dark eyes and lovely, delicate features for an instant made him forget that she was clad only in a chiffon robe which, half parted, revealed enticing glimpses of silken legs, and a body to which clung the caressing haze of sheer fabric that betrayed slender, olive-tinted curves . . . the amorous inward sweep of her waist . . . pert breasts that any hand larger than her own could conceal. . . .

Her lips were silently moving, and she was gesturing for him to leave at once. But she had overlooked her own loveliness. Connell was staying.

"I'm Walt Connell, and I think you're mistaken," was the retort. "Let me talk to your niggers. Someone of them might know about him."

That play was better than making a liar of Ducoin by mentioning Plato's flivver, half concealed in the shadows.

For a moment Ducoin's eyes flared with a light that Connell was certain could not be the reddish sunset glow; his qquiline features tightened, then suddenly he smiled and amiably agreed, "Do that in the morning. Too late now. This plantation reaches all the way out to the bay, and most of my crew is quartered at the further end. Take us an hour or more to go out, and it's getting dark. Make yourself at home — there is plenty of room here, and you can look in the morning."

A grim-faced negress served dinner in a vast, high-ceiled room facing the west. Fried chicken, Creole gumbo, rice, and corn bread. All tastily seasoned, except for an utter lack of salt. Connell, reaching for the only shaker on the table, noted that it contained pepper.

"Sorry," apologized Ducoin, "but we've run all out of salt. It's rather primitive down here on the Delta. We shop only once a week."

Dinner, despite Ducoin's easy cordiality, was a decided strain. Connell was wondering at the absence of the lovely girl who had warned him.

"Working many niggers?" he queried.

"A dozen or two," Ducoin carelessly answered. "Haitians: part of an odd lot brought to the West Indies a century or more ago. Sullen, stolid brutes, but good workers."

He changed the subject. Connell was relieved when the colored woman served night-black, chicory-tinctured coffee, and a pony of excellent brandy. Ducoin remarked, "We turn in early here. Plantation hours begin before sunrise. Aunt Célie will show you your room. In the morning you can make the rounds with me."

Connell followed the grim negress down the hallway. Her morose, stolid demeanor confirmed Ducoin's comment on the temperament of his negroes; yet Connell was distinctly perturbed. And as the door closed behind Aunt Célie, he received a distinct shock.

The moon was rising, casting a shimmering, silvery glow over the black expanse of open fields. Men were at work, digging and hoeing. Utterly unheard of, a night shift on a plantation. Connell heard the thudding blows of their implements, but not a murmur, not a spoken word.

There wasn't an overseer, yet they toiled on, methodically, as though motor driven, never pausing to lean on their hoes for a breathing spell. They advanced in an unwavering line, grotesquely combining the precision of military drill with the uncouth, ungainly movements of dummies.

Connell shivered and shook his head. Questioning such unnatural creatures would be futile. One glimpse of them and Plato would have taken to his heels. He wondered if his negro might not have abandoned his flivver, frightened out of all reason by the uncanny spectacle of Africans working without song and chatter.

A soft, furtive stirring in the hall just outside of his room made him start violently. Something softly slinking down the hall had paused at his door. By the moon glow that penetrated the shadows, he saw the scarcely perceptible motion of the knob. Something was stealthily seeking him. A silent bound brought Connell to the fireplace, and out of the moonglow. His trembling fingers closed on a pair of massive tongs.

He watched the door soundlessly swing inward. A nebulous spindle of whiteness cleared the edge of the jamb: a spectral, shimmering whiteness that for an instant froze Connell's blood. Then he saw the intruder was the girl who had warned him.

She paused to close the door, and as she turned from the threshold Connell for the first time realized how lovely she was. Her tiny feet were bare, and her shapely legs, gleaming like ivory exclamation marks through the sheer, gauzy fabric of her nightgown, blossomed into seductive curves that fascinated Connell.

The vagrant breeze shifted, drawing the misty fabric closer, revealing her perfections as though she were clad in no more than bare loveliness. The filmy silk clung to the inward curve of her waist, and caressed the firm, delicious roundness of her breast. She was a lovely unreality in the vague light that made her face a sweet, pallid mask, and her black hair a succession of gleaming highlights.

She advanced a pace before she saw Connell.

"Leave at once." As she spoke, she caught his arm. She was trembling violently.

"What's wrong?"

"It's not too late," she whispered as Connell seated himself, and drew her to the arm of his chair. "My uncle is out putting the night shift to work. "I'm Madeline Ducoin."

"I came here to get my nigger," insisted Connell.

"He's one of them now," said Madeline, shuddering. "A walking corpse."

"That's absolute rot! How can a dead man walk?"

"You saw them, didn't you?" Madeline countered, sighing and helplessly shaking her head.

As she leaned toward the window and gestured at the macabre figures that toiled in the moonlight, her dark hair caressed Connell's cheek, and he felt the supple flexion of her slender body. Madeline at least was real in the moon-haunted glamour. His arms closed about her, and drew her to his knee. She was still trembling, but at his touch, she snuggled up like a contented kitten.

Pillowing her head on his shoulder, she looked up and repeated, "Please leave, before it's too late."

Connell laughed softly and said, "Never had a better reason for staying."

For a moment they crossed glances in the moonlight. His arms tightened about her, and she did not draw away. And then as though by common impulse, their lips met, and Connell felt the ecstatic shiver that rippled down her silk clad body. She tried to catch his wrist, brush aside the hand that caressed the gleaming curves of her thigh.

Her inarticulate murmur of protest, breathed in Connell's ear, further inflamed his blood, and his possessive caresses for the moment brushed aside the hovering presence of mystery and horror. Each seemed to feel that the other was a haven of reality in the devil-haunted plantation.

The lacy hem of her gown was creeping clear of her knees. Connell's kisses were stifling her murmured protests. Madeline's breath came in ever quickening gasps. She was clinging to him, the pressure of her firm young breasts telling him that she really did not want him to desist.

If Ducoin was making the rounds of his spectral plantation where black automatons tilled the fields by moonlight, there was no hurry. Connelly's ardent caresses were calling to the surface all the fire and passion of Madeline's Latin blood. She was lonely and frightened, and his purposeful persistence thrilled and assured her. Her final protest ended in a sigh and a murmur and a silky embrace that became as possessive as Connell's enfolding arms.

"We'll soon leave, darling." As he emerged from his chair, she still clung to him.

"Aunt Célie is asleep." Her whisper was an invitation. "And Uncle Pierre won't be back for quite a while . . . ."

She caught his hand.

"You'll take me with you, won't you?" Madeline murmured, flinging back her disarrayed dark hair, and extending alluring arms. "When we leave. . . ."

"I'll take you away from here, forever and always," he promised.

FOR A LONG time their murmurings mocked the horrors that marched blindly across the spreading fields of the moon flooded Delta. Finally Madeline slipped from Connell's arms, and gestured toward the moon blot on the floor.

"It's getting late, sweetheart," she whispered. "We'll go to New Orleans as soon as I can pack up."

Connell followed her, and watched her hastily bundle together odds and ends selected from her wardrobe. A strange, mad night. Going in search of a stray nigger, and finding this incredible armful of loveliness. It was all fantasy, but Connell's lips still tingled from the fire of her kisses. Let Pierre Ducoin keep the secret of the uncanny walking dead men. Plato would eventually appear with some wild story accounting for his absence. It was utterly incredible that he would have lingered long enough to have left any clues. Amelia's African guile had fairly bludgeoned Connell into this mad search.

He watched Madeline dressing in the moon glamour. Once he reached New Orleans with that delicious loveliness, he would pension Plato for life.

They stole through the shadows of the orange grove to Connell's *coupé*. He took Madeline's suitcase and raised the turtle back. Something was stirring in the baggage compartment.

*"Mon Dieu!"* gasped Madeline.

"Is dat you, Mistah Walt?" whispered an African voice. Amelia Jones emerged. "Is yo' got mah Plato?"

Then she saw Madeline, and her voice trailed into reproachful indefiniteness. Connell was betraying his colored folks.

"What the devil are you doing here?" he sternly demanded.

"Ah jes' followed," said Amelia. "In case that no good niggah didn't want to come home."

Her plump, comely face was agleam with perspiration. It was a wonder she had not suffocated in the stuffy baggage compartment during that long search down the Delta. Connell helplessly glanced at Madeline who was nervously fingering his arm. Amelia painfully clambered out of the turtle back.

"Get back in there, Amelia," Connell abruptly ordered. "I'll fix the top."

But the negress shook her head.

"No, suh, Mistah Walt. I'se gwine to find him mah self. Ah knows yo' is too busy, and Ah's much obliged fo' de ride." Her glance shifted, and she saw the familiar model T. "Dat's Plato's Fohd. Ah'll git him. Don't yo' wait heah no longah, Mistah Walt."

Amelia's contradictory blend of stubbornness and humility got under Connell's skin. He couldn't sell his niggers down the river that way; neither could he leave Madeline another night in that fiend-haunted plantation house. But his indecision was costly.

Dark forms slipping from the shadows closed in on them. Ducoin's black laborers! Their eyes were not blind, but staring, unfocused and unseeing. Their faces were utterly devoid of expression. Walking dead men, moving with the slow, horrible motion of animated corpses.

"Get back, you black devils!" snarled Connell, thrusting aside a clutching hand and driving home with his fist; but it was like hammering the trunk of a tree. Not a gasp, not a grunt, not a change of expression. Madeline screamed as other hands clutched her.

Though Connell's fists crunched against bony faces, and chunked wrist deep into leathery stomachs, he made no more impression than on tackling dummies. Kicking, slugging, and gouging as the tangle of voiceless black men overwhelmed him, Connell's brain became a vortex of horror. He knew now why the *Cajuns* called them walking corpses.

They could not be alive. There was no resentment or wrath at his frantic, savage blows. Somewhere he heard a terrified wailing and a scurrying. Amelia was taking cover. The walking corpses seemed unaware of her presence.

Madeline's outcries were throttled. As Connell vainly battled, he caught glimpses of her silk clad legs flailing in the moonlight, heard the ripping of cloth as her ensemble was torn to ribbons by her captors. Then he was smothered by the irresistible rush. A sickening, musty, charnel stench stifled him. Iron muscles, leathery bodies, exhaling the odor of incipient decay, yet more powerful than any living thing, crushed him to the border of unconsciousness. They seized him and Madeline as though they were logs, and hauled them up the veranda stairs and into Madeline's room.

Connell heard Pierre Ducoin's familiar voice.

"Too bad," he ironically commented as the blacks dropped their burdens, and pinned Connell to the floor with their bony knees. "Aunt Célie told me something was going on."

Then he turned to the corpse men, and spoke in a purring, primitive language, more rudimentary than any Haitian patois: the old savage dialect of Guinea.

They bound Connell's hands and feet to a chair, and flung Madeline carelessly across her bed. Though half conscious, she was stirring and moaning, and instinctively trying to draw her tattered ensemble down about her hips. And then Aunt Célie appeared, black, sombre and malignant. The sinister negress knelt beside the hearth and struck light. In a moment she had a fire kindled and was heaping it with charcoal.

The walking corpses lined themselves against the wall, awaiting orders. It was only then that Connell fully realized what had mauled and pounded him and Madeline.

They were breathing; but their lack of expression reminded him of a dog he had once seen in a vivisection laboratory. The greater portion of the animal's brain had been removed; it lived, but it was a living log. And those black men had only enough brain left to let their reflexes function.

"How do you like my crew of *zombies?*" murmured Ducoin as the negress set a kettle of water over the glowing coals.

*Zombies!* That one word rounded out Council's rising horror. They were corpses stolen from unguarded graves and had been reanimated by a primal necromancy to serve as farm cattle! *Zombies,* toiling as no dumb beast could. Rich profits, farming a plantation with hands like those. He wondered why Aunt Célie knelt swaying and muttering before the kettle into which she tossed dried herbs, and bits of bark and roots and pebbles.

"Pretty nice, eh?" was Ducoin's satirical comment. "I learned the trick at Haiti, and I'm going to add you to my string of *zombies.* Once Aunt Célie mixes you a drink you won't be so interested in women."

Wrath blazed in Ducoin's eyes as his glance shifted to his disheveled niece.

"I don't know what you two were doing," he murmured, "but I can fairly well guess. Or else she wouldn't have been so willing to go away with you. Just another no-good wench. Shell be a very good *zombie* herself —"

"You damn' dirty rat!" snarled Connell. "Do you mean —"

"Certainly," answered Ducoin. "After fooling around with you, she's no niece of mine. In this day and age I can't give her what she deserves, but making her a *zombie* is different. Nobody will inquire out here on the Delta. And she'll not be playing around with strangers any more."

Another guttural command. The corpse men marched over to Madeline's bed as returning consciousness stirred her. Connell, struggling against his bonds, saw them stripping her dress to tatters as they throttled her into submission. Shuddering with horror at the grisly contact, Madeline finally surrendered, and the *zombies* methodically lashed her to another chair. Her dress was a pitiful rag. Her clawed breasts were half exposed, and her bruised legs peeped through the remnants of her hosiery.

Ducoin chuckled at Connell's frenzied struggles.

"That won't do you any good. I'll leave a guard here to watch you while Aunt Célie and I finish the brew that'll make both of you *zombies.*"

At Ducoin's command, all but one of the *zombies* filed out of the room. Before he and Aunt Célie followed, the Creole paused to remark. "You were looking for Plato. All right, I'm sending Plato in to help watch you. Now see how you like the white man's burden!"

They left. But presently, as the fumes from the kettle stifled and dizzied Connell, he heard approaching footsteps *clump-clump-clumping* down the hall.

The black apparition which stood framed in the doorway froze his blood. Plato had returned, a loose-jointed, shambling, lifeless hulk that moved in response to the *zombie* master's command.

"Good God in heaven!" he groaned.

"That's why I warned you," whispered Madeline. "I saw Plato before and after."

"If I'd only left —"

"I'm still glad you didn't, Walt. It was such a ghastly, lonely life. Becoming a living corpse is better than never having lived."

A wave of nausea racked Connell. He and Madeline would presently be the companions of that horrible hulk.

"Hitch your chair over, bit by bit," Madeline continued. "Maybe I can get you loose."

Connell's cramped efforts moved the chair a scant fraction of an inch. At the rasp of wood, the heads of the *zombies* shifted. They had their orders. Not a chance.

"Plato," said Connell. "Loosen my hands, Plato, don't you remember me?"

Over and over, he repeated the name. The blank, sightless face seemed to change for an instant.

"Maybe he's not been this way long enough to forget everything," whispered Madeline. "Try again —"

The oft repeated name got unexpected results, but not from the *zombie.* Plato's wife, Amelia, came slinking from the hallway. Her black plump face became slate grey as she stared into the ruddy glow.

"Where's mah Plato? Mistah Walt, was yo'all talkin' to him?"

Then she saw the hulk that had been Connell's nigger.

"Plato! Don't yo' heah me talkin' to yo'?"

Not a sign of life. That blasted brain could not absorb a new impression.

"Plato, honey, cain't yo' heah me?"

Finally, grey and trembling, the negress turned to Connell.

"Mistah Walt, Ah cain't do nuthin'. Mah Plato's am daid."

Connell realized that Amelia's persuasion had made less impression than his own authoritative voice.

"Untie us, Amelia," he said.

She had scarcely reached the chair when Plato's ponderous hand lashed out, flinging her into a corner.

"Mistah Walt," said the negress as she struggled to her feet, "Ah's gwine to de village to git help. Dat debbil don't know Ah'm here, and Ah'll get some white folks."

She stepped into the hall. Connell renewed his struggles. Once or twice Madeline contrived to jerk her chair a fraction of an inch toward him, but a *zombie* leaped forward, bodily picked her up, and set her in a corner. They did nothing to thwart Connell's struggles against his bonds. The orders had not covered that.

Finally Connell contrived to spread the knotted strands of clothesline.

"Hang on, darling," he panted. "I'll be clear in a second."

"But what good will it do?" moaned Madeline. "They'll block you before —"

"Maybe I can toss you out the window, chair and all."

He knew that he had no chance against his grisly captors, but anything was better than waiting for that deadly brew to receive the missing ingredients that would make them living corpses. Connell heard footsteps and relaxed his desperate efforts. His blood froze, and a stifled oath choked him.

It was Amelia. She had a small parcel wrapped in paper. Damn her black hide, why hadn't she run to the village?

"Plato, honey," she pleaded, "Ah's done brought yo' somethin' good."

"For God's sake, go to the village," shouted Connell.

"That would be wasted effort," said a sardonic voice. Ducoin crossed the threshold, accompanied by Aunt Célie and several *zombies*. His sinister presence, and the living dead seemed to freeze Amelia with horror. She had lost her chance to make a break.

"I guess we'll have a number three *zombie*," murmured Ducoin.

The living dead now blocked the doorway. Aunt Célie lifted the lid of the kettle, and added a pinch of powder from a small packet. She stirred the villainous potion, and drew off a cupful and held it to Connell's lips.

"You might as well drink it," said Ducoin. "If you don't —" His gaze shifted to Madeline's trembling bare body and he resumed, "These *zombies* will do anything I tell them. How would you like to see one of them —"

His words trailed to a whisper, but Connell knew what would happen to Madeline, before his eyes.

And then the last remnant of cord that bound his wrist yielded. His freed hand flashed out, striking the steaming beverage from Ducoin's hand. As the Creole recoiled, Connell's other hand jerked loose, gripping him by the throat. The sudden move caught Ducoin off guard. Since the master was present, the *zombies* did not interfere; and Ducoin, throttled by Connell's savage grasp, could not articulate an order.

*Sock!* Connell's fist hammered home, driving Ducoin crashing into a corner, dazed and numb. Connell struggled with the bonds at his ankles, but only for a moment. Aunt Célie seized his elbows from the rear.

Once Ducoin recovered his voice — !

Amelia was free. But instead of running, she approached Plato.

"Jes' yo' taste one, honey," she crooned, placing a salted cashew nut in the bluish, sagging mouth of her dead husband.

There was a mumbling and a drooling, a sudden flash of perception as the salty tidbit mingled with the saliva; then an inarticulate, bestial howl. Ducoin and Aunt Célie flung themselves forward.

"Stop her!" yelled Ducoin. *"She's giving them salt!"*

Too late. Burly, powerful Plato had become a raging maniac. Amelia thrust a dozen cashew nuts into the mouth of the other *zombie*. Another incredible transformation. Another slavering, howling black brute. A pistol cracked, but only once.

Ducoin's weapon clattered into a corner. Plato and his companion closed in.

The room became a red hell of slaughter. The insensate black hulks were pounding and trampling and flinging Ducoin and Aunt Célie about like bean bags.

They hungrily licked splashed blood from their black hands, and renewed the assault. Other *zombies* came from the fields, tasted a salted nut, and joined the butchery. And presently there was only a shapeless, gory pulp that they were trampling and beating into the floor. . . .

The *zombies* desisted for lack of fragments left to dismember. Then they clambered to their feet, utterly ignoring Amelia and the two prisoners. They shattered the window, cleared the sill, and dashed across the field. Against the moonglow Connell saw them burrowing into the ground like dogs.

Amelia, sobbing and laughing, was releasing him and Madeline.

"Mistah Walt," the negress explained, "when Ah saw mah Plato Ah remembered somethin' my ole grandmammy done tol' me years ago, about dem *zombies* cuttin' up dat way when dey ate salt. Den Ah 'membered de cashew nuts Ah done give yo'. Now, praise de Lawd, Plato am plumb daid, and all de other niggah is gwine to their graves lak Christians. Dey always does dat, when they gets salt. But fust they musses up de man what made dem *zombies*."

"But how did he do it?" wondered Connell as he helped Madeline into the car.

"I don't know anything about it, except that according to the law in Haiti, it's a capital offense to administer any drug that produces a coma. And I think that's the real reason Uncle Pierre decided to finish me — he found me reading an old book of Haitian statutes, not long ago, and was afraid of my suspicions."

"Mistah Walt," interrupted a voice from the rumble seat, "yo'll gwine to need a maid fo' de new missus, ain't yo?"

"Absolutely," assured Connell, "but you'd better take a vacation for a couple of weeks before you come to work. . . ."

# EVERY MAN A KING

"DO YOU have to go? At this hour?" Olajai turned from her mirror, but did not leave off unfastening the red velvet hood whose twinkling pendants trailed past her cheeks, and to her shoulders. "Couldn't it wait till tomorrow?"

Timur[1] frowned, which made it all the more certain that the King Maker's granddaughter had not married him for his looks. He snatched a shirt of link mail from a hook, and as he worked it down over his broad shoulders, he grumbled, "One of Bikijek's pets, and he's got the king's seal. Either be a good dog, or run out and join your brother at Saghej Well!"

Olajai said, wistfully, as she wiped off the last bit of dead-white makeup, "And I thought it'd be lovely, living in Samarkand."

Olajai was shapely of body, and exquisite of face; the Turki heritage, showing in the peach blow tinge of her cheeks, gave features whose every line was sharp and clean and delicate in its drawing. This was Timur's first and only wife, and thus far, he was glad that there were no others.

Though not quite twenty-seven, he looked older, for mountain blizzards and desert blasts had weathered his flat face. Wind blown sand and storm driven sleet had set the Mongol slant of his eyes in a permanent squint; and for all the blue Zaytuni silk tunic he put on over his shirt of linked mail, and his gold embroidery boots, and plumed pork pie hat, he seemed out of place in a palace.

"I'll get away as soon as I can," he promised, and limped out.

Bow legged, and never built for walking, he was further handicapped by an ankle which had stopped a well-aimed arrow. In the tiled reception room, he said to the waiting official, "Something important going on?"

The square-rigged Kipchak did not answer; he merely tapped the big four-cornered seal. In the court, a sleepy groom held his horse, and Timur's.

---

1    Editorial note: Tamerlane, the name we know so well, is a Persian-ized corruption based on a pun comparable to "Heel, Hitler." Timur is the true name; and "Bek," "Beg" is simply prince or lord.

They skirted the plaza of splendid Samarkand. The bitter clear moon brought out the blue of tile-fronted palaces, and the golden crests of tall minarets. Samarkand, the jewel of the Jagatai Empire, was now the prize of the Kipchak Horde who had overrun the land: and Timur was weary of serving invaders. But for luck, and a friend at Elias Koja's court, he might be an exile, like Olajai's brother, Mir Hussein. Yet, though his position as administrator of affairs gave plenty of enemies and little satisfaction, it at least enabled him to stand between Bikijek's rapacious clique of nobles, and his own conquered neighbors.

Timur trailed the official, instead of riding boot to boot. There was more than just the matter of rank involved. Then, wary ever since that first strange warning, he noted the stirring in the shadows of the archway to the left. Here the street was narrow; here he and his guide faced a cold, white moon.

A bowstring twanged, the strident note of a horseman's bow. Timur ducked. His sword was half unsheathed when the arrow thumped home, nailing the Kipchak squarely in the throat. The fellow made a choking sound, and lurched from the saddle.

Timur wheeled, chin in, and crouching low, so that there was hardly any vulnerable spot exposed. The Ferghana stallion stretched out in a great bound; hooves struck fire. When things happened too fast for thought, Timur Bek was driven by the instinct to close in, to cut down.

Then a man came out, barefooted and bearded. "Go home, Timur Bek. There was no other way to warn you."

The face was in shadow, but Timur recognized the voice and the figure. "Good shooting, for a scholar! But why?"

"Allah will enlighten you. Also, the man you were following won't be able to tell anyone you've been enlightened."

"What is this, Kaboul?"

"If all is well with your family, then this is a mistake. And the peace upon you."

Kaboul the Darvish turned into the shadows of the archway. On the ground, Timur saw a horseman's bow, but neither quiver nor arrows.

"One man, one arrow."

And now Kaboul was going back to his cubicle to write a Persian quatrain, or an ode in Turki!

Timur, retracing his course, held his horse to a walk, for in spite of the menace which threatened Olajai he could not risk the sound of galloping. When he finally reached the wicket which gave entrance to the rear court of his house, he hitched himself up and stood in the saddle. Then, catching the crown of the wall, he swung himself to the top, and dropped to the grass inside. His first move was to unbolt the little gate, and lead his horse in, for he dreaded the helplessness of being afoot.

His felt boots made no sound. As he hurried past the servants' quarters and down a hallway, he heard voices, in front: a challenge as of a drowsy porter, then brusque answer, and a scuffle which ended in a groan.

There was time. He hurried back, mounted up, and again felt complete. He nudged the stallion with his boot, and stroked the sleek neck, wheedling the bewildered beast into the tiled passageway.

A woman cried out, more in wrath and indignation than in fright. "Father of pigs! Get out of here or have you skinned alive."

"That's her, Olajai Turcan Aga!"

"Come down, *khanoum*; we won't hurt you."

"So you *do* know that this is Timur's house. You know, and come in?"

They laughed at the threat. "And we know where Timur is."

That was when the lame rider's scowl became a grin. "Come down, Olajai!" he called. "We're leaving town!"

The deep-chested hail made the men at arms whirl about. They had curved swords, they had maces; they wore peaked helmets, and armor of overlapping plates sewed on leather, but they were afoot, and they were surprised.

The stallion snorted. He quivered, then leaped as Timur's legs tightened. The heavy blade licked out, finding the gap between neck-guard and hauberk. As the stroke bit home, Timur traversed, so that the wall covered his left. He swayed in the saddle; a spike-headed "morning star" ripped his tunic, exposing the link mail beneath, and then his blade flickered, slashing the man's forehead.

Blood-blinded; that one was out of action.

"Come down; we're riding!" Timur shouted.

Some were scrambling now to get to the front court, and their waiting horses; several tried to close in with swords. Blades clanged. Timur hewed down, slicing off plates of armor.

Olajai snatched a tall Chinese vase from the landing and heaved it on the head of the rearmost. While his helmet saved him from a smashed skull, the impact dropped him in his tracks. She dashed down the stairs, and plucked the fellow's helmet from his head.

"Put it on!" she cried, crowding up on Timur's left.

"Grab a horse!" he answered, and booted the stallion after the handful who had raced for their mounts.

And when his horse got firm footing on the hard-packed earth, Timur charged with effect.

Olajai followed. She was not dressed for riding, but the ripping of her gown took care of that. And she picked a good mount.

Two of the raiders galloped across the square. Two others fled afoot. Timur snatched the bow whose case hung from the saddle of Olajai's horse. As he strung it, she passed him an arrow.

The hindmost of the footmen pitched on his face.

Timur grinned. "Good bow. Now keep behind me; there'll be the devil to pay at the gate."

There was, but it did not last long.

Guardsmen were turning out. The two surviving horsemen had attended to that. But the moon was bright, and Timur's bowstring twanged, once, twice, thrice: the deadly Turki arrows, released at a dead run, cleared a path. Then a whirl of steel, and the fugitives went pelting down one of the lanes which threaded the orchard girdle of Samarkand.

## CHAPTER II

### *The Beggar*

ONCE A bend in the lane furnished momentary cover, Timur pulled up. "Get Eltchi Bahadur and as many others as you can, and ride direct for Saghej Well. I'll keep the Kipchaks off your heels, and I'll meet you later."

Olajai had long since learned to think quickly, and to move while thinking; she waved, reined her horse down a cross lane, and galloped to notify the chief of Timur's fifty picked fighting men who had followed him from his home in Kesh. And since they lived outside the city walls, Olajai's task was safe enough.

Her brother, Mir Hussein, was at Saghej Well with forty-odd retainers. They had outraced the Kipchaks to find refuge in the wastelands, and their heads apparently were not considered worth the cost in horseflesh.

Timur dismounted. When he heard the approach of the pursuers, he pretended to be picking a stone from his horse's hoof. In a moment they came into view, and in the full moon, they saw him. Olajai could not be far away. The horsemen reined in. It was over, they thought.

The fugitive, having the advantage of the moon, fired from his own shadow. A man toppled. Timur swung into the saddle, and the Ferghana stallion took off in a falcon swoop.

He twisted, shooting as he rode. And this was not his second-choice horse!

They would stick. Speed was not the essence of this chase, since he had neither rations nor water nor a spare mount. As he gained a lead, he reined in a little, holding the distance just beyond arrow range. For all they knew, Olajai was ahead of him, just beyond sight.

Timur now had time to ponder on the reasons behind the raid on his house. Bikijek's resentment at a man who spent too much time blocking the sale of justice, blocking the extortion of doubled taxes, and the making of false returns: that was one fair guess. The other, plain court jealousy. Though the attempt to kidnap Olajai suggested a third answer — a blow at her exiled brother, or a stranglehold on Timur himself.

And as he rode, his memory reached back to that night when he had drunk his guests off their feet; it all came back, that survey at sunrise, of his littered banquet room.

He recalled the drums which had rolled and thundered across the broad maidan. They blotted out the muezzin's call to prayer. From a high window he could see the horsetail standards at Bikijek's door. The puppet king, Elias Koja, old Togluk Khan's son, let Bikijek play with the tokens of royalty, instead of setting to work with a running noose.

It would not, it could not last long, and when it ended, the Golden Horde of the Kipchak would restore order.

Order: herds eaten by Kipchak soldiers, granaries emptied by Kipchak officers, towns and farmsteads burned, and all Timur's broad acres in Kesh devastated with the rest. All because Bikijek, chief lord of the young king's court, had drums beaten five times daily before his palace.

Ten or a dozen local *émirs*, so busy battling each other that they had not stopped Elias Koja when his father sent him south to be Grand Khan of the Jagatai; that was the trouble. Rugged individualists, every man a king, and so now they had the Horde on their necks, and now their lands were the proving ground of an apprentice whose father had handed him the entire Jagatai heritage in which to learn the trade of kingship.

Timur had laughed aloud, for wine and fermented mare's milk had made him see the truth with a bitter clarity which his sober and busy days had never permitted. "First I fought Uncle Hadji, after Uncle Hadji and I drove Beyan Selduz out of town. Then they murdered Uncle Hadji, and I got an army to avenge him, and then the army divided into three parts and we had a war to settle the dividing of the booty. Every man a king. Allah! What we need is one king, and that one home grown. Too bad Mir Hussein's grandfather isn't alive."

He had smiled, in half drunken grimness and regret, thinking of the King Maker and the King Maker's grandson, handsome, hard fighting Mir Hussein, fickle, crackbrained, unpredictable Hussein who had the loveliest sister in the world.

"Allah curse Bikijek, Allah curse every man who does not curse Bikijek's religion and his father and his grandfather!"

He had spoken aloud. A grave voice had made him turn. There, in the arched doorway stood a ragged man with a snarled beard; the slanting rays kept his face from being any too clear.

"Who asks Allah to curse the religion of another true believer?"

Timur snorted. "I'm talking to myself. Only way to do, if you want to hear sense for a change."

Then his eyes became used to the glare: he saw the grimy *khelat*, the greasy skullcap, the girdle of frayed rope, the dirty hands which fingered a wooden bowl. Dirty hands, this beggar had, but fine and long, made for good penmanship. And he wore a writing case at his girdle, and a scroll carefully wrapped in a clean red silk scarf.

"Well, darvish!" Timur found a gold piece. "Guest of Allah, and a lot more welcome than these Kipchak pigs!"

Only then had his eyes a chance to focus sharply on the seamed face, shrewd, ironic, kindly; somewhat of a dish face, with broad, flat nose, Mongol features and melon head like Timur's own.

And Timur knelt on the littered tiles, catching the beggar's hand, too swiftly for any evasion; he kissed it.

"By the Splendor! I'd heard — I didn't recognize —"

The darvish freed his hand, made a gesture to decline the reverence. "Kaboul Shah Aglen, now the Guest of God and the least of the slaves."

Timur Bek had risen, to step back, entirely bewildered. Kaboul Shah Aglen, eighth in direct descent from Genghis Khan's son, Jagatai, begging his bread, and for shoes, growing callouses on his feet!

Kaboul smiled. "The darvish robe would fit you, Timur Bek. Last night's friends are this day's enemies. Become intoxicated by the splendor of Allah, and become His Guest, and the peace will be with you."

Outside, just then, horses had begun to squeal and snort; saddle drums rolled, for Bikijek was riding to the mosque. As the lordly sounds died out, Kaboul Aglen went on, "When Togluk Khan comes south to cure the disease which his son ignores, your palace becomes a mirage, and you'll be stealing sheep again. Get out, while you still can leave without killing too many horses.

"Genghis Khan, the master of all mankind, once had to steal a horse to keep from wearing out his boots. In me, the circle closes on itself. I beg my bread, as in the end all the race of Genghis Khan must do."

Timur's face darkened; Karashar Nevian, his ancestor, nine generations back, had been Genghis Khan's uncle and advisor. Then he laughed, and it was like trumpets braying before the charge. "See here! You're the heir to the Jagatai throne, you, not Togluk Khan nor Togluk Khan's son. I'll make you Grand Khan in Samarkand!"

The beggar shrugged. "No time; too soon, you'll be riding for your neck. You, not Bikijek."

Timur flipped the golden *dinar* into the bowl.

The beggar whisked it out. "What is nothing now will be your fortune soon, and the peace upon you!"

And here it was: hard riding pursuit behind him, while his wife raced to round up what fighting men she could find. So he laughed again, from thinking on the words of Kaboul Aglen, and the murderous bowstring a scribe could pluck.

FORTY-TWO horsemen, all with spare mounts, waited with Olajai when two days later, Timur's horse stumbled toward the rendezvous, where tents were scattered about a spring which kept the grass green.

Hashim, melon headed and scar-faced, came running to greet him; and he walked back, clinging to Timur's stirrup leather. "We ride again, *tura!*" he said, using the Turki word for 'my lord.' "It is like the old days again."

Then Timur saw Tagi Bouga Barlas, his distant cousin, hard bitten and grinning; Sayfuddin, the greatest archer of them all, coddling a bow; and roaring Elthci Bahadur whose strength and skill had thus far hacked his way out of all the traps into which he charged. They crowded about, grimy and sweat gleaming; jeweled collars and gold inlaid helmets and embroidered belts grotesque against greasy *khalats*, and sheepskin jackets.

"Hai, Timur Bahadur!"

Quickly they broke camp and rode, for they had rested while Timur led the Kipchak riders a crazy chase in circles. And now, being among friends, Timur dozed in the saddle; and Olajai rode beside him.

## CHAPTER III
### Battle

FIVE DAYS brought Timur to the Jihun's poplar lined banks; and swimming this river put the Jagatai realm behind them. At the Well of Saghej they found Mir Hussein, with Dilshad Aga, his wife, and some forty horsemen.

The King Maker's grandson was handsome as his sister was lovely; a small, pointed black beard, and high arched brows, and a high bridged, straight nose with nostrils whose flare made one think of a stallion scenting a fight. Until his army had been scattered, he had been King in Kandahar; now he had lost everything but hope.

There was no meat, so they ate cooked millet and buttered tea. Mir Hussein said, "*Bismillahi*, it could be worse."

Timur grimaced. "We can't eat sand very long. But with a couple good raids, I'll have an army at my back. The men of Kesh were giving me hard looks, you'd think I'd sold them out, just because I took the thankless job of trying to stand between them and those Kipchak hounds! But this fast ride has set a lot of them thinking."

"*Inshallah!* But I can't show up in Kandahar with a guard of forty men."

Timur chuckled sourly. "No, they've probably got a new king there. That's the trouble, too many kings, instead of one good one. Now, your grandfather —"

Mir Hussein sighed. "May God be well pleased with him! But do you think he could improve things? He used to pull kings out of his saddlebags, but this is different. Still, you'd do pretty well as Grand Khan of the Jagatai."

Dangerous ground. If Timur did raise an army to drive the present puppet out of Samarkand, he'd be quite a hero, but once he took the throne, jealousy would start feuds. Mir Hussein was good in battle, and good nowhere else. "You're the grandson of Mir Kazagan," Timur countered. "How's Tekil?"

"Hungry and looking for business. At least seven hundred Turkomans and the like."

"Our hundred will draw his following," Timur argued. "And with that start, we'll begin to make an impression."

So they rode through three marches of hell, across the black sands of Kivac. The scrawny oasis looked like a small paradise, for the lips of Timur's men were cracked from thirst.

The citadel loomed up, above the poplars. "I don't like it," Timur said. "No one working in the fields. No one tending the ditches."

Instead of pressing on to the city, they made camp at the fringe of green which marked the beginning of cultivation.

Timur beckoned to Eltchi Bahadur and Tagai Bouga Barlas, "We'll ride in and pay our respects to Tekil."

Hussein cut in, "No! Let me go. He knows I've spent a couple of months at the Well of Saghej, and he made no trouble. Let me talk to him."

Timur's eyes narrowed. "Hmmm . . . don't tell him I'm here. Just say you know where I am."

The deep-set Turki eyes sparkled. "So you've been thinking about that mess in Samarkand?"

Where Hussein had been the ill favored one, it now seemed that Timur's head was most in demand.

That night, Timur posted double guards and slept with his boots on. While his fame as a captain would always get him followers, it would also make his head a prize in a land where every man was a king, and allegiances changed overnight.

IN THE morning he heard trumpets and drums, and saw Mir Hussein's standard, and the riders who came from the gates, the fields and through the groves.

"Break camp, and be ready to mount up!" Timur commanded.

Then he rode out with twenty men to meet Tekil.

Ceremonious greetings: the burly governor fairly fell from his horse to be the first to dismount. A big, red-faced man, a hearty, smiling man. "Welcome, welcome, Timur Bek! Kivak is yours. You and your brother, I bid you welcome."

Tekil had an escort of perhaps two hundred horses. Timur wondered where the others were. He caught old Hashim's narrowed eyes, and made a twist of head and chin. The old fellow gave a gesture of assent; and unobtrusively edged from the clump of horsemen, to head back to camp.

More compliments. Hussein was smooth and smiling and affable. To-morrow, he and Timur would with pleasure and heartiness attend the governor's banquet. Today, Allah bear witness, things were in an uproar in camp. Horses, badly overtaxed, needed attention. And some of the party was still unaccounted for. *Ay, Wallah!* Some baggage animals, carrying all the gifts designed for His Excellency, were lagging a day's march behind.

Something was wrong, something was off color; Hussein's fluent patter confirmed Timur's earlier premonitions. He said, cutting in brusquely, "Allied-to-Greatness, we beg permission to turn from the light of your Presence!"

Words and music did not match. He was in the saddle before Tekil fairly realized that another speaker had addressed him. Tagi Bouga Barlas mounted up; and so did Hussein.

Tekil's face changed. And then came the great bawling voice of Eltchi Bahadur, and the pounding of hooves. "To horse, O Bek! They've got us hemmed in!"

"Swords out!"

And Timur had scarcely shouted his command when an arrow smacked home with a solid thump. Eltchi was shooting, shooting hard, fast, straight. "Get out of my way," he howled, "get out of my way!"

Timur and Mir Hussein were blocking his line of fire. Then the visitors and the host's men went into action, blades out; some lancers maneuvered for working space, while others threw their lances down and snatched maces from their saddle bows.

"To camp!" Timur shouted. "Archers fall out!"

There was no drill by command, as such; it was rather instinctive teamwork, based on many a pitched battle and running fight. Eltchi Bahadur charged headlong at the Tekil's guard. Hacking and hewing, he was swallowed up by milling horsemen and billowing dust.

Meanwhile, as though called by signal, half Timur's escort swooped to right and left, and the bows began to twang. Hard driven shafts laced the flanks of Tekil's tight packed traitors; murderous, close range archery; cunningly driven shafts, some picking men, others nailing horses whose fall would block the movement of other riders.

Stung by the ferocious archery, Tekil's men opened out. Timur and Hussein pressed in, head on, to divide the enemy. And from the rear came the brawling, booming voice of Eltchi Bahadur. He looked as though an avalanche had passed over him, but he was hewing his way back to meet

Timur.

Timur's archers fell back, shooting as they withdrew, and covering the retreat. Over the roar of battle, he heard the approach of his main detachment, and saw his chance.

"This way, you bawling bull!" he shouted to Eltchi, and pointed toward a low hillock.

In a moment, Timur's standard was on the knoll. Dust ringed the oasis. The rest of Tekil's men were closing in. It was now clear where the governor's force had been. It was all too clear that the riders trailing Timur out of Samarkand had been baiting him, while a courier rode directly to Tekil Bikijek, he now concluded, had known all the while where Mir Hussein was, and had counted on Timur's joining his brother-in-law: the two were to be settled beyond the border of the Jagatai territory.

Ten to one: Timur took a fresh horse, and looked out and down at the closing circle of steel. He said to his wife, and to Dilshad Aga, "Keep your heads down. There won't be many of us to block the arrows, not for long."

## CHAPTER IV
### Olajai

THE ONE sided battle was reaching its end as the sun slowly dragged down toward the horizon. Olajai, ignoring arrows, went about during lulls, carrying a goatskin jar of brackish water.

"Easier each round," Timur said, and licked the dust from his lips.

She laughed. "They're well whittled down, too!"

Of Tekil's men, scarcely fifty were able to fight. The others were dead, or they had left the field because of wounds. As for Timur, only seven were about his standard.

Charge after charge had been swept back, for in the beginning, Tekil's men had blocked each other, only a few at a time being able to present themselves to the enemy; and closing in on Eltchi Bahadur was a swift way to the mercy of Allah.

Those who first charged up the little knoll had struggled in sandy soil, facing a hail of arrows: and the next wave had been blocked by windrows of fallen horses and men. Finally, exhaustion took the heart from all but the strongest. Skill failed, and so did the will.

"Only seven to one now, my dear! Give Bahadur a drink!"

He turned to his sister-in-law: "I'll get you horse tails, tie them to the standard."

There were plenty of once splendid mounts who had no further use for their tails. Timur hacked, and Dilshad Aga set to work.

Timur waited. The ring of winded, wounded enemies waited. The air had the dead stillness of a well-fired oven, except when hot wind drove scorching sand. Tagi Bouga Barlas and Sayfuddin were now on foot. Eltchi Bahadur grinned, though wearily; blood and sweat and dust made his homely face a devil's mask.

"Hai, *Bahadur!* The sons of pigs would turn tail if someone knocked that Tekil out of action."

Timur snorted. "I've spent all day trying to get at him. I've been cutting meat till my arm's ready to fall off, he always gets someone between me and him."

Hussein came up; debonair, head cocked like the head of a falcon, eyes aglitter. "Why take down our standard, brother?"

"It's coming up in a second."

Then Dilshad Aga called, and Timur went to take the staff. Hussein saw the three horse tails. "The standard of Genghis Khan! By Allah, why not? This is our day. God does what he will do, and here we are."

Timur planted the staff, and said to Hashim, "Sound off!"

The one unbroken saddle drum rolled and grumbled in the hot silence; a hot wind made the three horse tails ripple, then fan out. Timur challenged the enemy: "Sons of Bad Mothers! Here is the standard of Genghis Khan, the Master of all Mankind. He rides again!"

Hussein mounted up, wordlessly, and with the smooth swiftness of a panther. Sword out, he raced down the slope. Then came Eltchi Bahadur's great voice; the drum stopped rumbling. Olajai cried out — many men had died, but this was her brother, and a clump of swordsmen had swallowed him up.

The others were at his heels. Tekil's standard, clipped in half, was trampled in the dust. Eltchi Bahadur smashed home with all his weight and steel. And as he raced, Timur plucked his bow. One shot. Just one. A single shaft, threading through the shifting fighters, caught Tekil between the teeth. The impact knocked him from his horse.

Then an arrow caught Timur's mount. The beast crumpled, flinging the rider asprawl. Timur rolled, recovered, and from the bloody sand he snatched a half-pike. Eltchi Bahadur had hewn a path to Tekil. Timur bore down on the pike, driving through armor, driving it through the man, and deep into the earth.

Whoever could run or ride fled to the fortress. Seven wounded victors left the field, to find whatever safety they could, before Tekil's men recovered from the shock, and began to think of vengeance.

They retraced their course. At the desert's fringe, three of the survivors said, "Lord Timur, Allah does what he will do, and with your permission, we go to our homes in Khorassan, while you raise an army."

This also had happened before, so Timur answered, "Go with my blessing."

Then on the night when they were not far from the Jihun, Timur said to Hussein, "There are not enough for any defense, only enough to be conspicuous. Better we separate. You go to Hirmen, and spend the winter with the Mikouzeri tribesmen. I'll go back home to Kesh, incognito, and I'll meet you in Hirmen, later."

So they parted. And when Timur was alone with Olajai, he said, "*Shireen*, you married a prince in Kesh, and now look! Not one rider behind me."

"I'm not worrying. Though I was scared silly, until you had that crazy notion of hoisting three horse tails!"

He eyed her sharply. "You quit worrying then? Mmmm . . . it did something to your brother, the crackbrain, he was off before I knew what was happening."

She nodded. "That shocked me, too. Then, suddenly, I knew that Tekil's men would break. For a crazy instant, it was as if Genghis Khan had come back through all these nine generations, and out of his grave."

"The sun, my dear. It was bad."

She shook her head. "I didn't see anything, I didn't hear anything, I just felt something. As though you had really had the right, that moment, to put up the horse-tail standard. And they felt it."

"You're giving Eltchi Bahadur and Hussein not much credit!"

"I notice you took the tails off before we left. I'm not worried. It's working out. What that darvish said. Only he didn't say *all*. Maybe he didn't know, maybe he couldn't see so far ahead. But I do."

"What's that?" His voice was sharp.

"My grandfather made kings. He unmade them. Always, he put on the throne of Samarkand someone of the direct line of Genghis Khan. And there was peace, the very name made peace. You know, he could have taken the throne himself."

"He could. And Kazagan Khan would have filled any throne."

"But he didn't, he wouldn't. Timur — don't you see what I mean? You have a right to the name, you've proved the right, back there."

They marched, from brackish well to dry well where there was water only by digging. Then the worst of the two horses collapsed. Timur dismounted and said "Take mine."

She stared, gaped. He said gruffly, "Mount up!"

"Why — darling — whatever— you're crazy."

Her incredulity was natural. A man tramping on foot would be too worn out to fight. It was plain sense that he should ride while Olajai walked.

"But —"

"Mount up!" he commanded and she obeyed.

He tramped along holding the stirrup leather.

And that afternoon toward sunset as they halted to rest he looked at his boots. The soles were gone.

"See! The darvish is right! Timur of the race of Genghis Khan is barefooted. This thing had to be. And now that I cannot go any lower I must go higher and the Power is with God!"

She was no longer worried by his seeming madness in walking while a woman rode. "You lied to me, you knew what happened on that knoll, as well as I did!"

They were coming near to a well, or to where one should be. The sun's level rays bent into their backs so that their shadows reached long and dark ahead of them.

Then he saw the horsemen riding into the glare. "How many?" he asked Olajai, very calmly.

"Ten — twelve — fifteen — too many, Timur, and you've been walking."

"Who are they — what are they?"

"Turkomans," she answered.

"I was afraid of that."

The Governor of Kivac's force had been largely Turkoman.

Olajai said, lightly, "We can't use horse tails again. We haven't enough horses."

She started to slide out of the saddle, so that he could mount up. He said, "Not yet. The glare keeps them from seeing that there are two of us."

When they reached the well, and its thin cover of scrawny trees, he made the horse turn, so that it screened the next move. Olajai slid from the saddle. He took his lariat and secured it to a root which reached from the wall of the well.

"It's dry. The water is in the other hole. Get down and stay down. You're near enough now to get to the river afoot."

Then he mounted up, drew his sword, and rode at them, shouting his challenge. He had no more arrows. The riders had fanned out to envelop the oasis, so as to block the escape of any other travelers who might be there. Every sign pointed to being cut down and robbed of his arms, his horse gear, the jewels of his belt and scabbard; so he shouted, "Timur, the Man of Kesh, Timur, the son of Tragai!"

A man cried an answer. The archers lowered their bows. That one man rode forward and dismounted.

"Timur Bek! Welcome, and the blessing of Allah, and the Peace of Allah upon you! We heard that you had gone this way, and we came to meet you."

So Olajai came from the pit. Timur gave her bracelets to Hadji Mehemmed, the Turkoman raider with whom he had ridden once, some years previous. And Hadji Mehemmed gave them horses, and an escort of ten men. Olajai said, that night, "This proves it — the horse-tails are still with you."

## CHAPTER V

### *"Spread the Good Word"*

AT BOKAR-ZENDIN, Timur left Olajai with friends, for being north of the Jihun again, he risked recognition, ambush, betrayal, which he would not have Olajai share. "More than that," he said, "if you went, I'd be recognized just that much sooner."

"Women's chatter? Well, men haven't done too well by you!"

Timur chuckled amiably at that painfully just quip. "*Shireen*, wherever we were guests, and we couldn't always refuse hospitality without making ourselves even more conspicuous, there'd be women looking at you. They'd guess, and much sooner than any men would, looking at us."

"Mmmm . . . yes, of course."

Now that the blame had been passed to superior feminine perception, Olajai felt better about it all. So the Lord of Kesh sneaked thieflike across the lands of his ancestors, not even daring to enter his own estate, for this choice territory was packed with Kipchaks.

A lone archer limped through the market place. Timur, being afoot, had the best possible disguise, yet the risk was deadly enough, since men of Bikijek's clique came in from Samarkand every day.

One by one, he cornered retainers who had ridden with his late father, *Émir* Tragai. These had to look twice before they could believe that this haggard footman was Timur Bek. Each one said. "Lord Timur, we thought that you had quit us. We were glad when we heard that you'd left Samarkand with a troop on your heels. Then we knew that you were with us in heart, and in the end, you would come back and wipe them out."

"What with?"

"We join whatever army you raise."

Close-mouthed, weather-beaten men listened to him and then spread the word. When he left Kesh, Temouka Kutchin rode after him with twenty horsemen ready for the field.

They took the trail for Badakshan. The story of his desperate fight against Tekil of Kivac had spread, and one chieftain after another joined him. There was Bahram Jalair, and a distant cousin, Saddik Barlas; Kazanchi Hassan with a hundred horse came seeking him. Mir Sayfuddin, whom he had not seen since the disaster in the desert, had meanwhile raised seventy picked men. Another kinsman, Koja Barlas, had a like party. Then came Shir Bahram, and Ulum Kuli with two hundred horse, Mamut Keli with as many footmen.

Timur's disaster and his barefooted march across the desert recruited more men more easily than any success had ever done.

Even the Kipchak Horde helped him: for with Bikijek's nobles now leading raiding parties over all the Jagatai territory, captain after captain fled to join Timur.

When he met Mir Hussein and they reviewed their combined forces, Timur said, "Now that the enemy has taught them that too much freedom is no freedom at all, they've stopped being kings."

Spies came, saying that the Kipchak raids were becoming more severe. Worse yet, Togluc Khan had sent some 20,000 of the Golden Horde to the north, to reinforce his son, Elias Koja.

"We're not ready. What we have is good, by Allah, but not enough. Time is against us," Hussein said.

"Time is the toy of Allah," Timur retorted. "He does with it what pleases Him."

"It pleased Him to have most of us wiped out facing odds of ten to one," Hussein pointed out, realistically.

And these men would follow Timur only as long as they willed, and no longer. Even Genghis Khan, more nearly an absolute lord than any man who had ever ruled men, had ruled only by the will of his captains: Asiatic democracy, masquerading as a despotism.

So Timur's frown deepened, and even more when he heard that Kesh was heavily garrisoned. Worst of all, spies said that Olajai, finally leaving Bokar-Zendan to him and her brother, had been recognized and trapped; she was a captive in Kesh, a hostage for his good behavior.

Timur asked the messenger, "Who else has heard this?"

"No one, *tura*, save yourself and Mir Hussein."

"I'll take your head," Timur solemnly swore, "I'll skin you and stuff your hide with straw if a word of it leaks out in camp. Is that clear?"

*"Aywah, tura."*

He gave the man a handful of golden *dinars*, and dismissed him.

Then, to Hussein: "I've got to get her out of there."

"I take refuge with Allah! My own sister, but can you risk a good little army against a walled city, just for a woman? Timur, that's not sense. Your men'll think you're crazy, wasting them on a woman."

Timur smiled. "That's something I'm not telling them."

"Allah! But what?"

"Listen."

The drums sounded assembly, and the trumpets brayed. Timur spoke from the saddle: "O Men! Friends of my father and my uncle, a saint came to me in a dream last night. Allah has promised us our city. Even though we had green boughs instead of lances, our faith would make us win.

"The Presence of Genghis Khan came into the desert, and our enemies ran.

"And if we take Kesh, every captain from Badakshan to Kandahar will join us to share in our next glory. When they join, who will stop us?"

He sold them as they stood there. And not even on the march, the hard forced march on Kesh, did a man of them wonder what Timur would do for siege engines.

"They're drunk," Hussein said. "Drunk and not from wine. How did you do it?"

"I don't know. It came to me."

"Well, if we do capture Kesh," Hussein countered, "they'll besiege us, and have you ever seen a Mongol or Turk who was any good, locked up behind walls?"

Timur laughed triumphantly. "*Hai!* Out of your own mouth, brother! The very truth that's going to make Kesh open up in no time. Go and spread the word! Keep them with a dream in their eyes!"

They rode so fast that there was no news of their coming.

Bivouac: and at dawn, far off, rose the gray walls of Kesh, high above the orchards.

"Now get busy," Timur said to his captains. "Cut off green boughs. Divide into four columns." He saw their faces change at this insane suggestion, but he gave them no chance to object. "Let each column mark the time, and do it in this wise —"

They listened, they grinned, their slanted eyes widened, and then they howled and drew their swords to hew limbs from the forest.

Timur with a picked handful emerged from the woods, and raced down into the plain, and toward the fields. He had all the musicians: and all were sounding off brazen trumpets and saddle drums and ear-slashing cymbals. Musicians on horse, musicians on camel back, and a picked troop of lancers: they moved at the pace of a polo game. Kipchak guards came from Kesh to welcome what they believed to be fellow invaders.

"Swords out!"

Though not caught entirely off guard, they might as well have been. They were cut down, and their horses galloped wildly home with empty saddles: and Timur resumed his bold race.

By now the gates of Kesh were closed. When Timur reined in, his archers shadowed him with a curtain of arrows. He demanded, "Surrender at once, and we'll let you march out alive."

A man in heavy Khorassan mail risked his head. Timur's archers ceased firing. The garrison commander came up to the parapet. The man was puzzled: a hundred horse seemed hardly the right force to take a walled town.

"You're crazy!" he raged. "Or drunk. Who are you?"

"Timur Bek, and what are you doing in my town?"

The bold challenge took the commander aback. "I am Daulat Ali, and I hold this in the name of Elias Koja, Khan of Samarkand, Son of Togluk Khan."

"You can become wealthy and famous by taking my head," Timur reminded him. "Bikijek wants it badly."

Daulat Ali was no drill ground soldier; Bikijek didn't send that kind out to hold a town. Yet he was worried. There must be a sizable army on the way, and there had been no warning.

Timur went on. "March your garrison out. One hour's delay, and I'll have the head of every fifth man, taken by count, with no regard to rank."

"You can't take a town with that handful!" Daulat Ali retorted.

"Only Allah knows what is in my hand! Trifle a bit longer, and not one of you leaves alive. Quick, man! You're up on the wall. Look around. Do you want a siege, or do you think you'd like to try a sortie?"

On the four horizons, great columns of dust rose. Each was drawing toward Kesh. Citizens were now on the walls, some of Timur's own people. They began to yell, "Allah! Armies from Khorassan! Armies from Kabul!"

Rioting broke out within the town. Timur grinned when he heard the shouting. "I won't have to take your heads, they'll tend to that before I can save you fellows!"

Heaving water jugs and roofing tiles from housetops may annoy soldiers, but such civilian resistance rarely gets far. That was what worried Daulat Ali. Timur must have promised his people four armies, or they'd never be crazy enough to stone Kipchak hardcases.

Timur could now see the dust columns from the ground level. "If you move fast enough you'll have a chance to warn the apprentice king."

Turning the garrison loose, instead of taking them prisoner or cutting them down would give Elias Koja and Bikijek a nasty shock. Only a strong army could afford such a gesture of contempt. And Daulat Ali, already shaken, signaled to his trumpeters; they sounded recall.

The disarmed garrison filed out, and rapidly enough not to see that they had surrendered to dust clouds raised by horsemen dragging green branches.

And when Timur found Olajai, he said, "Home again, *shireen*, but only Allah knows how long we'll stay."

## CHAPTER VI
### *King-Maker*

BY THE time his spies had caught up with him, Timur realized that though he would quickly have to abandon Kesh he had at least succeeded in more than a personal enterprise: his daring capture of the city was bringing hundreds of one-time doubters to his standard.

And then Timur learned that Elias Koja's army, strongly reinforced by his father's troops, had moved out of Samarkand. They were going toward the Jihun, to make a clean sweep of the Jagatai lands and possibly to invade Khorassan.

So Timur and his newly won recruits got out of Kesh before Elias Koja's general, Bikijek, could learn that green branches had swept his garrison out of town.

Timur won the bridge with a few hours to spare. Then from the Khorassan side, he saw *touman* after *touman* of Kipchak troops, each 10,000 strong, The apprentice king's father was out for conquest. "Brother," Mir Hussein said, "our army will scatter like dust, once we start running. They'll forget that trick at Kesh."

"Then we won't run."

"We can't face 60,000 Kipchaks, not when Bikijek leads them."

Olajai came from behind the red carpet which, hanging from its long fringes, separated her quarters from the reception room of the pavilion. "Remember the horse tails, Timur!" she cut in.

Hussein turned on his sister. "You little fool, how long will Allah's patience last! Bluffing Bikijek is not quite the same as scaring a blockhead out of Kesh!"

Timur scowled. "I've got an army. One retreat, and they'll go back to their sheep."

"Yes, and just one bout with the Golden Horde, and they'll be minced mutton. You can't keep on recruiting on the strength of glorious defeats like the one at Kivak!"

"The horse tails," Olajai repeated. "The Presence!"

Timur rose. "We can hold the bridge for a day."

So he went to dispose his six thousand against ten times as many.

From sunrise to sunset, troop after troop of Kipchaks charged the bridgehead, taking their toll, but going down before the stubborn defense. Timur and Eltchi Bahadur plied mace and sword; and the sight and sound of them steadied the little army. Yet when the sun sank, they were tired and battered: wearied from the very cutting down of successive waves.

That night, spies swam the Jihun. In speech and dress and face, they matched the enemy; and they could mix freely, grumbling about the stiff resistance, and muttering about Timur's reserves, spread out, well behind the Jihun. And they muttered about the fall of Kesh. . . .

Meanwhile, Timur was moving, He left only five hundred to hold the bridge: which picked men could do, for another day. The others divided, half going upstream, half downstream, well beyond hearing of the enemy, to risk the dangerous fords.

Bikijek could have made a similar attempt, but with his overwhelming force, it seemed far more sensible to hammer for another day, and drive through the troops who held the bridge.

Finally, there was the rumor of Timur's reserves; Bikijek was too good a general to risk being cut up in such fashion. Once he learned —

But Bikijek had no chance to learn.

Timur's losses by drowning were smaller than they could have been, had he and his captains not known every foot of the treacherous fords. Time and again, he went back, each time with a fresh horse, to lead the next detachment over. And on the final trip, he listened to a spy just returned: "Togluk Khan is dead! His son was about to go home when there was news of us."

Timur turned to Hussein, who commanded the final party.

"Allah is with us! There is a fear in Elias Koja. When he should go to Kipchak to receive the allegiance of his father's lords, and take the old man's throne, he stays here. The raid on Kesh has shaken him!"

Timur led his *hazaras* into the hills well behind the Kipchak camp. He spread them far apart. "Make fires," he commanded. "Many fires. As of many bivouacked *toumans.*"

That night, he looked down on the fires of Bikijek's six toumans. And that night, Bikijek looked backward and upward at fires which suggested a force at least equal to his own: and a force which had slipped up between him, and Samarkand, and the long trail to Kipchak.

At dawn, with all his men carefully under cover in the woods at the foot of the slope, Timur watched Bikijek's scouts patrolling the river. The Kipchaks were worried; they had not resumed the attack on the bridgehead. Fires behind them at night; and now they found hoof prints at the dangerous fords. As they saw it, Timur, with far more army than anyone had credited him with having, had held the bridge in order to make a night crossing to cut off their retreat, and so drive them into the river.

Bikijek's troops were soon in motion. First, they were going to withdraw; second, they were going to make the best disposition after what they considered a thorough outmaneuvering.

Then came Timur's charge: not from the distant line of the past night's campfires, but from the forest at the foot of the hills. Either too early, or too late, it could not have succeeded, despite the advantage of surprise; but Timur's lightning slash was timed to the second. He caught the Kipchaks when they were neither set for defense, nor fully committed to withdrawal.

Some tried to rush the bridge. Other *hazaras* fled along the bank. Those who tried to re-form and fight it out were blocked by disorganized units. And Timur's troops picked the heart of the opposition: Bikijek's *touman*, and the force led by Tokatmur.

Elias Koja's standard went down before the rush. Tokatmur, second in command to Bikijek, fell under the fury of swords which followed the final flight of arrows. And it was like the moves of a chess game long reasoned out in advance: one-two-three, and checkmate.

The apprentice king escaped, and so did Bikijek, one leaving behind him a throne, the other losing an army. And when the trumpets sounded recall from cutting down the fugitives, Timur formed his troops and raced on to Samarkand.

As he rode back through the gates from which he and Olajai had so narrowly escaped, the citizens who crowded the streets and packed the housetops, began to shout, "*Sahib Karan!* Lord of the Age!"

He had conquered a city by dust, and he had triumphed over an army by fire: and Olajai said, "When the Jagatai princes meet they'll make you Grand Khan of Samarkand."

She was right. Hussein had said as much; and the Barlas clan, Timur's uncle's kinsmen, were behind him. But as he rode toward the palace vacated forever by Elias Koja, Timur made plans of his own.

That night, serving men dragged monstrous trays into the banquet hall: camels roasted entire, and sheep; and there was horseflesh, and leather trays heaped with rice and millet. Others set out jars of wine, and jars of fermented mare's milk, and flagons that only a Mongol could drain.

Eltchi Bahadur was there, roaring as on the battlefield; Hussein, sleek and smooth and handsome as a panther; and the Barlas clan, flat-faced, grim and slant-eyed; Turki and Mongol in silken tunic and silken *khalat*. Though Togluk Khan the tyrant had died a natural death, horsemen still raced northward to deny his son any chance of an equally quiet end. . . .

It was complete; complete, except for two things: Timur Bek was not present, and the grand *khan*'s dais at the head of the great hall was empty. Lords and captains, *beks* and *émirs*, ranged in rank on either side, with that one high place vacant: election day in Samarkand.

Some laughed. Some muttered. Ali sniffed the savor of roasted meat, and wine ready for the drinking. But Timur, *Sahib-Karan*, the Lord of the Times, was late.

Then the drums rolled and the long trumpets brayed. Guards marched in, escorting a horse-tail standard. In the courtyard soldiers shouted, "*Hai, Bahadur! Sahib Karan,* Timur, Grand Khan of Samarkand, Khan of the Jagatai!"

The uproar of the rank and file told the *émirs* and the *beks* how they had better vote; and they knew that wholesale desertions would follow an unpopular choice. Most of the Jagatai princes agreed with their men; but some scowled. For Timur to make a point of delaying his entry until all the others had arrived was laying it on too heavily; and for him to have the horse-tail standard carried before him was taking too much for granted.

But the shouts from the court gave the lords no choice.

Then they saw who preceded Timur: a bearded man in the ragged robe of a darvish; a man who protested, a man who, though handled with respect, was being hustled into the hall, and toward the vacant high place.

At the foot of the dais, Timur halted with his barefooted companion. He raised his hand, and the shouting ceased. "O Men! In the days of your grandfathers, Kazagan Khan the Turk could have taken the throne of Samarkand but this he did not do; instead, he set up one of the blood of Genghis Khan, the Master of All Mankind, and used all his force to maintain one whom no one would deny or envy!

"Here is the darvish, here is the Guest of Allah, here is Kaboul Shah Aglen, directly descended from Genghis Khan's son Jagatai! Here is one who cares so little for power that he turns his back on thrones, and contemplates the splendor of Allah! Here is one with wisdom, not pride.

"Where we have each been kings, there has been no strength, and from too much freedom, we had an invader on our necks! So let this man be Grand Khan, for there is not one of us too proud to serve him!"

The shouting drowned the protests of the darvish. He could not deny his duty. They put an embroidered *khalat* over his ragged gown; they made him ascend the dais, and each prince in turn bowed nine times before him, as the ancient custom prescribed.

And when the banquet ended, the following noon, Timur Bek went to his own house, where Olajai waited.

"So you gave away a throne? After the Presence that came to you on the hill at Kivak?"

Timur was a little drunk, and he was tired, and he was hoarse from song and shouting. "He is the ninth generation, and all things go in nines with the race of Genghis Khan. Your brother and the others would soon turn against me — yet I can hold them together, serving him. And we won't have too many kings."

She looked up, smiling; her disappointment was gone. "The Presence will return to you, Timur." Then, just in the interests of discipline: "Allah, but you've slopped wine all over yourself, you're an awful looking mess for a King-Maker, you're as bad as my grandfather. You're ready to fall on your face!"

# REVOLT OF THE DAMNED

## I

NITA RICCO brought the wicker baskets of melons into her bedroom on the second floor of the filling station and carefully drew the shades. The gas pumps were locked, and below, the lights were out. Anyone wanting five gallons of regular could go elsewhere; to hell, for all Nita cared, or to Mexico, just south of the city limits.

She wished to God Blaze Hayden would come home. Torres, delivering the precious melons, had made her uneasy, with his snaky eyes. He had not even bothered to count the thousand-odd dollars in large bills. He had been watching Nita's every graceful move, trying to outwit the turquoise chiffon negligée whose half transparency gave tantalizing glimpses of her lovely legs.

The gown enveloped her like a scented bluish mist. The desert breeze that invaded a shuttered window made the frail fabric cling to the sweetly rounded curve of her hips. A little crucifix gleamed in the hollow of her firm young breasts; it matched the red-gold of her wavy hair.

The heels of her tiny satin mules sank into a thick-napped Chinese rug, which like the furniture, was costly but a bit garish. Blaze Hayden could never have bought those things for Nita by selling gas. Her gray-green eyes were somber as she emptied the melons on the hardwood floor, then knelt and split them with a knife.

Each cantaloupe contained several five-*tael* tins of opium.

A tap at the door made Nita start. She rose, and her smile reflected the sudden glow in her eyes. Blaze had returned. The blue chiffon trailed away from her thighs as she hurried to admit him.

Then she recoiled from the open door and hastily drew her gown together. Torres had returned. His eyes glittered from smoking home-grown marijuana. He licked his thick lips. "Señora, ees dangerous for you to stay alone —" Torres made a sweeping gesture as he crossed the threshold. "So I 'av return. We 'ave the drink, no?"

He produced a bottle of tequila. Torres was tall and swarthy and despite his loose mouth, not a bad looking young Mexican.

"Scram!" snapped Nita, putting on a bold front. "I paid you."

A snarl now bared Torres' white teeth. Cat quick, he flashed toward her. Nita dared not scream. If help did arrive, all those tins of Golden Pheasant opium would damn her and Blaze.

Torres was beyond mincing words. He had seen too much of Nita's white beauty to retreat. Desperate, she glanced about. There was the knife on her dressing table.

She lunged, but Torres intercepted her. She clawed his swarthy face. She almost wriggled from his grasp, but her frail chiffon robe parted in trailing shreds. Then her brassiere slipped. The opium smuggler was beyond fear or reason.

"You damn dirty lug," Nita panted. "Blaze'll kill you —"

Torres skidded on some melon seeds. Nita, peeled down to her scanties, flung herself toward the dresser and seized the knife.

"Drop it!" snarled Torres, recovering. "If you use it, the polees will know — about the opium — the beeg boss will keel you!"

That was Bud Worley's way. A foolproof racket is based on dead men's bones. One strike and out! No bungler lived long in Worley's mob.

Then Nita's fingers closed on a box of dusting powder. The Mexican, distracted by the gleaming blade, caught the choking cloud squarely in the face. She snatched the table lamp. But before she could smash it across his head, the door slammed open, and a tall man bounded in.

"Blaze — my God —"

"The greasy bastard!" He was lean, broad shouldered; wrath hardened his thin face into grim angles. "You black son —"

He lunged. His fist landed like a caulking maul. Before Torres could collapse, Blaze picked him up and bodily hurled him through the window.

The shattering of glass was followed by a grunt, a thud, a muttered oath in Spanish. Blaze, gun drawn, leaned over the sill. He turned away, grinning.

"Running like hell, honey." He caught Nita in his arms and stroked her copper-red hair. "That wallop sobered him, huh?"

"Blaze," she sobbed, "I'm checking out of the racket. I don't care what you do! It's lousy, stinking, putrid! Running hop —"

"Baby, we can't quit." Blaze's face lengthened, suddenly became old and weary. "The Feds'd get us. Worley, the rotten skunk, he'd turn us in."

This was an old story to Nita. First, a bit of easy money, smuggling perfume. Nothing wrong, nicking Uncle Sam out of customs duties he had no right to, anyway. Every tourist does it, or tries it. Then a load of Chinese. And finally, Blaze Hayden dared not refuse to run that filling station in Calexico, right on the border. Worley had said, "Play, or else."

They ignored the horn blast outside until it was repeated several times. Blaze started. He recognized the sound. Leadfoot Johnson had pulled up to get the northbound load of narcotics.

"I'm quitting. I don't care, I am!" Nita was half hysterical.

"Shut up, you idiot!" snapped Blaze, dashing to the door.

But Leadfoot was already clumping up the stairs. He was a big blond fellow whose tanned face was scarred from flying glass and metal; a racing driver not quite good enough for the big time, but a wizard on the highway, piloting a grimy old car with a supercharged engine.

"'Lo, Blaze." He eyed the disordered room and Nita's remaining tatters of negligee. "Listen, you two. It's none of my damn business you battling. But you was talking out loud. Forget this quitting idea. Bad for the health!"

"This racket's lousy," Nita bitterly observed. "Sure, I said it."

Leadfoot scratched his sandy hair, shrugged. "Ditto, toots. But you know what happens to saps that think they can walk out. Let's go, Blaze."

They loaded the junk. Then a gritting of tires, and the whine of the supercharger was swallowed in the roar of the big engine.

Nita turned despairing eyes to Blaze when he returned.

"I'll stick," she sobbed. "Any way we turn, we're damned. I guess you and me can't revolt. . . ."

"But you can keep a gat in your dresser," muttered Blaze. "If that hop-crazy spic ever makes another pass at you, burn him down and hide the junk before the cops get here. Anyway, I'll be on hand after this when Torres delivers a load. . . ."

Bud Worley's mob operated on Sacramento Street, just on the fringe of Chinatown. Behind the old gray building on the corner was a tangle of ancient alleys, and a fantastic huddle of old houses that offered an unlimited assortment of approaches and getaways. And on all sides were the hangouts of the junk peddlers, white and Chinese, who have infested that glamorous district since San Francisco became world famous for its Barbary Coast.

A wizened derelict shuffled up the steep street that led from the Embarcadero. His suit had not been cleaned for years. He was a Skid Row bum outwardly, but there was a purpose behind the furtive movements that took him across the street and into a dingy alley below the neon lights that emblazed the main stem of Chinatown.

He crept down the odorous gloom. Smuggled aliens were crammed in some of those foul warrens. In others, broken-down harlots made their last stand. Furtive pimps crouched in dark doorways. This was the sodden end of the trail that began in the glittering hot spots on Powell and Mason streets, or the gilded brothels disguised as fashionable apartments not many blocks distant.

They lived for their junk. The need was so great that Bud Worley had a bigtime rival and countless minor competitors. There was Smoke Keenan, the ex-pug. He might have been a success, had he not kicked the gong himself at times. Not often, but once is too much. . . .

It was one of Keenan's men who catfooted down the alley. Irish Annie used a lot of the stuff, and so did her customers.

"Wait a minute, buddy!" rasped a hoarse voice. A man emerged from the shadow of a pilaster. He snatched the bum's collar. "Hold it!"

The junk runner snarled. A skinny hand came out with a knife. Another man bounded from across the alley.

"Let him have it, Spike!"

The runner's yell was cut short. A length of armored cable crunched down on his skull. He collapsed. The two dark figures rolled him against the wall. They squatted; Spike kept watch while his partner went through the dead man's pockets.

"Uhuh. Loaded with it."

"Take it?"

"No. Scatter it. Teach these bastards a lesson. Maybe they'll quit working for Keenan."

Later, the cops of the Chinatown squad found a bum with a crushed skull. Packets of snow, and several tins of opium were half trampled in the grime.

"Maher," said the patrolman to the sergeant, "when the hell they going to clamp down on that lousy Keenan? This is the brand he peddles."

The sergeant snorted. Busting rackets is no harness-bull's job. A pavement pounder might as well learn that now as later.

"One of Worley's mugs done it, I guess," he said. "But what the hell, Barney? We ain't paid to make bum guesses. Not until a war pops up. Then maybe something'll be done about it. When it gets to be a big stink."

Later, Spike and his partner were entering a side door of the gray house on Sacramento Street. They found Bud Worley in a room whose ornate luxury was a glittering contrast to the dingy exterior.

He was dark and handsome, except for eyes set too close together; a suave, sleek fellow in costly imported worsteds.

"Hi, Spike! How she going, Benny?" He thrust a humidor toward his grim-jawed sluggers. "Luck?"

"Uhuh. Number ten conked," Benny reported. "But listen, chief. We been going strong. Cripes, I don't mind working. A guy's got to eat. But we been overdoing it, and Keenan's getting sore enough to blow the lid off."

Sitting somewhat apart from his chief, Rod Northup had been watching, stroking his straw-colored moustache. He looked like a collegian who ought to sell bonds. Thus far he had said nothing.

"Let him fight if he's got guts!" grinned Worley. "You mugs aren't paid to think. Or you'd starve."

"I don't know, Bud," interposed Northup. "Just so much of that, and the cops can't keep on reporting 'John Doe Number So-and-So, fractured skull sustained as result of fall while intoxicated.' And a war'll raise hell."

Worley smiled amiably. He always did, particularly when doing a fine piece of shooting. He was so proud of his marksmanship that he often took needless risks to prove that he was the best gunner as well as the best organizer in the racket.

"Well . . . why not?" he drawled. "Raise some hell. If Keenan ever pokes his nose out of that armored shack, I'll snipe it off myself."

A long-barrelled revolver blossomed like magic from the tailored coat that disguised its bulk. He scorned automatics; a double action Colt was the thing. As he spoke, he abstractedly dropped it into line as though to shoot the wart off Spike's chin.

"Uhuh, I'll cut the son down myself. Think I can't, Rod?"

Northup shrugged. "Sure you can. But for hell's sweet sake, don't. Live and let live. There's enough for all." He reached for a pearl-gray hat, carefully slicked back his wavy hair. "Be seeing you, Bud."

Northup reeked of hair tonic and shaving lotion. Worley chuckled, "You're too damn handsome to live, Rod. Cheating on Mae again, huh?"

"Nix, nix!" he protested, pretending horror. "Hell, don't a guy have to have a bit of fun?"

Worley straightened up, still smiling. But something about his expression made the two sluggers exchange glances.

"You better stick to blondes, Rod. Just a friendly tip."

Rod Northup pulled a long face. "What's the matter with Dora?"

"I don't say anything's the matter. I just got a sneaking hunch she's played around with one of Keenan's gang. I don't think she's on the level."

"Oh, all right, all right," conceded Rod. But as he headed for the door, he was adjusting his tie.

"Jeez," muttered Spike, as the door closed, "you think he's dumb enough to play with a frill like that —"

"Shut up!" snapped Worley. "Rod's all right. He ain't dumb. Now beat it, the two of you."

"Okay, okay!" Benny echoed Spike's assent, and they both left.

For a long time, Worley sat there, smoking monogrammed cigarettes. He knew better; a fellow never could entirely guard against absent-mindedly discarding an initialled butt in the wrong place, but he liked to flaunt handmade Turkish smokes that cost a dollar and a quarter for a small pack.

Finally, he dialed a number. A woman answered. Worley recognized the brittle voice and said, "Hi, Mae. How about speaking to Rod?"

"I don't know where the dirty so-and-so is!" she snapped and hung up.

Worley smiled quizzically and studied the ascending smoke from his cigarette. Rod and women just didn't mix right. Suppose Mae got jealous and ratted? He uncoiled his lithe length and went to a lacquered cabinet a Chinese hop distributor had given him. From it he took a small ivory-mounted automatic, which he slipped into his vest pocket.

Then he put on a dark hat, a brand new pair of rubber-soled shoes, and a cheap, dark coat. He left by a concealed panel that opened into a passage from which he finally emerged in the center of the block. Dense shadows concealed him until he reached an alley.

Worley was worried. Rod and his floozies. . . . Rod could do with a lesson . . . but Rod was too well liked by the mob. . . . Worley frowned. . . .

DORA SLAVICH'S apartment was neat, but very simple. Yet Dora radiated glamor. Somehow, her dark beauty made Rod Northup think of Persian gardens, tropical beaches, birds of paradise. When a Slavonian girl starts out to be lovely, she makes a job of it. Many have coarse features, square hips, stocky figures — but Dora was just right that way.

And in every way. The natural flush of her olive-tinted skin scarcely needed makeup. Her great dark eyes were pools of mystery; long lashes shaded them just enough to keep Rod searching their depths as she sank back among the cushions, breathless from the kiss that still made a passion flower of her generous mouth.

"Rod, darling," she murmured, "I've trusted you a lot, haven't I?"

"Isn't that a question!"

His glance traveled caressingly along the lovely body that smiled through a low-yoked nightgown of coral crepe. She had her fingers laced beneath her lustrous black waves; and leaning back among the cushions threw her breast into luxurious roundness. Northup bent over her, drew her close. He kissed her and thrilled to the convulsive pressure of her arms winding about his shoulders.

"Don't," she gasped, trying to free herself from his embrace. "I'm not trusting you that far — I won't —"

He drew back, bewildered by her sudden coldness. Her eyes, her dress, her voice had all been subtle promises.

"What do you mean?"

"If you'd quit Bud Worley," she whispered. "Get into a safer racket. Make books. Or gamble in the Peninsula night clubs. Or something."

Rod dimly sensed that that was not exactly what she meant. She was leading up to worming out details of Worley's operations. Maybe she had not really broken up with one of Keenan's men. Maybe the bitter quarrel had been a stall. Maybe Worley was right.

But Rod was a sucker for women. He had to have her. She reminded him of a bird of paradise. That didn't make much sense, but it sounded as glamorous as Dora looked. An allure and a mystery veiled her sensuous body. Every curve was a promise of something that no other woman could give him.

Hell, promise her anything!

She was looking up at him with glowing eyes. "Will you? Really?"

"Nuts for Worley!" he growled. "He don't own me! I'm his brains...."

He was, in a way. But that night he was not using them. And Dora was too elated by her triumph to use hers. Between kisses, she was tricking him into boasting to prove that he really was Worley's brain.

She did not notice the flutter of a window drape, nor the sudden intrusion of chilly air. She was too close in Northup's arms.

Her scream startled Northup, but he had no chance to go for the gun that lay on the end table near the lounge.

A dark man stood on the fire escape and shot across the sill. His glittering automatic reached far into the room. Its sound was small and dry and deadly, like the incredibly rapid snapping of sticks. Few men could accurately direct the fire of that short barrelled weapon, but this one did.

Rod dropped, coughing blood; his feet drummed against the rug. Dora had not a chance. She tried to duck, but her trailing gown was entangled with a dead man. When she jerked clear, it was too late.

The remaining four shots drilled her breast. Warm olive curves spurted red. She dropped, clawing at the lacy yoke. The silk crêpe was sticky. It clung to her flesh, and red froth gurgled from her gaping lips.

The man in the dark hat wiped the nickeled gat, flung it into the soft glow of the floor lamp. Pools of blood slowly reached for it.

"Just like I figured," Bud Worley told himself as he retraced his steps. "One job no mug could do . . . but now that it's done, I guess those skirt-chasing bastards will think twice."

They would. And Worley was right: this was one execution he had to do himself. Any torpedo who had killed Rod Northup would sooner or later brag about it. Bad stuff. But a mysterious death, like a mysterious woman, has a peculiar grip on the fancy.

Later, the new shoes, the hat, and top coat were consumed in an incinerator. They were beyond tracing, and so was the gun.

IN ANOTHER apartment, a blond woman in a sea-green slip lay sobbing into her pillow. Finally, she sat up, twisting a soaked handkerchief. Mae Allen's blue eyes blazed venomously, and wrath hardened her lovely face.

"God damn him, I'll fix his black-haired tramp! I'll claw him till he'll stay home for a week!"

She peeled out of her slip and stood for a moment before the mirror. A wisp of silk clung to her hips. A net brassiere outlined finely modelled curves. Her stomach was flat, and the flesh that blossomed from her hose-tops was firm and shapely.

"I guess I'm not good enough . . . the lousy — !"

When she emerged from the shower, she was clear eyed, glowing; she dressed carefully. Mae had lots of time. Her wrath strengthened her as it surged to white heat. Very deliberately, she went into the kitchenette.

There she found a knife. It was flexible, and keen from long whetting against a steel. When that Slavonian floozie got patched together, she'd never look the same again. Nor would that two-timing Rod be so popular.

She was guessing. But Mae knew as well as though she had seen him enter the apartment before whose door she stood, half an hour later. Whispers seeped through racketland.

She listened at the door. It would take a murmured endearment to give her the last touch. She worked the beveled latch-tongue back with the flexible bladed knife.

Simple trick, when people forgot to install bolt-latches.

A half stifled moan made her blood boil. But when she slipped into the room, she saw that it was the last sigh of pain. Dora Slavich had crawled to the telephone. There she lay, eyes glassy, teeth exposed in a grimace that made her beautiful features a horrible mockery.

Mae dropped the knife. For a moment she stood there, swaying. She was cold all over. Then she rushed toward Rod. Half way, she checked herself. He was all soaked with blood. She dared not touch him.

She had seen the ejected .25 caliber cartridges and the tiny gun. The wounds on the lovers told her the story.

Mae picked up the pistol and the knife she had dropped. She wiped the doorknob and jamb. With her handkerchief protecting her fingers, she closed the latch. And as the automatic elevator took her to the street level, she told herself what she had instinctively realized.

"No common torpedo did that job." She was dry-eyed, though grief choked her. New fury had blotted out all resentment against Rod and Dora. "Those dirty little guns aren't worth a damn except right close up. And from the way they were lying, whoever drilled them began shooting before Rod could get his gat off the table."

That took an exceptionally good gunner. She remembered that phone call from Worley; smiling, affable Bud. It fitted, like that.

So she shrugged, laughed bitterly when the racket captain called the next day to offer condolences.

"Thanks, Bud. Sure, it kind of hurts, but he might of known one of Dora's sweeties'd get hot about it."

Mae was certain that she had convinced Worley. As for the police hunting the murder weapon, as the papers claimed: she said, "That's good, isn't it? Funny they're not checking up on Dora's girl friend. The one that found the two of them dead."

So Bud assumed that the untraceable weapon had been stolen by someone who saw no reason for adding it to the police collection. A gun is a handy thing to have, but awkward to buy. Some foresighted person had just made the most of an easy chance.

He was right, but he did not realize how literally true his careless disposal of that question was. He now had his mob scared into line. His laugh became more affable, and his discipline more rigid, all the way from 'Frisco to Calexico. . . .

A WEEK later, Leadfoot Johnson was again pulling up to Blaze's filling station for fuel and a load of junk. He was on the second floor, putting the stuff into a container that would fit into the trick gas tank of his car.

"Well, toots," he said to Nita, "How's Torres behaving these days?"

"Damn nice," growled Blaze.

"I'd watch that greaser," Leadfoot lowered his voice. "A spic with a grudge is poison. His connections across the line make him more valuable than you. If he takes a notion to get square, all he's got to do is knife you to Worley." To clinch that, he told of the mysterious death of Rod Northup and Dora Slavich. He concluded, "If you asked me, and if I was telling you, I'd say Worley done it personally."

Nita shivered and drew her robe closer about her shoulders.

Blaze snorted, "Don't worry about us, Leadfoot. But what's eatin' at Worley? Going kill-crazy?"

"Jitters. G-men sniffing around. You see, he's getting too big. Blotting out Keenan's junk peddlers made him an all-time big shot out here. The damn fool. And he knows it, only he's stubborn."

"And smart enough to see his way clear, I guess," Blaze somberly added, as he helped stow the contraband. "Keenan taking it lying down?"

"He might as well," Leadfoot carelessly flung over his shoulder. "So long folks. Be back tomorrow night."

When Blaze rejoined Nita, she snuggled close.

"Darling," she said, "it's getting worse. Murdering his buddy on suspicion. God, if we could only take it on the lam."

"How far?" Brusque and bitter.

Nita's shoulders sagged. Her sigh seemed to deflate her lovely body. "Blaze, we're just like in those old pictures in a book I saw once. Some

Italian fellow wrote it. All about hell. Devils prodding people back into the fire."

She shuddered at the gruesome impression Dante's classic had made. And she was right. They were indeed the hopelessly damned. Lost if they revolted. Lost as surely if they stayed. Northup's fate clinched that. . . .

LEADFOOT Johnson loved his work. The deep-throated roar of the engine, the eerie whine of the supercharger, the whistle of tires: these were music to him. The money of it was nothing.

He would as soon have hauled passengers, if he could have made cakes and eggs that way. His work made him forget he had been an also-ran on the big tracks. He was in a racket, but he was no mobster; just a racing driver who did an Indianapolis grind every other night. This was something Worley did not suspect.

The long gray phaeton murmured lazily up the grade at whose midpoint Bud Worley waited for the cargo of junk. This was the time when Death crept into hospitals to slip up on those who had long outwitted him; when cops lounged in all-night restaurants, warming their bellies with coffee and thoughts of sunrise. . . .

The junk came to town in Death's rush hour. But Leadfoot Johnson did not think of this. He had made his fastest run, and Leadfoot glowed inside.

A savage clattering startled him. Slugs clunked against the car. A tire popped. The engine conked out. The dirty lugs had blasted the distributor to bits; she wouldn't take off.

He leaped clear. He was unarmed. Being flagged down could always be squared, but if a gat were found on him, the highway patrol would look further and find the junk.

He almost reached the middle of the road when his leg buckled. White-hot irons seemed to sear his ribs. A hail of bullets ricocheted from the paving. Blood from his creased scalp blinded him.

The hijackers were tearing into the car. They worked with mechanical precision. They had to, to get away before the Chinatown squad woke up.

Bud Worley's light sleep had been shattered by the riot. His gunners were there, but men booted out of the hay at that hour are dull and sluggish. The chief was the first into action. He dashed down a passageway that led to a deserted building that commanded the scene.

The murky glare of a street light almost touched the crippled car. He opened fire with a revolver. A hijacker pitched face forward. Cans of junk rolled down the grade. Worley cursed bitterly. They were beyond retrieving.

Answering fire blazed from behind a power pole. Another hijacker shot from the rear left of the riddled car. Worley's deadly skill got him; a slug lifted the top of his head. But as he dropped, the dead man's reflexes jerked a farewell shot.

That misdirected spurt of flame ignited the gas that ran from the slashed tank from which the junk had been taken. A tall column of flame roared up, three stories high. The raiders fled.

Police whistles shrilled. Cops came charging up the hill, guns drawn. A wounded fugitive stumbled, gun clattering from his hand. One lay roasting in the awful heat of the blazing gas, unable to crawl to safety.

Bud Worley lurked, eyes glittering. Dawn grayed, but the roaring blaze was brighter than day. The cops were picking up the cans of hop. Leadfoot Johnson was regaining his feet.

He lurched drunkenly. A cop started in pursuit. There was a man to question, along with the wounded raiders the others were rounding up.

Panting, coughing blood, Leadfoot headed for Worley's fortress and safety.

Then he saw a revolver barrel reflecting the flames. The wind whipped the blaze for a moment, giving him a view into the shadows of the building. He recognized the dark man who smiled.

"Bud, fer Christ's sake!" he yelled. "It's me —

His legs buckled. The cops were closing in. The revolver rose, and blackness blotted Leadfoot Johnson's terror. . . .

Worley Retreated before the cops could get between the flames and the window from which had come the shot that had picked a captive from their hands. As he reached his own house, which still was legally above reproach and could not be entered without a warrant, he exhaled a sigh.

"Close . . . damn close." He grinned amiably and set to work cleaning his revolver, washing his hands with chemicals to destroy incriminating traces of nitro powder. "Tough about Leadfoot . . . good driver, too. . . ."

He spent the day smoking and listening to the radio. From time to time, underworld gossip filtered into his house. He ran his gunners into cover. He knew now that Smoke Keenan, hopped up and reckless, had staged the reprisal; but the flareback had driven Keenan and his mugs into hiding.

EVERY JUNK DEALER was hot now. That the cops had not made a raid to round up every suspected racketeer was ominous. They were waiting. G-men were taking things in hand. When they cracked down . . .

But Worley smiled. Leadfoot Johnson could not talk about the source of his opium and snow. Suppose the narcotic squad did slug the pants off Keenan's wounded gunners? Their statements would only kick back at their boss, not Worley.

Some of his telephones were unauthorized extensions tapped into instruments a block away. Thus he got reports.

That night, things eased up. A few of his gunners returned. And Mae Allen came to the house.

"Bud, darling," she cooed, "Keenan's crazy-mad. I'm afraid he'll take it out of anyone messed up with you."

"Stay here," he generously invited. "I'll take care of you."

Come to think of it, Mae was nice looking. Her legs were gorgeous, and the way she had them crossed, he got peeps of smooth whiteness. Only the right thing to take care of Mae. . . .

They had a few drinks. Spike and Benny tended bar. Everyone had an alibi. Worley wished the dumb clucks would get out and leave him alone with Mae. She'd make a quick job of getting over Rod's death. Mob widows usually did. . . .

The phone rang. No name was mentioned, but Worley recognized the voice.

"Fer Christ's sake, watch yourself, Bud. Leadfoot sang before he croaked. He knew you tried to knock him off to shut him up, so he squawked. All about Calexico."

*Click!* Nothing more to be said. Worley's face tightened. Nobody could use Leadfoot's dying remarks as a peg for a murder rap. No D.A. would be silly enough to try to. But narcotic agents would nail Torres and Blaze and Nita. Not right away, no. Not until a new runner was put on the job.

Certainly not until then. For no one was supposed to know Leadfoot

Johnson had squawked. But for a crooked captain, Worley would have suspected least of all. He relaxed and began smiling.

"Drink, baby?" He squirted soda into the tall glass.

Mae snuggled closer, lifted admiring blue eyes. She had to build it up carefully before she used the gat that had killed Rod. She had not even dared bring it. If Worley began pawing her and found it, she'd be finished. He'd put two and two together; the answer was quick death.

Worley was pawing her, and she pretended to like it. Later, as she peeled out of her ensemble and stood before the dresser, all white and gold and silk, Worley said, "I could go for you, steady."

"Darling, do you mean that?" she cooed, snapping off the lights. . . .

THAT NIGHT, Worley got more phone calls. His plan took form. If he personally went to Calexico, he could pull things out of the fire. Instead of sending a pair of torpedoes to settle Blaze and Nita, he had a better idea. A keen piece of strategy. So keen that he kept it from Mae, who'd turned out to be a perfectly swell kid.

Worley smiled at the world as he listened to the pilot warming up a plane at the private landing field of an aviation club at San Carlos, some twenty-odd miles south of San Francisco. The cops and the narcotic agents still thought they had him bottled up in his fortress, huh?

He had discarded the idea of rubbing out Blaze and Nita, simply because they were too handy and too useful; he had them where they lived, and they dared not be stupid or talkative. And even though that lousy rat of a Leadfoot Johnson had squealed, Blaze and Nita would play a new role: that of decoy ducks!

"Let the feds watch 'em," he outlined to himself as the plane swooped south. "Let 'em chase suspicious cars with nothing in 'em. While I'm running the junk from Tecate . . . well, maybe Andrade would be better."

He was truly becoming a field general. This was strategy, making the feds believe that Blaze was really outwitting them. The continued flow of hop and snow to 'Frisco would drive them nuts! They'd end by folding their tails between their legs. He was so pleased that he forgot his bitterness against that yellow bastard, Leadfoot Johnson, ratting on his chief.

"And Mae's a nice kid. Damn near wished I'd brought her along." She'd begged for the trip, but Worley had compromised. "Listen, toots, I'll phone you from the hotel at El Centro. Uhuh. You don't think I'm landing in Calexico? Christ, am I that dumb?"

When he landed, he'd phone Blaze, and they'd meet at the hotel. That way, Blaze wouldn't get jittery and think, he, Worley, was sore.

IT WAS an hour after dark when he was set down in Brawley, which had a landing field. It was only fourteen miles to El Centro. He engaged a rental car and drove it himself. He needed no bodyguard in this apple-knocker section, where people had cotton and dates and rice on the brain.

Worley thus paid no attention to the car that passed him, just beyond the landing field, at Imperial, which was four miles from his destination.

At the Vista Real, he gave his keys to the porter and strode up to the desk. The house was small, yet tastefully furnished. Its lobby was spacious as the open desert. A tourist place, and the clerk was impressed by the debonair, carefully tailored young man who approached.

As Worley signed the register, the clerk said, "Lucky you reserved a suite. We're a bit crowded, and if you hadn't, we'd have had to give you something a bit less choice."

"Huh?" Worley looked up sharply. "Reservation?"

"Why, yes. Mrs. Worley hurried down to surprise you."

"Uh, sure." He brightened. Mae, the dizzy little doll, had flown down! After all, why not? "Listen, is this the best in the house?"

"Oh, yes, indeed, sir! Air conditioned — you know, it does get hot here, but it's clean, dry, invigorating desert heat. Lots of the movie people patronize us. Ah . . . I know I've seen your face on the screen, Mr. Worley." The clerk nodded wisely. The racketeer beamed. It tickled him, being mistaken for a movie idol, incognito. "The suite is sound proofed, Mr. . . . ah . . . Worley. Yes, indeed, sir. You'll not be disturbed."

Pretty swell. Pretty swell. And Mae's perfume and open arms welcomed him at one swoop.

"Darling, I hope you'll not be mad. I just got so damn lonesome."

He held her from him. Lord, she looked as good as she smelled.

"Shake up a drink while I clean up," he said, breaking from her followup kiss. "You little devil, you could get an airport plane ahead of me. But you took a risk."

"As if I care!"

A shower. A shave. His face smarted and tingled from windblown sand. He turned back to the medicine chest mirror, but there was Mae's handglass.

That quick move and the unexpected mirror gave him a glimpse of Mae's hate-distorted face and flash of nickel. Cat-quick, he hurled himself to the shelter of the jamb just as the little automatic crackled.

The tiny slug bit lightly. Mae's treachery infuriated him. She cried out, shudderingly, and desperately squeezed another shot. Worley flinched. God, that was close. He deliberately leaped out of cover, but crouched to make the most of the race against death.

He hurled the mirror. It caught Mae between the eyes, stunning her. She fell, a quivering huddle of white and orchid and red.

"You God damn dirty — ! So that's it?" Trembling, he seized the little gat, emptied it into the half-conscious woman's body.

Sound proofed room, huh? No one'd hear that pea shooter.

He dressed, very rapidly. He cut every label and laundry mark from Mae's garments and his own. Then he grinned, remembering the dumb cluck down below had suspected him of being a movie star. Sweet, huh?

But now he could not phone Blaze. Not by no manner or means! Especially not from a hotel in which an unidentified blonde would be found.

He stopped at the desk, slid a century note to the clerk and demanded change. That gave him a chance to add a few strokes to the register: changing Worley to Worleigh. Not that it'd make much difference. Why wouldn't an incognito movie star pick on his name? Not a dozen people in the state knew that "Bud" meant "Rudolph."

Presently, Worley was on a bus to Calexico, eleven miles away. When he reached his destination, he phoned Blaze Hayden: "Come on to the back room of the Mission Pool Room. Yeah, I know this is sudden, but I got a hot idea. Don't mention any names, see?"

"Listen, uh — listen," answered Hayden. "Nita's sick in bed. And that uh — well . . . that man — I'm afraid he'll sneak up on her."

Worley knew that Blaze referred to Torres. Leadfoot had told him that much, and no more; nothing about Nita's discontent.

"Aw, fer hell's sweet sake —" Then he abruptly checked himself. Much better to go to the filling station. It would not be as conspicuous. There was Mae, dead in her room. And since no junk-runner had been working the beat, the narcotic snoopers would not be watching day and night. It all flashed through his mind. He said, "Okay, Blaze. Be out right away. The back way, huh?"

Calexico was too small to make a cab necessary. The aristocrat got a kick out of walking, once in a while, like common people. He was whistling softly as he strode on air. He was invincible. Keenan's revolt had kicked back. So had Mae's lousy treachery. And she'd not squawked to the narcotic men. She was a mobster frill, sold on personal vengeance; not a louse like Leadfoot.

Can't sneak up on me. I catch 'em, even when my back's turned. Keenan. Mae. Not to make a horse's neck of the God damn feds . . . if they're screwballs enough to try to nip me.

He loved Blaze Hayden like a brother. Good old Blaze, helping making a monkey's so and so out of the coppers! He'd buy Nita something ritzy. Nice girl, Nita, but he had one blonde already. . . .

BLAZE HAYDEN was saying, "Now, honey, I tell you, Worley ain't mad. Cripes, if he was gunning us out, he'd not come down here, he'd send torpedoes."

Nita was buffing her finger nails long after they gleamed like rubies.

"I smell death. Look at Northup. Look at Leadfoot. We're hoodooed."

"He didn't croak Leadfoot," protested Blaze. "Keenan's mob did."

He was sore and got up to go downstairs and wait for Worley. Blaze was becoming shaky from Nita's day and night grousing. It was a lousy, stinking racket, but they were lucky, being so far from headquarters. It'd been different, if Leadfoot had squealed and told all about Calexico. . . .

A cheery voice hailed him. "Hi, Blaze."

"Hi, boss," answered Hayden, extending his hand. Hell, Worley was smiling, tickled to death with something. "Something big bringing you down, huh? How'd you square that mess up north?"

The telephone jangled. "Wait a sec. Be right back."

"I got it, honey," Nita called from the second floor.

"Oh, that?" chuckled Worley. "Listen, pal. It had me talking to myself, but believe me, when I get thinking, I think fast. Now take a load of this —"

He leaned across the kitchen table in the back room. A packet of maps jutted from his inside coat pocket. And the butt of his revolver peeped from under his armpit. But he was not thinking of that, nor of the gun in

Blaze Hayden's hip pocket. Hell, the boy was watching out for Torres. He'd have to warn him against quarrelling with such a valuable guy.

He did not hear the frou-frou of silk. But he did get a whiff of expensive perfume. He was still shaky about women in back of him. He had not laughed Mae completely out of mind. So he abruptly turned in his chair as he reached for his maps.

Blaze yelled, but that was drowned in the heavy blasts of a .38. Nita, white faced, was pouring lead into Worley. Slugs bounced screaming from the range. Some grazed Hayden as terror sent him ducking for cover.

Worley was cursing, rising to his knees, gun jumping into line.

Nita was crazy, but Blaze knew they were doomed. His own gun got into action. He finished what Nita's insane shooting had started. Worley dropped, his face a red blot, his revolver blasting wild. The blood fury gripped Blaze. He emptied his automatic into the quivering, dead hulk.

He shoved in another clip and emptied it.

Nita stopped him. Dazed, he said, "What'd you do that for?"

"Mae Allen — she phoned — from El Centro — the dirty son — shot her — she said just enough — to warn me — so — darling — we're not damned! We're free — thank God — free. Quick, get the car — I'll finish this."

As he rolled his bus into the drive and gunned the engine, he began to get the point of it all. Nita came out with a suitcase. A handful of large bills from Worley's wallet. The damned had revolted, and Satan's blood-soaked money would give them a fresh start.

Nita flung a match, then joined Blaze. "Drive like hell," she panted. "Before the fire gets too big. I soaked things with gas, lots of it. They'll think you shot Torres for making passes at me. And nobody'll care."

A tall red column rose high enough to touch the rear vision mirror of the roaring car. A pillar of fire celebrated the revolt of the damned.

"Baby," whispered Blaze, as he pieced it all together, "it'll work. When Torres hears of the shooting and fire, he'll stay away, so they won't nail him for killing me and running off with you."

SHE pillowed her copper red waves against his unwounded shoulder.

"Darling, you're awful smart. God, I was afraid I'd got you into trouble." She turned back, glancing at the far off fire that had made the undrained gas pumps explode. Then she sighed, "It's just like I read, once, about a pillar of fire guiding a bunch of people into the promised land, or something."

# CRYSTAL CLUES

"THIS DUMP'S got no more need of a house dick than Ethiopia has of a highway commissioner," Cliff Cragin told himself as he pocketed his first week's salary and planted himself in a chair in the lobby to wait for the arrival of a guest at the Westward Ho.

The hotel overlooked Bubbling Lake, not far from the volcanic park at Mount Lassen. The lake really did bubble, only no one gave a damn; and the bathhouse at the steaming sulphur spring had fallen to pieces without anyone ever missing it.

Then why a house detective?

Cragin, having at one stroke locked up his worries and the doors of the Golden Gate Investigation Service, dismissed the query and watched Glendora dusting her way across the vacant lobby.

Glendora's legs fascinated Cragin. The more he saw of them, the more he wanted to see of them. Their heart-stirring sweep was as tantalizing as the sway of her just-right hips; and whenever she stooped to touch up the polish on the arm of a chair, Cragin wished she would straighten up before he became absolutely cross-eyed trying to probe her tantalizing curves. She made all his treasured recollections of beautiful women seem somewhat uncouth.

Glendora was getting under his skin; and if he had to spend the rest of the summer doing nothing but watching that streamlined chamber maid, he'd end up gnawing doorknobs. . . .

The transparent, walnut tint of her skin was deceptive. She might be from the West Indies, or Central America. He'd seen quite an assortment of racial mixtures in New Orleans. He gritted his teeth and tried to think of other answers —

Glendora's lips were not thick; just lusciously full. And the flare of her nostrils was so delicate that it merely lent an alert eagerness to her otherwise placid loveliness.

Hell, she couldn't be an octoroon!

But Glendora's voice was a damnation. Her speech was a shade too slurred even for a New Orleans accent.

It was getting under Cragin's skin. Bubbling Lake. Empty hotel —

"Westwa'd-Ho House," he said to himself, mimicking her soft, slurred enunciation. "If this dump just had a bus with a colored driver, there'd be a land office rush when he went to the station and sounded off, "Dis way, gem'mum — de Wes'wa'd-Ho House —"

Cragin's outright laugh brought a sign of life from Gilbert Harris, the proprietor.

"What's so damn' funny?" he snapped. Harris was a small, sharp-faced man with black hair and shrewd, furtive eyes.

"Nothing at all, Mr. Harris," grinned Cragin. "I just thought of a way to keep everyone from going to Bubbling Lake Tavern."

"How?" snapped Harris, He was just griped; the answer did not interest him.

"Gimme one of those pencils, and I'll figure the details," evaded Cragin.

Harris had six sharp-pointed pencils projecting from his vest pocket, just in case the one over his ear should break. He was always calculating, on the desk blotter, and in large figures.

"Go —"

The retort was blotted out by the crunch of tires on the gravel drive. A long, rakish touring sedan with a Louisiana license had pulled up to the door. Twelve cylinders murmured sleepily under the hood that needed no nameplate.

Cragin had only a passing glance for the two men who emerged. The woman who preceded them was a double eyeful. She was tall and full-breasted and shapely, with sleek hips whose undulant action was subtle enough to make one wonder all kinds of things. She had a wanton red mouth and arrogant, trouble-making violet eyes that for a full moment appraised Cragin as though trying to decide whether his face was homely or interesting.

He forgot all about Glendora' mysteries, visible and suggested. This blonde bird from Louisiana fairly radiated invitation.

He emerged from the chair to give Harris a hand with the luggage. The proprietor nailed him with a blistering glance; and later, when the trio had been assigned to rooms, he said to Cragin, "From now on, you're a guest. Get it?"

"Uhuh," said Cragin. Only, he did not get it. Harris was more worried than ever.

The Westward-Ho House — anyway you pronounced it — was becoming screwier every moment.

That evening, in the dining room, Glendora made an awkward job of doubling as waitress. Cragin had no appetite. Too many eyes were covertly scrutinizing him. When it wasn't that blonde Lafourche woman, it was her ruddy, broad-shouldered husband, or the third member of the party, lean, saturnine Warren Dale.

Cragin, to end the misery, left the dining room. Harris ate in the office. In passing, he caught a glimpse of the proprietor lighting a cigarette from the butt of its predecessor.

When he reached his room, Cragin picked up a week old 'Frisco newspaper. As he began burning his way through a pack of butts, he read about Morton Sloane, the Louisiana sulphur mine promoter, who had escaped from the Federal jug in Atlanta.

"By God," he muttered half an hour later, as he re-read the inconspicuous squib, "that's when I got this cockeyed job . . ."

But the inevitable "What of it?" left him pondering.

Finally the phone tinkled. Cragin crossed the room and unhooked the receiver. Harris was speaking.

"Later tonight," he almost whispered, "I'll send Glendora up to move your luggage to the room next to mine. Get it?"

"Okay," assented Cragin, cutting short the impending explanation.

But before he could find new ways of telling himself how damn crazy it was getting, he learned that he had moved just in time. There was the dry snick of drilled glass, a hammer impact against the wall, and a spattering of plaster. Without thinking, he knew it was a bullet. He flattened to the floor.

Somewhat over a second later, he heard a sharp smack that was none the less vicious for being distance-blurred. Someone had trained a high-powered rifle on him.

"That sneaking little . . . !" he muttered, "calling me to the phone to get me plugged!"

His first impulse was to dash down and hammer the truth out of Harris; the second was to snap off the lights; but he did neither. A dead man isn't supposed to move.

Cragin rolled over on his back and inched himself toward the blind quarter of the room. There he noted the neatly drilled hole in the window. It was appreciably higher than the point of impact in the plaster. The sniper had fired from a level above the second floor.

Since the sound had taken just a bit over a second to reach him, the marksman must have been twelve, maybe thirteen hundred feet away. The bathhouse at the hot sulphur spring . . . only a guess, but a logical one.

Cragin bellied across the carpet, reached up and fingered the door-knob; but he had to wait. There were footsteps in the hall, and Adele Lafourche's ever-animated voice. She was poisonously tired from their long drive, and would she be glad to get to bed. Lafourche, pausing to bid someone goodnight, overtook her and reminded her she wasn't the only one who had had a weary drive.

Cragin edged his door open to slip down the hall and out the rear. Dale's room was in the opposite direction. The coast was clear: that is, until Cragin was well over the threshold. Then it was too late to retreat.

Glendora emerged from a room two doors down, and across the hall. Her eyes widened as she saw the house detective bounding from a crouch. Before she could yeep, he was at her side, one hefty hand muffling her mouth. He edged her back across the doorway.

"What the hell you prowling around for?"

"Mistah Ha'iss done tol' me to fix this room fo' yo'all," she explained.

Talk about lousy breaks! Harris, waiting for Glendora to use her key and discover a corpse, would get wise unless she screeched till the shingles shivered. No chance of a secret look-see at the sulphur spring by flashlight.

That, however, was not all that was disturbing Cragin. He had an armful of Glendora and he hated to let go. The past week's purely intel-lectual curiosity was becoming something more insistent and pointed. Whether she was a Creole, or an octoroon, or some Cuban blend that had picked up a southern accent didn't alter the fact that she had not recoiled from his grasp, that just south of the collarbone she was built like a bras-siere ad, that the curves where legs decide to become hips were round and warm and . . .

The shrewdness of a long line of level-headed Cragins came to the rescue.

"Tell him I don't answer. He phoned me the news a minute ago."

Before releasing Glendora so that she could step to the house phone, he shifted the unintentional embrace so as to leave her without any doubts that he wasn't fooling. She shivered, exhaled a sigh; and her assenting murmur did not entirely refer to Cragin's orders concerning the message to Harris.

"Hell," reasoned Cragin, as he heard her call the proprietor, "I couldn't get there in time to catch the sniper anyhow."

Glendora hung up the receiver, softly closed the door, and tiptoed through the half gloom to his side. He drew her to his knee; and as she clung like a wet handkerchief to a window pane, he decided that Glendora must have been reading his mind for the past week . . . she couldn't have gotten that way all in a minute. . . .

Ethnological niceties no longer bothered him. He was thoroughly convinced that she was a Creole; but before he could settle that question beyond any doubt, Glendora murmured something about having a drink first.

As she wriggled clear of his arms, she drew a half pint from her apron pocket. That, and her rapid breathing told him that she had been doing some thinking herself.

He watched her fumbling for a pair of tumblers in the darkness and wondered how she'd look if she shed that white, severely starched dress that failed to conceal her shapeliness.

The liquor was raw and blistering, but Cragin gargled it at a gulp. It should have sent Glendora through the roof, but it didn't. Instead, she seemed to be changing her mind about things that should have become more urgent every moment. Not that she was slapping him, but somehow she managed to keep him from going too far.

Finally, catching him entirely off guard, she slid to her feet, gave his hand a promising squeeze, and whispered something about being back in a minute. She tiptoed to the door, glanced nervously up and down the hall . . .

"Hell of a time to get the jitters!" Cragin grumbled to himself.

But a moment after she left the room, he ceased counting seconds. Maybe later on would be better . . . he was drowsy as a marathon dancer. . . .

And then a deep-seated instinct warned him. He was doped! Fear and wrath forced him to his feet. He could barely move, and when he did, he was like some wooden thing.

Glendora had paved the way for a second attempt. He gritted his teeth, bit his lips until the pain whipped him another wobbly stride to the door.

He was a walking dummy when he finally slumped across the threshold of his own room. He recovered, and dully dragged himself toward his suitcases.

If he had to hunt, he was finished.

But luck was with him. He found the tin of headache powders. They were an unadvertised brand confined to the west coast. They were loaded

CRYSTAL CLUES   103

with caffeine. He swallowed half a dozen. It was the equivalent of several pots of strong coffee, the best antidote for narcotics. . . .

And bit by bit, the sledge hammer jolt of that overdose of caffeine overcame Glendora's treachery. He was groggy, his heart was pounding like a bass drum, but he could carry on.

Cragin checked his .45, pocketed his flashlight, and crept down the hall. He heard the drowsy murmur and sigh from Adele Lafourche's room, but for once he did not take time out to wish he were someone else.

The crisp mountain air braced him.

Presently, he was approaching the sulphur spring. Looking back, he could clearly spot his still-illuminated window. But whoever fired must have used a rifle with a telescopic sight.

The porous ground was riddled with uncounted tiny jets of steam, spongy and in spots yellowish with fine needles of crystallized sulphur. By the glow of his flashlight he noted a man's footprints.

He followed them toward the decrepit bathhouse. Someone had pulled a boner, crossing that treacherous soil. The sniper wore shoes larger than Harris'. It would be a cinch, checking up on the footgear and nailing the owner of sulphur-caked soles.

It must have been someone from the hotel. No one else would have had Cragin's room spotted. But the motive?

"Wes'wa'd-Ho House! Hell . . . it's a madhouse!" he muttered, crouching behind a boulder.

The silence was broken only by the soft hissing of steam. Pistol drawn, he peered from the right of the rock as his left hand directed the flashlight around the other side.

The beam made a dull blur out of the vapors that surged from the bathhouse, but he could distinguish a man's feet and the trousers of a familiar checkered suit. He lay flat, face down. Warren Dale!

Cragin, bounding forward, muttered to himself, "The hot sulphur fumes knocked the dirty . . . out! But I'll wake him!"

Only he couldn't. Dale's hand was raised in a warding gesture. His Panama hat, crushed to his head, was a gory, bedraggled pulp. Nearby lay a rusty length of inch and a quarter pipe. Its end was dark with blood.

And in one corner, perilously balanced on the edge of one of the planks that bridged the sulphur spring, gleamed a rifle cartridge. Cragin, gasping and choking from the steam, missed his footing. He sprawled athwart the planks, missing a dive into a boiling pit; but the cartridge fell into the vaporous depths.

Dale's wallet was well padded with twenties and some hundreds. Oddly enough, in one compartment was a clipping from the New Orleans *Picayune*: "CONVICTED SWINDLER SWEARS VENGEANCE."

The article referred to Morton Sloane. The date line was a month older than the one Cragin had read in his room. He studied the terse summary of the case that had ended with Sloane's sentence to Atlanta.

The same old story: paying dividends out of money raised by the sale of stock. The payment of the faked earnings jacks up the price. Suckers buy on a rising market. Then . . . flop!

Only, someone got wise to Sloane, the president of the gyp outfit; and the missing fifty grand in bonds snitched from the company treasury had clinched the case.

"The dirty tug oughta get life, hooking those Cajun farmers!" muttered Cragin, pocketing the clippings. "But for hell's suffering sake, why did the guy that beaned Dale take a shot at me?"

He strode down the steep grade toward the hotel. Nothing to do now but phone the sheriff and watch the apple-knocker try get the answers.

"I kind of wish it'd been the other guy," reflected Cragin, wondering if Adele Lafourche wore pajamas or a nightgown. "Then there'd be a widow to console. . . ."

Maybe Harris had not called him to the phone to put him on the spot. Come to think of it, the boss was damn worried. But the two, clicking that way, had left an impression Cragin could not erase in a moment.

A light was in the office. He tiptoed up to the frame building to catch Harris off guard.

It was not the proprietor who knelt before the safe. Glendora, skirt hitched up and displaying those dazzling legs, was in front of the steel door, twirling the nickeled dial and frowning at a penciled scrap of paper. She shook her head, sighed, tried it again.

Cragin crept into the lobby. As he slipped past the counter, he saw that Glendora's shoes were marked with the peculiar volcanic earth of the hot spring. A fragment lay in the doorway. Sulphur crystals gleamed like topaz needles.

Cragin swallowed a mouthful of queries and bounded across the office. He throttled Glendora's dismayed outcry. Her face became all eyes, and though her color did not change, she went limp in his arms.

Had she gone to report to the mysterious sniper? Had he brained Dale for trailing Glendora? It was all too thick to make sense.

He was determined to put her over the hurdles when she recovered her wits. But as her blossoming curves pressed against him, he began to wonder. . . .

He compromised by tying her with a sheet and leaving her in her quarters just off the kitchen. Then he went upstairs to the proprietor's apartment, adjoining the room where Glendora had put out the doped whisky.

The door was not locked. A thread of light filtered between the edge and the jamb. He paused to knock, but before his knuckles reached the panel, Cragin's instinct warned him of a lurking presence.

He whirled, diving for his .45, but despite his speed, he was caught short. A gaunt, unshaven man with blazing eyes and mud-fouled clothes confronted him. He grasped a high-powered hunting rifle with a telescopic sight. He was crouched as though on guard for bayonet drill. His teeth showed in an inaudible snarl —

It ended the instant it registered. As Cragin's pistol cleared the holster, the rifle flickered up in a butt-strike — which refers to what hit Cragin, and not *where*. The walnut stock sank into the pit of his stomach, paralyzing him. He could not even yank a shot.

He doubled up, too numb to feel the ensuing smack across the head. It was not until a long time thereafter that he even realized that there had been a blow. . . .

WHEN HE finally became aware of the intolerable aching of his head, he wondered why the ragged madman had pulled his punch. A rifle butt or barrel could have smashed his head to a gummy pulp. And why had Harris not heard the thump?

Cragin tottered to his feet before he realized he was grasping a hunting knife whose blade was sticky. He blinked, dropped the weapon, noted the red splashes that stained his tweeds. He kicked open the door of the proprietor's room.

Harris was half in a chair, half sprawled across a table. The back of his coat was blood soaked. A darkening red pool drenched the floor and spread across the tabletop. Someone had pinned him to the oak, then yanked the knife out.

Westward-Ho House — hell, it was worse than a madhouse now! And when it came to bubbling, Cragin's brain was making a monkey out of the lake.

He picked his way downstairs, cranked the telephone in the office. The line was dead. No chance of calling the sheriff. It was a long jaunt to the Bubbling Lake Tavern, whose few lights winked across the black water.

If he had the keys, he could drive Harris' station wagon to Mineral Wells. He tramped back upstairs. As he approached the darkened head of the stairs, he reached for his pistol, just in case.

It was gone. Neither was it lying where he had dropped.

But before he could re-enter Harris' room, he heard a choked gasping, then a scream. A door slammed open, and Adele Lafourche burst into the hallway. Seeing Cragin, she stood there, blinking and gaping.

Cragin did the same. The strong side lighting from the door at her left made her chiffon nightgown look like the vapors that hissed from the volcanic earth about the spring. His initial ideas on Adele's structure were dazzlingly confirmed. Though full breasted, she was firm; and the incurve of her waist accentuated the roundness of her intriguing hips.

Double eyeful? That frail froth of chiffon and lace clung to a tapering sweep of ivory legs that would have dazzled a streetful of eyes.

"Oh — I had the most *awful* dream!" she cried. "I thought my husband was killing me!"

"Where the hell is he?" groped Cragin, wondering how she had managed to drape herself all over him in one move.

The longer and tighter she clung, the more urgent an answer became. That warm armful was making him forget his battered head and its whirling queries. And it wasn't entirely Adele's perfume, though that was a mighty sultry compound that probably was called *Nuit d'Ivresse* or something dizzier.

"That's what frightened me," she gasped, incoherent. "He's gone. Suitcase and all."

Though two plus two does not invariably make four, Cragin was willing to bet that the twelve-lunged Packard had sneaked from its stable after Lafourche had slipped the dripping hunting knife into his hand. That, of course, would cancel his first hunch that the shaggy-headed madman had finished Harris.

She seemed to sense his thought.

"He always leaves his keys on the dresser with his watch," Adele continued. "Do go and see if the car is in."

It took Cragin a few seconds over a minute to learn that the long locomotive was gone.

"Oh — I know something dreadful's happened!" she moaned as he returned. "Where's Mr. Harris? And where's Dale?"

She noticed that Cragin's head was battered and his face smeared with grime and blood.

"Tell me!" she persisted. Then, as he groped for words: "I know — Oh, good God! Maurice has been acting so strangely!"

She was rapidly getting out of hand. If he told her what had happened, the madhouse would be complete. And if he didn't, she'd guess, and it'd be just as bad.

"They're both deader'n hell!" he blurted out. "And someone damn near brained me! Now pipe down, sister, and pull yourself together."

She threw herself on the couch and lay there, a laughing, sobbing white length. Adele was plumb loco.

He kicked the door shut, and tried to remember how to snap a woman out of hysterics. He could not leave her this way while he went for the sheriff, and he'd go nuts it he had to listen much longer.

Cragin knelt beside the lounge and tried to draw her upright. His grasp slipped, and his hand brushed curves that set his blood racing.

That was no way to set a woman upright. Cragin regretfully shifted his grasp. But while his next attempt did not skid on curves, it was like taking a scoopshovel of pep tablets.

When Cragin did get her propped up among some cushions, Adele wouldn't let go. And what was pressing against his shirtfront was warm and resilient and resentful of pressure.

As soon as she calmed down a bit more, he might be able to find out why Dale and Lafourche had come from Louisiana to this lost corner of the woods, and how they tied in with Harris. Such was his intention; but about the time Adele became rational, Cragin couldn't stand it any longer.

He caught her in an embrace that squeezed her breathless, then kissed her until he himself had to come up for air. Before they broke, Adele was again making incoherent sounds, but this time it was not hysteria. It was something like a half-hearted attempt to say "Don't . . ."

Cragin gave her some bigger and better kisses; and judging from the shudder that rippled to her ankles, she forgot more than her nightmarish premonitions . . . .

Unfortunately, absent mindedness had likewise overlooked the latch on door —

When it slammed open, Cragin disengaged himself from a tangle of arms and chiffon and other odds and ends just in time to hear a wrathful oath and see two men standing in the doorway.

One was Maurice Lafourche. The other, viewing the show from behind a single-action Colt whose muzzle gaped like a sugar barrel, wore a slouch hat, a tobacco-stained moustache, and a nickeled star the size of a saucer.

"Er . . . ug — gug —" But gestures as well as speech failed Cragin, It was going to be hard as the devil to explain.

"Stick 'em up!" The sheriff's gnarled hand restrained the wrathful husband. "You're under arrest for the murder of Gilbert Harris."

"You're crazy!" Cragin cut in. "Someone sapped me as I was knocking at his door, and when I snapped out of it, Mrs. Lafourche screamed, and —"

"You might try wrapping a blanket around yourself," was Lafourche's frosty command to his wife. Then, to the sheriff: "I heard a disturbance and saw this fellow dashing down the hall with a knife in his hand. When I found Harris dead, I knocked at Dale's room, but he was not in.

"And so I drove out to get you. Didn't want to alarm my wife. I never dreamed he'd come back. By God, sheriff, if I had a gun —"

"All right, young fellow!" the sheriff interrupted, "stick 'em out."

Cragin knew that he had not a Chinaman's chance of proving that he had been sapped by a madman with a rifle, but he tried it.

"Get Glendora," he concluded. "Look in my room and see the bullet hole. Find out who killed Dale, up at the sulphur spring!"

"We'll look into that," was Sheriff Barker's noncommittal answer as he snapped on the bracelets.

"Dale, *dead?*" gasped Lafourche.

"Sure he's dead!" growled Cragin. "Ask Glendora. Look at the sulphur on her shoes, just like on mine."

Sheriff Barker, holstering his Colt, was caught off guard by his prisoner's vehement suggestion. He looked —

Cragin, nerves wire-edged, saw not only that the sheriff's glance had shifted, but that Lafourche was looking at his own sulphur-caked shoes.

*Smack!* The heavy circlets of steel smashed against Barker's head. He went down, his half-drawn revolver blasting the bottom out of his holster. Lafourche, stumbling as the sheriff dropped athwart his legs, took a nose-dive into the room.

Cragin, though manacled, snatched the sheriff's revolver.

"Get up, you louse-bound —!" growled the detective, cocking the ponderous Colt and shifting it to wrap Lafourche's stomach around his spine. "You killed Dale! You were at the spring. And you framed me after knifing Harris!"

The sheriff, though still out, was mumbling and stirring. Lafourche turned gray as he stared into the oversized muzzle.

But before Cragin could devise a way of keeping Lafourche covered while getting Barker's keys, the indiscreet wife took a hand. She had been lying on the lounge, face buried in the cushions to hide her confusion; but the way she hurled her overnight case would have made a goal from the sixty-yard line. And as the revolver was knocked out of line, Lafourche lunged, wrenching the weapon from Cragin's grasp.

"Tie them both and blow, darling!" said Adele, her voice tense. "Honest, I had to do *something* to keep him amused —"

"You didn't need to let him paw you over like he was taking lessons on a flute!" rasped Lafourche. Then, to Cragin, "Get up, you rat — if your hands weren't tied, I'd let you have it, messing around with my wife."

Cragin saw that Lafourche's nerves were at the cracking point. He also noted that Adele's overnight case had disgorged a bale of government bonds that would choke a sewer; but most important was that Lafourche was not familiar with a single-action revolver. It wasn't cocked.

Cragin lunged as Lafourche tugged at the trigger, catching him amidships and knocking him smack against his wife's richest curves. She tumbled nose first into the suitcase over which she was bending. The revolver skated under the bed.

"Never mind that gun!" barked a voice from the doorway.

Cragin, however, was moving too fast to stop; but when he did emerge, retrieved Colt in hand, he saw that while the sheriff was recovering, it was not he who had spoken.

The fuzzy-headed madman was in the doorway, rifle in hand.

"All right, Mr. G-man," he said to Cragin, "I surrender. Those bonds on the floor clear me."

"G-man?" Cragin blinked. Then, to the sheriff: "Here's your Colt. Grab Lafourche. He killed Warren Dale. Look at the sulphur crystals on his shoes."

"If you mean the fellow aiming this rifle at a window at this hotel," interposed the shaggy man, "you're wrong. I sapped him with a piece of pipe. I can beat a manslaughter charge. I was trying to prevent a felony."

"Sure you can," agreed Cragin, "but where do you get that G-man stuff?"

"I'm Morton Sloane, escaped from Atlanta. Harris was the crooked auditor who juggled the books. Lafourche and Dale cleaned up. I was the boob, taking the rap. For those stolen bonds. Those on the floor."

And then Glendora stepped into the room. She had slipped her moorings. She stared at the shaggy man and in wide-eyed dismay demanded, "Dad — what on earth —"

*"Dad?"* echoed Cragin, glance shifting from Glendora's dusky beauty to the not-so-madman's fair skin.

"This is just a paint job," laughed Glendora. "I followed Harris to recover these bonds, the theft of which is what really sent father to Atlanta. I had the combination of the safe, but he changed it.

"And this G-man business," she continued, "was what Harris told Dale and Lafourche. To scare them out of giving him the works for hogging all the loot. That fancy rifle is Dale's. I saw it in his baggage. Since he didn't expect a G-man, he must have brought it to kill Harris.

"I doped you," she concluded, "so I could go out into the woods and warn dad against making any attempts to capture the plunder."

"You can't prove I killed Harris!" flared Lafourche. "Sloane came out here for revenge. He did it."

"I guess Sloane put those bonds into your wife's suitcase!" snapped Cragin. "You went to the spring to check up on Dale's absence, found him dead, then found me knocked cold, and saw your chance to go for the sheriff and frame me."

"That'll make an indictment two miles long," rumbled the sheriff. "Sloane, I'm holding you for justifiable homicide, an' if you don't get a bounty for exterminatin' varmints, I'll eat the sights off my gun. Let's go."

He loaded his prisoners into Lafourche's big car. Cragin took the wheel, and Glendora joined him.

"Probably you're fed up on blondes," she whispered, smiling in sweet malice, "so I'd better wash off my false complexion along with my phony name —"

"Maybe you'd better," agreed Cragin, "Though we might go back and start where we left off . . . and sort of let the color wear off. . . ."

# NIGHT IN MANILA

THE broad-shouldered American who lolled in his chair and stared somberly at the colorful whirl of dancers in the ballroom of Chow Kit's cabaret was still sober, though he had spent all evening challenging native liquor to do its worst. His white duck suit was still neat, and he was clean-shaven, but his craggy, bronzed face was drawn and deeply lined, and his blue eyes were haggard.

Lieutenant Dan Slade, posing as a dishonorably discharged soldier, had come to Manila to find out how Datu Ali, the Moro rebel down in Jolo, was getting United States government ammunition.

Chow Kit was the answer: but try and prove it. His fleet of inter-island trading boats had a dozen times been searched for contraband, but in vain. The only remaining move was to get the low down on that crafty Chinaman by a flank attack directed through the chain of dance halls and bawdy houses that made him wealthier every day.

Slade spat disgustedly as he saw Chow Kit emerge from the private office of the cabaret. Suave, immaculate in a shantung suit, his slanted eyes inscrutable as the moonstones that gleamed in the only ring that adorned his long-nailed, thin hands. The Chinaman was sizing up the colorful whirl of *bailarinas* whisked about the pavilion by dancing soldiers, sailors, and white civilians.

Exotic girls of every shade from walnut to old ivory. Malay, Japanese, Chinese; Eurasians, and *mestizas* whose touch of Spanish blood gave them an inflaming glamour that no white woman can have. Those girls had the inside rumors of Manila — but try to get at the truth behind their dance hall smiles!

Chow Kit, seeing that business was good, turned back to his office, leaving Slade to continue pondering on a bedroom and bottle approach to of government ammunition.

Presently the office door again opened. The gift who emerged could have no more than a drop of Malay blood. The slant of her dark eyes was scarcely perceptible, and the faint flare of her delicate nostrils was just enough to be exotic. And as she picked her way to a table near Slade's, the American sensed that he was getting a break. She had the run of Chow Kit's office, and she might warm up to a white man, and tell him things.

Bell shaped sleeves, and a scarf of incredibly fine *piña* cloth about her shapely shoulders, and the tall, glistening combs that adorned her high piled, blue black hair gave an oddly foreign touch to the apricot satin of an evening gown, cut low in front, and lower in back. And the *piña* scarf cast a tantalizing mist about the warm, firm curves that smiled at Slade as she reached across her table for a match.

His glance shifted from the pert breasts that rounded out the shimmering bodice, lingered along the inviting curve of her waist and the blossoming richness of her sleek hips.

"Let's dance, *chiquita*," he proposed as he caught her hand.

Agata Moreno's clinging, supple curves aroused more than Slade's hope of information. At the end of the dance, as she headed for her table, he countered, "Nuts on that notion! Let's go home and talk —"

"About how nice a shack we can keep on thirty *pesos* a month?" mocked Agata in English almost devoid of accent. "Don't be stupid, Dan."

"Thirty *pesos*, hell! Wait till I fell you who I am, and then we'll get your suitcase and spend a week or two in Baguio."

Slade, short circuiting all arguments, headed Agata toward one of the square, bamboo houses on the main street of the village just off Paranaque Road, They're primitive things, these *nipa* shacks, with floors of split bamboo. The cracks between the slats made plumbing unnecessary, and they're high enough up on stilts to give a free range to the scavenging pigs and chickens. Agata's shack, however, was ritzy. She had wicker furniture, and an American style bed instead of a grass mat.

Agata's eyes narrowed speculatively as she regarded him for a moment. Then she said, "Let's not talk about Baguio. Why don't you go back to the States?"

His story had spread. She was sorry for him.

"To hell with the States! Not after the deal I got. Just pure luck I didn't get three years and a kick, instead of a straight bobtail. So I'm staying. From now on."

In the Islands, jobs for white men are as scarce as *bailarinas* who can say no. A *nipa* shack and a Tagalog girl to hustle the groceries is the only career left to a white drifter. Slade was paving the way for someone to hint that a rebellious Moro *datu* down in Jolo could use desperate American renegades as well as stolen ammunition.

Agata's dark eyes were troubled. She was white enough to sympathize with the American outcast in a way no native woman could. Which made her valuable.

"Don't be stupid," she whispered as she seated herself on the arm of his chair. "Go back. While you can."

"Go back with me?" proposed Slade.

Her brows rose, but her smile contradicted the shake of her head.

"Sure you'll go," Slade urged. "As soon as I can raise enough money for the two of us to travel."

And that was an offer that few *mestizas* can decline, coming from a white man, even if he is a renegade.

Agata's smile was becoming more personal, but she hesitated.

"We'll get married," he added. That was the ultimate bait. And the only way a bobtailed soldier could raise transportation across the Pacific would be in some illicit enterprise. She'd talk to Chow Kit, now. "How about it?"

And before Agata could answer, Slade's arms closed about her. Despite her parrying gesture, he found her unwilling lips. Unwilling — but only for a moment. She broke away, but only to be drawn closer, to have her mouth seared anew by that savage kiss.

Agata was a fragrant armful, and as Slade's embrace tightened about her, he forgot that he was searching for information. Her slender hands clawed at his face, but he evaded their attack, kissing her throat and shapely shoulders; and as he shifted back again to her crimson lips, she no longer struggled, but clung to him. Each supple, rounded curve was quivering, and as one hand probed the sleek folds of the apricot satin skirt that was working its way over her knees, Agata shuddered, and sighed luxuriously.

Slade broke away long enough to catch a fresh breath, but her questing lips followed his.

"Don't! Not tonight," she begged; but her dark eyes were misty with promise. "*And not here.* Stay away from here, Dan! It's dangerous."

Still holding Agata in his arms, Slade emerged from the wicker chair and headed for the further room, where a whirring electric fan was spraying a cool breeze across an acre of white counterpane.

"What are you afraid of?" Slade retorted, striding towards the threshold.

"Chow Kit," she tremulously whispered. "He's been making a play for me ever since I came here. I just about convinced him that I do nothing but dance — but if he suspects — oh, don't you see, I won't be able to stall him off any longer — I'll have to leave here — he'll kill me — and you —"

That rang true; which made Agata all the more worth a play. But as Slade barged across the threshold with his clinging, quivering armful, the munitions situation in Jolo became quite unimportant.

"Don't . . . you'll get my dress all rumpled up . . ."

Well, that might arouse Chow Kit's suspicions. Slade's embrace relaxed.

And then Agata let out a yeep that shook the *nipa* thatch. The sudden flurry of arms and legs caught Slade off balance and the treacherous footing of bamboo slats did the rest. He clutched at empty air and crashed to the floor. As he gained his knees, he saw the cause of Agata's sudden alarm: not Chow Kit but a bronzed American with shoulders as broad as a box car and a face like Gibraltar on a stormy night.

One glimpse of Agata's dismayed recognition and the newcomer's wrathful amazement told Slade that Granite Face was very much at home in that shack. Nor was there any time to spring the one about waiting for a street car; not after the ankle-to-hip display of ivory tinted flesh that had greeted him as he reached the threshold.

Granite Face crossed the room like a *carabao* charging through a cane brake. Slade escaped utter demolition by flinging himself clear of a devastating fist that would have lifted him through the roof.

*Sock!* — Slade's return bombardment. The explosion caught Granite Face like a pile driver, but it was like spraying a roman candle against the side of a battleship. They closed in as Agata, getting her legs, the counterpane, her streaming hair and other odds and ends untangled, gained the floor on the far side of her bed.

It looked as though she was screaming, but Slade couldn't hear. A sizzling hook had turned his head into something that sounded like a dozen cathedral bells shaken up in a basket; and the stranger's wrathful words were like thunder out beyond Corregidor, only louder and dirtier. Slade, lighter, was quicker on his feet; but his efforts were as useful as assault and battery against a locomotive.

The *nipa* shack now resembled the center of a China Sea typhoon, a roaring confusion with sound effects by Agata and the splintering furniture. They clashed in a savage clinch that ended in a power dive that carried them both under the table. They emerged, whirling. Then Slade broke clear, bounded back, side stepped, and gained enough space to time the *bailarina*'s jealous lover.

*Smack!* Granite Face took it, but it knocked him boarey-eyed and loop-legged. Slade followed through, fists hammering. Another concussion. For an instant the iron man looked silly. Slade's guard lowered. And that was a mistake. The refreshing pause was just long enough to let the enemy decide that swapping punches was an error. He recovered and flashed from a crouch. It was like feeding time at the zoo, with Slade at the receiving end.

The world became a blurr of bamboo slats, overturned furniture, *nipa* thatched ceiling, and Agata's bare legs viewed from the oddest angles . . . and then the room began blackening; but Slade's muscles still worked, though with a blind, instinctive stubbornness. He relaxed, absorbed a crushing punch, then got his hold. It was good. Granite Face catapulted half way across the room. Slade followed through – but so did Agata.

The three met in one spot Something sizzled past Slade's ear as he plunged forward to finish Granite Face. It smashed down on his shoulder, numbing him to his ankles. Agata, swinging the standard of a floor lamp, had missed her aim – and her boyfriend got the works.

The *bailarina* knelt for a moment beside her victim in error, then dashed into the other room to get water. Slade retrieved a cigarette case and wallet, automatically thrust them into his pocket.

Then he saw the fun was just beginning.

Half a dozen brown men came swarming up the veranda stairs and into the living room. Tagalog bouncers, drawn from the dance hall by the riot. At their heels was Chow Kit, narrowed eyes flashing from Slade's battered face and torn tropicals to Agata's streaming hair and rumpled gown. He chuckled silkily as she started, yeeped, and dropped the tumbler she was filling. The shock troops charged, clubs and bolos flailing.

Slade snatched a chair and slashed out at the advance guard, but the short, broad blades and pounding staves were too much for one man so near the end of his strength. He was forced back, raked and battered. They were now flanking him right and left. From the corner of his eye, he caught a glimpse of Agata's hand – but he had no time to wonder what her contribution would be this time.

It looked like payday on Paranaque Road –

And then the lights flickered out. Slade, milling the splintered remains of the chair, ploughed through the enemy's line. A long bound carried him to the veranda; and another flung him clear of the pack. He landed in a heap at the foot of the compound palisade, stumbled over a stray pig, and headed east. Native legs were not long enough to break his lead. As he reached the highway that led toward the Walled City, a grin crinkled his battered face.

For some reason, Agata had given him a break.

Nearing Cuartel d'Espana, he hailed a Red Diamond. As he boarded the cab, he fumbled for his wallet. He drew two from his pocket. For a moment he was perplexed; then he understood.

The extra item was Granite Face's roll.

Slade went through the contents. The wallet belonged to Captain Rupert Dwyer, Post Quartermaster at Fort McKinley. He had charge of enough ammunition to equip a *datu*'s army. Lord knows how many thousand rounds were stored at McKinley for the coming target season.

It *proved* nothing, but it was a strong hint.

And one card among the others that filled a compartment of that wallet upholstered with five hundred *peso* notes seconded the growing conviction that Captain Dwyer was not entirely what a well-regulated officer should be. *"Nomura-ro"* was engraved across the center of the card. Beneath it was a street address. At one end was a column of Japanese, and in a corner were the words, *"Shigashi San – O Shoku Kabu."*

Nomura-ro was the name of the last word in aristocratic brothels; and Shigashi San was the lady who had given the captain that card. The words that followed her name indicated that she was the reigning beauty of the house.

Such luxury might not be beyond the means of a captain, but Slade's suspicions became more pointed as he recollected that the Nomura-ro belonged to Chow Kit; that it catered to the wealthiest sports of Manila; *and that a patron who had established himself followed the oriental custom of running a charge account.*

What an officer does with his spare time is his own business; but once his taste for Asiatic diversions became noised about in the somewhat straitlaced military circles, it would be somewhat too bad. Evidence of indebtedness to Chow Kit would be more than enough to finish his career.

Chow Kit could thus demand government munitions as the price of discretion.

All this flashed through Slade's mind as he stepped into his room and set to work obliterating the marks of battle.

An hour later he was presentable. And Shigashi San's card, being unmarked by any handwriting, would get him an audience with the lady without arousing suspicion as to his right to be received. She wouldn't scratch or scream, and she'd know plenty about Captain Dwyer.

A hired car took him toward the lights of Sampoloc.

Nomura-ro was a rambling, two-story bungalow a block from the blazing lights of the quarter where the proletariat played with ladies whose greetings depended on their race. Crude places for crude people; whereas an evening in Nomura-ro was like being presented at the Court of Saint James, except a lot more entertaining.

Slade presented his card to the gray-haired, leather-faced *obasan* who managed the palace.

*"Irrasshai,"* she greeted, "You are very welcome."

The *obasan* consulted a register, nodded, pressed a bell button; and oriental courtesy somewhat lightened the ensuing shock as Slade's expense account for the evening was jacked up to astronomical figures.

No mere captain playing the Nomura-ro could be on the level!

A tiny, black-eyed *kamuro* — one of the several maids who attend a high class Japanese *oiran* to serve a seven year apprenticeship in the intricate art of becoming a courtesan — conducted Slade down a hallway and into a reception room.

Shigashi San, her slender body ablaze with brocaded silks gathered about her waist with an eighteen inch sash that one flip of her fingers and Lord knows how many silver *pesos* would unwind, sat in the sacred seclusion of her *zashiki* to receive her guest. Her glistening black hair, towering pagoda-high, was rayed with long fade pins and garnished with jewel-frosted tortoise shell combs.

Her gesture and bow and voice were the artistry of an ancient tradition; yet her smile was alluring, and her dark, oblique eyes animated the ivory and carmine painted mask of her face.

Shigashi San, famed from Singapore to Tokyo — and Slade saw how genius escaped the bonds of formal ritual and made that feminine toy a vibrant fascination, an infinite promise lurking behind screens of studied artificiality.

One of the *kamuros* knelt at Slade's feet to remove his shoes. Another prepared to serve tea. A third set a low table with trays and platters of Japanese hors d'oeuvres; the "august repast" itemized in the two yard long bill.

Three geishas entered the reception room to twang their three stringed samisens, dance and entertain Slade with Japanese ballads. And he had to like it. He tossed the chief *geisha* a fifty-*peso* note. She scooped up the extravagant tip, clicked her fan shut, and utterly ignoring Slade, turned to Shigashi San to say, *"Oiran maido arigato!"* — "Thank you, Madam, for your constant favors!"

Yoshiwara courtesy: entertainers don't thank the patron of the house for his liberality; they thank the courtesan whose fascinations have dazzled him. And Slade, though he did not know it, was to see an ironic play on those words before the evening was over!

Twice at long intervals during the *saki* sipping, Shigashi San retired to one of the further rooms of her suite, each time returning in lighter, more informal robes. And at last when the three bright eyed *kamuros* finally left their mistress, Slade, head buzzing from rice wine, followed her into an inner room whose ceiling was painted with an enormous phoenix.

A single subdued light cast the shadow of a six-fold screen across a foot-deep pile of silken quilts. At the head of which was a curious little cylinder of wood supported on carved legs: Shigashi San's pillow, which supporting the nape of her neck, preserved her mountainous coiffure.

Slade, thinking of Agata's passion-pulsing breasts and disheveled hair, suppressed an urge to dive for the door; but only for an instant: Shigashi San's artificiality was contradicted by the invitation of her eyes, the tantalizing, slow deftness of fingers plucking the bow of the *obi* that gathered the crepe gown about her waist.

Skill there, and the artistry of a thousand year old tradition. Figured silk caressed and shadowed and hinted unexplored delights in old ivory. One brusque hand could part the veil — but Slade, kneeling beside that gracious creature half sunk in the yielding quilts, hypnotized by studied ritual, could not make that impatient gesture.

His heart began rising into his throat, eagerness flamed in his blood; and as his eyes became accustomed to the scented dimness of the alcove, the gauzy gown seemed almost to melt before his hungry gaze.

Bought. Paid for. But through sheer artistry become infinitely more alluring than any woman won in a flare of passion. His brain was a surge of fire before that silken cincture finally yielded, and Shigashi San's mellow ivory body smiled from ambush . . .

Miraculously, it seemed, the lights dimmed to a fantastic twilight as her arms closed about him. Artistry that needed no mockery of ardor to make it perfect. And for a long time Slade was not worried about Datu Ali and the Christian dogs he was slaying with government ammunition, down in far off Jolo . . .

Shigashi San finally rang for *saki*. Time now for matching wits with that exotic toy imported from Japan; but a buzzer whirred, and one of the little *kamuros* entered.

A murmur of Japanese that Slade could not understand; and then Shigashi San apologized, in sweet voiced, stilted English, "August friend, the unexpectedness of your visit forbids me the pleasure of your company for the remainder of the night."

Heavy feet invaded the outer *zashiki*. Some guest with a previous engagement was entitled to her time. Slade would be ushered out a side door so that new arrival and departing playmate would not meet. He had to check the rush act, or the evening was wasted.

But Slade's knowledge of Yoshiwara traditions saved the night. He had but to follow the ancient precedent of many an infatuated Japanese *samurai*.

"I am going to my lonely plantation in Mindanao in the morning. Go with me. I will buy your contract and debts to the house."

As he spoke, he flashed a roll that fortunately was fronted with a five hundred-*peso* note. He replaced it before she could see that it was far from enough to withdraw a *de luxe* courtesan from her river of debt.

And if Slade met her terms, she would be well established for life. For a long moment she regarded him. Slade returned her gaze, and her loveliness put a convincing glow in his eyes.

Finally she beckoned to the little *kamuro*; but before she could tell her to cancel the newcomer's engagement, Slade interposed.

"Is there no *naki* leaf in your mirror?" The subtle question was to remind her that Hakone Gongen, the Japanese god of pledges between men and women, forbade her breaking her promise to the waiting guest. More than that, it told her that he knew the old traditions.

She smiled and murmured a few words to the *kamuro*, who conducted Slade to a further room of the suite. He could now wait for Shigashi San's visitor to leave. He could postpone the trip to Mindanao; and with the promised liberation ever dangled before her eyes, she would try to spur him to haste by hinting at another who wanted to buy her contract.

She might mention Captain Dwyer . . .

Slade listened to the murmur of voices. He opened his penknife and set to work on the partition that separated him from Shigashi San's bedroom. . . .

The *oiran*'s guest wore quartermaster collar ornaments; but he was not Captain Dwyer. Sergeant's chevrons were on his sleeves.

Yet that twilight shrouded meeting was more than it seemed. One of the sergeant's arms slipped clear of Shigashi San's embrace. He was reaching toward a low cabinet. Toward a small brazen Buddha that adorned its top.

The move was stealthy, not swift. The sergeant was placing a second image on the cabinet. Then he palmed its identical duplicate, the one that had originally been there.

The exchange could mean but one thing: the sergeant had either received or delivered a message or token of identification. All in one move which Shigashi San could scarcely have perceived.

Having seen as much as he had, Slade could not afford the risk of missing anything that took place in that room. This was more than the meeting of a soldier and an *oiran*; it must be the subtle hand of Chow Kit. But Slade gritted his teeth as he watched. . . .

Clear thinking became difficult . . . it all hinged on whether the Sergeant had delivered or received a message. If the former, wait and see who came to Shigashi San's room to get it; if the latter, follow the quartermaster man. But which?

An insurrection in Jolo depended on the right guess.

Finally the sergeant prepared to leave. Such haste confirmed Slade's growing certainty. Shigashi San accompanied him to the *zashiki*. That gave Slade his chance. He tiptoed into her bedroom, snatched the brazen Buddha, and turned to the exit. Ducking into an alley, he paused to scrutinize the tiny image by the glow of a distant streetlight.

A fine line indicated that it could be removed from its pedestal; but there was no time to seek the combination. He pocketed the effigy, rounded the corner, lurking in the shadows, where he could command a view of all approaches to the Nomura-ro.

Presently the sergeant emerged. Neither car nor *caromata* awaited him. He had trusted no one with his destination.

Slade followed. Ahead of him was a *tienda* from whose window a light gleamed. He reached for a handful of silver, stepped into the store and in a moment emerged with a pair of coarse socks and a cake of soap. Then, stretching long, legs, he narrowed the gap between him and his quarry.

Another block. The sergeant entered a saloon. Slade caught a glimpse of him as he stepped to a telephone booth. Aside from a bartender, and a few Chinese and Filippino loafers the place was deserted. Slade ordered a beer and edged toward the booth.

"Two-one six-nine six."

He recognized the number: Red Diamond Cab. Slade drained his beer, and stepped to the street. He slipped one sock into the other, then thrust the cake of soap into the foot of the inner one. Silent, effective, and harmless.

A moment later, the sergeant ploughed through the swinging doors. His tropic tanned face was tense, and his eyes instinctively flashed right and left as he cleared the threshold. Slade swooped from cover; but some sixth sense warned his victim. He jerked his head. The soap cake bludgeon missed by a hair, instead of laying him out for a long count; and for the second time that evening, Slade had his hands full.

Before he could drop his now useless weapon, the Manila night blazed into a carnival glow. Groggy and with legs limp as macaroni, Slade tried to block the sergeant's rush, but it was like boxing with a kangaroo. One more charge —

But before it connected, the sergeant, over reaching himself, tripped and sprawled headlong into the gutter. That gave Slade an instant's respite. When the noncom regained his feet, the mill began in earnest. It was touch and go for a moment, reckless, wrathful slugging; and then Slade blasted home with one that popped like a boiler explosion.

The sergeant was frozen before he hit the ground. Slade settled back on his heels and drew a long breath; but that was cut short in mid gasp. A brazen gleam from the darkness caught his eye. He made a dive for his pocket as he recognized the little Buddha lying in the dust. His own was still in place; it was the sergeant's that had rolled from cover.

Slade stooped to pick it up. The hidden springs of the trick pedestal had responded to the impact against the corner of the saloon! The Buddha's body contained a slip of paper. He struck a match.

"Sin Ban Fong is waiting," he read, which was damn little to learn for his trouble!

He stuffed the paper and the halves of the image into his pocket, regarded the prostrate sergeant, then used his victim's shirt and belt to improvise gag and bonds. That done, Slade stepped into the saloon, slid ten *pesos* across the bar, and struck a, bargain with the proprietor.

"Keep him on ice until morning," Slade concluded. "If he's here when I come back, it's five more for you; if he's gone, you'll get some of what he got. And when the taxi gets here, tell him it's the wrong number. *Sabe, hombre?*"

He did; and Slade dashed back toward the Nomura-ro.

The next play was to put the *empty* Buddha on Shigashi San's cabinet, and wait for someone to call for the one the sergeant had left.

*"Sin Ban Fong,"* he muttered as he slipped in through the back door. Then, with a bleak grin, "I hope the _____ enjoys waiting!"

Shigashi San, hearing him enter the further room of her suite, appeared from her bedroom. Her smile was cryptic.

He wondered if she suspected. She might not even know that the Buddha swapping had taken place in her room. The smile became alluring . . . it began to seem not such a bad idea after all to have the exalted blossom shed a few more petals.

All of which he worked into the discussion of his estates in Mindanao. But as Shigashi San luxuriously settled back into her heap of silken quilts, and reached for the bow of her *obi*, Slade put the empty bronze Buddha back on the lacquered cabinet.

And then the *oiran*'s draperies parted and her arms closed about him.

But that embrace was checked by the faint whine of a sliding panel. Slade was on his feet at a bound. Shigashi San, outraged at the invasion of her privacy, shed half a dozen hairpins as she snatched for the edges of her robe.

Chow Kit was in the doorway! Sallow, evilly smiling Chow Kit behind the muzzle of an automatic that yawned like a siege gun. He also had come by the back door; and at his heels were half a dozen Chinese and Gugus; murderous riff-raff, armed and leering and spitting *betel* juice on the mats as they waited for action. And two at the further edge of the cluster between them supported a woman in apricot silk. She was bound, and a gag masked half her face, but Slade recognized Agata Moreno.

All in an instant. *"Sin Ban Fong,* my dear sir," murmured Chow Kit, "is waiting with the patience known only to a ship. A Chinese junk whose concealed engines have fooled the revenue cutters. You and *Señorita* Agata will both take a long ride down the China Sea, where the sharks are hungry — don't make any false moves, please, or Shigashi San joins the party."

"Why wait for a junk ride?" snarled Slade, fighting for time, "Do it now —"

Chow Kit chuckled and explained, "Disposing of corpses on land is awkward and betraying, whereas the sharks are discreet."

Then he added, "One of my men works for the cab company which the sergeant called. The bartender was wise enough to ignore your warning. He phoned to inquire about his prisoner. The news reached me. And in the meanwhile, Agata's collection of American sweethearts had aroused my suspicions — so, we all go for a cruise in the *Sin Ban Fong*.

"With things turning out as they did, I really do not need the message the sergeant left here for me. I liberated him. He's getting the ammunition now."

Though Chow Kit was safe behind a pistol and Slade was empty-handed, the Chinaman's eyes did not shift as he purred a phrase in Tagalog, ordering his retainers to bind the American. Steady pistol, and unwavering eyes —

But Chow Kit's watchfulness worked against him. In watching the desperate American, he overlooked Shigashi San, and the *saki* jug she had stealthily plucked from a shelf.

A flash of white. A spattering of porcelain shards. The blast of Chow Kit's widely fired pistol. Slade's flying tackle carried him clear of the *oiran*'s bed as the Chinaman's weapon clattered into a corner. Flinging Chow Kit aside, Slade scooped up the six-fold screen and hurled it athwart the head-long charge of the Chinaman's armed retainers.

Wadding a silken quilt about his left arm, he parried a sweeping bolo slash, and hammered home with a blasting fist that knocked a Gugu smashing into an alcove. He shifted as the attack swerved to envelop him, seized a lacquered washbasin and crashed it about the ears of the flank guard. He ducked a hurled bolo, flung out the folds of the silken quilt to parry another, side stepped and snatched the first weapon by the hilt.

Slade now armed; but his breath was coming in jerking gasps, and the odds were heavy. Chow Kit, once more on his feet, was urging his shaken retainers to the attack. He had recovered his pistol and hovered on the fringe of the battle, watching Slade's blade dance in and out, steel striking fire from steel. The Chinaman feared to risk another shot; but as Slade's desperate charge swept the pack a yard to the rear, the weapon rose into line.

Shigashi San's voice shrilled high above the cursing confusion. Slade caught the warning, and his brain blazed red. The heavy bolo zipped point on, a streak of steel that ended at the Chinaman's chest as the automatic spurted flame. Slade won the exchange. Hot lead seared his ribs, but the bolo split Chow Kit's chest like a chicken for the grille.

Slade was empty-handed. Another saki jug, hurled from the sidelines by Shigashi San, bowled the foremost enemy end for end; and then the charge broke. They saw Chow Kit crumpled up on the matting, a red, twitching huddle. They scrambled madly for the door. No chief, no fight. Slade's reckless wrath had succeeded where caution would have been overwhelmed.

He bounded from his corner. As he snatched Chow Kit's weapon, he heard a pounding of feet, and a polyglot chatter that was submerged by a voice like a typhoon. An unpleasantly familiar voice — Captain Rupert Dwyer!

Slade's salvaged pistol jerked into line as the granite faced renegade burst into the room.

"Drop it, you rat!" Slade commanded.

Dwyer's hands rose. He recognized death when it stared him in the eye. But Slade's weapon dropped the next instant: behind Dwyer was a squad of military police, and the Provost Marshal.

"What the hell?" boomed Dwyer, eyeing the gory wreckage.

Then a cross-fire of questions, and Slade identified himself.

"And cut that girl loose — over there in the corner. That *mestiza*, with the gag in her mouth —"

Dwyer followed Slade's gesture.

"*Mestiza*, my eye! That's my sister!"

And Agata, when she was liberated, explained, "Dad was a colonel. And years ago, we were in the Islands, so it was easy —"

"But why that *bailarina* gag at Chow Kit's?" demanded Slade.

"When the old colonel died in the States, she came over to see me. And landed just in time to find me in a rotten jam," interposed Captain Dwyer. "Ammunition being lost by the case. And me responsible. You know what that would mean. I had to clear it up. We suspected Chow Kit. And Agata, damned little idiot, insisted on getting a job as a *bailarina* to do a bit of spying —"

"*Agata?*" echoed Slade. "But what's her real name?"

"Named after my stepmother: Agata Moreno Dwyer."

That simplified it.

"Anyway," resumed Dwyer, "I went out to Chow Kit's place to check up on Agata's hazardous game, and when I saw you two —"

"Rupert, you idiot!" interposed Agata, "you didn't see a thing! As if I couldn't take care of myself!"

"Listen, Dwyer," intervened Slade, "honest to God, I didn't mean a thing — and anyway, it was in the line of duty, getting evidence."

Dwyer snorted, and Agata's Spanish eyes glowed in fond reminiscence. Slade changed the subject to ammunition.

"Chow Kit was so busy with you, there in Agata's shack," resumed Dwyer, "that he overlooked me. And when I recovered from that crack on the bean, she was gone, and I checked up.

"That card of admission you took from my wallet was one the sergeant had dropped. That gave me a hunch as to his connections. I'd suspected him for some time anyway. And in trailing Agata, we tangled up with him, all beaten up, and hell bent for the warehouse.

"He explained plenty when I bluffed him about no honest enlisted man being able to hang out at the Nomura-ro. So don't bother trying to open the other bronze Buddha. That crook had arranged to have a tunnel dug to open into the warehouse, so he could load the whole works on a barge, in spite of the doubled sentries we'd posted about the place. That was the big raid — the earlier thefts were just petty larceny in comparison."

And then Slade remembered that Shigashi San's *saki* jug had given his chance to hang on until the M.P.'s arrived.

"Sorry about that plantation," he said, "but I'll buy up your contract."

"Death has canceled it," she answered, gesturing toward Chow Kit's body.

Slade dug out his wallet and handed the *oiran* the contents.

"Anyway, here's a ticket home."

Shigashi San had not missed the glow in Agata's dark eyes, and the glances she and Slade had exchanged. She accepted the present, then, utterly ignoring Slade, she turned to Agata to bow and say: "*Oiran maido arigato!* — Thank you, madam, for your constant favors."

Shigashi San, now a free woman, used Japanese courtesy as a harpoon; but only Slade caught the point.

"What did she say?" wondered Agata, sensing her mockery.

"She said," Slade falsified, "that you're a damn lucky girl to get a chance to carry on where we left off, in that *nipa* shack."

# MURDER SALVAGE

YVONNE yawned, and that made her white arms stretch like lovely snakes; the blue robe rounded out over small, firm curves. The stretch made her slimmer at the waist, and her legs straightened in a long, silky reach.

"Don't be tiresome," she said. "The car is mine, and I'm keeping it. I didn't tell Walt to dip into the till to buy it for me, and you can't prove that —"

"Look here!" Honest John Carmody hitched the spindle-legged chair a little closer. His face was a bit redder, and the more he saw of Yvonne's peep show, the redder his face became. "I know damn well we can't prove a thing. If you had the actual cash stuffed in your sock —"

She lifted a fold of the robe, and exposed the picot edge of a honey-colored stocking. "I haven't. It'd make too big a bulge."

That display made Honest John stutter. "I ain't browbeating you. I'm asking you, turn that bus over, it's worth a thousand bucks as it stands, secondhand. The bonding company's on Walt Crawford's tail. If he begs, borrows, maybe he can make good, and without selling his house."

"My dear man, I didn't ask him to clean the till."

Honest John growled, piled out of the chair, and stood there like an oversized cub bear in a shiny blue suit. He caught the glamor girl's shoulder, and jerked her to her feet.

"I thought you weren't browbeating me," she snapped. "If that fool's house is sold, that's *his* business."

Honest John made another quick move, and then Yvonne did yeep. He had the blue chiffon in his hand, and she stood there, peeled down to a bra and a bit of something about her hips.

"You fluff-witted dime's-worth of white meat," he boomed and shook the blue robe, "this and every other stitch in the house is what Walt Crawford bought you. You're still way ahead, even if you give him back that car. Damn it, he's got a wife."

"He never acted like it. Now, let's not wrangle," she purred and came closer. "I've been out of work for months, and what'll happen to me?"

She knew he was just another dick, a plug-ugly with half-soled shoes; but she threw her weight to make that bra stand out a little fuller, a little more alluring. She wanted him to go for her like every chump did. And she was succeeding. For a second, he did not know what to do or say. He dropped the blue robe.

She'd snuggle up and be sweet. Just sweet enough to follow up with a good laugh. Her big blue eyes, her drooping lashes told him that she was reading his face, and getting a kick out of her advertising campaign. "What'll happen to me, John?" she cooed.

"This."

He slapped her a hefty one. She landed smack on one of her best features. "I've seen some tramps that had a white streak in 'em," he growled over his shoulder and slammed the door. "You ain't one of 'em."

HONEST JOHN spent the next couple days in routine business: looking around hot spots for other chumps, hanging around race tracks for the same purpose. He was spotting tellers, cashiers, salesmen, assistant vice-presidents, all the white collar lads his bonding company covered. If they gutted the till, his company had to cough up and then try to recover as much loot as possible.

Throwing a man in the jug didn't bring the dough back. The company would rather have the chump on the hoof, paying off, which he couldn't do in jail. Sometimes, you can stop a fellow before he's too far gone and make him snap out of it.

Honest John passed Yvonne's apartment several times, but he did not go in. Appealing to her sense of decency wouldn't work, she had none. And she was too smart to be scared. Or was she?

Then, driving up the Ocean Shore road from Half Moon Bay, Honest John met Yvonne, though at first, he didn't know who the woman was. It's dark and lonesome between roadhouses; artichoke patches and little farm-houses dot the heavy black earth.

When he tramped on the brake, not far from where the new highway branches from the snaky old Montara Mountain roller-coaster, he said, "Aw, hell, I'm seeing things, I still got that floor show on the brain. Or maybe it's fog."

But it was a woman his headlights had picked out. She was lying on her face, and her blond hair gleamed. Her hands were all muddy from clawing the black soft earth. But a lot of her was white and round and hard to miss; you had to slow down for that sharp turn.

When he stumbled through the knee-high reeds in the ditch she had crawled out of, he saw that she'd been peeled right down. Not even stockings. He squatted and got a look at the face. It was Yvonne Latour.

As nearly as he could tell, two slugs had drilled her back, and a third, her head, behind one ear. Small slugs that did not tear her up. Then he looked into the ditch and saw a new, flimsy gray blanket; it had blood on it. His headlights didn't reach down, but a match made it all clear.

He was surprised that he could be sorry for Yvonne. Dumped into the ditch as dead, some lingering life had made her crawl toward the road. He made a move to get the blanket and thought better of that. He took off his coat, and laid it over the huddled corpse. She was cold, cold as the ocean mist, but he could not let her lie there utterly uncovered. Then he stamped away, snorting, "Dizzy — had it coming. Hah. Hope that fool of a Crawford didn't do this. Wouldn't blame him, though. She had it coming."

As he hightailed back to the nearest roadhouse to phone the sheriff's office, he began to understand a few details. Stripping Yvonne had been to prevent identification; hauling the corpse to San Mateo County would also help, though even in San Francisco, Yvonne was just another of a swarm of tramps playing the field when not taking turns at floor shows or hustling drinks. Finally, lying in the ditch in that lonely stretch, her weight would have carried her slowly into the mud.

All he reported was the actual discovery. He wanted to keep the inside track by letting the killer believe that there was no identification; also, he wanted to keep immediate suspicion from Walt Crawford. If the chump was guilty, turn him in. If he wasn't, let him have what little chance there was at getting a fresh start. He was really a nice guy.

TWO hours later, Honest John was in San Francisco, where an unidentified corpse in San Mateo County would not get more than half an inch in the classified advertising. The drive took forty minutes; the rest of the time had been devoted to making his statement and saying to the sheriff, "Hell, even if she'd been dressed, I wouldn't know her."

He had a thin ribbon of spring steel and a few assorted keys which were routine in his job; also, his stumpy fingers had a surprisingly slick touch. It did not take him long to get into Yvonne's apartment.

The feminine fragrance of the bedroom did not thrill his nostrils; he shivered a little, thinking of that dark ditch. Yvonne's silver fox coat was not in the house. There was nothing else he could check. There were half a dozen handbags, but none had a driver's license or keys. Honest John cursed bitterly and said half aloud, "She's deader'n hell, probably got no folks except some she don't keep track of. The public administrator'll take that sweet little convertible; the chump hasn't a chance at it now."

Then he began frisking every cabinet and drawer in the place; he was looking for the certificate of registration. Morally, the chump had a right to the car. If Crawford faked Yvonne's signature and peddled the bus he could make just that much more restitution. She was dead — who'd spill the beans?

But Honest John found no trace of any certificate. He found no evidence of a safe deposit box. Yvonne lived from chump to chump and didn't salt anything down. Not even a checking account.

In the living room he found two glasses of Scotch, one with a lipstick smear, and empty; the other, half emptied and a clean edge. Both glasses had raffia jackets. Some of the cigarette butts wore smears matching Yvonne's lip rouge. The others had been flicked out of a holder; a different brand. Some man had dropped in. He hoped it wasn't Crawford.

Then he saw the clipping from the advertising column: "'41 Packard 120 convertible, widow leaving town must sacrifice. Phone 2-2426."

That was Yvonne's number. It looked as if some fellow had come in to dicker with the "widow."

She wouldn't take it to a used car lot. She'd bet on being able to high pressure a better price through a private sale. He eyed the blue mules lying at the foot of the lounging chair, the depressions in the cushions, the robe carelessly flung over the arm.

"First she wore that glamor robe to get the guy dizzy, and then —" He shook his head. "Maybe he did offer her more'n it was worth . . . she always got more'n she was worth . . ."

But when, after further search, he found a threatening letter, he could not be too sure that the private customer had put two slugs into her back, and a third behind her ear. Not after that letter.

It was one for a postal inspector. But Yvonne hadn't crumpled the letter. She'd kept it for two weeks. It was worn from reading and handling. He pictured her there, enjoying the lines; she wanted men to go for her, and she loved to have women hate her.

Walt Crawford's wife had signed the poisonous page.

A woman's sized gun had finished Yvonne.

Honest John pocketed the letter. Maybe Linda Crawford was a sourpuss and pretty nearly deserved having Yvonne cutting in. But she didn't deserve having her house sold over her at a whacking loss, when another thousand in cash would have fattened the kitty. Selling the house even at a forced sale would leave her with a few berries after the payoff, but it was the principle of the thing. So he kept the letter.

Once on the street, he headed for the garage where Yvonne stabled the sleek red bus; the chump had told him where that was, in the ground floor of the building, which sat on a steep side hill. He barged in, found a young fellow in white coveralls polishing a big Cad. He had "Leo" worked on his coat in red letters.

"Hi, Leo." The young man looked up, and Honest John went on, "Miss Latour's car in?" He grimaced ruefully. "She's not answering."

Leo's swarthy face crinkled in a knowing grin. "She often don't. But this time, she's really out."

Honest John slipped him a silver dollar. "Who with, pal? Tell me."

"Sorry, I can't. She phoned, I drove it to the front and took the keys to her door."

"Didn't get a look in?"

Leo grinned. "A look, yeah. Man, man. Even if the door wasn't open more than this much —" He held his hands a few inches apart. "It was a good look, but I couldn't see past her."

"Past her what? Hell, keep the buck anyway."

HONEST JOHN stepped into a drug store and dialed Crawford. "This is Carmody, of the surety company, is Mr. Crawford in?"

A sweet, weary voice answered, "No, he's been out all day. Can't you quit hounding him? He won't run out."

"Now, Mrs. Crawford, I ain't hounding him, honest, I'm all for helping him, I been at it the past couple days. Can I come out and talk to you? I been working on that Latour woman."

"Oh. . . ." Linda Crawford's voice took on a peculiar lilt that Honest John could not quite make. "Yes, do. If there's anything I could suggest — I know you're just doing your duty."

Honest John kicked the starter a moment later and grinned. She wanted to get all the dirt on Yvonne, find out what the wench had. She wanted him to say Yvonne was a two-bit floozie. For pride's sake.

So he drove out to a section where white houses stood on terraces overlooking China Beach; not ritzy, but a damn sight better than he had ever afforded. Life was funny. With a little sense and honesty, Crawford would still be dug in solid in this swell little place. But Carmody, refusing to play ball with crooks, had been edged out of the police force; the fat boys winked, called him Honest John, and settled him.

So here he was, trying to give Crawford a chance. The man hadn't meant to be a crook. Probably Yvonne hadn't, either. Just two chumps. All this as he prodded the door bell.

He was prepared for something faded, perhaps washed-out pretty. But not this woman. She'd be swell if she took off that gingham house dress and put on wine-colored velvet to hug that creamy bosom and those round hips. She was no doll; there was too much character in that mouth, though not enough to spoil the kissing. But most of Linda Crawford was in her eyes.

This was while she was saying, "Come in, Mr. Carmody."

"Honest John," he corrected and got dizzy from trying to guess what was going on behind the dark eyes that sized up his pie-shaped mug. "Honest John, madam."

He followed her into a living room with ten-year-old furniture; good but old fashioned upholstery. When she faced him again, those eyes thrilled him and they puzzled him. But he could understand why they gave her something that Yvonne didn't have, couldn't ever have had; why her nicely rounded figure and her legs looked better every second; why she didn't need a fluffy robe to advertise nearly everything she had.

He fumbled for the letter. "You wrote this to that tramp. Sure you ought to cut out her heart and stuff it . . . ah, down her throat. Sure she's a . . . ah . . . ought to wear a brass collar and a license plate. But you hadn't oughta written that, Mrs. Crawford. Once she gets tired of feeling happy over it, she might put the bee on you for sending threats through the U. S. Mail."

As far as he could see, Linda's face hadn't changed a bit when he spoke of Yvonne as of a living person. Maybe Linda hadn't killed any one, *yet*, and was just full of murder inside.

She patted the chesterfield and moved over, saying, "Sit here and tell me why you've really come. I know that letter was foolish. I've never seen her. Tell me."

THERE was no sense-tickling bouquet about this dame, but she was exciting. He wanted to get ahold of her, and he had a funny hunch that she wouldn't mind; but that idea was crazy. She was a one-man woman, if ever there was one.

"Uh . . . you want me to tell you about Yvonne? You already know, don't you?"

She laughed softly. "Only what Walt told me, when he broke down, all stuttering and red and calling himself a fool, and telling me he really didn't care for her, it was all in fun."

"She's a hot number, built for modeling imported nightgowns, frilly and helpless-acting, and she'd act up for a cigar Indian if nothing else was around. People fall for it; I used to myself. Walt got a run for our money."

"Your company's, and —" She waved that slim olive colored hand. "And mine, too. I'll bet I have no clothes like she has."

"I ain't seen all your clothes. Now look here. Yvonne's sold that car. She stampeded, figuring maybe we could grab it. You game to help me try for the money? It'll be strictly unlegitimate. I wouldn't do it on my own account, that's why they call me Honest John. But I'll help you. It takes a woman playing the cards, I can't do it single-handed. I tell you again, it's risky."

"Am I game?" She drew a deep breath, let it out slowly. "Tell me how and when!"

She twisted, caught his upper arm, leaned closer. She couldn't have killed Yvonne, because if she had, she could not possibly look so eager now.

HONEST JOHN had to stall. First he had to find Yvonne's car. Already he was willing to bet that some slicker had asked for a demonstration and then knocked her off. Next, the slicker'd take the certificate of ownership, which Yvonne would have signed, and peddled the bus quick. That game had been played before, and the effort to prevent immediate identification clinched it. A professional touch; Honest John needed Linda Crawford to help him trap the crook and get the money.

He did not want to tell her about Yvonne's death. Not yet. He asked, "Where's Walt?"

"He's down on the Peninsula trying to raise money." That gave Honest John a chill; maybe Walt had knocked the blonde off. He shivered, glanced over his shoulder. Then he got a real shock. Linda pulled herself closer, still holding to him, and said, "Don't worry, he won't be back for quite a while; he phoned me."

He still couldn't believe it. Not this woman, telling him that her husband wouldn't be back for quite a while. He said, "Huh?"

She smiled at his amazement, and that made her lovely.

"I've been a fool long enough. I've been broadminded with him, and now he's given away the house, my house, mine even if he did earn the money. So for once I'm going to be broadminded with myself — don't stare at me that way — I mean it — I believe you will help me against her — so —"

When she kissed him, he had to believe her. He knew that he was only an accomplice, an ally to help her save her pride as well as her house. He caught her in both arms and said, "Lady, if this is your idea —"

"It wasn't, at the start. But when you told me about her —"

Then the forgotten woman told him to turn out the lights.

WHEN Honest John left, long after midnight, Linda understood the play he proposed; except that she believed that they would put the slug on Yvonne. Just a detail wrong, for the principle remained the same: get the price of the car before the seller had shot the roll.

In the morning, he made his rounds. For all the used car lots in San Francisco, the task was not as great as it seemed. Some dealt only in jalopies. Some worked on a shoestring and couldn't dish out a thousand bucks for one number. Others specialized in quick turnover items. And he knew enough insurance men to get all the angles to round out his own knowledge. So after a day's hoofing, he found that iridescent red bus.

His feet ached, and he was sweating. He stood there looking at the long, lean hood and narrow radiator shell. "Luck," he muttered. "If they'd kept it or caravanned it, I'd been outa luck. But not many '41 convertibles on the lots, so far."

A fat little man with a cigar and a smile came up and said cheerily, "Lots of class, real zip, only two thousand miles. Three hundred bucks down, twenty-four months for the rest."

"Too new to be full of cork dust."

The salesman laughed. He touched the starter. He beamed as Honest John listened to the silken whispering under the hood.

"Ain't many of these, how'd you pick it up?"

"Widow leaving town. Sure you've heard that one before, but it's a fact this time."

Honest John grinned. "Huh. Maybe I'd rather have the widow. Say, I've seen this bus before. Blond girl —" He made cupping gestures with both hands. "But streamlined, and legs. Mmmmm — and would she look swell in Bali, with a basket on her head." He looked at the registration slip on the steering column; he frowned. "You mean this is Yvonne Latour's bus?"

"Well, what does it say, friend?"

"I don't care what it says, how come she's selling this, last time I saw her, she had a Ford."

"You don't keep in touch. It was Yvonne Latour, in person. I gave her my check, then drove her to the bank so she could cash it, and —"

"Nuts! This belonged —"

"Yeah, to a blonde, you said." The trader was now pretty sure with the knowledge of his kind, that Honest John was not buying and didn't intend to buy. He cut the ignition and said, "Sorry, old home week doesn't click, this gal was a brunette."

Honest John swung around in the seat. He dug up his credentials.

"Tell me more, pal. I couldn't kid you long, you can't kid me long. I'm a surety dick, and I got an angle on this."

"All right, wise guy. I sent the certificate through, and if the registry bureau says the signature is okay, it is okay."

"Pal, it is okay by me, anyway. It probably was when the cops made their morning inspection for hot iron."

"Sure it was, so what are you interested in?"

"All you know about the dame. Play ball, or the cops may be back before you get rid of this baby."

That softened the salesman. He described the brunette woman; not Linda Crawford. At least, in her indignant display of her scanty wardrobe the night before, Linda had shown him neither hat or coat of the kind the man mentioned.

"Who was she with?"

"She was alone. I offered to drive her from the bank to her house, but she said never mind, she was shopping."

"I want to look a bit."

"Help yourself."

HONEST JOHN did just that. He found no bloodstains on the ivory upholstery, but wedged under the rear floor mat, he did find a .32 automatic cartridge. He pocketed it. In the front locker, on the driver's side, was a traffic citation made for Yvonne Latour. The time: 8:30 A.M., ten hours after Honest John had found the blonde's corpse. That meant that some dame had handed Yvonne's license to the cop. A dead woman was taking the rap for doing fifty in a forty-five mile zone, between the airport and South San Francisco.

"Huh. That stinking speed trap. And this smooth job, she'd not notice she was hitting fifty. And the cop didn't notice the dame's hair was black; those guys never notice anything but a chance to rook someone."

He walked away whistling. He drank a couple beers, ate a bowl of chili, and bought a handful of cigars. Then he headed down Van Ness to the used car department of a big dealer and spent an hour dickering for a late model. Since he knew the boys, he laid twenty bucks on the line and got the bus on three days' driving trial. The exchange of winks meant that they knew he wasn't buying; that if he wanted a joyride and was willing to forfeit his deposit when he returned it as "unsuitable," they wished him luck.

"Is she blond, John?" the friend asked.

"Nuh-uh. Dark and hot, Van. Red leather upholstery's just the stuff for a complexion like that."

So Honest John put an ad in every paper:

> '38 Cad sedan. Widow leaving Pacific Coast, closing
> house, sacrifice.

If he didn't hook them in two-three days, he'd chisel another bus and try again. The 'Frisco papers barely mentioned the murdered blonde near the artichoke patch.

THAT EVENING, he drove out to Crawford's house. The chump was in; big, blond, good-looking and worried; he had the face of a hurt child. He still couldn't understand why the world had kicked him. Honest John felt a bit squeamish about shaking his hand, and not because that hand had dipped into the company's till. But Linda was very smooth and without any of that fierce glitter in her eyes.

He knew that he'd never again kiss her. Her pride had been restored.

"I was telling Walt," she began, "that you came over last night to figure out a final chance to save the house."

"What is it, Carmody? God, I've gone around in circles."

"You keep circulating, nicking every friend who'll ante in a buck, five, or fifty. Keep away from this house. Mrs. Crawford is for the time being a widow."

"Eh? Widow?"

"Yeah." Honest John stepped to the window, pulled a drape, and pointed. "See that zippy big Cad? Your wife is selling that."

"I — I don't get it. How the hell can she?"

"It sounds unlegitimate, but it ain't. You be out of this house before the ad gets into circulation. Me, I got to stick around till someone comes to buy. To buy for the amount you're still short."

Crawford spent a moment perplexedly eyeing the beefy mug who didn't look too brilliant; the round faced man in box-car shoes; the kind of man anyone would leave alone with any woman.

"I still can't figure it out; you're not selling your car to help me."

"Me, a bus like *that*? No, it ain't hot, and I ain't really selling it. Listen, Crawford. Did you hear about a blonde woman being found dead around Half Moon Bay? A blonde girl, peeled down to the buff, with three .32s in her frame?"

"My God —" He jerked around. "Linda — Good Lord —"

His wife's color faded, her hands opened and closed. "Our gun is a .25, Walt."

He stuttered, "Get it — let's see —"

Linda wasn't any too steady when she went for the heater. Crawford said to Honest John, "I didn't know — I didn't — I stayed away from her — like I told Linda — and you — I would. Was it — Yvonne?"

"It was, and I found her. Keep your trap shut. If anyone should get a hunch and make you look at the stiff, say you never saw her before. If she's identified, you're sunk, your shack's gone!"

Then Linda came back with the gun. It was dusty inside and out. Honest John pulled the slide, jacked out a couple of tiny slugs. He said, "This gat didn't do it. All right, Crawford, move out before that ad gets a rise in the morning. Get a room."

"You mean, whoever killed her did it to sell — uh — that car?"

Honest John nodded. Crawford headed to the rear to pack a bag. When he came back, Honest John said, "Call the company and tell 'em you're moving out, blame it on your wife."

Crawford's desperation made him snap at the chance. He had sold his own car, and the garage was empty. He did not wait to see the cream-colored Cad take its place.

A few minutes later, Linda took the keys and said to Honest John, "You'll be back early?"

"Before sunrise, so I'll be planted way ahead of time."

Honest John waited all the forenoon, sitting in the kitchen, listening to Linda going about her housework. He wanted to smoke a cigar, but widows rarely use them. He burned up a pack of her cigarettes.

He wondered what Linda was thinking. Certainly not of that one evening. He wondered if it was well-controlled nerves that made her polish every bit of metal and enamel on the range, every inch of the sink, the refrigerator; or whether she was happy from thinking of the house she might save, or if she was taking farewell of a home she could not save. As the day wore on, he looked for cigarette butts to light, and he said, "Next guy says he understands women, I'll tell the _____ he's crazy, nobody does."

He jumped when the phone rang. He listened to Linda's sweet voice. Not a fumble, not a tremor; she said, "Fourteen-fifty" as smooth as silk. And then, "If you saw one the other day for twelve-fifty, you'd better buy it."

More calls. They all thought $1,450 was too stiff. Which it was. Only one kind of purchaser would come to the house: the guy who intended to tap the widow on the conk and get the car free.

That evening, things began to tick. She had barely said, "$1,450" when the speaker must have asked about seeing the bus. Linda answered, "Right away, if you wish."

She was not even breathless when she came to tell Honest John, "It's a man."

He felt foolish about asking her if she remembered her lines; but he did. She answered, "I'll know what to say when the time comes, I'll think of some way of getting to his house."

She didn't have any qualms about Honest John's ideas for keeping her from being knocked off in transit.

HE WAS in the room across the hall from the living room when the bell rang. A tall, thin-faced man was at the door. He didn't look like a cold-blooded killer; they seldom do.

He said pleasantly, "I'm Art Garth, Mrs. Crawford," and fumbled with a little square of newsprint he took out of his vest pocket. "It's a '38 Cad?"

She went on to tell him how swell it was, how her late husband had babied it, how it never had gone over forty; and she had to have cash, five hundred down on the line. Notes for the rest, any bank would handle it, she was sure.

Garth did not whimper. "Five hundred, Mrs. Crawford? Well. . . ." He smiled, turned a vest pocket inside out. "The funny thing is, I just hit a long shot at the races, but the money's at home. I expected to give you a check. Well, we can pick it up, and anyway, I'd like to have my wife try the car."

"I need cash, tonight."

Garth glanced about. "You have your certificate of ownership?"

She took it from her bosom, spread the yellow slip on the table. "Of course your wife should try the car, she'll love it. And you won't mind driving me back? I have so many things to do before I leave. Won't you phone, so she'll be ready when we get there? There is the phone, call while I get my coat. I'm so pressed for time."

Honest John heard him call the number, and penciled it on the wall. Then Linda was beside him. Squeezing his hand, she whispered, "You trace the number and get there ahead of us. Much better than trailing. I'm not afraid."

Garth followed her to the garage. Before the big engine was fairly rumbling, Honest John was telling the operator that it was police business, and got the address Garth had called. But when the long car backed out and made a U in the street, he clamped down on the cigar he had been saving all those hours. He ought to trail them.

But she said no, and her way was really best. Crooks fall into habits. This was a team. Garth got the victim, his woman sold the loot. One to drive, one to sit in the back seat with the owner, get her out in the sticks, and then pour it to her. As long as Garth was alone with Linda, she was safe enough.

So he took a short cut.

THE ADDRESS was off Allemany Boulevard, on a side street, where only a few houses dotted the hilly lots. There weren't any neighbors close enough to see or wonder. Just the spot, and handy to the highway leading down the lonely shore to Half Moon Bay.

He poured on the power, though he knew that Garth would take his time; a ticket was the last thing that Garth wanted. Honest John, uneasy because a woman had her neck on the block, kept telling himself, "Hell, I couldn't pinch him, I couldn't knock it out of him, only the longest chance that anyone could prove he was in Yvonne's house, much less knocked her off. And that wouldn't get the dough, the dough Linda needs."

Lights out, he skimmed silently past the house that must be Garth's: the only lighted one in that lonely block. He had checked numbers in his guide as he approached the district. Once past, he bumped up over a curb and parked in a vacant lot. From there he could watch.

Soon the long cream-colored Cad loomed up. Linda stepped out, and Garth slid from the wheel. He followed her into the house. Honest John waited and chewed his cigar. He had handcuffs; nail the two, shackle them together, when they came out. Then frisk them, frisk the house, get the payoff. They'd be afraid of banks. Get them both out of the house, off guard and thinking of a nice dark spot to cool Linda.

But minutes passed. He began to pace in the gloom. He was afraid. He wanted to give them time for chit-chat, time to dig out the five hundred cash for Linda, time to offer to drive her home, if "Mrs. Garth" liked the bus.

Suppose they varied their routine? They might risk conking her in the house. The more he saw of the place, the more he knew that it would be easy to bring a stiff to the car. He had not figured on such a nice spot. He had half considered trailing them, crowding them into the ditch, and putting the slug on them. Nailing them on their own steps was a last minute change.

God, how long . . . ?

He headed for the house. To hell with this. He couldn't take it.

He heard a scream, the dry, small smack of a pistol. Then no sound at all. Honest John went wild. He sprinted to the porch. He lashed out with his handcuffs, and swept the glass out of a French window, and barged into the living room, gun leveled. He shouted, "You lousy — ! I'll —"

THEN he checked himself, and stood there, gaping. There was a trim brunette in a red hat and fur coat, grabbing her shoulder. Garth, looking sick as the girl. One hand frozen in an unfinished grab for a table drawer. Linda's face was hard as her voice, and she was saying, "Get the other five hundred or I'll empty this gun into you. Hurry, Garth."

Honest John took charge. "Cut it, Linda, you fool, who'd you shoot? Garth, you and the dame poke out your hands, here, by the banister."

In a moment, he had them cuffed, and the connecting link passed through the balustrade. Linda lowered her peashooter, and said, "I saw the label of that coat, the coat that fool Walt bought Yvonne, he told me about that. So I knew — I couldn't be wrong —"

He eyed her, drew her into the hall, where the two cursing captives couldn't shout him down. He said, "With the right dress, baby, you could beat any rap. But I went wild, now they know I'm playing your hand. Even if they are caught with Yvonne's coat, they'll still squawk for that dough."

"I don't care, John. I'll face it out."

He told her to keep her gun on the prisoners while he frisked the house. In half an hour he had found plenty. Yvonne's rings on the dresser. Garth's girl had to grab them, and the coat. But in the basement was the payoff: a grave. They'd changed their minds about dumping the next victim. Discovering Yvonne's body so soon had scared them and had almost finished Linda.

Honest John was no longer sweating when he went to the captives and said. "Shut up, shut up! I got your prints on the glass in Yvonne's room. You grabbed the glass too high. Enough of her stuff is around here to sink you, and then there's the traffic cop in South City. But I'll give you one break, one break which maybe you can use."

Garth asked, "What?" The rat was scared sick, shaking.

"Maybe you can plead the old white flame stuff when you poured it to Yvonne. You can explain the blanket, easy. But that grave in the basement, way back out of sight, where I just stumbled on it. If the cops see that, it makes the both of you *premeditating* murder, it nails your girlfriend and you. I'll shut up, as long as you shut up about the dough we're taking. The price of Yvonne's bus."

"You mean — you'll — let us go?" the girl said, choking.

"Yes. To hell." He grinned. "I'm out to sink Garth. He's facing the works for Yvonne, but he has a chance for his life, pleading impulse or something, or she tried to shoot him first. You can claim he stepped out on you, and you didn't know the car was hot, and you're clear, pretty much. But sister, that open grave, that'll finish you, if I squawk."

SO THEY played it that way. Crawford, the chump, squared himself, and he's got a new job. Linda has her house, and she has clothes now. Lots of them.

Honest John? He's got memories. Which isn't bad for a guy that's red-faced, kind of bald, overweight, and not too smart-looking.

# TRIANGLE WITH VARIATIONS

EVERYTHING WAS strictly kosher until Valene invited Dan Slade to stick around for a drink, and headed for her bedroom instead of toward the refrigerator. And then Slade took a tumble.

While it was private stock she was breaking out, it wasn't anything kept in a bottle. He didn't actually see her slip out of the gown that for the better part of the evening had kept him wishing she had put it on backwards, but he might as well have, for while her negligee, when she reappeared in the doorway, could have covered everything a lady keeps concealed from all but two or three very dear friends, the edges of the filmy substitute for nudity weren't on speaking terms. . . .

There's an infallible way of losing one's memory and Valene's formula did the job in an instant. One eyeful — Slade forgot that she was Jim Tilford's wife, and that Tilford wasn't chained to the roulette wheel at Coppa's.

That eyeful was something like eating nine hundred dollars worth of pep tablets and then getting kicked into the Sultan's harem. Valene's silken legs were perfect from her dainty ankles to the guard stripe on her hosiery, and from there on the view became really good.

The white roundness of her thighs found refuge in a froth of lace just in time to give Slade a chance to observe that Valene's sighing inhalation threw her breasts in dazzling relief against the chiffon that caressed them like a lover's hand; and her scarlet smile was as inviting as her warm curves.

Then she remembered that the negligee had revealed everything but her wisdom teeth, but before she could do anything about it, Slade had an armful of Valene and a carload of plans for the evening.

"Oh . . . Dan! You're hurting me!" she protested, trying to withdraw from his embrace. Slade's crushing kiss cut her short, but her retreat was highly successful: it brought them a pace closer to a divan that was an acre of invitation — though it might have been the courthouse steps for all Slade now cared.

Her struggles suddenly relaxed. A shudder rippled down her body and her breath came in quick, short gasps. Valene's protests were becoming inarticulate murmurings, but she was doing her best to say no — in sign language, since his fierce kisses again stifled her objections.

Then the edge of the lounge made her knees buckle; and treachery from the rear was too much, with persistence from the front. A flurry of silken legs and chiffon — and then her arms closed about him to make the best of it . . . .

Bit by bit, Dan Slade's failing memory responded to treatment. He began to recollect that she was Jim Tilford's wife. Valene laughed softly at his tardy penitence. With feminine wisdom, she had repented in advance. And it was his fault anyway, and if she'd screamed, it'd have caused an awful scandal.

"Don't be stupid, Dan," she murmured. "Jim and I have all been all washed up for ages."

Which was true, and earlier that very evening, the Jim Valene armistice had flared into open warfare at Coppa's place. Tilford, sourly drunk, and as usual, bucking the roulette wheel. Valene, sweetly reminding him that he had lost a play after ignoring her winning suggestion.

That was always good for a fight, and it ended in an appeal to Caesar:

"Dan, for God's sake take her home! She's a hoodoo!"

And here they were: Slade and Valene.

"He's wild about Nancy Forrest," she added. "And he wasn't as drunk as he pretended. That quarrel was just a stall so he could ask you to bring me home so he could hang up with Nancy tonight — weekends aren't enough for them any more."

That was more than half probable; but Slade and Tilford were passably good friends and it was a rotten situation, All the more so, since an hour or so with Valene was enough to make it a habit with anyone — anyone but Tilford, and he'd in some way gotten out of the habit, as Slade had just deduced from one thing and another.

"Jim's drunker'n hell, and what's more," he countered, jerking away from her embrace, "he began winning as soon as you stepped to the check room for your coat. I'm going back to pilot him home. Been too damn' many holdups of gambling house customers lately, and —"

"Dan, don't be silly!" Valene was on her feet at a bound, but Slade, resolutely ignoring the ankle-to-collar-bone view, stalked to the door.

He stepped on the starter and tramped on the gas, driving wrathfully and recklessly, sending the *coupé* screaming to the outer fringe of the city and then hurling it out the highway.

It was going to be hell from now on, keeping away from Valene; and facing Tilford would be worse.

And then, three miles from Coppa's, Slade jammed his brakes to a screaming, smoking halt as he rounded the sharp curve. In the moonlight he saw a car that had smashed headlong into an oak that would telescope a battleship: Jim Tilford's canary yellow Packard. On the far side of the wreck Tilford lay sprawled on the ground. You could see with half an eye that he was dead.

Slade stepped to the running board of the sunburn special, and noted that Tilford, though drunk, had snapped the switch as he left the road.

And then, glancing back toward town, Slade saw the cause of the crackup; the self-luminous marker that indicated a sharp turn in the highway had been moved from the left to the right of the road. It would fool a sober driver.

"Accident, hell! It's murder."

Murder — and robbery. He had beaten Joe Coppa's wheel, but Death's roulette stopped at double zero.

Slade, as he reached for Tilford's wallet to verify his conclusion, saw a scrap of paper, hastily crumpled and half thrust into a vest pocket. He withdrew it. It was a penciled note, in crudely printed letters:

*Tilford:*
> *Better go home early tonight. You might see something worth looking at.*
> *A friend.*

"Good God . . ." muttered Slade. Robbery was bad enough; but this was fairly putrid! No wonder Tilford had left Coppa's, driving like the hammers of hell. But who had given him that damning note, that tip-off which but for Slade's belated qualms of conscience would have brought Tilford to his house before Valene could remember that the refrigerator was in the kitchen and not the bedroom!

"But maybe it's just a gag — it'll work with any married man." Slade assured himself. Still, it didn't quite stick, and he was hoping that robbery was the motive. Somehow, that would make him feel a bit better about it; better than thinking that somebody really had been wise and had in good faith sent Tilford to check up on his wife.

He reached for Tilford's wallet and the long, legal size envelope that peeped from the inside coat pocket; but his fingers did not quite make it. Something crackled behind him.

He started, heard a tense, short gasp, and from the corner of his eye saw a dark form lunging toward him. And as he whirled, he was knocked headlong across Tilford's body.

Something hard and swiftly moving crashed against his head and shoulder. His brain roared into a burst of flame, and then blackness blotted out all sensation. . . .

When Slade's consciousness finally returned, he struggled dizzily to his knees, rubbed the egg-sized lump on the side of his head, and resumed his search of Tilford's pockets. The envelope and wallet were now gone.

But in a side pocket of Tilford's coat, Slade found three small blocks of wood wrapped in paper. Odd baggage to carry to a gambling resort. They must mean something — but what? He took them, then picked up the penciled note which lay in the grass, near the head-bolt wrench which had felled him.

The ache of his shoulder told him why his skull had not been crushed as Tilford's had been. He had started just in time to rob the blow of a portion of its force.

As nearly as he could estimate from a glance at his watch, Slade had been out for about half an hour. He looked back toward town and saw that during that time the self-luminous highway marker had been moved back to the proper side of the road.

"Anyway, it was robbery — that note was just a stall," he concluded. "I happened along before they could roll Jim. And got cold-cocked."

But the fact remained that Tilford had headed home on a hot tip. And as Slade drove to Coppa's to phone the police, his thoughts were none too pleasant.

"That note may be evidence, but I'm keeping it under cover. Even if it's a fake, it'd sound like hell . . . or was Valene in back of this job. . . ."

Self-made widows aren't unheard of; and that spat at Coppa's began to seem tailor-made. Slade and Tilford had snapped at the bait. And for the last mile he suddenly hated Valene and himself.

SLADE FOUND Joe Coppa circulating among his patrons, his sharp black eyes missing nothing as his gold and ivory smile salved the losers and greeted the newly arriving optimists.

"Joe, how much did Tilford win?" he demanded.

Coppa shrugged and guessed it might be four-five grand; which was a trifle at his place.

"Any strangers? Any tough mugs hanging around?" snapped Slade.

Coppa's beady eyes contracted as he saw the sallowness of Slade's grim face.

"'Smatter, Dan? What the hell — maybe some of the crowd ain't social register, but I don't allow no rough stuff —"

"Jim Tilford's been run into the ditch and robbed. He was pie-eyed, and I came back to get him."

Slade touched only the high spots, and said nothing about having had his own brains well shaken up. Neither did he mention the three wooden blocks.

"Come to think of it," said Coppa, "there was a coupla hard-looking mugs eyein' Jim while he was taking us down the road, and then they parked themselves along the sidelines and begun reading a paper. I sort of think they did leave right after he did."

He indicated a now vacant row of chairs not far from the wheel Tilford had been bucking. A Chicago *Tribune* lay on the floor.

"That's it, lyin' there now," added Coppa.

"Nail it," snapped Slade. "May have finger-prints. There's not many stands that carry out-of-town papers. People don't come out here to read the news — unless they're damn' well interested in checking up on the hometown and don't care to write or wire. Get it!"

"Uhuh," agreed Coppa. "And by watching the down-town news-stands, you might grab 'em when they come for their next number. Particularly since we got good descriptions of 'em."

Slade phoned headquarters, then drove back to Tilford's wrecked car, to await the arrival of the police. He detailed his finding Tilford, and mentioned everything but the penciled note. He had forgotten the three blocks.

"And now that you've got something to work on," he concluded, "I'm going home — my damn head's about ready to bust."

But Slade returned to the city, he was certain that no out-of-town hangers-on at Coppa's had written that note to advise Tilford to come home early. And for the looters to take the long, white envelope from Tilford's pocket was distinctly a false note.

"And finally," demanded Slade, "why was Jim carrying a business size letter around with him to Coppa's? Also, what's he been so damn' worried about the past three-four days! That's what made him flare up and ask me to get Valene the hell out of there — that's what made him pile out, hell-bent, when he got that crackpot note."

He did not want to go home, nor did he want to see Valene. Valene last of all. He feared that he might read guilt in her smouldering eyes. Amorous — and spiteful — she might have done anything.

Spiteful —

And that reminded Slade of Tilford's secretary, and Valene's remarks. If anyone could give him the inside track, Nancy Forrest could. When Jim wasn't battling with his wife he was at Nancy's apartment. Slade stepped into a drug store and dialed her number.

"Dan Slade speaking. I want to see you. Right now. About Jim. Never mind why."

He hung up before she could argue. Ten minutes later he was punching the doorbell; and then he began to understand Jim's choice in sweethearts. He could hardly believe that this could be the trim, self-effacing piece of office equipment he had called an armful of nothing at all.

She was taller than Valene, and just as shapely; but unlike Valene, hers was a cool and restful loveliness. Her eyes were star sapphires, veiled by heavy lashes, and her smile was refreshing instead of inflaming. Yet the severe simplicity of her dressing gown could not quite conceal the fluent sweetness of her body.

They eyed each other for an instant. Slade knew he could not tactfully edge up to the subject.

"Jim just got cracked off," he blurted in a dry, hard voice, "Murder, sure as God made little apples."

Nancy's breasts for an instant swelled the silk of her gown. Then she froze — still lovely in her wide eyed, rigid incredulity.

"How?"

Slade told her. Everything — except the color of Valene's step-ins.

She listened in dry-eyed silence. Slade knew she was too hard hit to weep.

"All right, Nancy — you sing yours," he concluded. "What kind of letter would Jim be packing around in his pocket, even out to Coppa's? Why'd he want to mail it personally? And what's he been telling you about Valene?"

Nancy Forrest forced a pallid smile.

"He told me," she finally said, "that Valene was nutty about you, and he wished to God you'd take a tumble and get her off his hands — only, he'd kind of hate to have you tangle up with a hell-cat like her."

"Then he couldn't have been so damn' wrathful on his way home tonight."

Nancy agreed and then queried, "But why would the person who beaned you take the wallet *and* letter?"

"A guy in a hurry would grab the works. But what the hell was in that letter! You ought to know."

"Nothing but routine for the past few days, But he has been awfully up in the air about something."

Which got nowhere. And Nancy was beginning to crack under the shock. She'd be weeping all over his shirtfront in another moment. He could tell from the nervous twist of her fingers as they knotted the edge of her dressing gown.

Slade reached for his hat.

"Don't go," she said. "God — I feel — so damn' lost —"

She looked it. He wondered what Valene would say when she heard the news.

"Get a drink," he said. "You need it. So do I."

Murder or no murder, if that gorgeous armful draped herself all over him, and they began swapping condolences —

"Anyway," he grimly reflected as she turned to head for the kitchen, "Nancy still remembers the refrigerator isn't in her bedroom."

Which gave her the edge on Valene. And so did the bright lights as she crossed the threshold from the kitchen, playing the devil with Nancy's transparent gown.

But Slade's resurrected conscience balked at making the evening a study in comparative anatomy.

He resolutely ground a half-smoked cigarette into the ashtray, and fumbled in his pocket for a fresh one.

He found more than the smoke. With it he drew out the three small blocks of pine.

"What the hell are these?" he asked Nancy, catching her wrist just in time to keep her from depressing the lever of the siphon.

As he swallowed the straight Scotch, he watched her examine the odd cargo Tilford had carried to Coppa's — after he'd wrenched his glance from points of interest not far south of Nancy's shoulders.

In the bright light of the living room, he noted a red stain on the center of the cross section of the pieces. There was an unstained border not more than a sixteenth of an inch wide. It was perceptibly yellow — a decided lemon tint, and not the natural color of pine.

Nancy frowned, then answered, "Why — these are samples of *Wolmanized* wood."

"*Which?*"

"Wood," explained Nancy, "that's been treated with Wolman solution so termites — tropical wood-eating ants — won't touch it. Jim was shipping over five million feet of treated lumber down to a big job in Belize —"

"Fancy coloring," observed Slade, still a bit cross-eyed from noting that Jim's secretary was really stacked up.

"That red stain," she explained, "indicates the parts that weren't touched when the wood was put under pressure. The chemical in the wood bleaches that red testing dye. Good Lord, how Jim tore the office to pieces when some of the samples didn't come up to specifications!"

Nancy reached for a handkerchief. Slade reached for his hat. He wanted to think.

"Be seeing you," he said, striding toward the door. "And if the police ask you things, *forget about that screwy note.* Get it?"

Nancy sobbed an inarticulate yes. But Slade did not look back to catch the sudden narrowing of her eyes, and the tensity of her lovely face.

He had something on his mind; and as he took the wheel of his car, he wondered at Nancy's ignorance of the letter Tilford had carried with him in his pocket instead of including it in the outgoing mail.

"Something is cock-eyed," he summarized. "She ought to know about that letter. It was important enough to steal — then how could she have skipped it?"

Nancy might be holding out. Maybe she suspected him of having teamed up with Valene. In which case Slade would have the police on his neck for palming a few scraps of evidence. Slade wiped the sudden rush of sweat from his forehead. Nancy was business-like enough to be dangerous. It had the makings of a damn' nice jam.

He drove to police headquarters. The news he got there hit him squarely on the chin. It was too good to be true.

"Hell, yes," said the sergeant. "We got 'em. Two mugs with Tilford's roll. A packet of fifties, with the original bank wrapping band about them. Dated, and initialed by Coppa's cashier. They claim they found him dead, and frisked his pockets, that they didn't gum up the highway marker.

"They were going to knock him off, but someone beat 'em to it — only, they'll fry in a hurry. Nothing to do but give 'em cigars and chicken, and watch the lights blink."

"Let me talk to them," demanded Slade.

The two mugs were sweating and desperate. Caught with the plunder, there had been no need of sapping a confession out of them.

"Listen, Jack," said Slade, addressing the Italian. "Tell me something and maybe I can get you a break."

They eyed each other. The red headed ex-pug grunted; Pichetti answered, "Hell of a lot you can do."

"Take it easy, fellow," grinned Slade. "Just because you sapped me on the nut don't mean I got any grudge. I think someone else did it, and you birds are taking the rap. That's the guy I want. Now talk fast — or smoke, later."

"Dammit, Mac, how the hell can I talk?" muttered the wop. "We found him and his bus all cracked up. Which saved us the job. So we grabbed the roll. And we didn't sap you nor him."

"Oh, all right," grinned Slade. "Just stick to it then. The smell of roasting meat won't bother you, though the young news hounds'll park their lunches at their first execution."

"Listen," countered Pichetti, "whatta ya trying to work on us? You ain't no dick. We seen ya check out with the black-eyed broad. So what the hell can you do for us — and why'd you want to?"

"I have my reasons," retorted Slade. "Who talked to Tilford after his wife and I left?"

"Him and some short, stocky fellow with a red face chinned a couple minutes. Your buddy gave him a growl and a dirty look and told him to take a ___ for himself. He was madder'n hell, and he reached for his coat pocket, and I ducked, figuring he was goin' to pull a gat — your buddy, I mean. Then he shoved some more chips on the layout, and the other guy walked off. How would I know where? Me and Red was tendin' to business."

Slade handed the prisoners the remains of his pack of cigarettes. But when he reached the entrance, he retraced his steps and asked the sergeant if they had Tilford's key ring.

"So his secretary can get into his private office in the morning," Slade explained. "He had a stack of important stuff to get out, first thing. I work with Jim on a few deals."

"Better look somewhere else, Mr. Slade," said the sergeant. "We found nothing but his car keys in the ignition lock."

And that left Slade with but one play: go to the house, and ask Valene to find Jim's key ring. Somewhere in that office, despite Nancy Forrest's insistence to the contrary, there must be a clue to that letter for which someone had killed Tilford.

Slade was certain that Tilford had had words with a person who was interested in that envelope. If he could prove that, he would have an out for Valene — and himself — just in case Nancy began thinking things.

"Damn it," he growled as he headed his car to Tilford's apartment, "short, red faced fellows in a town this size are thicker'n bum tips on the races! But she couldn't have been screwy enough to team up with anyone to run Jim off the road!"

Valene answered Slade's ring. She was surprised and a bit incredulous. He was certain that she couldn't have heard the news. Her dark eyes widened as Slade broke it out.

"God, Dan . . ." She swayed, caught the table for support. Slade wondered what she would say if he mentioned the warning note which had driven Jim into a trap. Then she recovered, and soberly added, "We did battle an awful lot, but that does leave me wobbly."

She looked it. Then he wondered if it was from the strain of waiting, or whether it was a spark of friendliness that had survived the Jim versus Valene skirmishes for several weary years. That remained to be seen. She had the good grace not to paw him.

"The two thugs are nailed," he concluded. "See if you can find Jim's keys. He's got some blue prints of mine in his office, and some papers I don't want his successor to get in on."

He heard her stirring around in the bedroom. He stalked up and down the Chinese rug, clenching and opening his fists. Valene couldn't be messed up with that missing letter. There was a false note.

And then, just as he convinced himself that Valene was strictly on the level, and that the red faced man had turned the trick on his own account, Slade's glance shifted toward the telephone pad. The line of advertising printed on it matched the heading on the slip which was in his pocket. His heart stopped as he bent over to scrutinize the top sheet.

There were marks which had cut through from the sheet which had been torn off. He cocked his head, and saw the unmistakable trace of words shaped with a sharp pencil. And the signature was plain: *A Friend.* That note had originated in Tilford's house! Valene was it —

"Dan, I can't find his keys," she said as she reentered the living room. Then, eyeing him: "Good Lord! You're white as a sheet. Why — what's wrong —"

"You know what's wrong!" he rasped, tearing the sheet from the telephone pad and thrusting it before her eyes. "You wrote the message that sent him tearing home hell-bent to find out whose boots were beneath the bed — after that highway marker was gummed up to lead him into the ditch. You —"

"Dan —" She recoiled as from a blow. "That note — wait — I can explain —"

But if she could, it was to vacancy. The door slammed and Slade was heading for his car. He drove aimlessly. Valene was up to her neck, but despite the evidence against her, there must be other factors.

Why had Tilford's keys vanished? Why had that envelope disappeared? To cover Valene's trail was to share her guilt — and yet, after what had happened, he couldn't sell her out. The only way of finding out where he stood was to go through Tilford's desk. And Nancy Forrest would have a set of keys.

A QUARTER of an hour later he was jabbing her doorbell.

Her eyes were reddened, but she wore her grief well. Her cool, fragrant beauty subdued the wrathful surging in Slade's corroded brain.

"I'm so glad you came back," she murmured. "I've been thinking . . . and . . ."

"So have I," he said with a grim brusqueness that startled her, "And I'm damn' near ready to crack it wide open."

Her blue eyes suddenly became almost as dark as Valene's. Her fingers sank into his arm.

"How did *you* guess — it just dawned on me, and I've been following his work — know it almost as well as he did —"

She was leaning forward, her eyes blazing into his. Slade did not answer her question. The fragrance of her body intoxicated him, and the curved whiteness of her breasts dazzled him.

"I was shocked stupid," she continued. "But after you left, I caught the point of those samples. Those bits of wood prove that —"

And then she cracked. Too much poise to start, then giving away all at once. She was half laughing, half crying, calling him Jim and Dan alternately, and clinging to him as the one remaining link to the past.

"Steady — pull yourself together!" Which wasn't the most appropriate thing to say, but Slade couldn't think of anything else.

A full-blown case of hysteria was a new one on him. Plumb loco, and getting worse every minute. Not a chance to break away and get her a drink or souse her with ice water, or whatever you do to snap them out of it.

Jim was gone, and Nancy suddenly needed someone or something to hang on to. But as soon as she calmed down, she'd give him the missing kink she had doped out. Only, it didn't quite work out that way.

Slade gathered her in his arms, ignoring her clinging curves, the long, fine sweep of her legs, and the tantalizing pressure of breasts that every racking sob and its alternate laugh forced against him. He stroked the disarrayed, gold bronze ringlets as he tried to coax her back to balance. But things began to get complicated.

Valene had tricked him into a rotten situation — and the tighter Nancy clung the more sincere his indignation became. By the time his shirtfront was fairly soaked with tears and his ears jangled with bursts of laughter, he and Nancy were companions in misery.

And since whispered consolation had no effect, a shock might snap her out of it.

One hand slipped from her waist to the warm white curves that smiled through her filmy gown; but it was Slade who got that shock. Nancy shuddered and snuggled closer. It might have been hysteria, but it reminded him of something else — though the two are after all pretty much the same.

His next exploring caress made her breath come in short, quick gasps that weren't a bit like sobs. Then they were lip to lip, and Nancy's sighing murmur was quite rational.

As she sank back among the cushions, drawing him toward her, Slade told himself that if he broke away now, there was no telling what she might do. As it was, she did nothing more outrageous than snap out the floor lamp. . . .

FOR AN engineer, Slade had it figured out well enough. And when he finally extricated himself from Nancy's arms, they were both closer to rational thought.

"... You must think I'm perfectly awful ..." she whispered. "But ... Oh, for the time, I just didn't ..."

"Forget it —" interrupted Slade. "But what was your hunch? According to those test blocks, there must have been a shipment of five million feet of phony lumber about to go to Belize —"

"About? It's already gone. And with that faked wood — which'd rot overnight — costing the manufacturer about half as much as the real article, you can figure the profit someone would have taken if Jim hadn't cracked down on them."

"Get dressed and we'll follow it up."

A few minutes later, Nancy Forrest stepped into Slade's car and they drove downtown to the Federal Indemnity building. The janitor recognized Nancy and admitted them. He took them to the eleventh floor, and turned back to his rooms. Nancy unlocked the front office door and followed Slade to Tilford's private suite. They set to work searching Tilford's desk.

"Here it is!" exclaimed Slade, after five minutes of digging. He jerked a carbon copy from the center drawer. "A letter to the surety company that bonded the contract, telling them to pay off on account of the fraud. In other words, Union Wood Products is sunk — the bonding company'll burn 'em alive and —"

And then things happened in a dizzying blur of split second action. A click, and the faint screech of a hinge. Nancy's scream. Slade whirling. The blast of a pistol, and the searing scorch of lead. A stocky, red faced man, automatic in hand, standing in the threshold. *The killer had come back for the carbon copy of Jim's report.*

Slade ducked as the pistol again jetted flame. Something hit him in the shoulder like a sledgehammer. Nancy hurled a filing basket.

As the third shot blasted the plaster from the wall, Slade recovered and crashed home, driving the enemy into a corner. But he was dizzy from pain and the loss of blood, and the red-faced man was desperate. He felt his strength slipping.

Another pistol blast. As Slade forced himself to a final effort, he saw Nancy sink into a chair, clutching the red stain that blossomed from her side.

Slade's fingers closed on the armed wrist just in time to deflect the descending barrel He wrenched, and hammered home with his free fist. Red Face's head snapped back. He was out cold.

"Oh, Dan — !"

Valene's voice. She had arrived at the height of the party.

Slade staggered to his feet. Valene's face was pale and her eyes blazing. She dropped the smoking stand which she had picked up just too late to brain Red Face.

"I'm all right," said Nancy, pulling herself out of her chair. "That shot just raked me — Oh, you're bleeding!"

"Nuts!" grumbled Slade. He picked up the keys that Red Face had dropped at the threshold: *Tilford's missing ring*. And then the police followed the janitor into the office. Slade eyed Valene, and concentrated on Wolmanized wood.

"Damn' near a hundred thousand graft. This buzzard tried to beg off, but Jim couldn't give him a break. Finally he sat down and wrote the letter to the bonding company himself, to keep the mess strictly private in case he relented.

"Put off mailing it, hating to sink the fellow, even though he had pulled a fast one. And that cost Jim his life. That's what I make of it," he concluded.

"Now if you want to check his finger-prints and see if he tinkered with that self luminous highway marker, go to it. But his coming up here with Jim's missing keys is enough."

And that held the police. Before Red Face recovered, he was getting more from the cops.

There was a three cornered exchange of glances as Tilford's friend and two widows stepped to the hall.

"I guess we'd better get patched up a bit," was Slade's suggestion.

Nancy's glance was curious as she said, "I'll call a cab, Dan. It was only a scratch. You take care of Mrs. Tilford."

Then a brief, deadly crossfire as blue eyes clashed with black.

"What the hell are you doing here?" asked Slade, as Valene caught his arm.

"I knew you'd end up here, probably with her keys," said Valene. "So I came up — to tell you — you wouldn't listen — that Jim and I wrote that note. He knew he couldn't give me to you. Even if we broke, you'd steer clear of me, just for the looks of things.

"So he faked that message to catch us at it and make you like it. And to give Nancy a break. Jim knew you really liked me a lot."

And that was a lot for Slade to digest at one bite. He shot a long look at Nancy, then said to Valene, "Once the doc picks the lead out of my frame, you and I are going home — to give me a chance to find out what it's like with a clear conscience!"

# SCOURGE OF
# THE SILVER DRAGON

"THAT'S funny," muttered Gilbert Flint to the silence of his dingy furnished room, but there was no mirth in his frosty gray eyes as he watched a touring sedan emerge from the swirling mists of Chinatown and pull to the curbing of Jackson Street.

His craggy, suntanned face tightened into angles that were accentuated by the sudden grimness of his mouth. Crouched beside the sill of the flyspecked window that gave him a view from Stockton Street down to the Embarcadero, Gilbert Flint of the Federal Bureau of Investigation for a moment seemed to be a lurking tiger. It was time to strike. Twice during his endless prowlings as a shabby drifter in Chinatown, he had seen that six-wheel job pull up at the mouth of the alley that led to the rear of Yut Lee's "Abode of Felicitous Fraternal Association." And the third time confirmed his hunch that the Silver Dragon came to San Francisco by motor.

The same car, and the same driver: a hawk-nosed, swarthy man whose thin face, for a moment illuminated by the yellowish glow of the nearby electrolier, was deeply lined and haggard from hard driving. He stretched his lean, rangy body, then stepped to the side door of Yut Lee's place. He rang and was at once admitted.

Flint reached for a wreck of a hat, slipped into a shapeless, tattered topcoat, and resumed the role he had for a moment cast off. He bit off a chew of Rattle Axe and shambled down the two flights of creaking stairs. If a Chinaman emerged from the alley to remove the spare wheels from the fender wells, Flint wanted to be within arm's reach. Those tires — unless his hunch was wrong — would be filled with more than air.

He wondered how many five-*tael* tins of opium each inner tube could conceal. He wondered also what master smuggler was flooding San Francisco with Silver Dragon, the new brand that was forcing the old ones out of the market.

Flint slouched upgrade, crossed Jackson, and ducked into an intersecting alley not far from the parked sedan. He entered a gloomy doorway and ascended a flight of stairs. On the second floor hall he lifted a window, cleared the sill, and emerged on a balcony that overhung the court in the rear of Yut Lee's place.

While the Abode of Felicitous Fraternal Association was the center of the local opium traffic, Flint had larger game in view — the smuggling ring that supplied Yut Lee. The Chinatown squad, complying with a request from federal headquarters, arrested just enough peddlers and hop-heads to avoid a suspicion-arousing lull.

Across the court was a window, a blot of yellow glow in the gloom. Flint was looking into the inside of Chinatown. Lean, grizzled Yut Lee was earnestly conversing with a girl whose loveliness caught Flint's breath. She was not Chinese, and he doubted that she was Eurasian. Her blue-black hair was drawn sleekly back and caught in a lustrous cluster at the nape of her neck. Cream-colored skin and dark eyes perilously smouldering behind curled lashes; just a glimpse, but an unforgettable one.

This was the home of the Silver Dragon that had invaded San Francisco despite the airtight cordon of FBI men guarding the Embarcadero and searching every ship that came from the Orient.

A door silently swung into the murky gloom below. A Chinaman emerged. His felt slippers *swish-swished* as he shuffled across the flagstones. Same old routine. Haul the spares in, one at a time; then later, come out with other tires.

The Chinaman fumbled with keys. A latch click — but as the door to the street opened, the Chinaman froze for an instant. Then his hand darted forward, sending a silvery streak zipping on ahead of him. Screeching wrathfully, he drew another knife and bounded toward the street. That opened the show.

Flint, clearing the balcony railing, heard the tinkle of steel and the answering yell. He dropped to the shadows of the court, rocked for an instant on the balls of his feet to regain his balance. But instead of rising, he rolled back and to the shelter of a pilaster. The Abode of Felicitous Fraternal Association was waking up.

The hawk-nosed driver of the parked car came plunging into the court. As he reached the street, a pistol crackled. Lead thudded into the door. Wild shots spattered to whining fragments against the brick wall at the rear. A yell came, and the sodden thud of a man dropping to the paving.

Hawk-nose, ducking to the shelter of the jamb, cursed wrathfully and snapped an automatic into line. The blast of his heavy pistol drowned the spiteful rattle that came from beyond his parked car, but flame still streaked over the hood.

Flint caught it at a glance. Rival opium dealers were rising in revolt against the monopoly of Silver Dragon. One spare wheel lay on the sidewalk where the hijacker had dropped it to take cover as the Chinaman emerged from the court.

"*Cabron!*" roared Hawk-nose above the thunder of his .45, then he shifted to get a better line of fire.

His maneuver was good. Another shot, and the enemy's fusillade ceased. Hawk-nose bounded from cover. Sirens were screaming in the distance, and in another few moments the Chinatown squad would appear to mop up the disturbance. The iron gratings of windows opening into the court of Yut Lee's place were slamming shut; and when the police appeared, bland faced Orientals would be insisting: "No savvee. . . ."

Wisely enough, Yut Lee's highbinders were not taking a hand. There was no use. The car parked at the curb was Hawk-nose's funeral, not theirs.

Hawk-nose was losing no time. Even as the wounded hijacker dropped gurgling and groaning to the street, the opium runner leaped to the wheel.

Flint emerged from cover. Getting the license plate number was not enough. That would be changed; but by riding the rear bumper he could flag some traffic cop to tail the machine. But both Flint and the opium runner miscalculated.

Before Hawk-nose could jab the starter, a dark form jerked up from behind the front seat to meet him. A hand snaked up, striking aside his automatic, and a curved blade lashed upward. There had been two hijackers, one working on each fender well. And the one at the left had played a cunning game.

The interior of the car became a tangle of writhing bodies and grappling hands, and a relentlessly flickering blade that darted in and out of the confusion. Hawk-nose sagged to the floorboards.

Flint bounded to the running board. The hijacker, a short, stocky Chinaman, kicked clear of his wounded adversary and lunged to meet him. Flint ploughed in, his left hand catching the highbinder's wrist and deflecting his dripping blade, his fist popping home. The Chinaman, dazed but still kicking, sagged across the steering column.

Before Flint could regain his balance, the parked car began rolling downgrade. The emergency brake had been disengaged in the tussle. He jerked back, but the highbinder blocked his attempt to leap clear. The knife descended. Flint wriggled clear. Its red length stabbed the upholstery.

Flint drew his knee up to his stomach to boot the highbinder through the windshield — but gravity and the steep grade had been at work. The now swiftly, erratically descending car backed over the low curbing and crashed into a house on Grant Avenue, shattering the door. The impact pitched the highbinder and Flint to the paving. They came up fighting. A blade raked Flint from shoulder to hip. He jerked aside, struggled to his feet. Another vicious jab. Flint feinted, then ducked inside the highbinder's guard, planting him squarely on the jaw.

Hawk-nose, aroused by the shock that flung him from the floorboards, lashed out blindly with both arms.

The riot ended with a savage yell, a gurgle, and a gasp. Flint saw that the highbinder had impaled himself on his own blade.

Hawk-nose was still alive, though the ever widening pool of blood through which he was trying to crawl left his chances in the balance.

"Take it easy, Jack," cautioned Flint, kneeling beside the wounded man. "You got them both. I'll give you a lift — which way?"

Hawk-nose muttered, gestured vaguely as Flint lifted him from the paving. The car, despite its rear end crash, was worth a trial.

And then the Chinatown squad came pounding into action. Flint swallowed an oath, and obeyed the brusque command to surrender.

"Jeez, chief," he whined, resuming his pose as a drifter, "I don't know nuthin' about this. I was just helpin' this guy to his feet —"

"You look like it," growled the sergeant, eyeing Flint's knife-tattered coat and battered face. "Now shut up, or do I have to sock you?"

"Take it easy, cap," countered Flint. "Can't you give a fellow a break? I didn't have nuthin' to do with this, but the Chinks'll be waiting for me when I get out of the jug —"

"They'll be old men before you get out," barked the sergeant. "Now get into that wagon."

Flint risked a whisper as the police hustled him toward the department car. "Grab that spare tire halfway up the block!"

The sergeant glanced up Jackson Street.

"Spare tire!" he growled. "Try another one, fella!"

It was gone, but one still remained in the left fender well.

"Get that —"

But the Chinatown squad is hardened to artful dodges. Flint, now that his investigation had blown up, would have to start all over again, and he dared not continue the argument.

The next instant justified him. A blot of whiteness appeared from a second story window; then a pale, slender, jewel-sparkling hand swept out. A burning cigarette lighter landed in the pool of gasoline collecting under the crushed tank. A roar, a fierce wave of heat, and a surging gust of flame enveloped Hawk-nose's car.

Flint cursed wrathfully as the police machine pulled out. Before that blaze was extinguished, not a scrap of evidence would be left.

AT POLICE headquarters Flint identified himself. "Who is that hook-nosed guy, and will he live?" he asked.

"Henrique Robles, according to his driver's license," answered the sergeant. Then, after a moment on the telephone, he added: "They tell me he coughed himself to death on the operating table. The rest were cold meat before we got to headquarters. Three highbinders. Yut Lee, of course, claims he never saw the Chink that went out to get the spare tires — or the others that tried to beat him to it. Which is pure baloney. If there's not a tong war before morning, my name's not McDermott!"

"Worse than a tong war," grumbled Flint. "Damn sight worse! Anyone big enough to crowd the other brands off the market is not going to confine himself to opium. Hitting the pipe is comparatively harmless, especially for a Chink. The damnable thing about it is that this Silver Dragon won't stick to smoking opium. Deadlier drugs will follow. The kind that get at the white population."

McDermott's ruddy face lengthened. Flint's view had made a murderous tong war seem trivial in comparison.

While waiting for news of the exotic girl he had glimpsed at Yut Lee's place — the one he was certain had ignited Robles' car — Flint proposed inspecting the wreck.

They went. "Hawk-nose" Robles' machine was in the pound. The blackened remains mocked Flint. The blast of the half-emptied tank had sprayed it with blazing gasoline. He drew a jackknife and moved toward the still smoking wreck.

The hijackers had been interrupted before they could break the lock of the tire in the left fender-well. A slash, and the blistered rubber yielded. Flint's hunch was confirmed when he tore into the tube: it was filled with five-*tael* tins of Silver Dragon, each held in place with a rubber band vulcanized to the interior. But that confirmation was thus far useless.

The serial number had long been filed from the engine block, and no body number plate remained. The gutted interior was a total blank. Flame and the fire department had destroyed the ownership papers on the steering column.

"At the speed this guy was driving," said McDermott eyeing the insect-caked radiator, "he'd have to gas up about every hundred seventy-five miles. Watch towns that distance —"

"This is better!" interrupted Flint, abruptly checking his examination of the interior of the car. He pried a small metal plate from above the right corner of the windshield, "Somebody slipped!"

It was a greasing rack "tickler" with blank spaces for the speedometer reading at which oil should be changed and the chassis relubricated. The top of the plate was marked in red enamel, TIMOTHY'S SERVICE STATION – YUMA.

"Bullseye!" exclaimed McDermott. "That short-circuits the guesswork. Now we know where to inquire. First stop for gas, Fresno, hundred and eighty miles south. Then the all-night filling station at Mojave, three fifty-five. And Yuma —"

"Is headquarters," Flint broke in. "Close to the Mexican border. This tickler's never been marked. Probably not even Robles knew it was there. He'd grease up each round trip. Routine."

Flint then briskly ordered: "Get some mechanics to work on this heap. Fix it up with a used body the same color. I'm driving it south."

"Hell!" muttered McDermott. "You can't get away with impersonating Hawk-nose Robles! And the big shot — the Silver Dragon — ten to one knows by this time what's happened."

Flint's mouth relaxed almost to a smile. "McDermott, if it's got you guessing, this gag may catch someone else off guard. But unless I hit fast, I'll pile right into a buzz-saw. Shake it up. This is big stuff."

Flint, while waiting for the police to have Robles' sedan restored, listened to the radio network enveloping the Peninsula: but the incoming reports were a succession of blanks.

He returned to the pound. The mechanics were checking up the restoration.

"Put some bullet holes into the hood," he ordered, approvingly eyeing the second-hand replacement body. "Radio the highway patrols down the

San Joaquin to give me a clear block, and tell the small town speed traps to lay off, I'm going through.

"And while you're waiting for the radio in Yuma, find that black-haired jane with a quart of diamonds on her fingers and hell in her eyes. Just maintain contact, under cover. But don't grab her. She's been loose too long for a pinch to be any good. The beans must be spilled by now. She'll be worth more on the hoof than in the jug."

HALF an hour later the revamped car was hoisted bodily into a waiting truck. In a side street just short of the South San Francisco bottleneck, Flint took the wheel and nosed the powerful machine down the tailgate ramp and to the paving.

YUMA is sprawled on the east bank of the sluggish Colorado. Its adobe shacks and broad, dusty streets were replaced by granite and marble and asphalt when the Chamber of Commerce used the winter sunshine as tourist bait; hence the modern hotels, schools like Moorish palaces, and a post office that covers a quarter of the city. Yuma is the biggest small town in the country — or maybe it's the smallest big town.

Flint headed for Timothy's Filling Station. Six hundred and seventy miles in a little over ten hours, and the car looked it.

"Give her the works, doc," Flint ordered.

Despite his careless tone and the amiable grin that cracked the alkali dust coating of his craggy face, he was tensely watching the effect of his appearance.

The sandy-haired attendant's blue eyes narrowed as his glance shifted from Flint to the car, and the bullet holes in the hood. No doubt that the machine was familiar; but there was little chance that the attendant would know enough about Robles' business to be on guard.

"Robles got hurt," Flint remarked. "He tried to tell me who to get in touch with, but he passed out before I could get it. Know any of his friends?"

"Don't know anything about him, cap," was the answer. "But there's a fellow that drives up here with him once in a while. Perfesser Kane — the fortune-teller. Maybe you could find him in the phone directory."

Flint found that Alexander Kane was listed. That was something to work on.

"'I'll be back for the grease job later," said Flint, resuming the wheel.

But just in case the man at the filling station knew more than he seemed to, Flint rounded the corner, pulled up at a drug store, and called the telephone supervisor.

"Watch all calls going out of Timothy's Service Station," he ordered. "And report Alexander Kane's phone out of order. Police business."

Then he hastened to police headquarters. He arrived just in time to hear the sergeant at the desk rasp into the transmitter: "We don't know anything about that order —"

"You do now, sergeant," Flint cut in, flashing a federal badge. "Tell the phone supervisor to go ahead with it, and I'll explain a few things."

The order was confirmed; and presently he was conferring with Chief Fergus McDonald, lean and erect as the desert saguaros, and just about as thorny.

"What's the dirt on this fortune-teller, Kane?" he asked, after sketching the trail of the Silver Dragon.

"As far as we've had any occasion to know," answered McDonald, "he's just one of those pests that stay inside the law. He came to town six months ago, and there haven't been any complaints."

"I'm going to look him up," announced Flint.

ALEXANDER KANE'S squat, thick-walled, old-fashioned adobe house was a brown cube surrounded by an uncultivated grove of grapefruit trees. Though not far from the southern limits of the city, it was aloof, and isolated from the neighboring places. A dusty drive, winding in and out among the trees, led to a sunbaked yard fringed by flame-crested ocatillas and tall, towering sahuaros. At the right of the flat-roofed adobe was a stack of fire wood, lying as though just unloaded from a truck whose tire tracks were still plain in the yard.

Flint jabbed the pushbutton just below the brass plate that was etched, ALEXANDER KANE, PSYCHIC. No answer.

He circled the house. The professor's car was in the open garage. He returned to the stone slab at the threshold. Another futile ring. Then Flint went in. For a moment the cool dimness of the spacious room was too much for eyes dazzled by the outdoor glare. It was not until Flint had passed the table at the center that he perceived the thin, sallow-faced man who lay sprawled on the Spanish tiles. He had fallen, struggled to his knees, then slumped to his right. Life had ended with that last effort.

The flow from the dark splash on his gray coat, just below the shoulder, had made little progress across the tiles. His thin, pain-racked face was a mask of futile wrath, made grotesque by the froth that had drooled from his lips as he gasped out his life. Dried, blackened blood – he had been dead for hours.

Flint knelt beside the body, deftly probed an inside coat pocket and found a wallet. A glance at the contents identified the corpse as Alexander Kane.

"He might have been psychic," muttered Flint, "but not enough to keep from turning his back to the wrong guy."

Death had sought Kane with a smile and a knife. No mistaking that vengeful grimace; and the table runner, jerked awry, confirmed Flint's opinion. The psychic had died trying to reach his telephone. Another step, another moment of life, and he would have lived to speak a familiar name into the transmitter.

None of the living-room furniture had been disturbed. Then Flint noted that the trail of blood led to the rear. He followed it down the hallway. At his right was a door that opened into a room whose stucco walls were hung with astrological charts. In the center was a broad, flat-topped walnut desk on which were set, between brazen sphinxes, half a dozen occult books.

Without entering, Flint continued tracking the blood splashes in the hallway. They led to the kitchen and came from a trapdoor opening into a cellar. He descended a short flight of wooden stairs, found and snapped a switch.

"Hell's bells!" he exclaimed, noting the open door of a wall cabinet.

On one shelf were ten five-*tael* tins of Silver Dragon. On a table were several inner tubes, slit to receive their cargo.

Flint, examining the hot-patch kit used in vulcanizing the cans of opium to the inner tubes, saw that the psychic had been preparing to conceal fifty five-*tael* containers. Forty were missing. If it was hijacking, why leave ten?

"Flint retraced his steps, but this time he paused in the kitchen. It was large, neat, but scantily furnished – a refrigerator, a gas plate, and a shelf stocked with canned goods. In an alcove were two chairs and a dinette table.

The latter had not been cleared. There were two plates, both coated with a greasy, congealed, reddish brown gravy; and cups that contained coffee dregs. A bowl at the center was one-third filled with *frijoles* and *chili con carne*. Beside it lay a heel of bread and a square of butter.

He sniffed the chili. Home made. The real article.

But before he could look for some definite trace left by the unknown guest, Flint heard a muffled groan, as though someone, handicapped by a gag, were making an effort to call for help. He turned. It was repeated, choked and gurgling.

It might come from the mystic's study, but he could not be certain. No — it originated in the basement. The silence of the thick-walled adobe had an uncanny trick of distorting sound.

He paused, waiting for a recurrence of that deceptive cry of distress. He heard a sharp click as though a latch had either opened or engaged. No doubt about its origin. Regardless of prisoners, someone was on the prowl. Flint, pistol in hand, stretched long, stealthy strides toward the study door. Weapon leveled, he halted, peeped warily into the room.

It was empty. Nevertheless he sensed that he was by no means alone in that sinister adobe. The groan was repeated. Flint was certain now that someone must be beyond the door which opened from the study into an adjoining room.

Pistol still ready, he cleared the threshold; but as he bounded forward to reach the knob of the interior door, it jerked open to meet him. Simultaneously, something tripped him in mid stride, and a stick cracked down across his right forearm. His automatic slipped from numb fingers; yet swift as his headlong plunge was, he caught a glimpse of the short, moonfaced Chinaman who had lurked at the blind side of Kane's desk.

Only a flickering glimpse, as he desperately struggled to regain his balance: an unnaturally stolid, immobile face whose only animated features were the eyes, black fires that blazed in that frozen, yellowish mask.

Then, slipping on the tiles, Flint's efforts to regain his feet sent him plunging headlong across the threshold and into the darkness from which the choking sounds had come.

An adobe wall checked his lunge. Rebounding, he whirled to a crouch. But the door slammed, and a bolt snicked home. The solid panels fairly crushed his shoulder as he hurled himself against them.

Silence, except for his own hoarse breathing. He struck a match. He was caged in a cramped, dusty closet. The Chinaman, crouched at the blind side of Kane's desk, had by simple ventriloquism thrown his voice so that it seemed to come from beyond the door. And Flint had taken the bait.

His hands were slick and greasy, and so were his knees.

Butter! Taken from the square in the kitchenette. No wonder he had floundered on those tiles. And peeping through the keyhole, he caught a glimpse of a strand of wire on the floor of the study. That was what had tripped him.

He shifted and saw that blank face averted as yellow hands opened desk drawers and probed the contents. Without waiting to see what the raider was taking, Flint turned his back to the door. He braced himself against the knob, planted his feet against the closet wall, and heaved.

The panels creaked as he slowly straightened his arched body. He heard a soft, mocking laugh. Another heave, and then Flint settled to the floor. There, lying on his side, he could apply pressure.

But the groan of the wood was followed by the *slip-slip-swish* of shuffling feet and the locking of the outer door. And when the tongue of the lock finally tore the socket from the jamb, Flint was alone in a littered office. Escape was blocked by an iron-barred window and a door as strong as the first.

His gun was on the desk, every cartridge removed.

As he snatched a chair and began belabouring the remaining barrier, he wondered at the insane inconsistency of it all. Why such an elaborate trap when the Chinaman could have stabbed or brained him as he responded to ventriloquist's bait?

FLINT finally shouldered his way through the shattered panel. Although he knew that his captor had made good his escape, he nevertheless dashed to the front.

Robles' touring sedan was still there; but the top of the trunk at the rear was now braced open. Three prints of felt-soled slippers had registered before the emerging stowaway had reached the harder ground at the house. There were no tracks to show what direction the Chinaman had taken in flight from the adobe.

"That Chink followed me from 'Frisco!" muttered Flint.

In trying to outwit the enemy, he had carried one of the Silver Dragon's men with him for nearly seven hundred miles. Flint grimaced wryly and gave the sinking sensation at the pit of his stomach a chance to subside. Then he cursed wrathfully and strode back into the house.

"Funny," he pondered, stepping to the telephone to call the police, "that Kane didn't have this instrument in his office instead of out here."

He mentioned only having found the dead soothsayer. But as he started to the rear to resume his interrupted search, he heard a car coming up the driveway.

Flint turned again to the front.

A tall, swarthy man with a waxed black mustache emerged: a Spaniard or a Mexican. He carried a black leather bag.

Flint met him at the door.

"I am looking for Professor Kane," the caller announced. He was sleek and well groomed, and his purposeful dark eyes regarded Flint with sharp, querying scrutiny as he added: "Tell him that Dr. Alvarez is here."

"Did he call you?"

"Does it matter?" the doctor countered.

Flint suddenly stepped aside and gestured. He sharply watched Alvarez to note his reaction when his eyes accommodated themselves to the abrupt change from outdoor glare to indoor shadows.

Alvarez stared for a moment, then exclaimed and recoiled. He fixedly regarded the gray huddle just beyond the table, and the blood that blackened the tiles. Then, voice level and unwavering, he queried: "You found him this way?"

"How long has he been dead?" Flint asked.

Alvarez knelt, frowned and muttered under his breath. Finally, he arose, fumbled with his watch, stroked his mustache, and announced: "One couldn't say except roughly, without an autopsy. But —" he glanced again at his watch — "I'd judge he was killed around six o'clock last night."

"Thanks, doc," acknowledged Flint. "Stick around until the sergeant gets here. He'll want to ask you a few things —"

"I'm afraid," deplored. Alvarez, "that I won't be able to help much."

"We'll worry about that," said Flint.

Alvarez seated himself, fumbled for a match; then without hesitation strode to the far corner of the room to get a smoking stand. He evidently knew his way about the house.

McDonald, accompanied by the homicide squad, presently arrived; and as the medical examiner and fingerprint man set to work, the chief questioned Alvarez.

"Professor Kane," began the doctor, "has been my patient for the past six months. I called on him at irregular hours most adaptable to my time.

Either around noon, or in the evening. I live right next door, you know." His gesture indicated the northern side of the citrus grove.

"Did you see anyone call here last night, around six-seven?"

"Naturally not," answered Alvarez. "The grove doesn't permit me a view from my windows. Furthermore, Simon Carter — of Carter, Quentin and Carter — was dining with me. Thus, I'd not notice who approached the place."

McDonald nodded, asked a few routine questions as to the late Professor Kane's domestic arrangements and habits, then added: "That's all, Dr. Alvarez. The coroner will want a statement later."

"Another blank!" grumbled Flint as Alvarez returned to his car. "Remarkable how little that guy knows about his patient! But let's look the joint over. I'm still wondering who was eating chili with Kane."

His second survey of the house yielded no new information; but the fingerprint-man's findings gave significance to Flint's last question.

"Kane's prints are all over," he announced. "Except on the spoon next to that bowl on the other side of the table. And it's blank — wiped clean."

"How about the desk and that door knob?" Flint cut in. "Where the Chinaman was pawing around?"

"Wiped clean," was the answer.

McDonald nodded, for a moment watched his men carry on with their routine, then said: "Flint, that drive of yours, following a busy day in San Francisco, isn't going to help a lot with what's ahead of you. Get yourself a nap, and this evening I'll have all the dope sorted out for you."

McDonald was right. Flint took the wheel of Robles' car. And as he passed Alvarez's house, which adjoined the abandoned grapefruit grove that surrounded Kane's place, he saw that the doctor could scarcely have noticed the psychic's callers.

That evening Flint reviewed the evidence McDonald presented.

Alvarez's story checked perfectly. The coroner confirmed the Spanish doctor's opinion as to the time of Kane's death.

"The old Mexican woman who comes in several times a week to clean the house," said McDonald, "made that batch of chili. Kane liked it. And he always ate early, around six. Rarely left the adobe — naturally not, with the line he was running! Prepared his own meals. And according to the autopsy — based on undigested frijoles and chili — Kane was knocked off not long after he ate."

"That," growled Flint, "is damn helpful. But who wiped the spoon handles clean? And did that prowling Chink leave any marks?"

"Wait a minute!" McDonald broke in. "Till I tell you the rest. A Spic — Ramon Guevara — did odd jobs of gardening for Kane. Supplied him with cord-wood for the fireplace. And peddled a garden truck here and there in town.

"One of the neighbors saw Guevara in his Model-T truck heading down toward Kane's place with a load of wood. That was around six. And, not long after, he came out empty."

"Have you located Guevara?"

"No," admitted McDonald. "He comes from San Cristobal, right across the Mexican line. The customs inspectors tell me he hasn't crossed today."

"And from now on he won't!" declared Flint, "So I'm going over to get him."

SAN CRISTOBAL was a collection of squat adobe shacks centering about *Estrella Blanca*: the White Star, now agleam with light, blatant with music and laughter and the tinkle of glass.

Someone would know Ramon Guevara, and by now Flint had obtained a fairly good description of him.

Flint plunged into the smoke-banded air, picked his way among the dancers, and found himself a booth where he could observe the White Star and its patrons. The bar was to his left. To the right was a side door opening into the desert night. It afforded a ready approach to the adobe shacks facing on the side street.

He eyed the crowd as he waited for his drink. He heard a woman in the booth behind him saying in Spanish: "Ramon, you're so unreasonably jealous! That pendant isn't a present. I bought it myself in San Francisco."

A wrathful muttering; and then, still tinged with suspicion, came Ramon's warning: "Oh, all right, you bought it! But listen, Valencia — if I ever find out you're lying to me, I'll take you to pieces by hand!"

Ramon and San Francisco were decidedly intriguing. Flint moved to another booth. That cut off his eavesdropping but it put him in line with a back-bar mirror which reflected the speakers. He saw more than he expected.

The man was tall and rangy. The heaviness of his swarthy Indian features was relieved by a quartering of Latin blood. He was not much over thirty, and with his prominent nose and grim mouth he checked closely with the customs inspector's description of Ramon Guevara; but it was his companion who clinched it.

Valencia was the girl from Yut Lee's. She wore an acacia-yellow sports ensemble and entirely too many jewels, including a ruby pendant that blazed redly against her cream colored skin. But Flint, as he caught the reflection of those dark eyes and the heart-stirring loveliness of her face and figure, noticed no clash in her costuming. It sufficed that this was the woman who had been conferring with the grizzled Chinaman who was the Silver Dragon's vicar in San Francisco.

But which of the two was really the most important: Valencia or Ramon Guevara? Murder and tins of opium linked them both to Kane.

ANOTHER half hour of bickering, and they emerged from the booth to step toward the side door.

Flint headed for the main entrance and from the veranda watched them cross the side street that intersected the main stem of San Cristobal. Their destination was one of the adobe shacks in the center of the block; and if the wrangling became heated, it would be worth listening to. Flint strode toward the barbed-wire international fence, then swung south to approach Valencia's house from the rear.

The quarrel directed Flint to a listening post at an open window of the living room. It was illuminated by a kerosene lamp. Valencia's colorful length was draped in a chair. Guevara turned to step into the adjoining room. He thrust aside Valencia's detaining hand. Before she could follow, there was a wrathful growl and he came bounding back.

His powerful hand gripped a plush-lined cardboard box.

"San Francisco!" he growled, thrusting it before her eyes. "I knew you were lying. This came from a jeweler in Yuma!"

Valencia ducked, but not quickly enough. Guevara's free hand sent her sprawling, a tangle of silken legs and acacia-yellow skirt. And then the Mexican dodged a flashing sliver of steel that Valencia plucked from a calf sheath.

Flint cleared the sill. Knife work had already thrown too many obstacles in his way.

*"Basta!"* he snapped. "Hold it!"

Guevara whirled, but his hand dropped from his hip as Flint's automatic jerked into line with his stomach.

"*Que hay?*" growled the Mexican.

"Back up to the wall, both of you!" commanded Flint. "Why did you kill Kane after you dumped that load of wood in his back yard?"

"I did not kill him!" flared Guevara.

Valencia's color perceptibly receded, but her eyes narrowed venomously. He was risking a parlay solely on the chance that his surprise attack, coming on the heels of an interrupted quarrel, might result in an unguarded admission.

"Why did you go into the basement?" demanded Flint.

"I went to the office." Guevara started at the F.B.I. man's mention of the opium storage room, "where he paid me for the wood."

"And you knifed him."

"I did not. I will prove it. While he was taking the money from the desk, some wan call heem and he reach for the telephone —"

"He did *what?*" Kane must have an unusually long arm.

"Reach for the telephone," repeated Guevara. Valencia stabbed him with a glance, but the Mexican continued: "He was expect' some wan to see heem later. He write something on the desk blotter."

"What does that prove?"

"That he was expect some wan later. Find out who it was! That weel prove he was alive w'en I leave. *Verdad?*"

Valencia's face had frozen.

"Maybe it will," admitted Flint. "But the both of you take a walk with me. One on each side. And act natural. First sign of trouble from the White Star and you both get the works."

With arms folded, his left concealing the pistol that his right hand thrust against one prisoner, Flint could march them past the Mexican sentries at the International Line.

"All right, Valencia! *On my left.* Guevara, better be nice or you'll need a new girl friend. This is ladies' night."

The grimness of Flint's face warned Guevara that the American would make good his threat.

"Understand?"

"*Sí,* " breathed the Mexican.

"*'Sta 'ueno!*" Flint's clipped finality was steel hard.

He gestured for his prisoners to advance from the wall, but as they moved, he was warned by the perceptible shift of the Mexican's eyes.

Instead of stepping into line with the door of Valencia's bedroom, he jerked back and risked a glance to his left.

The Chinaman who had trailed him from San Francisco was lunging from the doorway.

As Flint whirled to drop the Chinaman, Guevara snatched a smoking stand and struck the pistol from his grasp. The American, sidestepping the highbinder's charge, lashed out with his foot. The Chinaman tripped, crashing headlong against the leg of a table.

That gave Guevara time to close in with his smoking stand. The weapon smashed down on Flint's shoulder as he turned, but it landed an instant too late. Though momentarily paralyzed with pain, he had weight behind his fist. The impact froze the Mexican in his tracks.

Valencia, scrambling for Flint's pistol, reached it as Guevara's legs sagged. But before she could jerk the weapon into line, Flint booted the Mexican against her. They pitched over the threshold and into the bedroom. Flint followed through.

Valencia was knocked breathless by the impact. Guevara was out cold, but the blank-faced Chinaman was stirring. And then the front door crashed open. Two bouncers from *La Estrella Blanca* bounded into the room.

Flint's pistol cracked twice. One dropped kicking, the other was howling for help.

Guevara was too heavy to haul; and Valencia seemed more important than the highbinder. Before she recovered her breath, Flint rolled her up in a blanket, caught her in both arms, and dashed toward the back door.

A crowd was pouring from the side entrance of *La Estrella*, but being directed by the shouts of the bouncer who had escaped Flint's fire, they did not perceive his direction until he was close to the international fence.

One arm squeezed his slender captive into submission as he halted and leveled his pistol. His erratically spattering slugs checked the pursuit long enough for him to slide his captive through the wire and dive after her.

He made it, with a length to spare. And once in a dry creek bed, he was out of sight. The customs guards on both sides, now aroused by the riot, would effectively block any pursuit.

Flint gagged his prisoner with a strip of his shirt, snapped a pair of handcuffs about her ankles, and left her where the dirt road dipped into the arroyo. That done, he dashed back to get his parked car.

FORTY-FIVE minutes later, Flint pulled up at the police station with his captive; but a patrol car had arrived just ahead of him. Two men in uniform were dragging a Mexican out of the wagon and carrying him to the desk. He was far beyond walking under his own power — dead drunk.

McDonald, still on the job, watched them search the prisoner.

"What have you got there?" Flint greeted.

"Too much *sotol*," explained a patrolman. "Making a good job of ganging up on the town and then it paralyzed him."

"Miguel Smith's the name," announced the other patrolman, digging a crumpled letter, a handful of change, and a pint bottle from the half-breed's pockets.

"You'll like it here," Flint jibed as he saw Valencia's perceptible *moué.* "Better change your mind and talk."

"At that, it's better than your company!" she flared.

Finally they booked Valencia on suspicion.

"Last chance," Flint reminded her.

But the slam of the cell door drowned her retort. Flint turned to McDonald and gave his account of the raid.

"If I knew when she got here from 'Frisco," Flint concluded, "I might dope out how she figures in this jam. But —"

"I've already covered that," interrupted McDonald. "We've been checking up the trains, bus stations, and airport while you were in San Cristobal. Just to find out how much more of Chinatown traveled south.

"A girl checking up with Valencia's description landed at the airport about one A. M. — about four hours after the riot broke out in 'Frisco. Her car was waiting. She'd parked it there when she flew north a couple days ago. And the inspector at San Cristobal says she didn't cross the line until nearly three A. M."

"That leaves an hour or so unaccounted for," Flint said. "If there's anything to Guevara's suspicions, she must have a number two boyfriend in Yuma — which might account for the missing hour."

"You mean Kane?"

"She might have found him dead," admitted Flint. "Valencia and Guevara didn't even pretend to be surprised when I sprung it on them. But neither of them seemed to know that that deadpan Chinaman was prowling around in San Cristobal. Guevara's startled look is what saved my hide, and —"

"But where does that lead you?" frowned McDonald.

"First the Chinaman was at Kane's place," explained Flint. "Then he pops up in Mexico, in her shack. As though he was checking up on Valencia and Guevara in connection with Kane's death. It's a cinch he couldn't have known I was going to be there."

McDonald conceded the significance of the mysterious lurker. Then, as Flint reached for his hat: "Calling it a day?"

"Hell, no! I'm going back to Kane's place. Guevara's gag about Kane being at his desk and reaching for a phone is so damn impossible that there must be something in it."

TEN minutes later Flint arrived at Kane's study. Drawer by drawer he examined the desk but found no hidden compartments. There were no dummy books in the cases; and after over an hour of thumping and measuring, he was convinced that the walls were solid. No chance of a concealed instrument.

The blank-faced Chinaman could have removed the desk blotter Guevara had mentioned, but he certainly could not have made away with an extension set.

From the living room came the tinkle of the telephone. Flint hastened to the front. McDonald was on the wire.

"Your prisoner checked out."

"What?"

"Yes. A bar sawed through. Miguel Smith — the bird we thought was paralyzed — is gone, too."

Flint swore. Valencia's disappearance confirmed his hunch as to her importance in the tangle.

"Why the hell call to tell me that?"

"So you won't be caught off guard," explained McDonald. "Remember, *that fake drunk was picked up before you brought Valencia to the station*. That deadpan Chink worked fast to have her sprung."

"What luck you having?"

"Just like yours!" growled Flint and slammed the receiver.

He turned to Kane's study to think it out. He finally shook his head, slumped back in the swivelchair, and swung away from the desk. His gesture of disgust ended in a jerk. There was something odd about the finish of that little patch of baseboard between the ends of the two book cases along the left wall. A squarish blot showed beneath the varnish.

In an instant he was on his knees. A fixture had been removed from the baseboard of the lath-and-plaster partition that now subdivided the original rooms of the old adobe into a more modern arrangement.

Then he found puttied screw holes, and one through which wires could have been run.

Flint dashed to the front. Flashlight in hand, he skirted the adobe. He traced the wires of the telephone still in service. There was no sign of tampering.

A trip to the cellar gave him the next lead.

Wedged in between the original dirt floor of the house and the wooden floor that had been installed in modernizing it he found three dry cells with wires that rose to the wooden floor above. They led to the left wall of the study. Then he distinguished, further back, almost beyond the reach of his flashlight beam, a weatherproof cable which, leaving that same partition, sank at an easy angle into the thick foundation of sun-baked bricks.

No doubt that that was what remained of a telephone set up: a private, local circuit of the kind used between the apartments of a building, or between house and garage.

He now understood the removal of the telephone. It had been a connecting link between Kane's study and the chief of the opium smuggling ring.

The Silver Dragon could not be far away; three dry cells would not carry for more than two thousand feet. Flint returned to the surface. He circled the house, inch by inch, scrutinizing the hard packed earth. Whoever had buried that line could not at the time have anticipated the necessity of removing it to block an investigation; and Kane's residence at the *adobe* had not been long enough for time to conceal the trench.

Yet the flashlight glow revealed not a trace.

Flint's jaw set stubbornly. You can't bury a cable without leaving a trace. The damn thing was there. It must lead to the Silver Dragon.

Then a white blot in the gloom at the edge of the grove caught his eye. It was the concrete lip of the underground irrigation tiles that honeycombed the citrus grove. Far down the dusky aisle his flash beam picked up another outlet that once had gushed an eight inch stream of water. "Got it!"

Flint bounded toward the nearest outlet. But the tongue of light he flashed down the tube touched only a bare bottom.

He looked again. The wall of the vertical riser had been pierced near the bottom. An obliquely drilled hole, not a trench, had led the line to the long unused aqueduct. Whoever had cut and pulled the cable could not have foreseen that Ramon Guevara's efforts to clear himself would uncover the trick.

"North — toward Alvarez's place," muttered Flint as he regained his feet.

Flint set out on foot for Alvarez's house. Despite the hour, the lights were on. The doctor himself came to the door. His greeting was suave, but his dark eyes expressed his unspoken query.

"Sorry to bother you, doctor," beamed Flint as he crossed the threshold, "but I'd like to use your phone. Yeah, I've been switched to the Kane case. The company disconnected the wire next door."

"A pleasure to oblige you," assured Alvarez.

Flint followed him through a vestibule and into an ornately furnished living room. A cigarette was fuming from the edge of a smoking stand at the arm of a chair just in front of an all-wave radio.

"In the next room, Mr. Flint," directed Alvarez. But Flint's pause had been long enough for him to note that the radio dial was set for police wave lengths.

On the mahogany desk of the doctor's residence office was a single telephone. Flint had not expected to find two; but his stall would give him a chance to look for the marks left by a recently removed instrument.

"Make yourself at home," Alvarez continued. "There's a directory — and let me give you some more light."

As he spoke, he stepped forward to reach for the chain of the desk lamp. It blazed to life. Flint, picking the telephone handset from its cradle, saw the doctor pluck an oversize fountain pen from the blotting pad.

Too late, he caught the meaning of the left handed gesture. A blinding, choking jet of vapor hissed from the black cylinder. Tear gas.

Something had warned Alvarez.

Before Flint could reach for his pistol, an uncontrollable cough and a devastating sneeze racked his entire body. He could not force his hand to his weapon. The involuntary catch of breath that followed drew in a gulp of the hissing vapor.

It was more than tear gas. It was a searing and corrosive narcotic. His head was already spinning, and his legs were sagging. One more gulp of that deadly vapor and he would be out. For an age-long instant, he fought the spasm that would have drawn in the finishing breath of the drugging mixture. He flung himself aside — anything to get clear of that hissing poison.

As he plunged out of that venomous cloud, a racking sneeze jerked every fiber of his body. Somehow, he forced his hand to his pistol butt. The effort was wasted. Before the weapon cleared the holster, an attack from his right knocked him from his feet.

A curved knife, and a blank, yellow face identified Alvarez's ally. There would be no betraying pistol fire to make the execution conspicuous.

The blade swept down. But that last inhalation of diluted gas stirred Flint's muscles to a spasm that no conscious effort could have equaled. The descending point nailed his arm instead of sinking hilt-deep into his chest. The shock of that biting steel prodded his whirling senses.

The knife rose again — but Flint's free hand jerked his pistol clear.

The blast was muffled by the yellow flesh it riddled. The Chinaman jerked back, then slumped forward. His wild thrust stabbed the floor. His dead weight pinioned Flint.

Flinging aside the now emptied gas tube, Alvarez closed in before Flint could extricate himself or disengage his pistol. The doctor knocked the weapon from his hand, but as they grappled, the concentration of oily fumes thinned into an agonizing mist that leveled off the odds.

The office became a hazy nightmare. Tear-blinded, sneezing, gasping, racked by coughs and seared by lung-corroding gulps of tainted air, they rolled and kicked and slugged.

Flint, almost overwhelmed during those first instants, saw red spots dance before his eyes, and steel-bright flashes that became raking cuts. The doctor must have seized the Chinaman's knife. He was no longer certain, but that warm flood that ran down his ribs and legs must be blood.

Voice in that murderous maze — Alvarez yelling — and then a droning, dry voice, like pebbles rattling in a gourd.

"Calling all cars! Miguel Smith — Mexican Mike — wanted for the murder of Ramon Guevara — heading for Telegraph Pass in a blue sedan. . . ."

McDonald broadcasting to the prowl cars and highway patrol. Miguel Smith — engineered Valencia's jailbreak and —

Another slash. That one didn't hurt. Nothing hurt. He found a man's throat and hung on. His fingers were weakening. So was Alvarez. Maybe his teeth would do the trick — got to get a look at that Chink's blank face.

Then a shriek. A low, tigerish feminine cry vibrant with wrath.

Some woman was helping Alvarez. But another stab wouldn't hurt. Let her help —

He felt Alvarez's sagging muscles perk taut and become iron. Flint lost his grip. Then he heard a strangled, gurgling cry. As he struggled to regain his hold, the doctor slumped to the floor, still clutching a knife.

WHAT followed was a hazy confusion seen through streaming eyes. Flint crawled toward the droning radio. A woman was weeping with rage and grief.

And as Flint gulped in clean air, he saw her lying in a huddled heap on the divan near the radio. A dripping stiletto was clenched in her red hand.

Valencia.

Flint slowly began to understand why she had not stabbed him. It wasn't a mistake, knifing the doctor.

"Yes. I came to help him, that dirty —" The next few words choked her. "Then I heard that police call. Miguel was one of Alvarez's crowd. Got me out of jail and brought me here. So I knew that Alvarez had tricked Ramon back across the line to give him the works."

"Afraid that Ramon Guevara might be tripped up and spill some beans?"

"Maybe," said Valencia. "But mainly jealousy. That rat over there probably told him how Ramon and I stood. I didn't care for Alvarez. And I don't care what you do with me. Ramon's dead."

"How'd he fit into things?"

"He smuggled the stuff across the line to Kane's place, concealed in loads of vegetables and firewood."

The arrangement was characteristic. Guevara, Kane, and Robles ran the risks of actual handling. Alvarez supervised by remote control. And Valencia, when not in Mexico, maintained contact with Yut Lee in San Francisco.

Then Flint remembered the blank-faced Chinaman. He turned back to the office, flung open a window, and as the lingering fumes thinned, he knelt beside the Asiatic hoodoo. A moment's intent scrutiny explained the facial immobility — a snugly fitting, lifelike rubber mask.

He jerked it clear, exposing the face of lean, grizzled Yut Lee — the Silver Dragon, who had come to Yuma to take charge.

"Who killed Kane?" Flint demanded.

She gestured toward Alvarez.

"He's got forty tins of Silver Dragon. He never kept the stuff in his house before. Figure it out yourself."

And that did not take long. Flint remembered the two bowls of chili and began to see their possibilities. He stepped to the telephone and called McDonald.

"I've got it, Mac." Then, after covering his discovery of the private wire, he continued, "Alvarez killed Kane after Valencia arrived from 'Frisco. . . . I don't give a damn about the autopsy. Suppose Alvarez dropped in to see Kane about two A.M. to talk shop and have some coffee and a plate of home-made chili. Then knife Kane.

"The autopsy would show he died shortly after eating. And with everyone taking it for granted Kane always ate around six, the alibi was holeproof.

"Why kill Kane? Nobody could be sure Robles died in 'Frisco before he had a chance to mutter anything while coming out of the ether. Knifing Kane and leaving ten cans of hop for us to find would make us think we had cleaned up the mob. And it would have worked if Guevara hadn't tried to prove he didn't kill Kane."

And then McDonald wondered why Yut Lee had not used his first chance to dispose of Flint.

"Simple, Mac. Bum play, blotting me out before he had a chance to find out just how much the D.J. really did know. Having Alvarez drop in was like getting a ringside seat."

He listened a moment, and as McDonald's voice burred over the wire, Flint eyed Valencia. Finally he answered: "The girl got away during the riot. We've got nothing on her. She was never caught smuggling hop anyway. The Silver Dragon is cold meat."

# DRINK OR DRAW

WEARINESS made Simon Bolivar Grimes' coffin-shaped face seem longer than ever. Spitting alkali dust, he muttered, "Another dang sign, DRINK RED QUILL BOURBON. Gosh, I wisht I was a hoss, they don't git thirsty for nothing but water."

Mile after mile along the wagon trail to Stinking Springs, Red Quill billboards had tantalized him by suggesting a bar, a free lunch counter, hard likker, and cool beer.

Some distance ahead, a freight wagon lumbered along. Instinctively, the kid from Georgia had sized up the country, a habit which had often kept him from being bushwhacked, and thus he noted a twinkle in the clump of post oak at the crest of a knoll. It was as though binoculars mirrored the blazing sun. Someone was spying on travelers.

The Stinking Springs region was the orneriest in Texas. Simon had a poke of gold pieces, the proceeds of the sale of some cow critters. If he were robbed, Uncle Jason would whale him with a wagon spoke; he'd claim that Grimes had spent the money on women and liquor.

"Dunno what in tunket else a man'd spend money for," Grimes grumbled as he pulled over to the whiskey sign.

Though the country was too open for ambush, nevertheless he wanted a look-see, so he peered through a knothole. "Ain't noticed me, they're still studying the wagon," he decided as the flickering continued.

He had brought Uncle Jason's binoculars in his saddle bags. Grimes had barely focused the powerful glasses for a bit of counter-espionage when two riders came pelting out of the clump of post oak, their guns blazing.

The wagon pulled up. The men dismounted. They tore into the tarpaulin at the back, exposing a cargo of barrels. A sharp faced man came toward them from the wagon. He was unarmed, and he made gestures, as if begging them to be reasonable.

One of the raiders smacked him with a pistol barrel, knocking him down.

The taller of the pair, who had a brace and bitt, began drilling at the keg. By now Grimes had read the lettering on the head: OLD VICKERY BOURBON, NELSON COUNTY, KENTUCKY.

Then a girl, apparently having remained on the driver's seat until indignation overcame her alarm, came racing toward the tail gate. She was blond, golden blond like a palomino filly. She bounded toward the man with the brace and bitt, and caught his arm.

He spat, grinned, thrust her aside. She recovered and smacked him. The other yanked her away; she tripped, landing asprawl in a puddle of whiskey. Liquor drenched her blouse and skirt.

Whatever was behind this insane business of letting whiskey run into the dust, Grimes decided that when people began slapping old men and girls, it was time to investigate. He mounted up and raced for the wagon. And then came the final horror: one of the ruffians touched a match to the whiskey, and flames began to lick the tarpaulin.

At the sound of his approach, the two whirled about, but seeing just one rider, they hooked their thumbs on their belts and waited. And when Grimes dismounted, they began to grin.

He looked as if he were about to fall over his own feet. Tall, gangling, with a straw colored cowlick reaching down to his china-blue eye, he did not look any too bright.

"What in tarnation you mean, burning good liquor?" he demanded. "And mauling that there lady?"

They chuckled tolerantly. The one with the brace and bitt explained, "Ain't allowed to haul nothing into Stinking Springs but Red Quill, bub. That's Colonel Delevan's orders. And we carry them out."

The other was rolling a smoke, and his amusement at Grimes was competing with his interest in the blonde, who wept in futile fury as she straightened her drenched garments. The old man, still dazed, was struggling to his feet. And all this was too much for Grimes.

"Hist 'em!" he commanded and went for his guns.

The man with the brace and bitt yelled, The other dropped his Durham and slapped leather. He was quick, but his Colt had not half cleared the holster when Grimes drilled him between the eyes.

Though the man with the brace and bitt made good time, his first shot went wild; and then, shifting, Grimes sprayed him with lead. He jerked one more shot, kicking up rocks. He lurched, fell across his gun.

The girl's scream made Grimes whirl: "Oh, they hit dad!"

The old man was clutching his side. "Ain't nothing, Melba, never you mind me, you help this young feller put out the fire."

Then he sat down.

SO GRIMES and Melba got blankets and whipped out the flames. That done, she gave him strips torn from her skirt, so that he could stop the flow of whiskey while he whittled plugs.

The old freighter said, "I'm mighty grateful, son. I'm Amos Hanford, and this here is my daughter, Melba. Baby, you get the jug for this gent, don't you fuss with me, I ain't more'n scratched."

Grimes started to protest, but Hanford's glance silenced him. As the girl hurried to the front of the wagon, the freighter said, "I don't feel none too spry, but it's no use scaring her. I can turn around and go back to Cold Deck instead of trying to get to a doctor in Stinking Springs; I'd probably get murdered there."

"Not if I go with you," Grimes countered.

"Bub, I never seen a draw like yourn and never heard of any like it," Hanford countered. "Fust one gets it betwixt the eyes, and the second musta had most of his heart shot out with them three slugs. But whilst you're watching me, who'd watch the whiskey?"

"Gosh, that's right," Grimes agreed.

Melba came back with the jug. Grimes hoisted a long one. "Is this here what you got in them kegs?"

"It is. You have jest drunk OLD VICKERY," Hanford said proudly. "The finest bourbon made at Bourbon Springs, Kentucky, ever since 1833. Drink up, suh!"

Grimes hoisted another. Melba, who had impulsively put an arm around his shoulders, became more beautiful than ever. Her voice sounded like angels playing harps, and even the landscape was no longer repulsive. "This is sure larruping whiskey," Grimes said, and wiped his lips. "Anywhere but a downright warped and perverted town, it'd be welcomed with —"

And then, he saw that Hanford had fooled him as well as Melba. Grimes caught the old man just in time. "Honey, it looks like that chaw of tobacco he stuffed into that wound ain't plugging it enough."

"Oh, why did you have to start shooting?" she cried, panic again gripping her. "I'd rather lose all the liquor in the world —"

Grimes tipped the jug and gave Hanford a swig.

"M'am, they was banging away at me, and it is downright unreasonable, blaming me for someone else's bad shooting. If you can prod them oxen, I'll make your pappy comfortable and do what I can."

"Oh, what can *you* do?"

"He's jest weak, he'll come outen it. And as soon as your pappy's took care of, I'm going to run Red Quill and Colonel Delevan out of that ornery town, and when I'm through, they'll be drinking Old Vickery in every bar in Stinking Springs."

"Baby," Hanford said to his daughter, "I'm all right, and Simon looks like the man that can do it."

## CHAPTER II
### *Recipe 309*

STINKING SPRINGS got its name from the hot sulphur spring which made the air reek with a rotten-egg bouquet; and the town itself, a sprawl of frame shacks and adobes centering about a plaza, looked pretty much like it smelled. Grimes dismounted at the Cozy Corner Saloon, which was between the Eldorado Hotel and Wing Lee's Restaurant.

Bellying up to the bar, he called for whiskey. The sour-faced barkeep set out a bottle of Red Quill. The stuff made Grimes choke and cough. "Gosh, this here tastes like soldering acid and sheep dip, ain't you got any good liquor?"

"Son," the professor retorted, "there ain't no other kind sold in this man's town. Lookee here, bad liquor makes you shiver like a dog swallering peach seeds; this here just sort of chokes you a bit."

The half dozen cowpokes who were watching looked as if this was an old and amusing story to them. One said, "Stranger, it ain't no use belly-aching about Red Quill. Mrs. Hopkins, she's a widow-woman, and the daughter of the Injun fighter that saved the hull dang settlement from the Comanches, and all she's got to live on is dividends from Red Quill shares, and there ain't a man in town low enough to drink any other kind of likker."

This was bad. While one might outpoint Colonel Delevan, the widowed daughter of a local hero was something else. Grimes bought a round for the house and went out, muttering, "Hell, they are all heroes in this town, I'd ruther fight a passel of Comanches than a bottle of that rotgut." Once on the boardwalk, he decided to head for Wing Lee's; the only civilized person in Stinking Springs would be the Chinaman. And then he saw that even this ornery town had its good points.

A redheaded girl was stepping out of Lem Bigg's General Store with an armful of packages cuddled against her bosom. She was an exquisite creature, slim-legged as a race horse; she wore silk stockings and store clothes. The group of small boys who sat on the curbing playing stud poker and chewing tobacco quit their game and stopped cursing. They chorused, "Evening, Mis' Hopkins."

The smile and voice which acknowledged the greeting were smooth and lovely, and as heartwarming as Old Vickery. For a moment, Grimes forgot that Doreen Hopkins, the Red Quill heiress, was a stumbling block in the pathway of good liquor.

She tick-tacked along on high heels which flattered her trim ankles, but a knothole in the tricky boardwalk played the devil with her alluring footgear. She snagged a heel. Her stride broke, and her ankle twisted.

Grimes lunged. Eggs poured from one of the paper bags, but he got an armful of the widow, and managed to keep her clear of the uncooked omelette and coffee on the boards.

Regretfully, he let her slide to her feet as he straightened up. Then, as she clung to him for a moment to steady herself, he asked, "You ain't sprained your ankle, I hope?"

"Thanks, no!" After the full impact of dazzling smile and greenish gray eyes, he helped her salvage the groceries and stow them in the rubber-tired buggy. Doreen waved, smiled, drove down the dusty street. No dang wonder that Colonel Delevan was looking out for her interests!

Grimes stepped into Wing Lee's restaurant, ordered a steak, six eggs, and a slab of apple pie, and settled down to studying it out. Finally he asked, "Wing, can you get me a couple empty whiskey bottles with the labels washed off?"

"Catchee quick," the pigtailed proprietor said, and shuffled to the rear.

DARKNESS had fallen. After wiping the egg from his chin, Grimes went to the hitching rack, and got his jug. Then, back in the restaurant, he said, "Look here, folks tell me that all Chinamen are honest fellows."

"Thass light, Clistian Chinaman, watchee want now?"

Grimes stepped into the kitchen. As he filled the bottles, whose Red Quill labels had been soaked off, he said, "You keep what's left in the jug, don't tell no one, and I'll give you five bucks."

186 ඏ E. HOFFMANN PRICE

"My savvee plenty, Missee Glime. Allee-time, lynch whiskey sell-man, allee time thlow blicks in my window. Town no damn good."

Wing chuckled gleefully. Grimes demanded, "What in tunket is so funny about getting bricks flung through your window?"

"I gettee even, I spit in coffee."

"Someone oughta spit in their whiskey. Wing, have a drink."

He offered one of the quarts. The Chinaman poured a shot into a tiny teacup, and downed it. "Vellee nice. You take dlink, Missee Glime. *Ng ka pay*, China whiskey."

He dug out a stone jug and poured a shot of reddish and syrupy liquor. The stuff tasted like kerosene and orange shellac. It was almost as bad as Red Quill. But Grimes, having met the only civilized man in Stinking Springs, downed it and said, "Mighty good."

Wing wagged his head. "You velly nice man. Evly-one else thlowee locks when I give *Ng ka pay*."

"How long ago was this?"

"Mebbe-so five, ten yeah."

That was odd. Today, they drank something worse and didn't even blink.

"Wing, who hauls whiskey to town? Where do they keep it? Who dishes it out to the saloons?"

"Wagon tlain bling-ee Led Quill. Keep-ee in big house by jail. Ev-ly-body catch-ee whiskey flom Colonel Delevan."

"How about Mrs. Hopkins?"

"Velly nice lady. Colonel Delevan fix-ee all business, him savvee plenty."

Grimes went back to the Cozy Corner Saloon, after taking his horse to the livery stable. The same bunch of cowpunchers were playing poker in the corner. They dropped their cards, and eyed him as he went to the bar.

Grimes said, "Belly up, gents! I'm buying!"

There was a whoop and a jingle of spurs. The sour-faced professor set out glasses and Red Quill.

Grimes pulled a quart from his hip pocket. "Gents," he said, and slapped a gold piece on the bar, "I'm buying the local likker. Only, I am gal-danged if I can drink the stuff, try some of this."

He filled the glasses with Old Vickery.

The cowpunchers blinked, eyed each other; one said, "Stranger, you're violating a local ordinance, Colonel Delevan had the mayor pass a law agin foreign liquor."

"Ain't I paid for Red Quill? Ain't I doing right by the widder-woman?"

"Pardner, that's gospel."

They thrust out their grimy paws to grab the glasses.

The swinging doors slammed open. A stern voice shook the house: "Drop that, right now!"

Two men had entered. The foremost wore a star. He had a sawed off shotgun leveled at the group. The man beside him was tall, distinguished; slouch hat, frock coat, a pique vest, and flowing tie; drooping mustaches, and a neatly trimmed beard, an Imperial, perfectly tailored. And just for emphasis, he had a Colt .45 pointed at Grimes. He looked as if he could shoot.

Grimes demanded, "What's this, suh, breaking into some sociable drinking?"

"I am Colonel Delevan," the man in the frock coat answered. "And my companion with the shotgun is Mr. Frost, the marshal. Selling liquor — without a license —"

"I am giving it away."

The colonel fingered his silky beard. "Ha! That also is in violation of a city ordinance. Giving or selling, or causing to be given away or sold, without first having it tested for wholesomeness and purity, is a violation of the law. Mr. Frost, be pleased to seize the evidence. Young man —"

Grimes shouted, "This here is good whiskey, the finest dang whiskey I ever drunk, that Red Quill is sheepdip, it's poison, it ain't fit for human consumption!"

"If you were not a beardless boy," the colonel retorted, "I would challenge you to a duel. Mrs. Hopkins, the daughter of a local hero, sponsors Red Quill."

Mr. Frost seized the bottle of Old Vickery. Grimes saw no chance of shooting it out; and as Amos Hanford had observed, shooting a customer doesn't improve sales.

LATE that night, Grimes decided to get to the bottom of things. If everything else failed, he'd set the Red Quill warehouse afire.

"Arson," he told himself, "is genrully agin' the law, but this here is an extenuating circumstance, every time you take a drink of that stuff, it's committing arson on your gizzard."

Wing's description made it easy for him to find the warehouse. The place was of adobe, thick walled, with small windows high up and barred. Ceiling beams projected far out and supported the eaves whose overhang kept the rains from cutting into the adobe. Grimes had brought his lariat; it was simple enough, roping the end of a ceiling beam. Then, in the gloom at the rear of the adobe, he went up, hand over hand, and in a moment, he was on the roof.

As he had expected, this was of clay tamped over bundles of cotton-wood saplings which had been laid athwart the massive ceiling beams. Such a roof, unless constantly maintained, deteriorates, and this one had been neglected; thus Grimes had less work than he had anticipated. He found a patch of bare saplings and very quickly worked them right and left, until he could, being lean and lanky, wriggle through.

His lariat, let down into the whiskey-scented darkness, was as good as a portable stairway. In a moment, Grimes was down in the stockroom.

He struck a match, lighted a candle stump, and with hat and bandanna, shaded the flame. Along the wall furthest from the door was a row of barrels which were marked "proof spirits." On a table was a plane, some paint, and a stencil which read, "RED QUILL BOURBON." There were several empties, freshly stenciled. But what most interested Grimes was the cabinet in the corner.

There he found a bucket of stewed prunes, some one-pound plugs of chewing tobacco, and a jug of wine vinegar. Also, there was a pail of beef blood. Hanging from a nail was a paper bound book entitled, AMERICAN BARTENDER'S GUIDE. A glance at this last item confirmed his suspicions; he read, "To one hundred gallons of proof spirit, add four ounces of pear oil, two ounces of pelargonic ether, thirteen drachms oil of wintergreen, and one gallon of wine vinegar; color with burnt sugar."

But what prodded Grimes to a high fury was *"Recipe 309; Bead for Liquor. For every ten gallons of spirit, add forty drops sulphuric acid and sixty drops of olive oil previously mixed in a glass vessel."*

"There ain't no Red Quill Distillery," he said to himself. "There ain't any likker hauled to Stinking Springs. That sculpin makes it right here, outen chemicals and acids."

Such being the case, how could the daughter of a local hero be dependent on dividends from Red Quill shares? Instead of setting the warehouse afire, it would be far better to expose the fraud and drive Red Quill forever from the market.

## CHAPTER III
### *A Risk To Be Taken*

THERE was a lot of excitement in Stinking Springs when two horses came into town without riders. Grimes, going from bar to bar, drank Red Quill and listened to the news. Dusty and Pecos, gunslingers protecting the whiskey market, had heard that a rash freighter was heading for Stinking Springs, and they had gone to meet him.

And now this.

Most of the population galloped out to investigate. They found, after chasing away the buzzards, enough odds and ends to identify beyond any doubt the remains of Dusty and Pecos.

Thereafter, when Colonel Delevan appeared in public, he had Buckshot Frost at his heels. Grimes, barging into a saloon, caught a snatch of conversation: "That long lanky galoot that don't look like he had sense enough to come in outen the rain. . . ."

Silence. Dripping silence. Then the boys began whooping it up again. They could not believe that he had cut down the two gunslingers, and yet, there was something odd about it all. So Grimes began to catwalk about town. People were wondering about his protests on the whiskey question.

Stinking Springs got another sensation when a shapely blonde came driving down the main street in a rattling buggy. She looked sweet and helpless. Her somber mourning accented the pallor of her face and the pale gilt of her lovely hair. Grimes, sitting with the hotel lobby wall at his back, heard her say to the cowpoke who carried her carpetbag, "Thank you so much! Never mind the things in the buggy, it's just a sewing machine, would you mind taking the rig to the livery stable?"

She signed the register. Then, to the clerk, "Oh, what is that *horrible* smell?"

Grimes chimed in, "M'am, that there is Red Quill Bourbon."

The girl was Melba Hanford. Her dainty nose rose a degree or two, and she sniffed. The clerk said, "M'am, that there is the hot sulphur spring, it ain't bad when you get used to it."

THE HOURS dragged. Grimes watched Melba come down the stairs and sweep past him, head high. He watched her return from the restaurant. He heard the muttered speculations of the cowpunchers who lounged on the board walk.

"Widder-woman . . . Sure looks like a lady . . . proud as a queen . . . hell no, she ain't fixing to work in the dance hall, not that gal . . ."

THAT night, Grimes went to bed with his boots on. But the real novelty was that he did not sleep. He was on edge, alert, and at the first faint scratch at the panel, he was on his feet. Just for luck, he had a gun ready.

Melba edged in when he opened the door. "Simon, it's the craziest thing, I nearly died when I came to town, with everyone eyeing me."

"How's your pappy?"

"He'll pull through, though I hated to leave him. What have you found out?"

Once Melba had found the settee in the darkness, he seated himself on the floor at her feet. "Honey, it's thissaway —"

He told her everything and concluded, "The hull dang town's against us. I'd figgered a gal like you might have a chance pertending you was a orphan or widder, but that there Doreen Hopkins is mighty purty for a old woman dang nigh thirty; these jaspers worship the ground she walks on, account her pappy, and I jest don't know what to do next."

"You mean, if you did prove that Red Quill is just chemicals and acids, you'd be casting reflections on a hero's daughter, and that would not help us?"

"Correct, honey." Grimes sighed gustily. "But there's sumthin' salty about it all. That Mis' Hopkins looks like a honest woman. She don't look like the kind that'd have cowpunchers drinking sheep dip and soldering acid and sechlike. This here Red Quill musta once been fitten to drink, account they nearly lynched Wing Lee for offering them *ng ka pay* on Chinese New Year.

"And this Colonel Delevan, you call on him, tearfullike, and whilst he's listening to you sobbing, I'll sort of make a *pasear* around the house, he's a bachelor."

THE following evening, Grimes lurked in the shelter of a weeping willow until Melba drove up to Colonel Delevan's big white house. He came from cover when the colonel went to admit his lovely visitor.

"Good evening, m'am. What is your pleasure, Miss Hanford? You had scarcely arrived in town when I took the liberty of ah . . . inquiring at the hotel."

"You're very kind, colonel. I hardly know where to begin —

Grimes crept to the window. Delevan was stamping down the hallway and bawling, "You, Tomas! Paca! Where are you?"

The only answer was echoes; then, returning, he said to Melba, "I had hoped to have one of the servants offer you refreshments, m'am, but the scoundrels have, so to speak, folded their tents like the Arabs. But I make a very tolerable mint julep."

Grimes grinned. Delevan had merely made a loud show of assuring Melba that they could have a cozy chat. And when he went to the rear to prepare juleps, Grimes tapped gently at the window, and whispered, "Do your best, and if he gits familiar, I'll pistol-whip him."

Delevan lost surprisingly little time in coming back with a silver bowl and tall glasses.

Melba said, hesitantly, "Colonel, I hope I don't seem rude, but I don't drink strong liquor. I might take a sip of Madeira, though I really shouldn't —" She dabbed her eyes with a lace edged handkerchief. "Not so soon — after — poor father's death."

As he poured Bourbon and added sprigs of mint to garnish his tall glass, Delevan said solicitously, "M'am, it was all too evident from your mourning — ahem, if you'll forgive my saying so, it is most becoming — you remind me of the late Mrs. Delevan, when her distinguished father passed away."

He sighed gustily. "I am a very lonesome man and have been for many years now. Pray accept my heartfelt sympathy, m'am, for I also have been bereaved."

The man was magnetic. Grimes' trigger finger began to itch. He said to himself, "That goat-bearded sculp-in's got a routine for widder-women and orphans, I 'low he ain't ever asked Mis' Hopkins to marry him, not with them notions for preying on bereaved gals."

The colonel was on the sofa beside Melba. He barely touched her further shoulder with his fingertips; he was waiting for her grief to get out of control before he offered consolation.

"You're so kind, colonel. I almost hate to bring up a matter of business —"

"Consider me your servant, m'am."

"It's about — *whiskey*."

"Whiskey, m'am?"

The lovely blonde head inclined in a nod. "My poor father, practically ruined by railroad competition, was freighting a number of barrels of OLD VICKERY BOURBON into new territory, and — and —"

Her voice broke. He patted her shoulder. Melba went on, "Bandits — road agents — held us up. There were two of them — I begged him not to resist — but he fought like a lion — he killed them both — but his wounds — he succumbed, and here I am, trying to sell — that whiskey — and I've been told — that nothing but Red Quill is allowed in Stinking Springs.

"They gave me to understand, Colonel Delevan, that you are a stockholder in the Red Quill distillery, and that this ban on other liquors is to — well — protect your interests."

She eyed him reproachfully; but the colonel's glance did not waver. "M'am, I have been put into a false position. Pray let me convince you. The truth is, I am protecting the interests of a widow, the daughter of that gallant hero, the late Cyrus Barlow."

Melba rose. "Colonel Delevan, it is not gallant to put the blame on a widow!"

The colonel's face became red. "Madam, I have been put in a false light! I shall challenge the dastard who put me in such false light! Pray let me convince you."

The colonel stalked out, and in a moment came back with a tin box which he unlocked. He took from it various papers, and began, "M'am, this should convince you that years ago, as a gesture of gratitude, I conveyed to Mrs. Hopkins' gallant father every share of my Red Quill whiskey stock."

"I know so little about business —" Melba wavered, her knees buckled; she would have fallen had he not caught her. "Oh — I'm sorry — I'm dizzy — I think I'm about to faint —"

The colonel scooped her up in his arms. "Let me make you comfortable in the late Mrs. Delevan's room — there are some smelling salts —"

Melba protested feebly, but the masterful colonel insisted that nothing was too much trouble. And he had barely started up the stairs when Grimes tiptoed into the living room.

Melba's voice filtered down from the upper darkness: "Oh, colonel,

I'm so confused and worried and lonely . . . I don't know whom to believe . . . I'll be all right in a moment —"

Grimes scooped up the papers. The first one seemed to bear out Delevan's contention, but as he riffled his way through the file, Grimes found a letter of earlier date, on the stationery of the Red Quill Distilleries. The colonel's thousand shares were to be assessed $5 each, and in return he would get one thousand new shares. Grimes muttered, "Participating perferred, gosh it sounds worsen the time Uncle Jason got hornswoggled outen that mine in Arizony."

Another paper: a notice of bankruptcy, dated a year after the assessment. Grimes, listening to the murmuring upstairs, was assured that Melba was holding her own. Delevan, while a scheming scoundrel, was in his own way a gentleman. And so Grimes hurried out to make a move which neither he nor Melba had planned.

There wasn't and there had not been any Red Quill whiskey for some years, except in Stinking Springs. Bit by bit, Delevan had cut the stock of Bourbon, so that the local cowpunchers had gradually become accustomed to rotgut bearing the label of a once drinkable brand. And he had used Doreen Hopkins as a front.

Exposing Doreen as a crook would be tough work. It might end in an all around shooting scrape which would not help the sale of Old Vickery. But Grimes had to risk it.

## CHAPTER IV

*Challenge!*

WHEN Doreen Hopkins came to the door, the lamplight put a flame-gold halo about her red hair; it played tricks with her white robe, which had been made out of an embroidered Chinese shawl.

"I rarely have visitors — if I'd been expecting you —"

"M'am, you look scrumptious thatta-way. And if you ain't too busy with your embroidering, I'd admire to talk business with you."

He thumped a buckskin poke of gold pieces into the heap of embroidery silk. "It's about your pappy's Red Quill shares. The Old Vickery Distillery craves to buy your interest and good will."

"It's paid such splendid dividends, I'd have to consult Colonel Delevan. He's advised me ever since father died."

"How many shares you got?"

She shrugged. "Good heaven, I don't know! But wait a moment."

When she returned, she had a thousand-share certificate made out in her father's name. The date was prior to the dates of the letters announcing the assessments. Grimes, scrutinizing the late hero's name, saw what only a keen eye could have noted: there had been an erasure, and *Cyrus Barlow* had been written, letters widely spaced, in the space once occupied by, as a good guess, *Worthington Delevan*.

"M'am, when'd you know your pappy had it?"

"Colonel Delevan found it among father's papers, after the estate was settled. I guess it hadn't paid dividends for some time, but soon after the colonel found it, I began getting checks, in my own name, he said he'd written the company that I'd inherited the stock."

Grimes picked up the poke of gold. "Thank you kindly, m'am, but that there certificate ain't wuth the paper it's printed on."

"How can you say that?" she flared up, "when the dividends have kept me in comfort? I'd never believed you to be a slicker, trying to cheat a widow out of her legacy, trying to tell me it's worthless, so I'd accept an absurd offer."

"Ma'am," he persisted, "there ain't no distillery, it's jest a fraud Colonel Delevan's worked up to palm off pizen likker on poor, honest cowpunchers, keeping good whiskey like Old Vickery out of town. I come here to see you account of a orphan lady whose pappy was shot down by gunslingers the colonel sent out to keep him from bringing honest Bourbon into Stinking Springs. If you got any conscience, let it guide you, m'am."

"You wait till I get dressed, I'll see if you dare repeat that statement to Colonel Delevan!"

That was just what Grimes wanted. Catching Colonel Delevan consoling Melba would drive a wedge into Doreen's trust and admiration. Hearing Melba's story of her father's death would finish the job.

"That there stock is wuthless," he repeated.

"It's been keeping me in comfort!"

"What you mean is, Colonel Delevan's been keeping you in comfort," Grimes retorted.

"You dare say such a thing!"

She slapped him, one-two-three. And as he recoiled before her stinging blows, he tried to amplify the statement she had interrupted. "M'am, what I meant —"

THEN the door slammed open. Colonel Delevan, with several peculiar and long scratches on his handsome face, stamped into the room. "I heard my name bandied about, and fortunately I did not enter until I heard the atrocious reflection you cast on Mrs. Hopkins! Please stand aside, m'am, do not sully your hands, I'll shoot him down like a dog!"

Grimes yelled, "Go for your guns when this lady's outen the way. Or keep your hands in sight whilst I tell you what I was aiming to say when she started slapping my teeth loose!"

"That vicious slander can't be explained! Doreen —"

Then Doreen, who now clung to Grimes with both arms, cried over her shoulder, "Colonel Delevan, I am surprised that you would want a gun fight in my house! Need I remind you of the light in which that would put me?"

Delevan bowed. "M'am, my indignation made me forget myself. Mr. Grimes, if you have any manhood left, you will not precipitate a shooting array in this house."

"I'm agreeable."

Flushed and breathless, Doreen broke away.

Grimes went on, "M'am, what I was starting to say wasn't a reflection on you, if'n I'd said all of it."

"Silence!" the colonel thundered. "My seconds will wait on you. We shall arrange this so that I can demand satisfaction, and without any slurs on a lady's name. Your remarks, made in several bars, casting aspersions on the integrity of Red Quill Bourbon, are ample cause. Good evening, sir."

ON HIS return to the hotel, Melba was waiting for Grimes in the doorway of her room. "I couldn't help it, darling," she said, "but I simply had to claw him crosseyed, the old reprobate!"

"And then he come over to the widder-woman's house, and we had words."

Melba's eyes narrowed. "Simon, someone has been clawing *your* face," she said coldly. "Am I to understand that you were making love to that middle-aged creature."

"Honey, when I kiss 'em, they don't kick and claw."

Melba rose. "You do take things for granted! I didn't claw or slap you, did I, which makes me — oh, get out! You and your fool ideas, putting me in such a humiliating position."

She flung herself face down on the sofa and began to sob. When he patted her hair, she cried, "Get out, or I'll scream!"

So he got.

HE WAS ready to shake the dust of Stinking Springs from his boots. "Every dang time I open my mouth, I put my foot in it," he muttered, and he stamped his way down the hall. "The gent that said silence is golden was speaking gospel."

After having risked his life in a gun fight, after having defied an entire town, he'd been misunderstood by the very girl he was trying to help. And with an impending challenge, he could not run out.

That challenge would settle everything. Smoking out the colonel would only confirm Doreen's grudge; Delevan's cronies would continue making Red Quill using the lovely widow as a front. One remark with an unintended double-meaning had killed his chance of appealing to the widow's better nature. Then he remembered the bottle of Old Vickery which the marshal had seized for testing. He went down the backstairs and down the alley.

Half an hour afterward, when he had finished the rounds of the saloons, he went to the jailhouse, where the turnkey asked, "What you looking for?"

"Back up, pappy! I know jest where to find what I want."

He walked to the door marked "Town Marshal" and kicked it open.

Frost jumped up. His sawed off shotgun was well out of reach. In one hand, he had the confiscated bottle, and judging from the level, he had been testing it.

"Marshal, that there's my likker, get your hooks offen it."

Frost went for his belt gun; but the gesture froze before it was half completed. He was looking into the muzzle of Grimes' .45, and it was entirely beyond his imagining how such a thing could have happened. His color changed, and he raised his hands.

"Bub," he stuttered, "that jest wasn't possible."

Grimes replaced the gun, and with a move little slower than his draw. "Marshal," he said softly, "what you seen don't prove I can hit anything when I come out smoking, does it?"

"I ain't craving proof. Lookee here; your name's Grimes?"

"I ain't denying it."

"I mean Simon Bolivar Grimes."

"I ain't saying I am, I ain't saying I ain't."

"Help yourself to the whiskey."

Grimes reached for the bottle. Edging about as a guard against surprises from the doorway, he took a quick snort. The gaping turnkey, who had seen the draw, made no effort at trickery.

"This here," Grimes said, as he lowered the quart, "ain't been tampered with. How you like it?"

"It's sorta nice."

"Get busy and drink."

The marshal took a shot.

"When I say drink, I mean, drink deep."

Another hefty one.

"Take more."

"Bub, Colonel Delevan told me to save him some."

"Drink or draw!"

*Gurgle-gurgle-gurgle.* Finally Frost said, still gulping, "Uh – um – I'll get plumb plastered, hogging it down thissaway, and I'm a lawman, it ain't right –"

"Come up," Grimes commanded, "with a drink or with a gun."

There was still an ounce left when the marshal fell forward on his face. Grimes handed the remainder to the turnkey. "Down it!" he commanded.

"I ain't a drinking man, I ain't touched a drop since –

"Since how long?"

"Nigh unto seven year. When I start, I jest can't stop, I dassent, so I took a pledge."

"You ain't teched a drop for seven years? *Drink up!*"

Tremblingly, the turnkey obeyed. He licked his lips. He hitched his pants. He cocked his hat at a rakish angle.

"You went and done it! Now I'm a-going on a bender, I'll be staying drunk for three-four weeks, and gosh, it's going to be fun!"

"How'd it taste?"

"Finest Bourbon I ever wrapped around my tonsils, and I been drinking, man and boy, for thirty year afore I took a pledge."

He headed for the door.

"Where you going?"

"Aiming to get dead-drunk quick as I can."

"You ain't going to like it, not if you ain't used to Red Quill," Grimes solemnly promised.

He went from bar to bar to size things up before he forced some group of cowpunchers to drink Old Vickery. This would be his revenge, and let the results be what they might; since Melba had turned against him, nothing mattered.

PRESENTLY, he stepped into a place just as the turnkey, already roaring and stuttering, staggered to the street. Grimes could feel a difference between the guarded looks which now searched him and the open stares of only an hour previous.

The turnkey, it seemed, had babbled between drinks. When the tin piano's jangle stopped, and the silence caught some speaker off guard, he heard, from a far corner, the voice of a man who had an instant earlier been talking against the jangling music: "— I'm betting he kilt Pecos and Dusty."

Two men marched in, shoulder to shoulder. Both were hard cases. Their eyes restlessly covered the entire saloon; though in home territory, instinct kept them on guard. One said, "Mr. Grimes, we are speaking direct to you for Colonel Delevan. Being as how you're a stranger, you ain't got seconds to repersent you."

"That's right, gents, I repersent myself."

The spokesman went on, "The colonel challenges you to a duel and wants to know whether you aim to fight, or get hoss-whipped outa town account of saying Red Quill ain't fit for man or beast."

Grimes set his quart bottle on the bar. "My compliments to Colonel Delevan, and say that I am tickled silly to fight. And is he game to let me pick the weapins?"

"On hoss or on foot, shooting or cutting. What style do you take?"

The whispered debates as to whether this was or was not the original Grimes had ceased. The answer seemed very loud: "Gents, tell the colonel that it'll be drink and shoot."

"What's that? You aiming to be funny?"

"That's up to the colonel. What I aim is a duel like Clay Allison fit with Wild Bill Hickok. I know the old marshal can explain."

"Drink-and-shoot," they muttered, still puzzled.

"Speaking of drinking," Grimes went on, "this here bottle is the only one in town with likker in it that's fitten to drink. Belly-up, gents."

"We ain't drinking with anyone that's insulted the — uh — tastes of Stinking Springs."

"You are drinking," Grimes asserted, "or I'll be taking my own answer to the colonel."

He held his hands well away from his sides. "Take your choice, gents, grab that bottle or slap leather."

The two exchanged a side glance. One said, "Slim, this fool is asking for trouble, and if we give it to him, there won't be anyone for the colonel to duel with."

SLIM went stubborn. He sidestepped toward the bar. "You suit yourself, Top Rail."

And Top Rail crossed from his pardner's right to get the bottle, passing in front of him. He was in no position to draw, and Slim was blocked. They had backed down, and they had covered themselves by saying that they had to save the victim for the colonel.

Or so it seemed to the cowpunchers in the corner, until guns blazed.

Slim, sidestepping from the bar as his pardner moved toward it, had drawn during the split second in which he was masked; but during that same shred of time, Grimes had gone for his .45s. They smoked and bucked as he advanced on the gun slicks.

Slim stumbled, tried to level his weapon again, but a third slug knocked him down. And Top Rail, whirling when he sensed that something had gone wrong with the whipsaw play, barely reached his holster.

His vest jerked three times from impacts before he doubled up and dropped in a heap against the brass rail.

Grimes turned in his cloud of smoke and faced the customers. "Gents, two agin one, and they aimed to whipsaw me. Anyone here see it any other way?" There was no answer. "Being as how Colonel Delevan's fust second and second second ain't talkin', I'd admire to have someone tell him we'll fight a drink-and-shoot duel, unless he's leaving town."

He picked up the bottle, took a swig, set it down. "That there is real Bourbon, it ain't Red Quill rotgut. Help yourselves, gents."

Then he went to Wing Lee's restaurant. Half-emptied plates showed how the sound of gunfire had cleared the counter. And Wing Lee's face showed that he was not surprised to see that Grimes, while waiting for half a dozen scrambled eggs, jacked expended cartridges first from one Colt, and then the other.

The Chinaman said, "You gettee flee glub, Missee Glime."

"Slim and Top Rail used to throw rocks at you?"

"You savvee plenty."

Grimes could not positively assume that the dueling colonel, unable to back down in issuing his challenge, had planned for his seconds to settle the matter, yet the whipsaw trick which the gun slicks had attempted did indicate that the turnkey's account of Grimes' dealing with the marshal had left its marks on the town.

Whether Melba deserved it or not, old man Hanford deserved a break. Grimes was going to make one final attempt to pave the way for honest whiskey in general, and Old Vickery in particular. He said to Wing, "I'm giving a barbecue the day of the duel. You fix everything. Exactly like I tell you."

"Me savvee plenty," the Chinaman answered, and Grimes settled down to explaining.

## CHAPTER V
### Doctored

FOR the next three days, Grimes camped on the open range. Some thought he was taking precautions against being bushwhacked before the duel; others, hearing the pistol blasts, checked up with field glasses, said that he was practicing his draw and popping the heads from quail and rattlesnakes.

But his campfire, each night, assured the curious town that he had not run out. And then Stinking Springs became interested in the Chinaman's preparation for a barbecue out in the plaza.

When Grimes rode back to town, Melba pushed her way through the crowd which lined one edge of the plaza, and ran to meet him as he dismounted.

"Simon," she cried, catching him with both arms. "I was worried to death, thinking you'd be dry-gulched."

"Honey," he answered, "I was purty sure they wouldn't, account they wanted to see a drink-and-shoot duel."

"But that fire!"

He whispered, "That there was so the Chinaman could find me."

The marshal advanced to the center of the plaza and began, "His

Honor, the Mayor, asks me to announce to all and sundry that this here drink-and-shoot duel concerns itself entirely with the aspersions Simon Bolivar Grimes has cast on the good name of Red Quill Bourbon, and that Colonel Delevan is defending the liquor he has sponsored. And anyone claiming a lady is involved is a liar and a skunk. Is that clear?"

A shout of assent answered him.

He went on, "Colonel Delevan, you got anything to say?"

The colonel bowed ceremoniously, raised his hat, and answered, "Suh, I am ready to defend my honor."

"Mr. Grimes, you got any statements?"

"I'm buying a keg of Red Quill for the public. Jest to show I ain't got any hard feelings. Instead of each one drinking outen his own bottle, me and the colonel share the same keg."

The colonel's handsome face tightened a little. "I cannot drink with a man I am about to meet on the field of honor."

Grimes grinned amiably. "Colonel, you can make that right by giving me back half of what I paid out for the keg. Thataway, we are both contributing alike to the cheer of our feller citizens. Me, I got some Old Vickery, but I'm meeting you half way, taking your brand. Or mebbe them bottles in that basket your hired man has got ain't got Red Quill in 'em?"

The colonel had no argument left. The marshal cut in, "If you gents are ready, get to your posts."

Grimes and the colonel marched toward each other, arms folded, until they were within three paces of each other, with a whitewash line separating them. Two cowpunchers rolled the little keg to the line and drove in a spigot, then gave the combatants tin cups. The marshal went on, "Ladies and gents! This here duel is a test of skill and endurance. Once I pass the sidelines, taking away the empty cups, they can draw without warning, any time till I come back with a fresh drink, and then all shooting's cut until I get over the side line again. The idee is, who can shoot the straightest when he's drunk the mostest."

The only one who paid no attention was Wing Lee. He shuffled about the barbecue pit and monkeyed with a pot of sauce.

Grimes raised his drink, and when the marshal had backed away, he said, "Colonel Delevan, your good health, suh! Beef blood, prune juice, plug terbaccer, chemicals, and acids."

The colonel gulped his cup, shuddered, lowered it, glanced about him. Grimes, lips barely moving, said, "Your choice, colonel. Drink or draw?"

"Fill them up, marshal!" Delevan demanded, loud and strong.

SILENCE ringed the square. Then, in the dusty and deserted main street, they heard the turnkey whooping it up.

"Gimme more likker! Put rattlesnakes and trantlers in it, I want it hot and strong! *Wheeeee!*"

After seven years, he was making up for lost time.

Grimes whispered, "Colonel, this here ain't what you use in your juleps. You know what they'll do if I ever tell 'em what you put in them barrels?"

Delevan did not answer. Straight as a ramrod, he accepted his cup of Red Quill. Each eyeing the other over the rim, they downed their poison.

"Suh, you can't stand this here likker much longer, and if you fall on your face, I'm telling 'em why."

The colonel raised his voice. "That was delicious, marshal. Fill them up again."

Arms folded, they faced each other; once the marshal crossed the sideline, each had the option of a quick draw, or else waiting until the other had faced another jolt of forty-rod.

Grimes' cargo of Red Quill was raising ructions. He was beginning to wonder how long he could endure his own contest. He had no qualms about his gunnery. As long as he stayed on his feet, his trigger finger would work by instinct. But winning an exchange of lead, shooting down the widow's sponsor would gain him and the Hanfords nothing at all, for the town would forgive the dead and coddle the Indian fighter's daughter.

Gun to gun, he had the colonel bluffed. It had worked just too well. Delevan would not draw, and if Grimes was the first to collapse, the duel was lost.

Already, the plaza began to weave a little. Grimes was sweating from the effort to keep his attention focused against the instant when he could make his play.

Finally, he caught the first sign of the colonel's wavering, and Grimes risked letting himself go a little. He sagged, his legs went wobbly.

Delevan's draw, considering all, was very good. But Grimes' was better.

His gun blazed as it cleared the holster. The slug smashed against the cylinder of Delevan's heavy Colt, and lead fragments tore his hand. The weapon was useless, and so were the gunner's fingers. And then Grimes yelled through the smoke, "Knock 'er loose!"

The Chinaman swung the axe with which he had been chopping fuel for the pot of sauce. The whiskey barrel's hoops burst. They had been filled almost to the breaking point the night before the duel. Wing Lee had seen to that.

Grimes pointed at the scattered staves. When the crowd saw what came out on the flood of liquor, they howled, "Putting trantlers and rattle-snakes in it!"

The colonel saw and turned a sickly pea-green. He doubled up. Doreen Hopkins rushed from the sidelines and cried, "Oh, you scoundrel, poisoning all these people! I'd rather starve than take dividends for such filthy liquor!"

Delevan was too sick to protest, and the shock of a bullet-torn hand did not help him. Doreen clawed and slapped him, ripped his flowing tie and his fine shirt. "I hope they lynch you — putting snakes and tarantulas into their liquor, just to make more profit!"

There was talk of lynching, but Grimes and the marshal won Delevan a chance to get to his house to pack up for a trip. And then Grimes went to get the bottles of whiskey which Melba had concealed in her rig.

"Drink up, gents; it's this lady's treat. Old Vickery, the best dang Bourbon ever come outen Kentucky, and no chemicals and acids in it. Jest repeal that ordinance, and her pappy'll haul in a wagonload of it."

Outraged citizens smashed all the other barrels of Red Quill. And an hour later, when Grimes and Melba drove back toward Cold Deck to tell old man Hanford the news, the blonde pillowed her head on his shoulder and asked, "Simon, how did you stand it, knowing Wing Lee had put rat-tlers and tarantulas into every barrel in the warehouse?"

She shuddered. He drew in the reins, and his arm closed about her.

"Honey, when I was in Arizony, I et rattlers. They ain't bad when you get used to the idee, and the trantlers was some Wing Lee made up outen black darning cotton, they sure looked good enough to turn the colonel's stomach more inside out than if'n I'd shot him there."

# SHE HERDED
# HIM AROUND

SCOWLING, the boy from Georgia stamped out of his hotel room and down the hall. A straw colored cowlick reached to his china blue eyes; he was lean and long, and a black frock coat hung from his shoulders. He stopped at the door next to his own, tapped with a ham-sized fist, and barged in without waiting for an answer.

"Ain't no woman on Earth can herd me around," he began.

The girl sitting in the rocker let out a yeep and cried, "Simon, you might wait to find out if I was dressed."

She bounded to her feet and held a red silk dress in front of her to cover the most conspicuous bare spots.

Simon Bolivar Grimes stuttered, "Dang it, Elma, how'd I know you'd be plumb . . . ah . . . uncovered-like?"

He backed toward the door, but the dark haired girl said, "Might as well stay, if there's anything you've missed, I'd love to know what it is."

She turned her back and proved her point. There was a fluff of chiffon about her hips; it didn't reach very low in one direction or high in the other. Her back and shoulders had a creamy richness. She was plump and shapely; her legs were sleek, and her garters made luscious indentations. Just a single graceful move, and the red dress was slipping over her head and sinking down to her hips. A pat, and it rustled past her knees and cut off his view of her calves, which tapered down to dainty ankles.

"How'd I know?" Grimes repeated.

"I guess you wouldn't." Elma sighed, then winced. "Ouch!" She picked a needle from the red dress. "Never occurred to you I'd have to patch the only dress I have. And you're as ragged as I am, after riding a hundred miles in a frock coat!"

A frown again tightened Grimes' coffin-shaped face. "Look here, Elma, ain't no woman on Earth can herd me around. I am damn-blasted if I aim to be a cowpuncher just account you got a notion I'm too dumb to reckonize gold if I stumbled over it."

"Simon, darling, I don't mean you're stupid. I mean, you just don't know a thing about mining. Anyway, mining towns are poison, and miners are the lousiest ruffians."

"Huh! When I found you, you was hustling drinks in a dance hall!"

Elma slapped him with both hands before he could dodge. "Yes, and I got you out of jail, I got you the horse you escaped on, and you were a small town lawyer when I found you, you long-legged idiot!"

She began crying and clung to him. "Simon, mining towns are poison! Claim jumpers shot my dad. Anyway, your uncle's a cattleman, if you weren't so stubborn you and me could get a start with him."

"Aw, honey —" She was close enough now for him to be delightfully aware of her generous curves, and she snuggled closer; but the Grimes stubbornness won out. "Look here, I ain't got more'n a couple hundred dollars, and my uncle'd mock me, coming back thattaway, after I busted outen that jail wheah that crooked Jedge Hillman flung me fo' contempt of court. I got to get myself some gold, and I'm a-going to."

She jerked back, wiped her eyes. "Simon Bolivar Grimes, you weren't too proud to have me smuggle saws into the jail!"

The boy from Georgia straightened up. He dug into his pocket and brought out a buckskin poke and emptied half the gold pieces on the dresser. "M'am, I am mighty sick of these here reminders." He looked at the heavy gold watch his grandpappy had given him just before he was hanged for shooting a revenue officer. "It is jest about time for the stage coach to get here. You kin keep both the hosses you got."

He turned to the hall. She snatched the coins and flung them. They hit the panel just as he closed the door behind him.

"Ain't no woman herding me around," he repeated. He knew he'd miss Elma, and he had to build up his courage.

Grimes stepped into his room and shouldered the saddle bags which contained his razor, a quart of whiskey, and a pair of field glasses. Then he went down the creaking stairs and stood in the doorway.

Cowpunchers yelled when, a few minutes later, the stage came clattering down the dusty main street. Hostlers brought out the new relay and took the sweating team to the stables. The driver leaped down, and so did the shotgun messenger who guarded the heavy box of gold coin. A blond girl stepped from the stage.

There was a seductive rustle of skirts, a coy flash of shapely legs; the slanting rays of the sun twinkled on the sheer silk of her hosiery. The sweetness of her perfume warmed Grimes' heart; he felt a little less bleak inside.

Grimes watched her walk into the stage station. She lifted her skirts a little and picked her way daintily across the dust and among the bottles and cigar butts that littered the dirt sidewalk; but she looked at home, for all her frilly garments and the little hat with the blue plume. Neither did she grimace when she entered the dingy dining room.

Grimes bought a ticket for Skull Gulch. He had barely stuffed a few ham sandwiches and a slab of apple pie into his coat pocket when it was time to board the coach. He held the door open for the fascinating stranger and then followed her to the coach; now that she had walked the cramps out of her legs, she needed no assistance.

Grimes looked up at the window at the end of the second floor hallway of the hotel. He caught a glimpse of Elma, and for a moment he felt like a skunk. Then he said to himself, "Ain't no woman kin herd me around."

He had half hoped she would fling her few odds and ends into her carpetbag and follow. But she had not, and it was too late to back down. Then the driver cracked the whip; the stage lurched forward, flinging the lovely blonde all over Grimes.

She had curves in the right places, even though her prim blouse hid them from the eye. The momentary pressure, the warm contact of her hand, the fragrance of her garments: they all made Grimes tingle down to his boots.

They were alone in the coach, but the girl might as well have been surrounded by a board fence. He could not get up his nerve to edge her into one corner and slip an arm about her; that puzzled Grimes, and fascinated him. She was sweet and friendly, and she wasn't stand-offish, but he kept his hands clear.

He said, after the exchange of names followed the untangling of accidentally scrambled limbs, "Miss Anne, I knowed you belonged out here, the minute I seen you picking yo' way, calm and placid-like into that there station. Me, I'm a miner, but I usta practice law. I'm aiming to make a pile fo' myself at Skull Gulch."

Anne Parsell made a gesture of dismay. "Why, Simon, that's the murderingest town in Arizona."

"I reckon it ain't too wild," he answered and hitched about a little, for the .45s in his leather-lined hip pockets were a nuisance. Now that he was through being a lawyer, he'd wear his guns on belts again. "Anyways, a fellow can face a few risks for a saddlebag full of nuggets."

SHE laughed merrily. "Well, they do say gold is where you find it. You know, there's the New Golconda, where I live, in Broken Axe. For years, it's been completely played out. And do you know, now they're taking ore out of it so rich they don't let the miners leave the mine, or else they'd fill their boots with nuggets whenever they headed for town."

Grimes sat up straight. "Miss Anne, mebbe I been a mite hasty about Skull Gulch. Reckon I oughta go to Broken Axe instead."

"You won't get rich on miner's pay. Since you've practiced law, why don't you work in dad's bank?"

"Yo' pappy own a bank?"

"No, he's only president of it. Brad Thorman owns a bit of stock, and he wants to marry me, but he's old as the hills. I wouldn't be surprised if he's thirty-five."

IT WAS dark now, and above the clatter of the stage, Grimes heard the yip-yip of a coyote, and the answering howl of another. Anne's profile was exquisite in the gloom. The noise made conversation lag. She sat up, lovely and straight; but finally, as the hours wore on, her lovely head nodded.

She leaned against the arm rest. She gasped, murmured an apology as a jolt flung her against Grimes, but she did not take her head from his shoulder. She pillowed her blond curls against the black frock coat, and Grimes said to himself, "Jest like a dang-blasted angel, gosh, she's beautiful. . . ."

To hell with Skull Gulch! He was going to Broken Axe. He hoped Elma wouldn't follow him to Skull Gulch, it'd be too bad, going so far out of her way.

Grimes must have been dozing, for the screech of brakes startled him. Then there was a shot. Anne cried, "Good Lord, a hold-up!" Men yelled, rocks clattered down the moonlit slope of the pass. The guard cut loose with his carbine, and then a volley raked the coach.

The driver was trying to swing clear of boulders heaped in the trail. Grimes caught Anne by the shoulder and thrust her to the floor. "You scrunch down, honey," he yelled and drew his .45s.

She cried, "Simon, you'll get killed — oh!"

Two slugs had zinged from bolts inside the coach. Grimes leaned out the window. Four men were pelting down the slope. Their horses struck fire from the rocks. Their guns blazed. The driver was whipping the team, sawing the lines, weaving in and out among the boulders, trying to get back on the trail. Grimes fired. A man slumped over in his saddle, then rolled off; his horse galloped with the others.

Then the messenger lurched from his post.

The lead team piled up. A horse screamed. Grimes yelled, "Cut them loose, I'll hold these here ____s!"

The driver answered, and Grimes' Colt blazed again.

The nearest road agent doubled up, clutched for support, and thumped to the ground. Grimes shouted to Anne, "Honey, get out on the other side, get outen here and hide yo'self afore you git a stray bullet."

And then a hammer blow knocked the breath out of Grimes. He had many times before now felt the paralyzing smash of a bullet, but this was different. He could not feel a thing from his collarbone to his knees; the moonlight blurred and blackened.

He never did know how long it was before he heard Anne cry, "Oh, he's not hurt at all, really."

The driver, head bandaged, knelt beside her, with a lantern. Grimes sat up. "M'am, what in tunket you mean I ain't hurt none?"

"Why, the bullet hit the big gold watch in your vest pocket."

"They busted that heirloom," he muttered, looking at the wreckage. "If ever I ketch that sculpin, I'm staking him out on an ant-hill. How's the hosses?"

"One kilt, I had to shoot t'other whilst Miss Anne was looking for bullet holes in your gizzard. And they got the gold."

Anne recoiled. "They got the gold? Oh, good Lord."

Grimes hoisted himself to the seat and leaned back against the bullet-riddled upholstery. "Huh! Tain't yo' gold, is it?"

AT THE next town, Ojo Caliente, the driver got a lead team; but Anne refused to go on.

"Simon," she said, "you've got to see a doctor, you got an awful wallop, watch or no watch. And I'm going to stop over to see that you're taken care of."

Once the coach was on its way, Grimes muttered, "Shucks, nothing wrong with me, here I am letting a woman herd me around again."

Before he reached the head of the hotel stairs, he did think his gizzard had been knocked out of place; but he told the doctor, "Ain't nothing wrong with me, get me a quart of liquor and a cigar."

IT WAS perhaps an hour or two before dawn when he awoke, a gun in each hand, and sweat pouring down his cheeks. He looked around, realized that he had been dreaming of a second hold-up, and took another swig of rye.

Then he heard the sobbing next door; Anne was crying, tossing restlessly. It was all plain through the thin partition. He got up, put on his boots and coat, and tapped at her door. When she answered, he said, "Honey, it's jest me. I done heard you weeping like yo' little heart's busted wide open."

"Oh, just a minute —" There was a flurry of bare feet, the scratch of a match; then, "Come in, Simon, I'm so worried."

She wore a filmy robe over a lace-paneled gown; the two garments together wouldn't have been enough to wad a shotgun. Her hair was shimmering gold in the light of the smoky lamp. For all her reddened eyes, Anne was the loveliest creature he had ever seen; through the frail garments he could just distinguish the shadowy roundnesses of her slim figure.

He caught her in his arms, gritted his teeth for a moment, then let himself down into the rocker.

"It's that robbery," she said, snuggling against his shoulder.

"Huh. Tain't yo' money."

"But the loss will hurt dad's bank, there may be a run on it."

"Shucks, ain't the stage company responsible?"

She shook her bead. "The bank owns the stage line."

Grimes stroked the golden hair, slipped an arm about Anne, and kissed her. She did not protest, and before he could marvel at that, she was clinging to him, murmuring, "Simon, when you were half conscious from trying to defend me from the road agents, you said the sweetest things."

That kiss inspired Grimes. "Honey, all the more reason fo' not working in yo' pappy's bank, and going to the New Golconda instead. I'll give him the gold, and I wont ask fo' my money until the bank's earnt enough to stand the loss of the robbery."

"Simon, darling, miners just get pay."

Grimes chuckled. "Not me. I'm a-filling my boots with nuggets every shift I work. They ain't keeping me locked up at any mine!"

"Oh, but that'd be stealing."

"Huh. Tain't neither. It's downright stingy, expecting a fellow to dig and drill and blast all day long, and then holler if he stuffs a couple nuggets into his pockets. Did the owner of the New Golconda put the gold into the ground in the fust place? You jest hush up, honey, I'm saving yo' pappy's bank if I have to high-grade two-three mines."

Anne didn't have an answer. Then he was kissing her until she couldn't say anything for a while. At last Grimes said, "That there light's too dang glaring. . . ." He got up and blew it out. When he got back to the warm white shape in the gloom, he went on, "Who'd you say owns the New Golconda?"

"Brand Thorman."

"Huh. He's the gent that thinks he'll marry you!"

IT WAS dawn when Anne said, "Simon, you better go back to your room, folks might start talking."

He wrote a letter, telling Elma he was not going to Skull Gulch; but he did not tell her what his destination was. No woman was going to herd him around. . . .

When the following stage brought Grimes and Anne to Broken Axe, the town turned out. The marshal and half a dozen cowpunchers surrounded Grimes and Anne, demanding a first-hand account of the vain but valiant defense of the coach. Anne's father, Jim Parsell, joined the crowd. He was a tall, ruddy man with a blond mustache. He wore boots and store clothes and a battered Stetson jammed down on shaggy white hair.

"Simon," he said, "I done heard all about it, and I'd sure like to have you be chief counsel for this here bank."

Grimes answered, "If it's jest the same to you, suh, I'm plumb sick of law and I'd ruther work in the New Golconda mine."

Anne said, "Dad, why don't you ask Brand, Simon was defending his interest, too. It was bank money."

"Well, I reckon I could, if Simon insists."

And then a dark man with a close-cropped mustache came up. His thumbs were hooked in his green satin vest; a good looking fellow, except for his gimlet eyes and too-hearty smile.

Anne said, "Hello, Brand, Dad and I would like for you to give Simon a job in your mine."

Brand Thorman cocked his head and eyed Grimes from dusty boots to bullet-riddled hat. "So you're Simon Bolivar Grimes, the Texas gunslick, eh? Nice work, smoking out two road agents."

"Huh? What's that?" Grimes scowled; he didn't like the man. "I ain't no gunslick."

Thorman chuckled. "No offense, Simon, no offense. And I'm sorry, but I don't need any more miners, I've got plenty." He lifted his hat, "Goodbye, Anne."

Grimes watched him mount up the slim-legged palomino in front of the Thorman House Bar. Then Anne's father said, "Simon, let's liquor up a bit and see if I can talk you into working for me."

Anne cut in, "I wish you could persuade him, dad."

Though Grimes stepped into the Thorman House Bar, he was still determined not to have any woman herd him around.

After two or three quick ones, he said, "Lookee here, Mistah Parsell, you got to get me into that mine, I'm plumb set on mining, I allus craved to learn the business." He omitted any mention of his plans for pocketing nuggets; he sensed that rugged Jim Parsell would have the same childish ideas that Anne had. "Though mebbe I ought to help the sheriff run down them robbers that ruined my grandpappy's watch."

Jim Parsell's craggy face tightened. "I'd sure love to see them dancing on the business end of a riata. Forty thousand bucks, and if the news gets out how hard we're hit, no telling what'll happen."

THE following morning, cattlemen came driving into Broken Axe, supposedly to buy groceries; but each one went to the bank and drew out cash. Grimes watched Jim Parsell through the fly-specked windows; the tall rancher was saying to each depositor, "Your *dinero*'s safe, neighbor. But if you drag it down, you might get held up, same as the stage."

Parsell was sweating. Some depositors did return most of the money they had drawn, but some got stubborn. It was touch and go, all day.

Grimes was impatiently waiting for night. He and Anne were driving out on the mesa. She was bringing a lemon pie, some cushions, and a Navajo rug. Anne would pass by the hotel to pick him up.

Brand Thorman drove down the street in a buckboard and pulled up in front of Cy Daley's General Mercantile, Hay, Grain & Feed Store. He did not notice Grimes, and Grimes barely noticed him; the passengers sitting on boxes set on the wagon bed accounted for that last.

There were two Mexican girls built like Percheron mares, three chemical blondes, and a redhead. They were painted up like a carnival parade, their perfume drowned the main street's odor of stale beer and horses, and their low-cut dresses made Grimes gape.

The redhead said, "See anything you ain't seen before, dearie?"

Grimes answered, "Not yet, m'am, but if that there wagon hits any bumps, there's jest no telling."

She laughed and patted the deeply cut yoke of her dress, just by way of checking up. One of the Mexican girls said, "*Señor*, you are too fonny!"

"Where you all ladies going, to a picnic or suthin?"

"Picnic?" A blonde turned to her nearest neighbor. "Sure, and he thinks it's a picnic, up there at the mine."

Then a little gray man with a blue apron came out of the store carrying a case of whiskey. Brand Thorman followed, a case on his shoulder. Grimes asked the girl nearest the tailgate, "Gosh, m'am, is that there liquor for the miners?"

"Miners get thirsty, don't they? Listen, dearie, come up to see me Friday night, I live right next to the post office."

Thorman took the reins and cracked the whip. The cargo of girls and whiskey rolled down the street. Grimes said to Cy Daley, "That gent sure treats his miners mighty nice."

The storekeeper said, "Finding nuggets the size of steers, he can damn well afford to! It beats all, bub, the luck of some folks. Mine's been given up fer years, and Brand snoops around and finds the lost vein."

Grimes watched the dust cloud rising from the desert. As he went to the hotel to wait for Anne, he said to himself, "No dang wonder these gals holler when a fellow aims to work in the mines. Some of them ladies was right pert looking, too."

He ate a steak and four eggs and half a dried-apple pie. But thinking of Elma took the edge from his appetite.

"After all," he said to himself, "she's got them two hosses, and I gave her half of my roll. No, I ain't being herded around by no woman."

It was dark now, but he sat there, trying to devise an approach to the problem of getting a job from a man who did not want more employees. Finally he brightened up: "If Thorman don't break all the likker out at once, which he wont, supposing I snuck in and opened a case? Them miners ain't going to know their own names fo' a week."

WHEN Anne Parsell drove up in her father's buggy, Grimes took the reins, and flicked the high-stepping bay's rump. "Sure a scrumptious night, honey."

Anne sighed, leaned back against his shoulder.

Well out on the mesa, Grimes pulled up at a *tinaja* whose slow ooze of water filled a small rocky basin just enough for the grass that covered the thin soil for a few yards about the basin. He spread out the Navajo rug, and Anne snuggled beside him, in the lee of the boulder that sheltered them from the cool wind.

The silence finally made him look up from the girl in his arms, for all that she clung to him, lips eager and misty eyes veiled by drooping lashes. "Gosh, honey, I could almost grab them stars and put 'em in your hair."

She sighed ecstatically. "You're so poetic, Simon." And then, needing both arms, Grimes was unable to reach for the stars. . . .

The way it ended, he forgot all about the chicken sandwiches and the lemon pie until Anne exclaimed, "Oh, it's getting late, we ought to get back to town before everyone turns out for the westbound stage."

He helped her to her feet, sighed regretfully, and then became practical. "Better let me brush the burrs offen your skirt, honey."

There weren't any to speak of, but it was nice work.

On the way back to town, Grimes asked, "Why in tunket don't Thorman put up gold brick and save your pappy's bank?"

"He's offered to, if I'll marry him."

"That old buzzard, I bet he's dang near forty. Your pap can't make you marry Thorman, can he?"

"Oh, it's not a case of *forcing* me to, Simon. But dad's worked so hard with that bank. He's carried so many ranchers through bad years. I just can't let him fail now. I'd be letting all our friends down."

Grimes flicked the whip. "Look here. Suppose you and me cut up so scandalous that Thorman'd not want to marry you, and then maybe your pappy could deal with him reasonable."

Her eyes brightened. "That would be fun, darling." But the smile faded quickly, and she let go his hand. "Only Thorman'd kill you. No, that's not the way — oh, hurry! Here comes the stage!"

He plied the whip. The bay stretched his long legs. The buggy bounced and careened over the rough road; but for all his gallant effort, the stage beat Jim Parsell's trotter. And when Grimes pulled up, all of Broken

Axe had turned out.

Grimes gave Anne the reins. "Shucks, mebbe we coulda made it through the arroyo instead of to town, I musta been absent-minded."

"I'm afraid not," Anne said, "without going miles and miles around."

Even so, the late return might have been inconspicuous, but for one passenger who had stepped out of the stage. In another moment, she would have been in the hotel. As it was, she stood there under the lights at the door. Elma Austen had followed Grimes.

She saw him, and she saw his blond companion. She dropped her carpetbag and darted toward the buggy. Grimes leaped to the street and said, "Anne, you hurry —"

The crowd, however, blocked her way, but it did not block Elma. She said, "You jailbird, maybe you think I didn't see this blonde bait get on the coach with you! Maybe you thought I'd not hear of that robbery and know where you'd gone?"

She bounded to the step of the buggy and said to Anne, "If you think you can take advantage of this long-legged idiot, you're crazy! Not after I got him out of jail."

Grimes caught Elma's shoulder. "Look here," he stuttered, "you can't talk thattaway, this lady's totally respectful, she's a banker's daughter."

That did not soothe Elma a bit. "Banker? Oh, you low-down coyote, you fortune hunter, after all I've done for you!"

She smacked Anne. Grimes, trying to drag her from the buggy step, tore Elma's red dress to the waist, and Elma turned out a good display. A crowd of cowpunchers cheered.

Then Anne took a hand. Two hands, in fact: both full of brunette hair.

Elma's feet slipped. The buggy step was too narrow for footwork. That threw Grimes off balance. Anne could not let go in time, and Elma would not: the pair of lovelies landed between the buggy wheels and on top of Grimes.

"Grab that there hoss!" he yelled, "and git these gals offen me!"

He was submerged in a flurry of legs, skirts, tattered outer and under garments. But someone did grab the bridle, and the wheels did not mar either girl's curves.

Grimes dragged Anne clear. Elma came up clawing. Before he could shake her until her teeth rattled, Anne was driving away with a Navajo rug about her shoulders to keep the breeze from her bare spots. Her chin was in the air. She did not say good-night.

"I barely get you loose from a judge's daughter," Elma stormed, "when you get tangled up with a banker's high-nosed baggage!"

"Her nose ain't all that's high," Grimes retorted and stalked away. Broken Axe had become complicated. He would have left on that very stage, but no woman was going to herd him around.

IN THE morning, be got a livery nag and rode out toward the buttes whose gold was making Brand Thorman rich. He reasoned, "Now that Anne ain't got no use for me, Thorman won't be refusing me a job outa spite."

Gold he had come for, and gold he was getting.

Presently, he heard the wheeze of a steam engine, the pounding of the ten-stamp mill. But he could not see any miners. There were no ore cars coming out of the black tunnel to feed the mill; no ore cars took useless rock to the dump. All Grimes knew about mining could have been written on a postage stamp, but even so, he felt that there should have been more activity than that thump-thump-wheeze.

He might never have thought of ore cars had he not seen three of them on the rusting rails, up there along the butte's eroded side.

Then there was activity aplenty. That puff of vapor from the engine house might have been steam, but just on the off chance, Grimes piled out of the saddle. Two seconds later, a slug buzzed past. He heard the rumble of the gun. As he clawed dirt, he muttered, "Either that coyote's shooting a cannon, or they jest fired a blast in the mine."

A second shot kept Grimes from taking his horse to a sheltering dip. The animal toppled over, kicking. A third shot from the buffalo gun drove the rider scrambling for cover. He pitched and rolled. Then, minutes later, he took off his hat, held it well to one side, and cautiously crept toward the lip.

A .55 caliber slug drilled the Stetson. He tried to crawl in the opposite direction to reach an arroyo that seamed the mesa. A slug fanned his ear. Grimes' Colts were outranged by a good 600 yards. He was bottled up. He could not get at the canteen hooked on the saddle.

The sun was beating down. Horn toads raced among the hot rocks. Grimes' mouth became dry; his lips cracked in the searing wind. He began to doubt that anyone could get a job at the New Golconda.

At hourly intervals during the blasting afternoon, Grimes tried to creep to the arroyo. The final attempt cured him. Another quarter inch, and he'd have had both lungs torn out by a 550 grain slug. Brand Thorman wanted to make sure that snoopers didn't return with reports on the lay of the land.

The sun was low, and Grimes was fairly perishing of thirst. Little whirlwinds blinded him with dust and burrs. The whole mesa danced crazily. He took some mesquite sticks, tore his shirt into strings; he peeled out of his coat and pants.

"I'm getting into that mine if it takes till Judgement Day," he mumbled as he set to work. "Mebbe I ain't working there, but I'm getting a look, and I'm getting a nugget."

He made a dummy of mesquite branches tied together. He dressed it and put his hat on the dummy. Then, crawling on his belly, he caught a wooden "ankle" in each hand and made the scarecrow simulate cautious peeping.

No one fired. He wondered if the watcher was looking. He tried again, making the dummy pop up once more, a little nearer the point where a man might make a dash for the arroyo's protection. Grimes reasoned that a man who had baked in that deadly heat all day would not have patience to wait until dark; he might be too crazy with the heat. Indeed, Grimes was practically that, or he would have let well enough alone.

Once more he managed to put his double up to spying.

The dummy jerked. An ounce slug had smacked it between the shoulders. A big puff of dust rose. Grimes lay there, flat on his face, the scarecrow just ahead of him. From the mine, it must have looked like that final, perfect shot. Mirage and sunset haze had kept the sniper from seeing that he had plugged a dummy.

PATIENTLY, Grimes waited for darkness. Then he went to his dead horse to get his canteen. The hot water tasted better than any beer. Once in the arroyo, he headed upgrade, toward the now silent stamp mill. Lights gleamed in the buildings. As he came nearer, he could hear voices; there was laughter, some feminine, some masculine, and all drunken. A foghorn voice bawled.

> "Three gals came down from Canada,
> Drinking rum and wine,
> The subject of conversation was,
> Your hair ain't as red as mine —"

It was the chorus that shocked Grimes. He muttered, "They sure weren't ladies," and picked his way up the grade. Soon he was at the narrow-gauge line for ore cars.

He got a look through a crack in the nearest shack. Four miners were paralyzed, one was nodding, and one was bawling another verse of the song. The second case of whiskey was open, and the half dozen girls had most of their garments scattered all over the tangle of bottles and tin plates and pack saddles. One was doing a dance that fascinated Grimes.

"Gosh, I never knowed a gal could wobble in so many places at once."

The nodding miner prodded her hip with a cigarette butt. She cried, *"Chinga'o borrego!"* and smacked his mustache. He toppled over. The song went on. So did Grimes. But the life of a miner sure did have its high spots.

The other lighted shack was new. The lumber had not yet turned gray in the blistering sun. The narrow-gauge tracks ran right into the building; it had apparently been whacked up with no regard to ore cars. That was odd. But not half as odd as what went on in the large room.

There were three-decked bunks, horse gear, a sheet iron stove. Three men sat on packing cases; Brand Thorman sat on a solid oaken chest with a shattered lock whose express company seals still hung from wires. The fifth man knelt before a little crucible under which there was a charcoal fire; sparks flew as he pumped goatskin bellows and sweated in the red glare.

There was a box of black sand in which ingots cooled; there was a depression in the sand, ready for the next crucible of melted gold. The man with the bellows said, "Dump in a bit more, Brand."

Thorman straightened up, took a double handful of coins out of the chest, and dumped them into the crucible. By then Grimes understood the whole game. One of the gang was familiar; he had taken part in the stage robbery.

No wonder Thorman kept his gang of miners dead drunk and did not want strangers prowling around! The miners and the stamp mill were to fool the natives of Broken Axe. The mine was a fake; a hideout for bandits to melt down stolen coin and palm it off as gold from a lost lode. Thorman was sinking the bank and then offering to ante in enough to save Jim Parsell, marry Anne, and also get control of the bank. Simple as pouring sand out of a boot!

These men were sober and armed. Even for a surprise party, five to one was too much to bite off. Grimes retreated up the rusty tracks. Fifty yards upgrade, he came to an ore car. He released the brake and heaved to free the rusty axle. It squealed. The car began to roll. Grimes vaulted into the steel shell. Creaking and groaning, the car picked up speed.

The clump and clatter warned the gang a little too soon. Two men dashed out, guns blazing. Slugs zinged from the sides of the car. Grimes rose, a Colt in each hand. Light from inside the house silhouetted the gunners. One doubled up and rolled down the grade. The other stumbled.

Brand Thorman's buffalo gun cut loose from the window. Grimes, however, was already ducking. The next instant, the car ploughed into the cabin. A lantern smashed. The crucible and furnace tipped over. It was the oaken chest that derailed the ore car. Guns laced the murky glare. Slugs smacked and screamed; Grimes came up shooting, but two men escaped.

Horses clattered down the grade. The wrecked cabin began to blaze. The drunken miner and one of the Mexican girls still sang, *"Three gals came down from Canada, drinking rum and wine. . . ."*

Brand Thorman and one accomplice had escaped. Grimes thrust his guns into his leather-lined hip pockets and bounded toward the tunnel where the horses had been stabled. He lost time catching a saddled nag; the fugitives had stampeded the dead men's animals. When he set out, he could no longer hear the pounding of hooves across the mesa. But he quirted a dead man's mount toward Broken Axe.

Thorman couldn't leave Broken Axe. Thorman could scarcely suspect the identity of the snooper; neither could he double back to recover the unmelted coins from the blazing shack. So Grimes galloped on.

HE DISMOUNTED in front of the Thorman House Bar. None of the horses at the hitching rack were blowing or sweating. He was sure that Brand Thorman had come down a side alley and gone either to some bar or to his quarters in the hotel he owned. Grimes poked his head into several saloons and decided, "He'd go to his room and pertend he's been in all evening. Fust find him, then find his hoss."

Grimes bounded up the narrow stairs to the second floor. "Mistah Thorman," he yelled drunkenly, "if you think yo're marrying Anne Parsell, yo're crazy — yo're crazy, you sidewinder, you ain't fit for Anne!"

There was no action from any hall door. But men in the lobby heard the bawling challenge. Someone shouted, "Brand'll shoot your gizzard out, kid! You better go home to bed."

Grimes repeated the challenge, then answered the men below: "I'll be any dirty name if I back down, he ain't marrying my gal!"

Just then two doors opened; one at his left, near the head of the stairs; the other at the further end of the hall. Elma came dashing out of the nearer door. She wore a transparent nightgown, and her dark hair was streaming. "If you're that crazy about her," she cried, "go ahead and good luck, you jughead!"

Brand Thorman stamped into the hall. His boots were dusty, and he saw the dust on Grimes' boots, the alkali and rust and dirt on the frock coat; he saw, and his face changed. He understood.

Elma screamed, "Simon, watch it!"

But Grimes was already whirling from that lovely distraction. Thorman's guns were clearing leather when the kid from Georgia cut loose. No one, Thorman least of all, believed that any man could get a Colt from a hip pocket and clear of a long frock coat in time to win the exchange.

But Thorman learned. His own shot went wild, just as Grimes' Colt bucked a second time and knocked a second jet of dust from Thorman's green vest. The big man spun, his knees buckled, and he fell face forward; his smoking gun skated down the hall.

Elma clawed her breast. Her gown was soggy, blood-soaked. Before Grimes could catch her, she caught the door jamb, missed, then slumped to the floor.

"Simon — you fool — I told you — mining towns — are poison — did he get you —?" She shivered, held to him with one arm. When he supported her in the crook of his elbow, she smiled. "Kiss me, Simon, you idiot — it's been fun — herding you around —"

The men who came pounding up the stairs checked up short. One said, "Hell, the pore gal's been shot, get a doctor."

"Shot, hell!" Grimes choked. "She's dead, and so is that son of a —!"

HE WAS right. Later that night, he rode to Jim Parsell's house with the marshal and told of Thorman's trick to palm off stolen coin as gold from a high grade mine. Anne came out, wide eyed, and laid a soft hand on his arm.

"Simon, darling," she said, "I'm so sorry about that poor girl. And I'm not angry about the way . . . the way she called my hand. You saved us all, Simon, and —"

Grimes kissed her, then gently thrust her from him. He said to Anne, and to Jim Parsell, and to the marshal: "Folks, you all been mighty nice, but I'm leaving tonight. I'm going back to my uncle's spread, like Elma wanted me to —" He choked, blinked, then jammed his hat on and ran down the front steps. As he stumbled toward town, he muttered, "Damn it, I wish I'd let her herd me around."

# YOU CAN'T
# FIGHT A WOMAN

"SLIM — DON'T!" the red haired girl protested. Her voice was tremulous, and her eyes were misty in the moonlight. "I've got to get home before dad gets back from town. He'd kill me if he knew —"

Reluctantly, Slim Crane let Madge slip from his arms. For a moment, he watched her pat her disheveled hair into shape, and smooth out the blouse that a close embrace had pulled all awry.

"Shucks, honey," he answered, broad month twisting ruefully, "what do you low *my* old man'd do if he knew about *me*, sneaking away like this!"

Madge's sigh, and the way she laced her fingers behind her finely poised head as she leaned back against the rock that sheltered them brought pert young curves into charming relief as her blouse drew taut.

Slim watched the play of moonlight accentuate her beauty. He abstractedly ran his fingertips over his thumb, as though still trying the texture of a fine fabric. He was thinking, "Gosh . . . she's wearin' silk . . . an' she smells nicer every time. . . ."

Madge Daley in gingham was fascinating enough to make him a traitor to every cow country tradition. As she slowly rose and smoothed out her rumpled skirt, he caught her hand. "Honey — I don't think my dad's going to have time to cut your bob-wire fences again, not fo' a spell, no-how."

A frown puckered her smooth brow. They had not until this moment mentioned the feud that forced them to meet on the sly. Then her eyes brightened. "Oh — Slim! You mean, he's getting reasonable?"

Slim Crane loved Madge enough to swallow the unintended jab. "No, dang it! There's a passel of skunks beefing our critters. Killin' 'em and hauling 'em off."

"And that," Madge said, a sly bit of malice creeping into her voice, "is even worse than a nester putting a fence about his lawful property?"

"Aw, blazes, honey!" He tried to be grim, but he simply could not, so he tried to laugh it off. "You and your pappy don't understand nothing. Look-ee here. My dad and his'n, afore him, fit the Injuns to get this yere country. They starved, froze, kilt varmints and Mexicans and brought cow critters into this corner of what used to be forsaken hell.

"Now a bunch of galoots in Washington pass laws, giving nesters the rights to settle down, put fences aroun' the water holes our critters need —"

"But Slim, darling." She sadly shook her head. "Your cows aren't hungry and they're not thirsty!"

"Makes no difference!" He stubbornly shook his tow head. "Fust drought that comes along, the Diamond C critters won't have a thing to drink except whar your pappy's squatted."

"He's not a squatter!" she flared. "He's a homesteader!"

"I don't give a tarnation damn!" He snatched his hat and jammed it on his head. "Between homesteaders and this new passel of varmints that's beefing our critters and selling 'em in Paso del Norte, we'll git shoved to the wall."

"Why — you — you — putting my father in the same class with beef thieves!" She slapped him, and it sounded like a pistol shot. "Thieves, are we! You listen here, Slim Crane! Your father, the pig headed old fossil, he's a thief! Tearing down a mile of barbed wire that cost dad every cent he made —"

"Made outen hogging our water hole!"

But Madge was in the saddle, galloping recklessly from the grove toward the section that Herb Daley, lawfully enough, had "proved up." Crane, just as sore, mounted his blue roan, and growled, "Gol dang my hide, she's a snake, like all them nesters! Thief, huh?"

But as he rode, he had more and more difficulty in keeping his rage white hot. He could not forget those stolen moments when Madge looked up, lashes drooping and lips half parted for a kiss; he could not forget how a runaway team had flung her into his arms, that day before he knew that she was the daughter of the first nester to come to Arroyo Rojo.

For the next few days, he tended strictly to business, scouting around the vast Diamond C spread, ready for a clash with beef thieves. The coming of the railroad to Paso Del Norte had started a boom; hundreds of pilgrims, gamblers, dance-hall women, business men and railroad contractors had poured into town, and all the newcomers needed steak — principally, it seemed, from the Diamond C herd.

Brand inspectors, supposedly, were scrutinizing each hide at the slaughterhouses, checking them against bills of sale. But the inspectors were either drunk, blind, or bribed. And old man Crane was madder than a hornet. His line riders had made no progress. Thus Slim's father was in the saddle, stalking thieves as he once had tracked down marauding Comanches.

"Way I figger it out," the old man said, pointing, "is that they're fixing to turn a trick over yonder. Judgin' from old wagon tracks, and the lay of the land, it's got to be."

"Why'n't y'all put our riders over there, then?"

Crane spat, shook his grizzled head. "Son," he said, patting the stock of "Jezebel", his buffalo gun, "when I tends to varmints, I tends to 'em. Jails ain't wuth a damn! Less company, the better. Now, you ride over that-away, up through that gulch."

Stealthily, with muffled hoofs and curb chain to silence his advance, Slim went up the gulch. The full moon cast black shadows, but in the open, the shooting would be good, if it came to that. He hoped it wouldn't. It had been bad enough when Madge's dad had just missed stopping a hatful of .45s, that day when the first fence had been destroyed.

He rather wondered why Madge had continued meeting him. She probably reckoned he'd saved her life, or something. Then, because he'd indirectly called her old man a thief, she'd gone hog wild. Women are sure as hell funny critters.

When Slim heard vague sounds some distance ahead he crept forward on foot, his Winchester ready. If he got the drop on them, a killing might be avoided. His father would not shoot unarmed men, not even thieves. The old man liked to startle them into going for a gun, which was pretty nearly always fatal — for the other fellow.

Slim wondered if his dad's skill was what it had been, thirty years ago. A man couldn't keep that up forever. Not even a good one. He was vaguely worried. A premonition urged him to hurry, and to hell with noise.

A wagon was just discernible in the shadows of a grove, out there in the open. The very silence was ominous. Slim squatted, straining his eyes to outwit the treacherous blend of shadow and blue-white glare. A twig crackled. Someone whispered, "There's the old son of a —! Yonder —"

The thunderous boom of a buffalo gun cut into that. A horse screamed, wood splintered, and wagon tires rattled over the rocky outcropping as the team bolted.

Then Slim went wild. It would take the old man just a split second to shove another cartridge into "Jezebel", but three rifles were crackling, and Crane, enraged by his bad shot, was roaring more loudly than his .60 caliber gun.

Slim raked the flame-stabbed shadows with his Winchester. A man yelled. The kid's gun jammed. He drew his Colt and charged, cursing as he fired.

The silence in his father's quarter froze him. They'd killed him! A man broke from the shadows. He doubled up, cut down by a pair of slugs. Then Jezebel's blast drowned every other sound.

The old man bobbed up from cover, a .45 in each hand. But two men escaped his wrath. They reached their saddle mounts, and galloped hell bent. When father and son met at the overturned wagon, they found only one raider, his own blood mingled with that of three butchered beeves.

"Had ye worried, heh?" old man Crane chuckled.

"Gosh, pap, you sure did!" Slim was shaking all over.

Then he felt sick. His mouth sagged, and the gun fell from his hands. His father, striking a match, was kneeling beside the dead man, and sombrely shaking his head. "By God," he mourned, "I shore *am* gittin' old. Wan't old Jezebel that got this jasper, after all. Yes, sir, I'm shore gittin' old, when all I kin hit is a pore, helpless hoss." He looked up, sharply. "Whut in tunket? Ain't you never seen blood afore!"

"Ug — uh —" Slim choked, gulped. His face was gray green in the moon glow. "That's — um — that's the — nester. Herb Daley —"

"Mighty nice, son." The old man rubbed his hands together. "Smoking out a double action varmint. Though it's too bad, him having a daughter."

He scrutinized the wagon and the horses. He was saying, "Brands blotted out, so's they kain't be traced. 'Tain't Daley's rig."

Slim went to get his horse. When he returned, he said, "I been thinking mebbe I could go to Paso del Norte and find out who's behind this crooked stuff. It's a cinch Daley ain't the head man, and we didn't ketch no one to question."

"By gravey!" This after a moment of pondering. "That's right. Arter daylight, when I kin study the sign, I'll tell you what size jasper to look fer, and what kind of hosses they was riding."

That would be an open book to an old scout. Slim nodded, then said, "Pappy, why'n't you tell the sheriff and the coroner you done this yourself? Thattaway, won't nobody suspect me, if anyone hears I'm going to Paso del Norte. Being as these yere are your critters, on your spread, ain't no one going to as much as axe you a cross question."

Old man Crane straightened up. He appreciated modesty in a young squirt. "They allus lowed you was a easy going jasper and none too dang smart, nohow." He slapped his thigh, chuckled. "I allus looked dumb too, when I was your age. Which fooled a lot of folks. You go right now, and I'll write you to Paso del Norte, telling you what all I larned."

That helped. "Good God," the kid told himself, later that night, "I'd ruther be shot than face Madge. And onct I help pappy outen this mess, I ain't never coming back."

Then his face hardened, and looked older, years older, than it had an hour ago. Even if Madge never learned he had fired the fatal shot, she'd still hate him for his father's sake. . . .

ALL THE hard cases in the southwest had come to Paso del Norte. Longhaired trappers in buckskin, frock coated gamblers, waddies in faded levis, all busy with their own pursuits; and none, as far as Slim Crane could tell, with an eye for him.

As the sun dipped lower, Slim saw the women who had flocked to town. They leaned from windows, beckoning and smiling; they lounged in doorways, clad only in kimonos whose thin fabric and loosely gathered folds seconded the wearer's brazen invitation.

Somewhere in hell roaring Paso del Norte, Crane expected to get a direct lead to the beef thieves. His father had mailed him descriptions of the fugitives who had survived the melee at the Diamond C. Hoof-prints, bits of hair rubbed off on trees, human hair in the sweatband of a hat lost in flight; boot prints, and the length of strides, all these built up the picture. A short, heavy man whose feet were cramped by new, tight boots, had ridden a *grullo*; a long legged, red haired man with a slight limp had escaped on a strawberry roan with one defective shoe.

From one saloon to the next, Slim hunted the pair. Appealing to the law was useless. The beef contractors, the railroad builders, the slaughter house operators were hand in hand. Unless he found overwhelming evidence, he had not a chance.

The only way was to catch the thieves with Diamond C hides in their possession. That would justify cutting them down in their tracks; a frontier jury would acquit him.

"And to hell with the jedge and his whereas-nevertheless-buts!" Slim told himself, as back prudently planted against the wall in the corner, his biting glance covered the smoke filled barroom.

One thing Slim had not overlooked; though leaving Arroyo Rojo by night, he could not hope to have reached Paso del Norte unheralded. Two fugitives had ridden ahead of him. Thus, his back was to a wall.

Slim watched the dancers whirling about the rough-hewn floor, and the girls who hustled drinks to the tables along the further wall. They were trim wenches, fresh and shapely; too subtle to wear short skirts. Slim had seen that type in the saloons of Arroyo Rojo, and they seemed downright indecent. But these girls stirred his blood.

Before Slim realized it, he drew a slow, deep breath. The glass in his fingers spilled little drops of whiskey. He shook his head, as if to clear it of dizziness. When a blonde girl with hair that was more silver than yellow came lithely toward him, he could not avoid her glance. Nor did he want to, when he smelled her perfume and heard her voice.

She seemed almost shy, like Madge, the first time they met by moonlight, and she nervously fingered a concha on his vest.

"I wonder if you'd not take a table, over there." She gestured. "We could drink together." She looked up, and hesitancy blossomed into a smile. "Wouldn't it be fun, pretending we're old friends? I'm . . . well . . . a newcomer, and it's awfully hard, playing up to these tough customers. I never realized it would be like this."

A tall man with a drooping black mustache stood in the corner, arms folded. He nodded as he watched her accost Slim. This was the proprietor. The girl flashed him a glance as Slim followed her.

Then he saw a red haired man, long legged and limping a little. Slim remembered his father's description. He wondered if the cowpuncher had a strawberry roan outside.

"Listen, Sally," he whispered, as they approached the table in the corner, "I'm waiting for a fellow, and I can't see much, from here."

A waiter was bringing the drinks Sally had ordered before leaving the bar. One glass, Slim realized, would be cold tea, but he didn't care.

The tall redhead's face went sour, then black when his glance shifted toward Sally. The blonde shrank, caught Slim's arm. Her hip would have brushed him, but for the holster tied to his thigh.

The redhead moved swiftly, despite his game leg. He spat and wrathfully said, "Well, you towhaired tramp, I guess he's handsome, huh?"

Slim did not want to quarrel and make himself conspicuous; his job was to follow the lame man, "Now, look-ee here, pardner." He raised his left hand in a placating gesture; Sally still clung to his right arm. "That ain't no way to talk to a lady."

"Please do go away, Randy," Sally implored.

Between them, they only managed to get him hostile.

"Why, you long legged son of a —"

The music had stopped, and Randy's voice filled the entire place. Sally cried out, and Slim thrust her away from him. That move was enough to start Randy for his gun.

He was quick, but he delayed a little, to give Slim a chance to get shed of Sally. This was from over-confidence, and the desire to make it clear that he had not drawn first. His face made that all very plain; Slim knew that this man had moved in for a kill.

So did everyone else. Men were scrambling, and girls were diving for cover.

Randy's eyes suddenly bugged out, and his jaw sagged. That was when Slim snapped, "Drop it, you polecat!"

The gun in his left hand enforced that. Randy, too intent on timing the kid's right hand reach for the holster at his right hip, had missed the Colt which Crane had flashed from the waist band of his pants.

Randy's smoke pole chunked to the sawdust, Men and women began breathing again, murmuring; it seemed almost funny, that surprised gunner's gaping mouth and popping eyes.

But what followed capped a good start. As he holstered his Colt, Slim closed in with his free fist. Randy was cold on his feet, and he had no time to lower his hands to defend himself. He crumpled, cracked his head on a cuspidor, and lay there, not even kicking.

The spectators shook their heads. A bouncer said, "Shucks, Randy won't know his own name fer a couple days." This was as they hauled him to the rear, his scalp deeply gashed.

Slim said to Sally, "M'am, I'm pow'ful sorry, but I can't tarry and drink with you."

He went to the street. A strawberry roan was hitched at the rack. By the saloon lights, he could plainly see the hoof prints: half the near front shoe was missing.

"That gent was fixing to kill me," Slim reasoned, and with certainty. "But ain't nobody around here that's got ground for thinking I know it."

Randy's studied attempt to make Slim draw first indicated that the law was biting into this tough town's hide. Self-defense had to be pretty

228 ⌒ E. HOFFMANN PRICE

clearly proved. So, as he headed for his hotel, he chuckled and said to himself, "Nothing to do now but see I don't get myself shot in the back. And whilst Mistah Randy is trying to recollect what his right name is, there's a chanct of finding his pardner."

Once in his room, he thrust his gun under his pillow, and began unbuckling his spurs. He was thinking, "Mebbe if I fixed myself up like a Mexican, I'd have a better chanct of sneaking up on Randy's pardner."

Winning a few gunfights would not expose the chief of the cattle thieves; that would only block the trail. He sat there, thinking it over; he recollected that Sally knew Randy by name. . . .

A furtive tapping at the door brought him to his feet before he removed his boots. A feminine voice whispered, "It's me. Sally."

He let her in, and replaced his gun when he saw she was alone.

"Oh, I'm in a terrible predicament," she breathlessly began, a hand on his arm.

Sally still wore her blue satin gown. Lamplight reached down into her low cut bodice to model the loveliest curves. A backward move as his boot closed the door behind her. She let go his arm when he offered her the only chair in the room. When he seated himself on the bed, Sally resumed, "I've been robbed — I mean, someone went through my room — over at the Buckhead Saloon — I'd just saved up enough to pay my fare home —"

"Ma'am, I sure would admire to help you." Slim was touched by her distress, "But I'm dang nigh busted. If ten bucks'd help —"

"Oh, but it's worse than that!" She buried her face in her hands, and her white shoulders for a moment were shaken by sobs. As Slim seated himself on the arm of the chair and stroked her head, Sally went on, "I married a man — who advertised — he was a wealthy rancher —"

"What? A gal like you, looking for matrumonyal advertising jaspers? That jest ain't reasonable."

"But I lived in Cross Plains. Everyone that amounted to anything left town, except those that got killed in feuds."

He began to catch the point: a lovely girl, one of the many extra women in a town depopulated by adventure and the interminable quarrels of the post oak country, had snapped at the first prospect.

"Uh — what's wrong with your — um . . . mail order husband?"

"He's a drunken bum. He's one-eyed, and positively filthy! Most of the time, he's in jail. I told him I'd pay his fine and give him a hundred dollars in cash if he'd promise to leave town and never look at me again!"

Slim, touched to the heart, tried to offer a consoling arm. The chair nearly upset, and in the scramble, Sally ended on his knee. She clung to him, curled up in his arms like a kitten. "Gol dang it, m'am," he gasped, "in another second, I'll be busting right out crying myself. But where in tunket I can get the money — onless mebbe I win myself a reward —" He was thinking fast. "For nailing rustlers or road agents or something."

"Oh, you're wonderful!" Her generous kiss made him realize he had really discovered something. "Slim, if you can just keep an eye on things and protect me until I can save up some more money —"

Sally was built to arouse protective instincts, and her voice encouraged such emotions. That sufficed to start a reckless exchange of kisses; and the fact that her father's thievery and violent death had erected an impassable barrier between Madge and Slim clinched things . . . . He turned the lamp low.

But Slim was surprised when the door slammed open, and Sally screamed, clawed herself out of his arms. "Oh, my God! That's him!"

One of the men revealed by the hall light was the proprietor of the Buckhead Saloon. Slim scarcely more than noted his black mustache and twisted mouth and craggy jaw. It was the drunk at the threshold who held his attention.

So this was Sally's husband, strangely released from jail? A chinless, one-eyed beanpole whose weak mouth twitched and slobbered tobacco juice as he screeched, "You dirty — Sally, you lousy stinking —!"

Sally cried, "Look out, he'll shoot," and flung herself clear across the room, legs for a moment twinkling as she vanished in a flurry of silken slip and streaming blonde hair.

But Slim hardly heard that. A fellow hears nothing when a .45 is weaving into line with his gizzard. The drunk lurched a pace. Slim had no time to debate. His hand came from beneath the pillow. The drunk was slow and fumbling. Sally's boss made a move toward his hip.

Slim cut loose, and the room shuddered from the rolling blasts of his Colt. The drunk's hammer thumb slipped, and he dropped with a cold gun. Men were tramping and shouting down the hall. They had been attracted by the two who had barged through the lobby, hunting trouble.

Sally's boss did not shoot or even draw. But a deputy marshal was advancing behind drawn guns. Slim knew that that hard bitten specimen would never back down; they'd kill each other.

"Hist 'em, bub!" His icy eyes covered everything; the dead man, the disheveled girl who came from cover, crying out that it was not Slim's fault. "Mebbe 'twarn't his fault, defending hisself," the law allowed. "But smoking out a gent that's pertecting the sanctity of his home is downright murder, m'am, and yo're a disgrace to yore sex, yuh shameless hussy. Mr. Kenyon bails the pore feller outen jail, and look whut you was doing!"

Sally's boss was smiling contentedly, and stroking his mustache. That told Slim a lot. The blonde had not deliberately betrayed him; she had been no more than a cog in the machine. And the marshal was bona fide; also he was stubborn in his notions on a husband's rights.

It looked like a hanging. At the very best, more years in the *juzgado* than any man could endure. Sally was paper white, wide eyed; she made inarticulate sounds as she swayed, uncertain on her feet. Slim wondered when she would collapse, or burst out with insane laughter.

The marshal was coming forward, one gun now holstered, so that he could search his prisoner. There was no help for this. Slim saw a man approach Sally's boss, Burt Kenyon.

Kenyon started, cursed, whirled from the scene. That brief distraction left Slim wondering what had happened. A gun blast shook him. Flame from the marshal's Colt set his shirt afire. Glass had spattered. Kerosene fumes thickened the air. The lawman was buckling at the knees.

Slim could not put these details into their natural sequence. Things had happened too quickly, and he was already in motion. Sally was slamming the door, bolting it, screaming, "Run, darling! Before he gets on his feet!"

She had snatched the lamp from its bracket and smashed it across the marshal's head. Slim picked up his gun and bolted for the window. Men were yelling in the hall. Sally cried, "They can't hang me for this! Run, you fool!"

The door was splintering. The bolt was yielding.

SLIM LANDED in the alley. They could not do much or anything to a woman who had become hysterical. Sally's laughter was clear above the uproar in his room. And before the alarm could spread, he was forking his unsaddled horse.

He was well out of Paso del Norte before a posse combed the town. But Slim Crane's mission was blown all to hell. Whether a warrant would follow him was another question. He'd better talk it over with his father.

That urge drove him toward Arroyo Rojo, the town he had resolved to quit. And quit it he would; he'd get a fresh horse, some money, and his dad's blessing, then head for New Mexico before Madge could ever curse him for being in on her father's death.

As he rode, he wondered what news had startled Burt Kenyon.

Then, hearing hoof beats far behind him, he had no further time for thought. How in tunket could a posse have picked the trail so surely and quickly! With his start, that was all wrong.

Someone might have guessed his next move. Certainly, his identity must have been blazoned all over Paso del Norte.

Slim, however, outwitted his pursuers. His horse, unburdened by a saddle, carried less weight. So he gained for a while, then doubled back; from cover, he watched them swoop past him.

"Dang funny, only four of 'em!" He shook his head, frowned. "And that damn' sure of where I'm going, they ain't bothering to track me!"

He mulled that over. He could not get the full significance. However, his best guess led him toward home, though along a short cut. It was a toss up whether he'd get there before or after the posse. Still, that really made little difference, so that they did not meet.

"Just as long as I can put a bug in pappy's ear. If Kenyon ain't in the beef business, I'm a polecat's uncle!"

When he reached the Diamond C spread, after swinging wide of Arroyo Rojo, it lacked less than an hour of dawn. The cook was not stirring about, nor was anyone snoring in the bunkhouse. Slim guessed that the riders, including his father, were out patrolling the range. That made it bad. He did not know whether to go out to find them, or stay and wait.

A horse whinnied. Even in the gloom, Slim could plainly enough discern the silvery mane and tail of a *palomino* at the hitching post; and the Diamond C had no animal of that coloring in its entire string. Then he noted the glow of light from a side window. Something was dead wrong. Whoever the stranger might be, there should have been some sound of conversation, and dominated by his father's voice.

But Slim's unwary approach had given warning. As a window rattled up, he flung himself from his mount and landed behind the grindstone. A woman cried, "Stay right where you are, or I'll shoot!"

Madge Daley was at the sill, ready to slide to the ground and get to her *palomino*; though only Slim would have recognized her in the shadows that blotted out all but the white blurr of face and throat, It seemed that the desire to escape without recognition had spurred her to that desperate outburst; her voice was tense and tremulous.

She was the last person on earth he wanted to see. He wondered whether, vengeance bent, she had come to assassinate his father. Finally, he contrived to croak, "Madge — what the blazes — what you doing here?"

"Slim!" She choked, and there was a metallic gleam as she lowered a pistol. "Good God, I thought — I've got to get out of here before your father gets back — don't ever tell anyone — dad would kill me!"

She was scarcely coherent. Slim vaulted to the sill. "Get back in. I'm alone. What's wrong?"

For a moment she clung to him, trembling and groping for words. Then she tugged at his arm, urging him to the lighted room. She said, "Slim, I'm so ashamed. I don't know what to say. But that —" She gestured toward the table, "That'll prove — but don't ever tell dad!"

She did not seem to know her father was dead. He regarded her disheveled hair, the torn blouse that trailed in tatters, exposing a good deal more than she realized. But as she hid her face on his shoulder, Slim's eyes popped out of his head.

On the table were bills of sale, which he recognized from their legal appearance. There were a dozen squares of rawhide, cut from as many freshly peeled hides. Each piece had the Diamond C brand!

"When we quarreled that night," she went on, haltingly, "I was furious. But the next night — oh, I hate to say it, but I learned that dad was beefing your cattle. To get even for that fence you cut. And for good measure — well, I realized why he'd bought me so many nice things, so suddenly. So I left, Wednesday night. To steal evidence, in Paso del Norte. I tricked a watchman there, and —"

She flushed, grimaced wryly. But Slim didn't notice that. He was too busy with his thoughts. While her father faced fatal bullets on the Diamond C, Madge had been in Paso del Norte, on the prowl. Slim demanded, "You mean you was fixing to sell your own pappy to the law! Why —" He thrust her from him. "Why — you damned low-down —"

"Slim, don't look at me that way! Don't you understand, I came to throw this stuff in through a window. But no one was in. So I put it here, where he'd find it. There's nothing against father, only against Burt Kenyon. A politician, beef contractor, saloon owner."

"Oh." Slim understood. "Trying to save your pappy, huh!"

"More than that! Trying to get him out of crookedness and revenge.

I'd begun to see the cattleman's side of it."

Then Slim's misery returned a hundredfold. Madge was honest to the core, and brave as they made them. And he had killed her father. He didn't know what to say or do. Even if it never leaked out, he could not face her. The glow in her eyes burned him when she went on, "You and I can make peace between our parents, can't we, Slim? I hated you for what you said, but it set me thinking."

"Sit down, honey," he muttered, sinking into a chair.

"I can't. I've got to get home to dad. I'll lie out of it, somehow, so he won't suspect, right away, what I did."

"I'll ride with you." Slim could not evade the issue, or let her go to an empty cabin, to wait until the news reached her. "I got — uh — a heap — to tell you."

She regarded his drawn face. She sensed something was dreadfully wrong, and apprehension gripped her. "Slim, what is it? Tell me now. Right here!"

But Slim had no chance to explain. A rifle blast and the shattering of glass were sounds prolonged by Madge's scream. His side went numb. He did not realize that the distortion of the pane had spoiled the marksman's aim. Other slugs thudded against the heavy walls, and sprayed the room with flying splinters.

As he went for his .45, Madge snatched a poker and swept the lamp from the table. It crashed in the fireplace. She smothered the blazing kerosene with cushions from the lounge. Slim steadied his pistol barrel on the sill to squeeze lead at the tongues of flame that spurted from the woodpile and from the corner of the barn.

When the fusillade slowed down to futile sniping, Madge crept to Slim's side and said, "We can slip out the other side. There's only four shooting at us."

"We can't," he muttered. "They got my hoss and yourn. It's too close to dawn, anyway. We'd not get far."

A man shouted from the murky shadows, "Throw out those papers, and we'll go away."

Slim leveled the Winchester Madge had located. As he did so, he thought, "Gawd, if I had dad's buffler gun, I'd bust hell outen the grindstone that son is hiding behind." He fired, heard the futile whine of a ricochet slug, then a mocking laugh.

"Don't be silly, you young fool. Throw out the bills of sale. We know exactly what she stole. We trailed her, and you."

"Come in and get 'em," Slim challenged, wrathful at having ridden into a trap. The enemy had craftily lurked to learn the entire sense of that baffling alliance they thought it was.

There was a furtive stirring outside, but gloom still protected the besiegers. Slim did not realize what was in the wind until he smelled burning hay. Flames first yellowed, then reddened the gaping door of the barn.

Dry as it was, it would go up like gunpowder. Worse than that, the first gray of dawn brightened the open ground. If he or Madge tried to make a break on foot, they would be hunted down.

The barn was smartly ablaze. Choking fumes billowed in through the broken window. Gusts of furnace heat lashed the besieged. At any moment, Slim expected the shingles to catch afire over his head. And the flames would now expose him, whichever direction he tried for flight.

"Honey," he choked, catching her hand, "you try slipping out yonder whilst I go out, shooting, tother way. You got a chanct!"

"I won't," she said. "It's my father's fault all this is happening. If you're killed, I'll feel like a murderer, and he'll be one!"

That whipped Slim to desperation. He caught her shoulder, shook her violently. "You damn little fool, get out! Your pappy's dead. I shot him the night you was in Paso del Norte. I didn't know 'twas him that was beefing our critters, but I kilt him!"

Horror widened her eyes. He repeated, "I kilt him. Now git out; you got no call to stick with me. Git, you fool, I'm going out a-shooting!"

He had found and loaded a second .45. Gun in each hand, he bounded toward the side furthest from the fire. He had thrust the evidence in his shirt. Grimly he saw that his death would still nail Kenyon. The'd not search his riddled carcass; they'd assume the evidence had gone up in smoke. But when the old man found him, they'd be sunk, the _____s!

Though four men had circled to await his break, regardless of direction, he still caught them momentarily off guard. His long legs seemed to cover yards at a stretch as he zigzagged, ducked, guns blazing for an instant, then silent during another bound. The enemy fired as they concentrated to cut off his flight.

Lead whipped past him. One of the raiders jerked back, and lurched into the open. Then Slim caught a glimpse of big Burt Kenyon. He shifted, spraying lead. He missed, and a hammer impact from the other flank made him spin, numb and helpless; his guns would not work any more.

Kenyon shouted, "Where's the girl? You, Hubbell! Doran!"

"Watch it!" someone howled above the roaring flames.

Kenyon ducked. Somewhere, Madge screamed, but no one heard. Pounding hoofs shook the ground. Slim, recovering a little, saw two riders charging hell bent. His old man and Whitey Harris, a cowpuncher, had been attracted by the flames. They could not have distinguished pistol shots from the crackle of blazing wood, tinder-dry.

They were riding into a trap. Slim tried to yell, tried to shoot. God, wouldn't they see it was more than just a fire!

Kenyon, thinking Slim finished, was turning his fire on old man Crane. Hubbell's gun was dancing. The two riders piled from their saddles, pulling iron as they dropped; but the roll of the ground was their only cover. The raiders' slugs kicked up spurts of dust. Answering fire whistled over Slim's head; the buffalo gun was roaring.

Then Slim cocked his gun with his teeth. He yelled a challenge, and as Kenyon jerked up, the kid's .45 did its work. And the smack of a Winchester, tying into the roar of the Colt, cleared the deck.

Madge, coming out of the house, flung the rifle on the ground.

"It was empty," she cried, "and I fumbled the shells till the last second. Why didn't you wait?"

Slim, staggering toward his father, hailed Whitey Harris. The cowpuncher, wounded by that first volley, was clawing a red splash on his chest.

"We seen the blaze," he choked.

Madge caught him as he sagged. He thrust her aside.

"Look to Dad Crane, he's damn neart finished."

Slim knew that, even before Whitey spoke. The old man forced a grin, tried to speak, then slumped in a heap. Madge, now at Slim's side, caught his arm.

"Are you hurt bad? What can I do?"

The kid's drawn face twitched.

"Fix Whitey. I just got a rib knocked loose and my shoulder drilled. And what the hell you doing here? I told you — I told you what I'd gone and done. Get out, I can't stand looking at you. You know what I done!"

"I know." Her lovely face was pained and weary. Tears gleamed in her eyes, and cut white paths through the dust and smoke stain of her cheeks. She shook her head, very slowly. "First I couldn't believe you. Then I went wild, but when I got the gun loaded — Slim, I couldn't hate you enough, so I fired at them, instead."

"Uh — what!" He couldn't believe all the implications.

"No," she solemnly went on. "All this, tonight, is what my father's pardners led him into, using his resentment for their own gains. Look what you've lost — from *our* fault —"

Slim scratched his battered head. "Honey, you forgiving me, you mean!"

"You didn't do it on purpose, and he was in the wrong. You and I can't carry on a feud. We've no relatives to keep it up."

Something told Slim that some day she could smile at him, and that she would. His own grief left him too numb for hatreds, and perhaps she felt that way, too.

"Honey," he finally said, "you can't fight a woman, so the feud's off, if you see things thataway. Orphants ought to stick together."